Rising Darkness

by
Roger Thomas

In memory of Michael Nicholas Richard
Colleague, critic, and friend

I'm looking forward to hearing all the stories you have to tell

Books in the *Watchful Sky* series:

Under the Watchful Sky

Rising Darkness

The Wounded Land

The Tattered Web

Published by JCK
Fort Gratiot MI

ISBN 978-1-7330809-0-3

This is not a story for children. This is a story about the struggle between good and evil in the midst of the decaying remains of what was once Western Civilization. It grapples with the types of evils that arise in such moral environments, which requires describing them. These descriptions are done plainly, with no choreographing, special camera angles, or other embellishments that are used by the entertainment industry to make evil appear glamorous and alluring. Those who have never encountered unretouched descriptions of evil may find them shocking, dismaying, and even revolting – as well they should, for that is what depravity looks like. This story deals plainly with kidnappings, rapes, beatings, murders, and other brutalities.

But why describe such things? Certainly not to revel in or celebrate them, nor to shock or affront deliberately, but rather that the reader might appreciate the good that rises to combat the evil. For there is good, though the weapons of combat are not the glowing sabers or technological super-suits or magic hammers so beloved by modern legend. Instead they are the only weapons that have ever been effective against evil: humility, longsuffering, determination, obedience, forgiveness, and most of all love. This story and the others in the series are also clear about the cost of the struggle, the fact that the Faithful of every age "fill up those things that are wanting in the sufferings of Christ." Redemption costs.

This story and others in the series also present plainly the Unseen Real. This is not in the interest of making them Fantastic Stories (as we moderns like our tales categorized), but because the Unseen is as real as the tangible reality present to the senses. The Seen and Unseen Real stand closer than we moderns like to admit, even in the face of St. Paul's warning that our enemies are not flesh and blood. Because of this, and because "where sin abounds, grace abounds all the more," I believe that we will see both evil and good, hitherto unseen, manifested more and more plainly in the times that are upon us. These stories reflect that belief, and those who read them should be prepared for that.

Roger Thomas, Easter 2019

The Thumb Region of Michigan

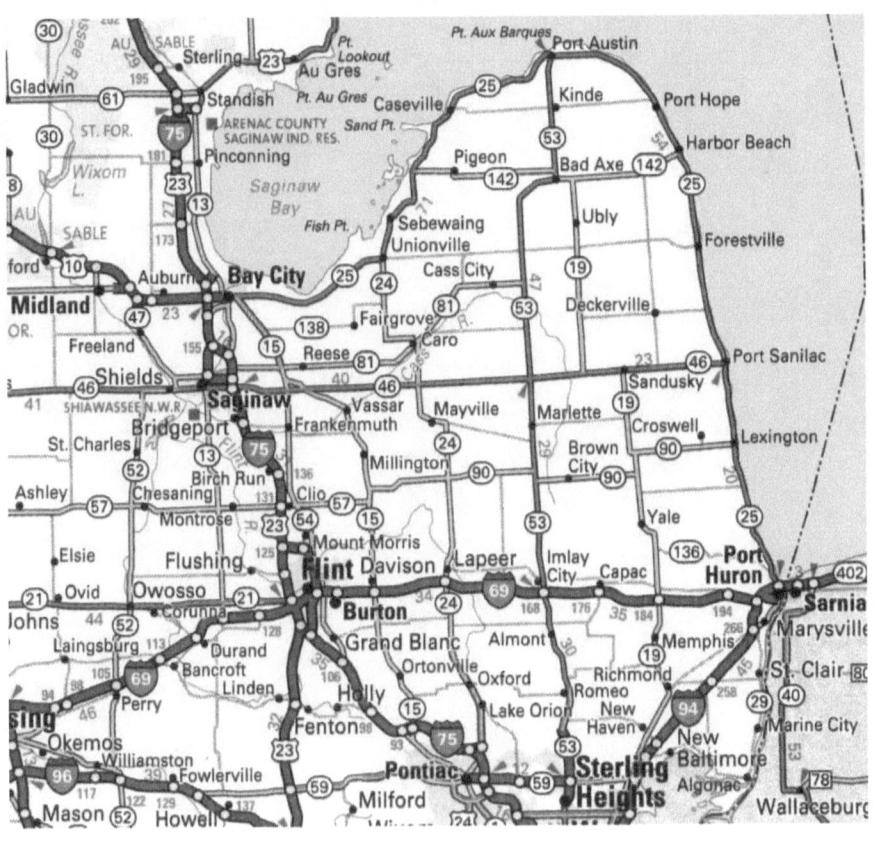

Voluntary Exile

"God bless, Grace. We'll miss you."

"I'll miss you, too, Jake," Grace Kyle replied, giving her brother a firm hug and a kiss on the cheek. She'd said her tearful goodbyes to Mom, Dad, and her other brothers back at home. Jake had offered to drive her up to this wee-hours rendezvous just east of Croswell, and now it was time for him to head home. Grace blinked back a few tears. This would be the longest time, and the farthest distance, she'd ever been away from her family. It wasn't all that far geographically, but numerous factors would make it difficult for her to run back home on a whim.

The biggest factor being an international border. One they had to cross without anyone knowing they'd done so.

"At least I'm leaving you in good hands," Jake said with a half-wink and a grin, glancing over to where Todd Beck was working with Ben Stover checking and tightening the straps securing the boat to the trailer. Since Todd and Grace had met under unusual circumstances the prior autumn, Todd had been a not-infrequent visitor to the Kyle home – but only when Grace was there.

"Get going, before I start bawling again," Grace retorted, giving her brother a playful smack. He returned another quick hug and headed for his car. Grace sniffed a little as his taillights receded down the road, then walked over to where Felicity Peterson was pacing while the guys did the final checks. They were behind a house, hidden from the road. The only light was from the security lamp on the front of the barn. The sky was still pitch dark, though the eastern horizon would soon begin to lighten. It was 4:00 a.m., and they wanted to be underway by 4:30.

"Hey, Feliss," Grace said as she took her friend's hands.

"Hey, Grace," Felicity replied a little huskily. She looked a bit red-eyed and kept sniffing.

"Did your folks drive you up?" Grace asked. Felicity had been here already when Grace arrived.

"No, we said goodbye back home. Cletus drove me up – he's used to early mornings."

Grace nodded and looked at the ground. The girls stood silently for a minute before Felicity spoke.

"So – this is it, eh?"

"Looks like it," Grace acknowledged.

"Remind me again why we're doing this?"

Grace smiled. The two of them been over this question so many times, first when the representative from St. Anselm's had come to explain the program, then when they had been selected, and then again when they had both agreed to go. But it made sense that now, in the predawn chill when they were actually setting out, the question would come around again.

"Because even in times like these – especially in times like these – we cannot lose touch with the foundations of our heritage and civilization," Grace recited with a smile. "Which is why we're going to Canada to study Homer and Shakespeare and Euclid and Plato and Austen and Lewis for the next year."

"Don't forget the Latin!" Felicity chided.

"And the Latin," Grace affirmed.

"And not quite a year," Felicity reminded her. The girls again fell silent for a minute before Felicity spoke again. "Do you think she'll be okay?"

"Who, Janice?" Grace replied. "I think so. She seems to be doing better since Easter, and I think this move she's making is a good idea."

"I hope so," Felicity said. "She still seems so…fragile."

"She'll be in good hands," Grace assured her.

Then the guys jumped down from the boat and walked over to them. "Okay," Ben said, wiping his hands. "It's just like we explained yesterday: you'll be in the cabin below decks until we say you can come out. It's pretty cramped in there, but above all, we need you to be quiet and still. You need to sound like an empty boat cabin, no matter what happens."

"Even before we launch," Todd added. "Trailering this boat with you in it is illegal, so in the unlikely event we get stopped, don't come popping out. Ready?"

The girls nodded, and the guys helped them up the ladder and into the boat. They made their way to the cabin and shut themselves in. It felt strange to be heading off for a school year with only the clothes on their backs, but it was important that they not look like they were carrying anything. They crouched in the dark and rocked with the slight swaying of the trailer as the truck rolled out onto Peck Road and turned east toward Lexington Harbor.

Lexington. Grace hadn't lived there since she was a little girl, but she had fond memories of it – the little shops, the old homes, the long pier of big limestone blocks. She'd see nothing of that this trip. They were stuck in this hold until they were out of sight of the harbor. It wasn't too bad – they each had a bench seat, and only had to bend over a little as they sat.

They endured the drive to Lexington, trying to guess at their progress from the turns and tilts. They stopped for what seemed like an inordinate length of time while the guys scrambled about the boat, releasing straps, shoving around objects that made loud clunking noises, and generally behaving like a couple of deep-water anglers preparing for a day's fishing expedition. Then there was another long wait before they felt the boat tipping and moving backwards, followed by the slap of waves against the hull and the sensation of being afloat. This was odd for both of the girls, neither of whom had ever done much boating.

They could hear someone on the deck outside, but remained quiet in their hold. After a long wait someone else jumped aboard and the engine rumbled to life.

"Not long," Grace whispered in Felicity's ear. They were both getting a little stiff. The boat did some maneuvering and cruised for a while at low speed, then made a turn and accelerated. They felt the stern tip down and the boat acquire a new, irregular movement.

"Clear of the harbor," Grace whispered. "Open lake now. Just a little longer."

"Feels weird," Felicity whispered back with an odd look. Grace gave a sympathetic nod. This was Felicity's first time boating on the open lake. She was a farm girl totally unaccustomed to her environment rocking, and even on a relatively calm day she might be feeling a bit worse than "weird" before the trip was over.

The doors from the deck opened and Todd stuck his head down into the cabin. "We're clear of the harbor, but you should stay below until we're well out of sight of the pier – maybe another fifteen or twenty minutes. Then you'll be able to come up on deck."

"Great," Grace replied. "Any chance you could leave those doors open so we can get fresh air circulating down here?"

"Um…sure, as long as you don't stick your heads out," Todd acknowledged. "And if you can lie down, that helps."

The girls did the best they could on the short, barely padded benches. What sky they could see through the doorway was still dark, and the breeze blowing down was cool, carrying the unmistakable scent of the lake. Felicity wasn't talking, and Grace knew what that meant. She lay still and hoped they wouldn't need a bag.

After what seemed like a long while, Todd stuck his head down again. "We're well out from shore, and Ben says that there are no boats about, so you can come up." The girls sat up stiffly and Todd helped them through the hatch and onto the deck. It was still night, but the eastern horizon was lightening with a pale shade of rose and the thinnest edge of a crescent moon hung just above the horizon. It was a morning of quiet beauty, and Grace felt her heart rise despite her uncertainty and queasy stomach.

Ben was at the boat's wheel, his eyes moving between the horizon and some instruments on the dash. Behind them Grace could see the dark outline of the shore, occasionally punctuated by lights on homes or docks. Before them was open water – it would be a while before the Canadian shore would come into view.

"How long will it take us?" Grace asked Ben.

"Just over two hours, under these conditions," Ben answered, not looking up from his instruments. "We're only turning for fifteen knots to save fuel."

"Will it be this choppy all the way across?"

Ben gave her a quick glance, edged with the slightest bit of scorn. "Choppy? These waters are the next best thing to calm. Couldn't ask for better weather."

"Oh," Grace said. "Well, some of us have lived all our lives on farms, and don't have much experience with boats." She nodded back to where Felicity was sitting on a bench with her head down. Ben glanced back at her and grunted.

"Hmm. Tell her to stay near the gunwales. I don't want to have to clean up the deck." He reached up and threw a switch on one of three identical-looking devices fixed at the top of the dash. The device sprang to glowing life and displayed something on its little screen. Ben consulted this, grunted again, and adjusted the wheel a little before turning the device off again.

"What are those things?" Grace asked, wanting to know as much as she could about this new environment.

"Location finders," Ben answered shortly.

"Why do you have three of them?"

Ben gave her a slightly impatient glance, but Todd interrupted before he could respond.

"Grace, why don't you come and sit down? I've got some juice and wraps for breakfast, if you'd like."

Grace dropped back to sit on the bench. Todd had a little cooler open, and fished out a package which he offered first to Felicity. When she just shook her head without looking up, he handed it to Grace.

"You'll have to forgive Ben," Todd whispered. "He's good at this, but transporting people makes him nervous. The location finders are to identify where we are on the lake. The problem is that they all have transponder circuitry which will respond with the current position if interrogated. If someone knew the circuit identifier of the locator device, and if it was always on – which they usually are on most boats – they could interrogate it and trace the entire path of your journey."

"Really?" Grace asked. "How could anyone get this – circuit identifier?"

"It's embedded when the device is manufactured. Every identifier is unique, and the government has ways of learning it," Todd explained. "It's unlikely that anyone would interrogate our locator while we're on this trip, but if we leave it off, then they definitely can't. And when we have three different ones which we use alternately, then it's almost impossible for anyone to track us."

"Oh," Grace said, still a little confused. "Is the boat motion going to calm down soon?"

"It should," Todd answered. "The wind is from the south, which means the closer we get to Canada the calmer the waters will be.

"I hope so," Grace said, glancing back at the stricken Felicity who was now holding her hand to her mouth.

"Maybe you could tell her," Todd whispered. "If she's feeling sick, just...let it out. It'll only get worse until she does."

Grace slid over and passed along this message as delicately as she could. Felicity nodded, stood up – and barely made it to the side in time. Ben glanced back over his shoulder with a bit of a smirk, but Todd moistened a paper towel and handed it to Felicity, then gave her a bottle of water to rinse her mouth.

"Lying down helps, too," Todd assured her. He and Grace moved to the side benches so Felicity could lie down on the bench which stretched across the stern of the boat. They chatted about minor things while the horizon continued to lighten and the boat cruised steadily eastward. By the time the sun rose in its full magnificence, the dark edge of the Canadian shore was clearly visible.

"Under an hour now," Ben assured them after checking their position. Felicity sat up and they reviewed the steps they'd follow once ashore, as well as the various fallback plans in case anything went wrong.

Soon the shore was drawing close, and they could discern individual houses along the beach. Ben slowed down and angled toward where a river flowed into the lake. "Port Franks," he said, pointing up the river. "The marina is only half a mile in, so we'll be there shortly."

Since the girls were going to disembark here, they didn't need to stay below or hide any longer. Ben cruised slowly up the river, chatting on the marine band radio, and finally pulled into an empty slip along a long stretch of dock. The plan was for Todd and Ben to go ashore and hit the marina store like a couple of noisy Yanks looking for beer, bait, and fishing tips. Once they were inside, the girls would hop off and go to the marina restrooms.

The guys tied the boat to the dock and headed up to the store. In their pockets were their passports, driver's licenses, and U.S. and Canadian fishing licenses, just in case they got stopped. In the girl's pockets were their rosaries.

Once the guys were inside, Grace and Felicity jumped onto the pier, trying to look as relaxed and casual as Todd and Ben had. They instinctively sought cover, dodging under the trees as they made for the restrooms. Once finished, they stepped out and looked toward the parking lot.

There it was, just as planned – a red mid-sized SUV. The driver sat in the shadows, her eyes shielded by sunglasses. The girls strolled toward the car, chatting lightly, until they could see the beads hanging from the rearview mirror.

Blue.

The final signal, the last go/no go for the transfer. Black beads would have been a wave-off: get back on the boat and go home. Red was for caution: don't go, but be careful. Blue was all clear – no problems detected, climb in and go.

Still trying to appear nonchalant, Grace and Felicity ambled up to the car and hopped in like they'd just gotten out.

"Ladies," the driver said with a quick nod and a smile. She started the car and pulled away, not speaking again until they were well clear of the marina. "I'm Amanda Pride, business manager of St. Anselm's. Which one of you is Grace?"

"I am," Grace identified herself.

"Then you must be Felicity," Amanda said. "Welcome to Canada. I presume both of you have been here before?"

"Just day trips," Felicity confirmed. "Only then it was –"

"Legal," Amanda interrupted with another brisk nod. "It's about two and a half hours up to Hanover. If either of you are hungry, there's a cooler and hamper in the back. Since I suspect you were up very early, feel free to nod off along the way. We'll be driving though farmlands, which I imagine you've seen before. I'm happy to chat if you wish, but I hardly need the company."

Amanda's tone was cordial, but clipped enough that the girls took her at her word and didn't try to engage her in conversation. Besides, they were both tired, and were soon dozing as the car sped north through the fields and woods.

They finally pulled into a drive that circled around a large farmhouse – nearly a mansion – made of dull yellow bricks. Inside, they met the cook, Susan Beaker, and Dr. Hennington, the dean. Jim, the groundskeeper, was somewhere outside. Dr. Hennington explained that there were eighteen students this year, most of whom had yet to arrive. Grace and Felicity would room together in the main house, upstairs with the rest of the girls, while the guys would all bunk half a mile down the road in a ranch house grandiosely named Cluny. They were shown the parlor, and told of the basement at Cluny, where the seminars would be held. They were taken to their room, already stocked with the clothes that had been purchased for them and the textbooks that had been provided. The furniture consisted of a wardrobe and a dresser, both of which they would share, a bunk bed, and two study desks with straight-backed chairs. They were told that lunch would be served at 12:30 p.m. and left to themselves to "settle in."

Grace sat beside Felicity on the lower bunk, her heart heavy. The strange house and spartan room contrasted painfully with the memory of her familiar home and loving family. The school year which just days earlier had seemed like such an enticing adventure now lay before her like a long, bleak road stretching out of sight. Felicity was also silent for some minutes, then tentatively reached over to grasp Grace's hand. They fell onto each other, clinging and sobbing their hearts out from sheer homesickness.

Glad Tidings

Derek packed his gear into the all-terrain vehicle's cargo bins and zipped up his heavy jacket tightly. The already cool wind would get colder once he got moving, which he needed to do quickly. This call had taken longer than he'd figured it would, and the light was fading quickly. The equinox had "turned", as his farmer friends put it, just weeks before. The darkness was coming sooner each evening and lasting longer each morning. If he didn't hustle, he'd be caught by the night – and this four-wheeler wasn't one of the ones with the powerful headlights.

Starting up the four-wheeler, Derek turned onto the wooded trail that would take him home. He'd been working near a little hamlet named Valley Center, just a little southeast of Brown City. He navigated carefully – he didn't want to get lost and have to call his family to come rescue him. Besides, he was tired and just wanted a hot meal and his own bed. Though the idea of running all over the Thumb on a four-wheeler excited eleven-year-old Jude Schaeffer no end, the thrill had long since faded for Derek. It was just a way to get around – and one with no protection from inclement weather, at that. Truthfully, he preferred to ride his horse Kilroy when he was working close to home, but that wasn't a practical option for longer circuits. Not only were horses slower, but few of his stops had the facilities to care for them. Furthermore, on an ATV he could reasonably wear a helmet with a full face shield, something that would just look strange on horseback. Horses drew enough attention anyway, and the last thing Derek needed was more attention.

Especially since he was dead.

In fact, it was just about a year ago now, Derek mused as he navigated the tree-shadowed trail. A year since he and his friend Janice Boyd had been taken captive by a mysterious, dangerous government agency which had been quietly executing certain old and infirm people across the region. Derek had become involved with a clandestine network of families who had been secretly

11

working to rescue the intended victims and sweep them into hiding. When the agency had learned of this underground network, and that Derek knew something of them, it had been prepared to do almost anything to force Derek to betray his friends. Through a bizarre set of circumstances, Derek and Janice had been rescued from the hands of their captors by their friends Kent Schaeffer and Gil Peterson. The only reason they hadn't been immediately chased down and recaptured was due to the heroic sacrifice of another beloved friend, Sam Chapman, who had detonated a devastating explosion that had destroyed the enemy and himself in the process.

Their rescue had relieved the immediate problem but had had an unintended side effect. Since Janice and Derek's ID cards had been found at the blast site, it had been presumed they were among the dead. This had simplified circumstances for both Derek and Janice, since the government agency saw no point in pursuing dead targets (and also because most of the agency leaders were dead themselves), but it also had dramatically changed both their lives. It wasn't as if they had retired from public life, or moved to a far-off place. Officially they were *dead*, under dramatic and suspicious circumstances, which meant they couldn't legitimately show up anywhere without triggering extremely difficult and dangerous questions. Only the families who had rescued them knew that they still lived. To everyone else – friends, former coworkers, even their own families – they were dead and had to remain so.

This had far-reaching implications for them both. Neither Derek nor Janice could drive any more, since that required a driver's license. Bank accounts and credit cards were out of the question. Phones could be used, but never to contact anyone they knew before their "deaths". Even going into cities, particularly cities near where they'd lived and worked, was strongly discouraged, since the risk of being recognized by someone was too high. Even among those who were hiding, only a few knew who they really were. Fortunately, in the circles they now belonged to, concealed lives and masked identities were commonplace.

Those who'd been rescued from execution by the government agency – sometimes from right under the noses of the executioners – also needed to vanish completely from public life. Mostly these were older people with no living or close relatives. They were hidden in a network of homes and facilities known as ranches. These ranches had their own communications and transportation network and were not only scattered throughout the immediate area but, as Derek quickly learned, were sited across other regions within Michigan and in neighboring states. Where Derek lived and primarily worked, the "Thumb" region of eastern Michigan, was code-named "Eastfarthing". Beyond Saginaw Bay, across a broad swath of the northern area of the state, lay densely wooded but sparsely populated "Northfarthing," where people could live in hiding for generations. Farther down I-75, in northwest Ohio, lay "Southfarthing," and in northern Indiana, stretching west from I-69, was "Westfarthing". There were no firm boundaries or administrative structures, just loose networks of families who helped each other spirit away those in danger and hide them from harm.

It was into this hidden world that Janice and Derek had vanished when they had "died" in what had been officially declared an industrial accident. This meant that they both lost their livelihoods, he as an assistant medical examiner and Janice as a nurse. But their skills were in high demand, especially in this environment with so many elderly people who could no longer receive medical care by usual means. Though a few courageous practitioners helped the effective refugees, it was a prosecutable offense to provide medical care outside official channels. Thus, a trained physician's assistant who didn't officially exist was a godsend to the far-flung community, and Derek quickly found his days filled with what amounted to a circuit-riding medical practice. He could be driven places, or he could ride vehicles like four-wheelers or snowmobiles (or the occasional horse) off the public roadways. As his reputation spread, he began taking sweeping tours across the region that could last over a week, staying with families and serving as many ranches as he could cover. It was demanding but gratifying, and he suspected that he was practicing more actual medicine than some MDs he knew. Of course, he lacked the most up-to-date examination and treatment tools, and had to make do with what could be bought, borrowed, or scrounged from medical practices that were closing. One unexpectedly useful resource was older medical texts and manuals, some dating back seventy-five or even a hundred years, from the days when it was presumed that a doctor made "calls" with only the instruments in his bag and the knowledge in his head. When Derek realized how precious these texts were, he put out a call for them through the network of contacts that supported the ranches, and was soon flooded with a library of old books. These kept him up late many a night as he researched how to treat some challenging conditions.

Of course, since most of the "guests" at the ranches were elderly and already in frail health when they arrived, Derek had to accept that many would die under his care. The simple conditions of care, scant resources, and shortage of medications meant that there was only so much that could be done for them. One thing that helped, about which he hadn't learned until after he'd been "practicing" for a while, was that there was an active and growing pharmaceutical smuggling operation managed along the Canadian border. This scant but somewhat regular trickle helped Derek do what he could for his patients.

At a personal level, Derek had seen a lot of changes beyond the practical outfall of his official "death". The shattering events surrounding his brush with catastrophe had forced him to reconsider everything about his life. Falling into the power of such malicious evil, then being unexpectedly rescued by such towering heroism, had made clear to him how little he knew about life and the workings of the human heart. Humbled and challenged by the example of those who risked so much to help others, he'd undertaken to learn what made them the way they were.

That began with their religious faith. Having been raised in a non-religious household, Derek had always considered religion something done by other people, like belonging to a fraternal organization or a community charity. He'd known almost no one who took religion seriously, and his impression of religious people, especially Christians, had been formed by online sites and shows. Thus, he'd thought them prickly, narrow-minded people hung up on rules and looking down their noses at anyone who wasn't like them. Derek had assumed that anyone who was Christian was automatically a hypocrite. He'd never thought seriously about them, or their religion, or their god, deeming it all irrelevant to his life.

Yet now he owed his freedom, and indeed his life, to a group of these same people – not just Christians, but Catholics, an even stranger type of being. They broke all his stereotypes. Far from being judgmental, narrow-minded, and cliquish, they were open, loving, and accepting. They were even fun – Derek felt like he'd laughed more in the last year than he had in in the prior decade of his life. Sure, they had a moral code, but that's what made them so honest and trustworthy, and caused them to value every human life so highly that they were willing to take great risks to save them – even lives of non-Christians like himself and Janice. Far from being hypocrites, they were honest and genuine. In fact, it was Derek who often felt like the phony, the guy wearing a mask. Oddest of all for Derek, at least when he was first getting to know them, was how they spoke of God. They didn't talk of Him as if He were some abstraction or philosophical principle. They spoke of Him – and often *to* Him – as if He was right there in the room. To them, God was close, even intimate, involved in the smallest details of their lives.

Part of Derek had been (and occasionally still was) tempted to scoff at what seemed like such simple folly, but his experience witnessed otherwise. These people were neither simplistic nor foolish. In fact, they were the ones whose lives were marked by focus and determination. They were the ones who had done the heroic deeds, facing down dangerous enemies to save lives. All

Derek's accomplishments had pertained to mastery of video games. Beside them he felt like a schoolboy, still learning the fundamentals of how life worked.

This was particularly true when Derek dealt with Grandpa, the venerable patriarch of the family. Grandpa had undertaken not only to instruct Derek in the faith but to mentor him. Though Grandpa was easygoing, and Derek never heard him utter a harsh word, there was a quiet authority about him that made Derek keenly aware of how much he had yet to learn about being a man. From Grandpa's careful lessons and engaging conversation, Derek learned to look at the world, his life, those around him, and all existence in a new light. His own experience made it easier to grasp the elements of the salvation story. Still fresh in his memory was the brutal reality of being in the hands of powerful and malicious forces, too weak to help even himself, much less his friend. The example of a savior who sacrificed himself for those he loved had been powerfully modeled by his friend Sam. The living example of a community of love was provided by the families who had taken him in.

These personal experiences combined with the new rhythm of his life had eased Derek's transition from his old existence to his new one. A few weeks after their rescue the prior autumn, the solemn season of Advent had begun. It had been a new experience for Derek, who had only ever known the gaudy, noisy "Christmas season" of the shopping centers. The quiet, meditative atmosphere of Advent was perfectly suited to the introspection and self-evaluation in which he was engaged. Even the daylight cooperated – he found the shortening days and lengthening hours of darkness conducive to reflection. Like many of the households, the Schaeffers with whom he lived had been trying to restrict electricity usage, so often the dark hours were lit only by the quiet light of the Advent candles, if at all. Derek had read, meditated, written in his journal, held quiet conversations with Linda or Kent, and tried to learn how to pray.

When Christmas had come with its joy and cheer, Derek had celebrated with the rest, but had not completely shared in their cheer. He'd made a point of going out in the snow to stand before the stone monument they'd erected in Sam's memory. Looking at his name, the dates, and the simple inscription – "The Lord is my strength" – Derek had pondered the fact that but for Sam's sacrifice, he might not have seen this Christmas. Oddly, he'd also missed his mother. Though they'd rarely talked and were effectively estranged, Derek had realized that there was a difference between not calling her because he just didn't want to and never being able to call or see her ever again.

After the turn of the year, Derek had moved out of the guest suite in the Schaeffer's home and into the apartment which had been Sam's. The workshop had continued to be used, but the apartment beside it had stood empty and just as Sam had left it when he'd charged off on his rescue mission. Derek had felt strange moving into the apartment – almost like he was unworthy – but everyone had decided that the space was there, and Sam wouldn't have wanted it to stand unused, especially as any kind of shrine. Since Derek was *de facto* medical provider for an increasing number of the ranches, he needed the quarters. So, weeping all the while, Derek had carefully cleared out the shelves, packed everything away, remade the bed, and settled his gear into his new quarters.

Derek had spent most of the winter expanding his medical responsibilities, so the season of Lent had snuck up on him. Ash Wednesday had fallen toward the end of a dreary, cold February. Derek had found that he didn't like Lent much. There was a dry grittiness to it, with the fasts and penances and sacrifices. Grandpa had assured him that this was part of the point of the season – coming face-to-face with one's smallness and inadequacy. Derek had certainly experienced that, encountering many setbacks and frustrations in his personal life. He'd even started wondering if he should go through with being baptized. Grandpa had listened to and encouraged and prayed with him through this time, helping him regain his bearings and focus. Then had come Holy Week, which was like a condensed Lent, followed by the awe and beauty of the Easter Vigil. With

Grandpa at his side, Derek had been solemnly baptized and took the name Luke at his confirmation. Thereafter he was publicly known as Luke Peterson, though among the ranches he was already known simply as "Doc".

During all this time, Derek had also been gravely concerned for his friend Janice. She'd been rescued at the same time he'd been, but had suffered torture and the threat of rape and worse at the hands of their captors. Also, she had been drawn into the group responsible for the murders, and had killed three people while under their influence. The trauma had caused her to have a breakdown after her rescue, suffering emotional damage as well as self-inflicted injuries. Derek had nursed her back to physical health, but the lingering terror of what had happened, guilt over what she'd done, and confusion from the massive disruption in her life had all combined to smother her beneath a cloud of gloom and despondency. She had spent a lot of time talking to Grandma, who'd effectively adopted Janice. She'd also spent a lot of time with Felicity Peterson and, oddly, Grace Kyle. This latter friendship mystified Derek, since it had been an unexpected and extremely irregular first meeting between the two women that had ultimately precipitated the crisis that had put them here. Derek would have thought that Grace would be the last person around whom Janice would have been comfortable, but he was clearly mistaken, since Grace had been a regular visitor through the year, spending long hours conversing with her new friend.

The long, cold winter had weighed upon Janice, who hadn't seemed to be making the same kind of progress back toward normalcy that Derek had. Even Kent and Linda had quietly wondered if Janice had been psychologically damaged by what she'd been through. The guilt was certainly real – she had three murders on her conscience, a situation so grave that Grandpa had brought in a moral theologian from the seminary in Detroit to evaluate the case. After hearing all the circumstances, the man had explained that while Janice's spiritual guilt would be washed away by baptism, there remained the matter of corporate moral responsibility. Under other circumstances, the proper thing would have been for her to turn herself into the civil authorities. But there was more to the story – Janice had been coerced and deceived into doing the murders, and circumstances made it nearly impossible for her to submit herself to civil justice. Not only would it endanger many innocent lives, but it was highly unlikely that she'd be justly treated. The shadowy group which they'd escaped would certainly seek to silence her, possibly to kill her, in order to safeguard their secret. Since civil justice was effectively out of reach, and Janice was sincerely contrite and repentant, the theologian had judged that she had no responsibility to turn herself in. Besides, her "death", which had cut her off from her entire life to that point, was effectively a permanent exile – which had once been the sort of punishment meted out for crimes like hers. So, in a sense, she was already serving what amounted to a sentence.

This ruling had settled some questions but hadn't lifted Janice's spirits. She'd remained morose and withdrawn through the winter and dreary spring, helping out by serving as a nurse to the guests in the house where she lived and occasionally accompanying Derek on his rounds. Her lingering depression had distressed Derek, who'd done what he could to help her, but she made so little apparent progress that he'd felt helpless before the weight of her struggles. He'd been particularly concerned when Lent began, worried that the somber atmosphere of the penitential season would exacerbate her already downcast spirits. And indeed, things had seemed to begin that way – on Ash Wednesday Janice had gone forward eagerly for the ritual marking with ashes, and then didn't wash them from her forehead for several days. Derek heard that she would spend long hours in the chapel at the Big House, sometimes far into the night, holding vigil in the cold darkness by the light of a solitary candle. She'd been responsive enough in her daily activities, and interacted with those around her in a brisk and functional manner, but to Derek she'd seemed personally withdrawn, turned even more inward than she'd already been. What conversations he'd had with

Felicity and Linda indicated that they were as concerned for Janice as he was. Only Grandma seemed unworried.

For Holy Week services they'd traveled up to Peck, just north of Yale, so they could attend services celebrated by Fr. Gabriel Stover. Janice had thrown herself into the events with unusual intensity, especially in light of her recent emotional lethargy. During the lengthy Gospel reading of the Passion, she'd stood with taut anticipation, attending to every word and joining in the common acclamations with almost gruesome vigor ("Crucify Him! Crucify Him!") On Good Friday, with the sanctuary stripped of every decoration and echoing stark desolation, Derek had worried that this would so resonate with the desolation in Janice's soul that she'd never recover. He'd been even more concerned when they'd brought the crucifix with the life-sized corpus down the aisle, chanting "Behold the wood of the cross!" When the crucifix had been set up for the worshippers to come forward and venerate, Derek had watched Janice out of the corner of his eye to see how she'd respond. As he'd feared, it was dramatic enough to be worrisome. She'd been among the last to come forward, and had thrown herself at the foot of the cross, sobbing as if her heart were breaking. She'd stayed there almost to the point of embarrassment, crying and pressing her forehead against the wood and nestling her head next to the feet of the corpus. Finally, Grandma and Felicity had come forward to lift her gently and lead her away to a pew where she'd collapsed, her face buried in her hands and her shoulders heaving.

Concern for Janice's emotional state had overshadowed the final preparations for the Easter Vigil, when Janice and Derek were to be baptized and confirmed. They'd sat close together, with Grandma and Grandpa beside them as their sponsors. Janice had been transfixed when the tall Easter Candle had been brought down the aisle of the darkened sanctuary and placed at the front, where the crucifix had stood just the day before. She'd watched the flickering light with almost hypnotic intensity while Fr. Gabriel had chanted a lengthy prayer, and her gaze had remained on it through the many readings from Scripture. Then had come a point when the lights all came on and bells were rung and a great song was sung, and things had proceeded more like the Masses Derek had grown accustomed to. But through it all Janice had remained focused on the candle.

Then had come Janice's turn for baptism. She'd requested her full head be immersed, which apparently was valid, and she'd stood up dripping, her hair soaking her dress but her eyes shining. When Fr. Gabriel had confirmed them, he put a little of the chrism oil on Derek's forehead, but he'd slathered so much on Janice that it ran down the ends of her eyebrows, dripping down her face to mingle with the streams of water from her hair and with her tears. Janice had wept quietly for the rest of the Mass, but it hadn't been the broken-hearted gasping that Derek had heard so often over the prior months. It was a quiet, steady stream of tears that gave her eyes preternatural brightness as she'd continued to gaze up at the tall candle. When communion time had come, she'd seemed reluctant to go forward, but Grandma had taken her elbow gently but firmly and brought her forward to kneel at the rail and accept the host and chalice.

After that night, Janice hadn't completely changed, but she'd definitely turned a corner. She was still quiet, but she smiled more often and even laughed occasionally. She still spent time alone, but instead of being in darkened rooms it was more likely to be in the warm twilight under flower-laden trees or sitting beside the pond behind the Big House. Derek and Felicity had even managed to coax her into a horseback ride, which she'd enjoyed. Mostly, Derek had noticed that the shadowed look which had haunted her eyes since before that fateful day seemed to be gone. He began to wonder if he'd missed something during the Easter Vigil, something which Janice had found.

"Possibly," Grandpa had told Derek with a wink when he'd asked about it. "Don't worry – you'll catch up. Those who have been forgiven much love much."

Therefore, Derek had not been concerned when Janice had announced just after Pentecost that she would be moving up to St. Anne's House near Deckerville, about an hour north of the campus of Rivendell where they'd been living. A small group of religious sisters with a ministry of medical care had set up the house to tend to guests in need of more care than could be provided at the ranches. Janice had been talking to Grandma and Jan Peterson about it, and wanted to try working in a place where her medical training could be most useful.

"Does this mean you'll be taking the habit?" Derek had asked Janice at lunch before she was driven up to her new home.

"I don't know," Janice had replied. "I don't think I'm supposed to worry about all that just yet. I'm just supposed to work and learn."

"Just be careful to stay upbeat," Derek had cautioned. "More smiling and laughing and less morose weeping!"

"I can't promise about the weeping, but I'm trying to drop the morose," Janice had assured him.

"I'll miss you."

"I'll miss you, too, dear brother," Janice had said with a warm smile. "But I won't be that far away, and your rounds will bring you by fairly often – in fact, they'll have to."

"I'll be certain they do," Derek had assured her.

And so they had, Derek pondered as he guided his ATV along the final, familiar mile of the trail. Since Janice had moved up to St. Anne's House the prior spring, he'd managed to swing by there at least twice a month, doing as much training as patient care. This on top of his increasingly busy medical "circuit" had kept him busy through the summer and into the autumn. The run he was just completing had taken him far west, over beyond Caro, up past Cass City, and down by Marlette. Now he was nearly home, for which his chilled fingers were grateful.

Coming into the familiar yard, Derek drove right past his quarters and up to the back door of the home of his adopted family, the Schaeffers. He'd unpack later. Right now, he wanted to get warm, get fed, and see some familiar faces. He didn't have to wait long for those – stripping off his gloves and helmet, he stepped through the back door into the brightly lit kitchen to be mobbed by gleeful children shouting, "Mr. Derek! Mr. Derek!"

Three-year-old Matthew, shrieking with delight, grabbed his leg in a death grip while seven-year-old Tabitha pulled on his opposite arm in excitement. He was accustomed to happy homecomings, but this seemed unusually enthusiastic.

"Good to see you, Derek," Kent Schaeffer said, wading through the crowd of children and gripping his hand. "We were beginning to get a little concerned."

"Sorry – my last call took a bit longer than I'd anticipated, and I didn't think to message you," Derek said apologetically.

"No matter – Linda's kept a plate warm," Kent replied, ushering him to the now-cleared dinner table. Derek wondered if it was just his imagination, or whether Kent was grinning more than usual. For that matter, Linda looked quite bright-eyed as she brought over his plate. Was something up?

Derek didn't have long to wait. Giving him just enough time to say a quick grace, Linda plunged in as he dipped some fresh bread into the thick stew. "We told the kids at dinner, and have just been waiting for you before we made the news public," she said, nearly bouncing in her seat in excitement.

"News?" Derek asked.

"Linda's expecting," Kent affirmed with a broad grin.

Defeat

It had been two weeks, and the memory of the face still haunted Dennis Rayman.

He'd only had a brief glimpse in his right outside mirror as he'd been pulling away, but the image remained graven in his mind. Maybe it was because it was so unusual to see such a face at that site. Maybe it was because of the expression the lad had been wearing – a mixture of curiosity, innocence, resignation, and weariness beyond his years. Dennis had no idea who the youngster was, or why he'd been at that window, but there was something about him that made Dennis want to reach out and help.

Not that that would be possible. Not at that site.

Dennis had paid his dues doing long-haul trucking over the years, so when the position with Premier Trucking out of Saginaw had opened up, he'd jumped on it. It was all short haul jobs, one day there-and-back runs. It meant a lot of runs between Detroit and Grand Rapids, or between Detroit and Chicago, and occasionally over to Toronto, but he was back in his own bed most every night. He liked that most of the runs were routine, with familiar faces at familiar docks, regular loads, and predictable schedules.

Even the Bad Axe run was predictable. But nobody liked that one, least of all Dennis.

They called it the Bad Axe run, but it actually was to a site north and east of Bad Axe, almost to the tip of the Thumb. The run was every week or two, but since nobody ever volunteered for it, the dispatchers tried to rotate it around so no one would have to do it too often.

The run itself wasn't that hard, and no more monotonous than many. It was always the same – driving bobtail down US23 to Toledo to pick up a trailer parked in the same out-of-the-way lot just off the turnpike. The trailer was always a container chassis holding a forty-foot shipping container. This was hauled up to the site and dropped off, and an identical trailer holding an identical shipping container was picked up and run back down to the lot by Toledo. It was a simple, mindless task – a little long for one day, but not if you got an early start. No, it wasn't the trucking that was troublesome about that run. It was the site itself.

Dennis had talked to the other drivers about it, but none of them had ever been able to figure out just what the site was. It was almost certainly some sort of factory – it was about two stories tall and had a loading dock with three bays. There were translucent windows up toward the roof and a smaller one-story side building of the sort that held offices. But this structure was set back on a heavily wooded lot, far from any cities or other factories or suppliers or services. He even had to drive miles on dirt roads just to get there.

But most bothersome were the people. The site had a heavy gate across the drive right at the road that was always chained shut. Usually there were a couple of punks in a UTV waiting behind the gate, though sometimes they weren't there, which meant Dennis would have to call the office, who'd call the client, and eventually the punks would show up. They'd unlock the gate, let him through, and lock it again behind him. They'd escort him down the narrow, curved drive through the woods to the site. The trees were so close around that there was barely enough clearance to turn the truck so he could back the trailer up to the dock. He'd unhitch the trailer he'd brought and hitch up the one he was taking, all under the unsmiling supervision of the punks.

Dennis and the other drivers called them punks because that's what they seemed to be: sullen, ill-groomed kids in their late teens or early twenties who muttered to each other or checked their phones but never talked to him other than to bark instructions. There was nothing friendly about them or the entire site – no joking, no coffee offered, no chance to hit the john, none of the human interactions that usually accompanied a delivery. In fact, the one time he'd really needed to use the john and asked the punks about it, they'd just smirked and pointed him to a cluster of bushes. It was as if they tolerated outsiders on the site only long enough to do their job, then wanted to hustle them away as quickly as possible. In fact, there were never even any people around but the escort punks.

Except for that one glimpse two weeks ago.

Dennis had been pulling away from the dock, glad to be seeing the end of this place again. In his mirrors he could see the side of the building which he presumed was the offices. It had tall, floor-to-roof windows through which he'd never seen any activity. But this time he saw the head of a young black kid, maybe in his early teens. The head was low and kind of sideways, as if the kid was sitting in the offices and had leaned over to look out the window. Dennis watched the kid, who was gazing at the truck with plaintive yearning. It made Dennis want to comfort him, whoever he was, but there was no chance of that. The punks were leading the way, and he had to keep up. He watched in his mirror until he took a curve and the face in the window vanished behind the thick leaves.

Now Dennis was headed back up to the site on another run. It would be the same punks, the same drop-off and pickup, everything the same. The chances of seeing that face in the window again were next to nothing, but he'd look anyway. That kid was the only person other than the punks which he or any of the other drivers had ever seen on that site. Dennis kept wondering who the kid was, what he was doing there, and whether he was all right. He'd probably never know, and certainly couldn't do anything, but he could wonder.

*   *   *

Sheriff Chip Keller watched the county clerk's site with increasing dismay as the precincts reported their counts. His spirits, and those of the handful of people at his victory party, sank lower by the minute as they beheld the unthinkable unfolding.

Chip was losing his reelection bid.

It wasn't unheard of, but it was very, very uncommon. In rural counties like Huron, typically once a sheriff was elected, he had the job for as long as he wanted. Barring some kind of major scandal or gross incompetence, he would hold the office until he retired or resigned. He'd have to go through the reelection mechanics every four years, and the opposition party would nominate an opponent as a formality, but the incumbent would usually win by a margin of over sixty percent, with over eighty percent not being unusual. That's just how things were.

Which was why Chip had been blindsided earlier in the year when Andy Klein had started a serious campaign. Andy Klein! He'd had no experience managing law enforcement – he'd served as a street cop in his youth, and had once worked at a private security firm. But suddenly he was the opposition party's nominee! Chip had many friends in that party's leadership, and in private they professed astonishment at how things had unfolded. At the turn of the year they hadn't even been thinking about the sheriff's race, but by early spring everyone was buzzing about Andy. He turned in enough petition signatures to file for the race, and was nominated at the party's county convention. But even then nobody expected him to have a chance.

But then the "Andy Klein for Sheriff" signs had started popping up all over the county, bearing a picture of him with his smarmy grin and his meaningless campaign slogan – "Time for a Change" – on walls and in yards and staring down from billboards. Then had come the radio ads and web videos, almost but never quite attacking Chip. There were interviews with citizens testifying to their "disappointment," and those who thought they could have been treated better (you could always find some people with a complaint against the sitting sheriff). The carefully-crafted image being painted was that after three terms, Chip Keller had lost his touch.

Chip didn't take this seriously enough until it was too late. Not only that, but his election team, who'd run his campaigns and had honed everything until it ran like clockwork, was hit with a series of problems. Fred got diagnosed with cancer, which took

Elaine out as well. Chris and Judy were rumored to be having marriage trouble – at least, he moved out and she wasn't returning calls. Jack and Amy's son-in-law lost his job, so she'd had to move down to North Carolina to help with the grandkids. The result was that when Chip needed to ramp up his campaign in response to the unexpected challenge, he had fewer than half his usual volunteers and almost no experience. Meanwhile, the Klein campaign was papering the county from Sebewaing to Harbor Beach and flooding the airwaves and sites with their "Time for a Change" message. Chip wondered where Andy was getting the money. He knew how much it took to run a campaign, and Andy was far outdoing Chip's most extravagant effort. But it didn't matter. By the time Chip had run what campaign he could, it was "a day late and a dollar short," to use his grandfather's phrase.

Tonight, election night, Chip was watching the end game. His workers were quiet and downcast, but he was stunned. What was he going to do? Perhaps it was foolish for an elected official, but he'd presumed he'd have this job until retirement. His résumé was hopelessly out of date, and he hadn't even been exploring contacts – what were they going to do? Erin still had her job at the courthouse, but with Eric off to college and Heather about to graduate from high school, they had a lot of expenses. It wasn't like he could draw unemployment. What were they going to do? Maybe he could call Al Corrigan down in Sanilac County, or Amanda Morris in Tuscola – one of them might have a deputy slot opening.

"Tough luck, Chip," Ken Williams said, walking up and putting a sympathetic hand on his shoulder.

"Yeah," Chip shook himself. "Thanks for all the help, Ken." He needed to work the room, thank people, wish them well, see them off. There'd be time to hash out details later, but right now he needed to be gracious to his workers.

What was he going to tell Erin?

Betrayal

The St. Clair River wasn't technically a river, any more than the Detroit River just to the south was. Being long, narrow passages of water connecting two larger bodies of water, geographically they were straits. But they were called rivers anyway, and since an international border ran down the middle of them, they were heavily patrolled and constantly monitored.

For all the good it did.

Both sides of the hundred-mile waterway between eastern Michigan and southwestern Ontario were thick with rivers, bays, and inlets, many of which were navigable far inland. From where Lake Huron narrowed at Port Huron to where the Detroit River widened into Lake Erie, there were thousands of mooring spots, public and private. On a fine summer day there might be over fifty thousand small craft plying these waters, as well as larger commercial traffic.

Practically speaking, the border was a sieve. That had been proven back in Prohibition days, when heavy patrols and constant observation hadn't prevented the locals from getting rich by bootlegging liquor. Granted, the enforcers back then hadn't had the advantage of video cameras constantly watching every foot of the rivers, surveillance drones, and sophisticated communications between agents ashore and afloat. But then, the bootleggers hadn't had mobile phones, internet communications, and GLN positioning. Getting contraband across the border was a constant game of cat and mouse.

This sunny April morning, Todd Beck and his companions were the mice.

The gaudily decked-out pontoon boat looked a bit odd for this time of year, but not outrageously so. Pontoons weren't considered serious watercraft, so it was expected that anyone who owned one would be a little strange. Granted, the quasi-Polynesian motif was eccentric even for a pontoon, with the faux grass skirting hung about the edges of the hull, the "thatched" awning over the center deck, and a large blue plastic parrot perched atop the thatching. Nobody would think that the gaudy frills had a very specific purpose (except for the parrot).

Todd was in the chair in the bow, doing his best to look like he was diligently fishing while keeping a keen eye on the water ahead. This was his first time helping with a "wet" pickup, which meant pulling a shipment from the water. They were cruising just off the city of St. Clair, where in the center of the river there was a shallow section that was ideal for such exchanges. Earlier in the morning, a Canadian boat had traversed the area slowly, releasing as they passed a cargo that sank to the river bottom four feet below. The shipment was packed in two tightly-sealed cubes that were connected by white polypropylene line, which floated. The goal was to drop the two cubes just the right distance apart so that the white line floated between six and nine inches below the surface – close enough to be visible to an alert lookout, but not shallow enough to float on the surface where it would be visible to all, or so deep that it would be invisible to the most diligent search. It was this line that Todd was watching for.

"We're approaching the release location," came Ben's voice in Todd's earpiece. Todd scanned the rippling waves, his eyes aching from the glare cast by the morning sun. Behind him Paul had set his pole in a mount and was kneeling on the deck. Beneath the cover of the awning, he'd thrown back the large hatch in the deck and was preparing to lower a chain with a grapnel.

"Anything yet? We should be coming up on it," Ben said.

"Maybe a little left. There could be something about twenty, thirty feet ahead."

Ben angled gently and eased back on the throttle. His locator told him that they were almost on top of the coordinates that the drop-off vessel had sent him.

"Definitely something there," Todd reported, still brandishing his rod to protect his cover. "Well below the surface, though. A bit more left."

"Ready here," Paul reported from the deck, grapnel ready to drop through the hatch.

"Definitely rope, about a foot down," Todd relayed. No wonder it had been so hard to see.

"Todd, let us know when it passes under our bow," Ben muttered.

"Fifteen feet," Todd answered. "Ten. Five feet – passing under."

"Drop," Ben said sharply, and Paul let the chain slip through his fingers.

"And…got it!" Paul announced, hauling back the chain and pulling a good bight of the white line through the hatch. He put a couple of wraps of the line around a pulley and began cranking a winch to haul in the cargo. "One package free," he reported as he felt the line take the weight of the first cube. "Second package free, first package visible." Ben had cut back the throttle so that the boat was drifting gently.

"First package…in," Paul reported as he hauled the first cube up through the hatch and cut the line. A little more cranking brought up the second cube, and Paul quickly closed the hatch. It wouldn't do to drop their hard-won cargo back into the river.

Todd and Ben maintained their angler cover while Paul, hidden from overhead view by the thatch hanging from the awning, sliced open the packaging that made up the cubes. He deftly transferred the cargo into the waiting coolers then lay down camouflage in the form of a layer of ice and beer cans.

"What've we got?" Ben asked casually.

"Insulin, of course. Looks like some blood thinners. Bunch of other stuff. Doc will be excited," Paul replied. "All done – now what?"

"Enjoy your fishing," Ben said. "We'll idle out here for another hour or so, then ease up the river." The Pine River flowed through the city of St. Clair and wound back into the country beyond. A couple of miles up the river was a riverside house with a pier, where a van would be waiting to take the medicines for distribution across the ranches.

"Pretty smooth, for the first pickup of the season," Paul added.

"We're not home yet," Ben cautioned. "But things are looking pretty good."

Todd's rod jerked. "Oops – I think I've got something," he said, starting to reel in.

"Hope you remembered to pick up a fishing license for this season," Ben grinned, reaching for the net.

*   *   *

Sitting in her cubicle at the New York office, Brandi McCormick looked at the image on her screen with a mixture of annoyance and yearning. Her birthday was approaching, and Linda never forgot it, though it had been years since Brandi had visited her and Janine back in Michigan. It was a message of the usual type from Linda, sent from a random e-mail address that would never be used again. There were no names, only a brief text, and a picture of the family. They'd made their choices and she'd made hers, Brandi thought as she stared at the bevy of smiling little faces. Part of her argued that they weren't trying to make her feel like a single, childless freak. But hell, *another* kid? When would they quit?

"Eww," came a sneering voice from over her shoulder. "Who's the breeder?"

"Oh," Brandi hadn't known Karen was there. "My effing sister. It's her idea of birthday greetings – sending me a picture of her snot-nosed kids," Brandi scoffed.

"Yuck," said her coworker Karen. "How many is that? Five? Six?"

"Six," Brandi confirmed. "And she's due again in a month or so."

"*Seven* kids?" Karen asked in astonishment. "You'd think they'd have some regard for the environment. Don't they know what causes them?"

"Oh, they know. They're fundamentalist Catholics, so they think their job is to populate the world."

"The worst kind," Karen affirmed. "Where do they live?"

"Over in Michigan. Right near my other sister Janine, who's a similar type but not as bad – she only has four kids."

"So – eleven kids between them?" Karen asked incredulously. "That shouldn't be legal."

"I think so, too, but what can you do?" Brandi said with a shrug. "Best thing I ever did, getting out of there before I ended up as some sort of brood mare." Both women gazed at the image full of smiling faces, each thinking her own thoughts.

"Do you...have her address?" Karen asked casually.

"Her address?" Brandi asked with a puzzled expression. "Why would you want her address?"

"Maybe nothing," Karen said. "Maybe a little harmless pranking."

Brandy was a bit suspicious, but another glance at her sister's smug face in the picture was all it took. She tapped up her address book and grabbed a sticky note. "Sure, here it is," she said, handing the note to Karen.

"Thanks," Karen said, taking the note with a smile.

*   *   *

"What's that noise?" Jude Schaeffer stopped concentrating on the soccer ball that his sister was trying to maneuver past him and looked toward the east.

"What noise, Jude?" His older brother Phillip, who'd been preparing to defend the goal against Elizabeth's assault, stepped over and looked toward where Jude was gazing. They were silent for a moment before Phillip shook his head. "I don't hear anything."

"I don't, either – now," Jude acknowledged. "But I thought I did for a second. Kind of a low, regular hum – listen! There it is...no, it's gone again."

Phillip, Jude, and Elizabeth were all listening now, but didn't hear anything beyond the gusting breeze ruffling the spring leaves. Finally, Phillip shrugged. "Could've been anything. You know how sound travels out here." That was true – they often heard noises echoing off the wall of trees half a mile across the field.

Just then Tabitha and Matthew came running out, wanting to join in the game, but Phillip noted the time and started hustling them in to prepare for dinner. Jude glanced once or twice over his shoulder, but then gave it up and went inside.

*   *   *

In the drone control room in the Department of Homeland Security's Border Security and Domestic Terror Division, Sergeant Abigail Danvers finessed the controls to lift the helidrone back above the tree line. She'd gotten a little careless, lingering too long to capture video of the kids out in the yard. It looked like one of them had heard something from the drone, because he'd abruptly stopped his play and looked toward where it was hovering. The drone was well muffled, but keen ears could still hear it, even in gusting wind. She'd had to drop it down behind the trees, running the risk of getting struck by a branch. But when she'd edged the copter back up, the kids were all heading inside, so apparently they hadn't gotten suspicious.

It didn't really matter. She'd caught plenty of good footage, and was running a bit low on fuel. Time to bring the helidrone back to the barn. Sergeant Danvers hoped this would satisfy them. A week or so earlier, they'd gotten a request to do some flybys of a road in rural St. Clair County, just north of their location at Selfridge Air National Guard base. When they'd sent in that footage, they'd received a follow-up request to monitor a particular address along that road, in particular to capture footage of children. That had mystified everyone, and Major Collins had grumbled about wasting resources, but had acquiesced in the name of interdepartmental cooperation. Apparently, the request had originated with the local Child Protective Services office, but had come through the Department of Health and Human Services. Sergeant Danvers had no idea what it was all about, but she now had several hours of video showing lots of kids in and around that house – certainly five, maybe six. She'd caught a few shots of the parents, too, and from the looks of it, mama was expecting again. Danvers hadn't known anyone still had families that large.

*   *   *

A couple of days later, Janine Peterson was tidying up the living room when movement on the road caught her attention. It was early evening and raining fairly steadily; one of those gray spring days that seems to soak everything. Through the front window Jan saw a small caravan of cars and vans, including several sheriff's cars, racing down their dirt road. Jan gasped and ran to the window, but she could only see so far up the road. She held her breath until she saw the cars drive past the driveway to the Big House right next door. But then to her horror she saw the red glow of brake lights just a little beyond – right in front of the Schaeffer's house.

Jan dashed for the phone in panic.

"Young lady, please hang your dripping jacket somewhere other than the kitchen chair," Linda Schaeffer called. Martha had just returned from chores and had dumped her jacket where she could.

"Yes, Mom," Martha called from the laundry room where she was scrubbing her hands.

A loud, hammering knock came at the front door just as the phone rang. Kent Schaeffer, who was sitting in his recliner reading a book, looked up with annoyed mystification.

"Could you get the door, honey?" Linda asked as she "lumbered" (her term) to the phone. As she answered the phone, the harsh knocking came again, causing Kent, who was halfway there, to call out angrily, "I'm coming, I'm coming!"

"Hello?" Linda said into the phone handset.

"Linda, get out, get out, there's a whole bunch of police turning into your drive!" came her sister's terrified voice. Linda's eyes widened and she turned to see Kent just reaching for the door handle.

"Kent, no!" she screamed, but it was too late. He cracked the door only to have it thrown open in his face. What seemed like a mass of wet people, some uniformed and some not, burst into the living room.

"What – what's all this?" Kent demanded, but just then the back door flew open and several people piled into the kitchen, one with a gun drawn, causing Martha to shriek in alarm. Then all the kids were piling into the main area to see what was going on, and little Matthew began to wail and run for Linda.

"Kent George Schaeffer and Linda Margaret Schaeffer," boomed one deputy, reading from a piece of paper in his hand. "I have a warrant for your arrest on charges of child endangerment and abuse, along with probate authority to take your children into protective custody."

*   *   *

Derek and his ATV had been stranded up near Kingston by the rain moving in, so Phillip had hitched up the small trailer and driven up to get him. They were on their way back, just turning east on Old M-21 at Imlay City, when Phillip's phone rang. "Hello?" he answered. Derek swiftly knew something was very wrong. Whoever was on the other end was talking in a panicked frenzy that was so loud that Derek could almost hear it from the far side of the truck. Phillip listened in stunned silence, his eyes growing wider, and suddenly pulled onto the shoulder to concentrate on the call.

"Oh, no," Phillip whispered, his face ashen. Derek felt a chill of fear knot his insides – he'd never seen strong, confident Phillip look so stricken.

"What – what can we do?" Phillip whispered, then listened some more while Derek waited anxiously. "We're about fifteen minutes away. Okay, we'll do that." There was another bit of the caller speaking. "All right, see you shortly." He hung up and put his head down on the steering wheel, looking utterly defeated.

"What's going on?" Derek asked, almost afraid to hear.

"Mom and Dad have been arrested," Phillip gasped. "There was a raid – they don't know much – Aunt Jan heard some of it over the phone."

"Oh, my God," Derek whispered.

"It's worse," Phillip struggled against sobs. "The charges had something to do with child abuse, so they took the kids, too – all of them – into some kind of custody!"

"Oh, *no!*" Derek cried, his vision narrowing and his heart hammering. His family, his beloved family! "What can we do?"

"Aunt Jan and Uncle Gil are working it," Phillip said as he pulled the truck back onto the road and roared down it. "They've called Fitz."

Derek was stunned into silence. Kent and Linda arrested? The children taken? He glanced at Phillip, who was staring down the rain-drenched road and muttering under his breath. "Phillip, if there's anything I can do…" Derek began, then trailed off. He couldn't think of a thing, and didn't want to waste Phillip's resources by asking him to think about it.

"Thanks," Phillip said distractedly. "I think…I think it'd be best if I dropped you at Uncle Gil's, or somewhere other than the house. It's likely the house has been watched, and may still be, so it's best if you lie low. You can make your way to the workshop by the back ways."

"Good thinking," Derek replied. They drove the rest of the way in silence, Phillip muttering either prayers or curses – or both.

By the time they arrived at the Peterson's, the rain had stopped. Phillip pulled into the circle drive while the family ran out to greet them.

"Fitz is at the district court right now, filing for their release," Gil explained hastily, handing Phillip a phone. "Use this unit – Fitz is speed dial two."

Derek jumped out of the truck and helped Chris Peterson unhitch the trailer. Phillip drove off toward Port Huron while the Petersons hustled Derek inside.

Gil and Jan gave Derek dinner while they explained what they knew about the situation. Derek was still stunned, but he could see that Gil and Jan were nearly frantic. Not only was Linda Jan's sister, and her kids Jan's beloved nieces and nephews, but this kind of seizure was everyone's worst nightmare. Derek had been told of families whose children had been taken from them on flimsy pretenses. Complicating matters was the fact that all of the Schaeffer children save Phillip were "off the grid" – not officially known by the government. Beyond the record of birth with the county clerk, the children from Martha on down hadn't been claimed on taxes, received Social Security numbers, been enrolled in the health care system, or been sent to public school. This strategy had kept them out of the government's eye, but nobody knew how it was going to affect the handling of the children by probate court and Child Protective Services.

The tension was thick in the air around the little campus. Since nobody knew why the Schaeffers had been so unexpectedly targeted, nobody knew which door might be the next one knocked on. All the children in the Peterson and Winters households were off the grid, and Derek could hear plans being made to distribute them out across the ranches. Derek could sense that his presence was giving the Petersons one more thing to worry about, so he retired to his workshop to await any developments. He resettled his gear and tidied his rooms, then said evening prayers and did pretty much anything he could think of to occupy himself, but his mind and imagination kept obsessing about what had happened to his adopted family. He wished he could go talk to Grandpa about it, but he was sure the patriarch had enough on his hands.

Shortly after 10:00 p.m., Jan called to tell him that Phillip and Fitz were bringing Kent and Linda back. Derek got over to the house, made coffee and tea and some sandwiches, and tensely awaited their return. When he heard the truck pull into the drive, Derek dashed out to help them in. Phillip and Kent were supporting Linda while Gerry Fitzgerald, whom everyone just called "Fitz", followed looking grim. Derek let the guys help Linda inside while he collared Fitz.

"What's going on?"

"I was able to get them released on bail," Fitz explained tersely. "The kids are in the hands of CPS – I'll be down filing with probate tomorrow."

"Any idea why? What could have caused them – "

"Clueless," Fitz replied. "Linda's taking this hard, and Kent isn't much better. Come on – they may need your help."

Inside on the living room couch, Linda looked ready to faint. Derek realized he should have brought his stethoscope and blood pressure cuff, and even now wondered if he should run and fetch them. He knelt by her knees and took her hand, trying to feel for her pulse.

"My babies, my babies," she was muttering in a thin whisper. She was pale and her breathing was fast and shallow.

"Mom, Mom, try to calm down," Phillip encouraged, patting her other hand. Kent said nothing, but just stared at her, his mind elsewhere. Derek noticed a rather severe contusion on his right cheek.

"Linda, try to lie down here," Derek said, knowing it was futile to tell a woman who was eight months pregnant to put her head between her knees. Though Phillip tried to help her, it was no use – she just kept staring at the floor, muttering "My babies, my babies."

Suddenly, Kent stood up and began stalking about the room, then burst out the door and onto the front porch. Alarmed, Derek glanced at Phillip and Fitz. Phillip nodded that he should follow Kent, so Derek got up and went out. He found Kent pacing the front porch in agitation, running his fingers through his hair and rubbing his face.

"Kent, I –" Derek began.

"The bastards, the bastards," Kent was muttering as he stamped to and fro. "Cowards! Picking on kids and pregnant women! They tore Matthew from her, screaming, and threw him in the van!" Kent collapsed on the bench, and Derek sat beside him, tears streaming down his face. Cheerful little Matthew was especially close to Derek, and the thought of him being manhandled tore his heart.

"I couldn't even protect my own family," Kent choked through his sobs. "They'd handcuffed me, and when I saw what they were doing and tried to go to them, they kicked my feet out from under me. Cowardly bastards."

Well, that explained the contusion. "Kent, don't torture yourself," Derek urged him.

"Why would they do this?" Kent pleaded to the air. "Who would target us? Why would He let this happen?"

"Kent, I don't know any of that," Derek replied. His heart was breaking, and he wanted nothing more than to comfort his friend, but there was no time. "What I do know is this: Linda's almost in shock."

"She nearly fainted twice," Kent said bleakly. "Gutless bastards. Couldn't even protect my own family."

"I know, Kent, but this is my point: you can't afford the luxury of self-recrimination. You have another child to worry about." Kent looked at him, bewildered, and Derek continued though it was hell to do so. "If Linda gets distressed enough, her body and the baby's might come to the conclusion that it's time to bail. She could go into early labor. She's thirty-five or thirty-six weeks along, which isn't a catastrophic premature birth, but it's early enough. The midwife couldn't do it – she'd have to go to the hospital, into the system, and then you'd have another of your children in their hands."

Kent stared at him, dazed with shock and pain, grappling with this new complexity. "What…what do I do?"

"Get in there and try to calm her down. I'm going to contact the midwife to see what she recommends, while I research what medicines we have that I could use. Kent, I know you're hurting, but Linda and the baby need you right now."

"Calm her," Kent muttered, heaving himself to his feet.

"Right. I'm going for some gear – be right back." Derek dashed off to his apartment while Kent went back in to Linda.

The night held little rest for any of them. Fitz left soon, promising to be at the courthouse first thing to fight on their behalf. Derek consulted the midwife, Fran, who recommended an herbal tea mix to help Linda relax and promised to be down in the morning. Derek was back and forth between the house and his quarters, monitoring Linda and the baby's status and reading everything he could about delaying early labor under conditions of maternal distress. Unfortunately, almost everything recommended either medicines or facilities he didn't have access to, but he gleaned a few suggestions.

The other two houses were quietly busy as well. From time to time, Derek could hear four-wheelers or UTVs, and he knew what that meant: the children were being sent away to safety under cover of darkness. Roads were being avoided in case of surveillance. They'd use the same network of trails and hidden roads that Derek often used in his travels.

The next day was tense, but there were no significant developments. Messages of support were pouring in from across the area. Parishes across the Thumb offered Masses for the safety and swift return of the Schaeffer children. Linda was weak, but resting and not showing any signs of going into labor. The midwife stopped in and looked Linda over, prescribing complete bed rest and a battery of herbal teas and scents. Phillip walked around looking like he was ready to spit nails, but Kent was nearly catatonic, sitting by Linda's bed, holding her hand, and not responding to much except his phone. Grandpa was in and out, but Grandma just sat by Linda's bed, crocheting. Over in Port Huron, an increasingly-frustrated Fitz kept bouncing back and forth between district court, which was handling the charges that had been filed against Kent and Linda, and probate court, which was handling the cases of the children. He was making little progress in either place, but if there was one thing Fitz was, it was doggedly persistent, so he kept at it until the courts closed.

Fitz was back down first thing the next morning, first to the probate court with another filing. Oddly, the clerk handed the paperwork back to him, telling him that there had been some "developments" in the case and that he should go over to the district court. This he did, and what he found out there sent him right back to the probate court, where he argued and demanded but to no avail. He made calls to contacts who promised to do what they could, but that such an unusual situation would take time, and no outcome could be guaranteed.

Finally, sitting in his car parked in front of the courthouse, Fitz knew he had to make the call he'd been trying to postpone. Sighing, he keyed the Schaeffer's number.

"Hello?" Kent answered.

"Hi, Kent. Are you there with Linda?"

"Yeah – and Phillip and Derek and Grandma, too. Here, I'm putting you on speaker."

Fitz winced, but supposed they'd all have to learn eventually. Better to hear it directly from him than through Kent. "Listen, there have been some…developments…in the case."

"Developments?" Kent asked guardedly.

"Yes. First, they're dropping all charges against you and Linda. Everything, dropped, as of this morning."

"Dropped? All charges?" Kent asked with a note of disbelief. "But why – that's good, isn't it?"

Fitz drew a deep breath and blinked back tears. "In one sense, yes, but in another sense, not at all. This is a very difficult and complicating development. They're dropping the charges because – because they're now claiming that there were never any children for you to abuse."

"No…children?" Kent whispered.

Fitz closed his eyes, fighting the tears no longer, and just said it straight out. "It is now the stand of the courts that you were

44

arrested in error. Since there are no official records of any of your children, they do not officially exist, and therefore you could not have abused or neglected them."

"Not – exist?"

"Since your children do not exist in the eyes of the law, the probate court is not handling their case. I can file till the cows come home, but it won't make any difference."

"But – their birth certificates?" Kent asked weakly.

"The contention is that the weight of evidence discounts them. The fact that your children have no other, later records from other sources is being used to argue that there are no such children. Legally dubious, but it would take a protracted court battle to contest it," Fitz explained.

"Then – where are they?"

Again, Fitz caught his breath. This was the hardest part. "I don't know. They've vanished into the foster care network maintained by CPS. Without probate authority, not only can I not petition for their return, I can't discover their whereabouts or status or anything about them. All we know is what Child Protective Services wants to tell us, which isn't going to be much."

Fitz winced as the sound of Linda's scream echoed through the bedroom.

Violation

For the third time in ten minutes, Felicity jumped up from her desk and paced the small room in agitation.

"Feliss, I understand your turmoil," Grace offered from where she sat on her bed outlining her paper. "But you're going to wear the floor out. Why don't you take a walk? It's a pleasant evening."

"I've taken two walks already today, and I really need to study," Felicity answered. "But it's so hard to concentrate on Euripides with...all this..."

The residents of the little college had learned of what had befallen the Schaeffer family through the circuitous channels they used for cross-border communications. They were all aghast, but Grace was stunned and Felicity nearly frantic. Both girls had wanted to return immediately, but reason had prevailed – not only was there nothing practical they'd be able to do, but the tremendous risk of crossing and re-crossing the border made it next to impossible. They'd not even returned home for Christmas and Easter; taking such a risk now for no practical purpose was out of the question.

The little group of students and faculty, who were by now a close-knit community, rallied around the girls in sympathy and support. Masses were said, prayer vigils were held, messages of support were sent, and word of the tragedy went out through the Canadian side of the underground network. While the girls appreciated the support, the emotional burden was still heavy, particularly on Felicity, who was very close to her kidnapped cousins. She was almost sleepless with anguish not only over their fate, but for her aunt and uncle, and what they must be suffering.

"I hate to remind you – again – of what Grandma Del used to say," Grace finally said after watching Felicity pace. "But..."

"I know, I know. Worrying is praying to the wrong god," Felicity completed the statement as she sat down on Grace's bed.

47

"But – and I don't mean this irreverently – I've done so much praying, and I still feel like I ought to be doing more." She wiped her eyes with the back of her hand.

"I know," Grace said sympathetically, handing her a tissue and gripping her hand. "When you've done all you can and haven't seen any results, there comes a point when the prayers are as much for you as they are for those for whom you're praying."

"I suppose so," Felicity acknowledged.

"I know I'm praying for you as well as them," Grace assured her.

"Thanks," Felicity replied, smiling through her tears and giving her friend a hug. "Oh, Lord, please let them be safe."

*   *   *

Martha and Jude agreed that wherever they were, it was a bigger city than they were used to, though maybe not a really big city. That meant it was likely either Port Huron or Lapeer, and they were guessing Port Huron.

Not that it made much difference.

Everything had happened so quickly – the policemen and strangers, the confusion and shouting, Dad being handcuffed and Mom being held by those two deputies. Martha, Jude, Tabitha, and Elizabeth had been hustled into a van despite their tears and protests. They'd been taken to a building and had spent much of that evening sitting in bleak conference rooms. People had come in from time to time to look at them and type things into tablets. They were asked no questions other than their names and birthdates. When they'd protested that they wanted their parents, or were hungry or tired, or needed the bathroom, there had been no response. Finally, in the middle of the night, they'd been taken downstairs to an underground garage and loaded into another van. They'd had a brief glimmer of hope that they were being taken home, that all this had been a misunderstanding. But that hope had been crushed when they'd been brought here and dumped – and here was where they'd been stuck ever since, for nearly a week now, though it felt like a grim eternity.

"Here" was Ms. Florence's house. It was an older two-story house with a small yard in an older neighborhood – not that they got to see much of either. They weren't allowed outside at all. All the doors had locks on them, the type with a numeric keypad where you had to know the code to open it. The doors leading outside were always locked, but their bedroom doors were on some kind of timer. Every night they were locked in their bedrooms from 10:00 p.m. to 7:00 a.m. There were three bedrooms upstairs, as well as some kind of loft in the attic that was reached by a narrow staircase at the end of the hall. Martha was put in one room, Tabitha and Elizabeth in another, and Jude in the third. Downstairs, there was a family room in the back of the house, the kitchen in the middle, and a small living room in the front. Ms. Florence's bedroom, and a small adjoining room that she used as an office, were off the kitchen.

The children presumed that Ms. Florence was supposed to take care of them, but there was no care provided. She spent all her time watching the huge television that covered one wall of the family room, or talking incessantly on her phone. Sometimes she'd duck outside to smoke and talk, at times for nearly an hour. When asked about meals, she pointed the children to the cupboards and refrigerator and snarled that she didn't want any messes in her kitchen. Martha and Jude were both adept cooks, but the house had little to work with – cans of vegetables and soups and spaghetti, cheap fruit drink rather than milk, and cheap white bread rather than Mom's homemade. Meals were bleak affairs.

For that matter, just about everything about their imprisonment was bleak. There wasn't a book in the entire house, no workstations except the one in Ms. Florence's office. Nobody wanted to watch the inane shows that blared incessantly from the television – not that Ms. Florence would have tolerated their presence. She made them do menial chores like cleaning (with pitifully inadequate tools) and collecting trash, but otherwise they were left to themselves. None of them wanted to spend any more time than they had to in their stuffy rooms upstairs, where all the windows were screwed shut, so they usually huddled miserably in the living room, trying to console and encourage one another. Martha sang every song she could remember while Jude told stories from his repertoire of myths and legends. They began and ended each day with prayers that their ordeal would soon end, and that they'd be reunited with their family.

*   *   *

Melanie Gibs took another sip of her drink and tried to relax after her frustrating shift. Honestly, it was getting to the point where anything like a normal day was the rare exception. With the increasing demands and decreasing resources, everyone at Child Protective Services was overstretched. Caseworkers were badly overloaded, supervisors were trying to oversee too many caseworkers, and compliance inspectors like Melanie were expected to cover far too many care sites. She was spending so much time running down grievances and non-compliance complaints that regular audits were getting short shrift.

At least there were outfits like Wondercare. Not many, but hopefully the trend would catch on.

Melanie was currently awaiting Andrea Stevens, the compliance officer for Wondercare. Andrea had messaged to say she'd be a little late for their appointment, but that Melanie should relax and order a drink. They'd taken to meeting after work hours, when Melanie wasn't technically on the clock, and thus could relax a little. Over the years Andrea had become as much a friend and confidante as professional colleague. She had a caring demeanor and would listen sympathetically as Melanie poured out her woes. Of course, they transacted business as well, but it was so different from the press and rush of her regular workday that Melanie looked forward to their periodic meetings.

Wondercare ran a network of foster care homes across the region. Unlike so many small-time operators, Wondercare was efficient and well managed. They had a website, a wide array of care locations and qualified providers, and a shuttle that could transport kids to and from appointments. They even had a staff physician! Of most interest to Melanie was their full-time compliance office, whose job it was to ensure that all staff qualifications were current, all certification paperwork filed on time, and all relevant laws and policies followed. Oh, how Melanie loved dealing with Wondercare, especially after a career full of contending with little mom-and-pop operations that didn't even bother to read the manuals that came with their contracts! Working with Wondercare's compliance staff meant no more unanswered e-mails or vanishing voice mail messages. Calls were returned promptly, questions were answered, data was provided. If all providers were as efficient as Wondercare, Melanie's job would be a lot easier.

"Hey, girl!" came a familiar voice just as Melanie was pondering ordering another drink.

"Andrea! Good to see you!" Melanie answered.

"Sorry I'm so late," Andrea apologized as she slid into the booth. "I had to dash back from Midland. We're opening up some new homes over there, and I had to insure they were all ready for the initial inspections."

"Wow – Midland. You guys are really expanding, aren't you?" Melanie asked. "Here I thought you were just in the Thumb area."

"Well, that's our bread and butter, but even that takes in Flint, Saginaw, and Bay City," Andrea explained. "From there, it's an easy and logical reach out to Midland. But the bosses are already setting their sights higher."

"Higher?"

"Yes – the tri-county area. Lots of opportunity there, but lots of competition, too."

"I don't know, Andrea," Melanie said, shaking her head. "Metro Detroit has a lot of problems. Not that they couldn't use

51

an organization of your caliber – I have a friend who works for CPS down in Wayne County, and her job drives her mad. But it would be a very tall order, even for Wondercare. Besides, I'd never see you."

"Oh, I'd make certain that never happened," Andrea assured her. "What are you drinking? It looks good."

They ordered a round of cocktails, and then another, and then a good dinner with delicious wine. They chatted and laughed and shared their respective struggles. Andrea sympathized when Melanie shared her deepest heartache: that she feared her marriage was dead, and was contemplating calling a lawyer. It was a long, wonderful time of heart-to-heart sharing that Melanie was sad to see come toward a close. When the waiter left the bill, Melanie did the obligatory fishing in her purse only to have Andrea wave her off as she always did.

"I've got this, Melanie. It's been my pleasure, and I wish we could go on for hours. Before you go, I've got a couple of things for you." Andrea slid two items across the table. One was a pretty little folder which Melanie didn't recognize. "I know your birthday is coming up, and since you've been under so much stress recently, I thought you might appreciate this. Go ahead, open it."

Melanie picked up the folder and saw that it contained a gift card good for a full day's treatment at the spa in town.

"Oh, Andrea, I've never...thank you so much," Melanie said, gripping her friend's hand.

"I just hope it helps you get some much-needed relaxation," Andrea replied. "And I hope this eases your burdens in other ways."

Melanie looked at the other item. It was a storage chip, and she knew what was on it. It had files for all of Wondercare's facilities in the county, files that exactly matched the required fields for the compliance inspections which Melanie had to submit. Andrea had started this a few years earlier as a way to help Melanie be more efficient. It had begun with just the basic administrative details about the sites – date of opening, license numbers, staff qualifications, and the like. But once Melanie had accepted that help, more and more data had been added each time: prepared answers to questions, text descriptions of facility conditions, even photographs. The last set of files had essentially been pre-completed compliance inspections which Melanie could copy and paste right onto the official forms, and then just sign and submit.

"As usual, this is just to save you grunt work," Andrea said casually. "Take what you can use, let me know what you need to eyeball directly, and we'll schedule the appointments for your visits. I know midyear is fast approaching, and you'll be up to your ears, so I wanted to lighten your load as much as I could."

"Thanks, Andrea," Melanie said, slipping the chip into her purse. They both knew what would happen: Melanie would start out with the best of intentions to perform physical inspections on all her sites, including the Wondercare homes, but she'd hit delays and unexpected demands which would clog her hours. As the submission deadline drew closer, that chip and its contents would loom larger in her mind until at last she'd pull it out and dump the contents onto her official forms. That was what Melanie had ended up doing last cycle, and though she'd never told Andrea, it was clear that she'd never scheduled any site visits. Melanie had no ethical qualms about it. Her supervisors demanded the impossible – rapid responses and thorough investigations and impeccable write-ups and outrageous compliance percentages, along with perfect inspection reports with every "i" dotted and every "t" crossed. Well, they'd get those, at least for the Wondercare sites. After all, it was Wondercare, who always kept things above board and squared away.

*   *   *

When the children had been at Ms. Florence's house for just over a week, Cliff showed up. Nobody explained where he'd come from or why he was there. He looked to be in his late teens or early twenties, with curly brown hair and a scruffy attempt at a beard. He wore dirty t-shirts and jeans and a sullen, resentful look. He spent all his time either in the family room watching television or in the kitchen scrounging food or outside smoking. He and Ms. Florence were always yelling at each other, but for some reason she never sent him away.

Jude didn't like it at all. He noticed how Cliff shot sideways glances at Martha – sly, ugly glances that made Jude want to hit him. He noticed that Martha didn't like to be in the same room with Cliff, and would find an excuse to leave any room he entered. But there was only so much space in the house, and wherever she went, he would soon find some pretense to follow. He wouldn't even talk to her – he'd just loiter about, pretending to be doing something but eyeing her constantly.

One evening, they went upstairs early to escape, which was a trial because their rooms had effectively no ventilation. With the windows sealed and no air conditioning vents, the only circulation came through the grids mounted in the bottom of the doors, which were pitifully inadequate. They all huddled in the middle room to say evening prayers and then clung to each other for comfort until Ms. Florence came up to shoo them to bed.

Martha went to her room and closed the door, knowing she was locked in until morning unless Ms. Florence keyed the code to let her out. She prepared for bed and lay down on top of the sheets; it was so stifling already. She lay in the dark for a while, listening to the noises of the house. Eventually she heard footsteps clump up the stairs, down the hall, and up to the attic. Cliff. Martha suspected that he secreted beer up there. That was fine by her, so long as he kept it there. What a creepy guy. She drifted off to sleep eventually.

"Oh!" Martha sat up suddenly, not knowing what had awakened her. Glancing over, she saw that a shadowed figure had entered and was just closing the door, leaving the room in complete darkness.

"Who…who is it?" Martha stammered, her heart pounding.

"It's me, baby," came Cliff's slurred voice.

"H-how did you get in?" Martha asked, grabbing for the covers.

"I work here, baby. I know all the codes," Cliff replied, walking toward the bed.

"What do you want?" Martha's mouth was going dry and she pushed back against the wall, trying to escape.

"What do I want? I want you, baby," Cliff said, dropping his jeans to the floor and lunging for her.

"No, *no*," Martha began to cry, but then he was on her, pinning her legs and covering her mouth, stinking of sweat and beer and tobacco.

"Now, now, don't you be making a fuss," he whispered hoarsely. "You don't want to be scaring your little sisters next door. And if you put up too much of a fight, I'll just go over there, yes I will."

"No, no, no," Martha moaned, shaking her head, unable to believe this was happening. He pulled his hand away from her mouth and tried to kiss her. She turned her face aside, revolted by the coarse brush of his whiskers against her skin. She tried to push him away, but he grabbed her wrist with one hand while groping her chest with the other. No, Lord, no, this couldn't be happening, this couldn't be happening.

But it was. His weight was on her and he was pulling at her clothes. She struggled but he pinned her down.

"No noise, now," he laughed. "Besides, where you're headed, you're in for a lot of this. May as well lie back and enjoy it."

Then darkness flooded Martha's mind and heart as he did his vile deed. So deep was her shame and revulsion that she didn't even notice any physical pain, at least not then.

Then he was rolling off, standing up, and pulling his jeans back on. He keyed the code into the lock and opened the door, letting a shaft of light onto the bedroom wall.

"Remember, baby," he said over his shoulder. "Our secret." Then he was gone, leaving Martha in the darkness to curl up against the wall and sob into the pillow.

The next morning, Jude knew immediately that something was dreadfully wrong. Normally Martha was up first, coming around to the other rooms to see how everyone was. This morning, as soon as the doors unlocked, Martha dashed for the bathroom and stayed in there for a long time. Eventually Tabitha, who needed to use the bathroom too, knocked and asked Martha when she'd be out. Jude wasn't close enough to hear the conversation, but was disturbed by what Tabitha reported when she came back.

"She's crying. Why is she crying in the bathroom?"

Jude didn't know, except that it was one more terrible thing about this whole terrible situation. Eventually Martha came out and went back into her room to dress. Jude caught a glimpse of her face and knew his suspicions were correct. The normally cheerful and happy Martha wore a desperate, hunted look. Her eyes were red, her hair was in disarray, and her expression was grim. She looked no better when she came out and they headed down for breakfast.

"Martha, are you all right?" Jude asked. She shook her head, saying nothing but bursting into tears and hugging him fiercely.

Jude watched Martha carefully all morning, trying to discern what was wrong. She hardly talked at all, but seemed to murmur to herself a lot. She'd hug the others, mostly the girls, tightly if they came near, but at the same time she wanted to be alone. She seemed restless, no sooner settling in one room before she'd get up and go into another – though she never went upstairs to her bedroom.

When Cliff finally came downstairs and into the kitchen, Martha fled – literally fled – into the living room. It wasn't anything Cliff did – in fact, he looked more subdued and downcast than usual – but when Jude went in after Martha, he found her curled in a chair in the corner of the room, her eyes darting about like those of a cornered animal. Jude knelt beside her and hugged her and promised he'd stay right with her. She clung to him and sobbed into his shoulder and said nothing.

Jude knew then that it was up to him. He had to "put on his thinking cap," as Mr. Sam used to say. Until now, they'd all looked to Martha as the eldest for comfort and reassurance. Now something had happened to her, something horrible, and from the looks of it, she was going to be struggling to get through the day. Unless she got better soon, which didn't look likely, it was up to him to figure a way out of this horrible situation.

Before more horrible things happened.

*   *   *

Back at Rivendell, the campus of households normally so full of harmony and peace, the atmosphere was charged with desperation and fear. Linda was on full-time bed rest, closely monitored by Derek, and Fran when she could drop by. There was no sign of labor beginning, but Linda's pulse and blood pressure worried Derek. The midwife said there seemed to be no indication of fetal distress, and though Linda was effacing slightly, she didn't know whether that was due to the extraordinary conditions or just because it was Linda's seventh birth. Derek was determined to do all he could to get this baby to term.

The overriding concern was locating the children. Every resource was being tapped and every option exercised, but with no results. Fitz was almost living at the probate court, and tried to bring encouraging reports, but everyone noticed that his assurances were getting increasingly desperate. Almost two weeks had passed, and every attempt to learn the children's status or whereabouts had been stymied. They were completely at the mercy of Child Protective Services, which wasn't being merciful.

The days crept by. Messages of support trickled in, prayers were offered, word was spread. Grandma kept vigil at Linda's side, knitting or saying a Rosary or quietly reading Psalms. Kent tried to go into the office but admitted that he couldn't concentrate on calls. He couldn't get his mind off his children. Where were they? Were they safe?

*   *   *

After a couple of days, Jude noticed that Martha's fearful mood seemed to abate a little. She still looked miserable, and obviously wasn't sleeping well, but was a little more attentive to things around her, and even managed to smile a few times when the girls worked hard to cheer her up. He noticed that she seemed to spend an inordinate amount of time in the bathroom, and was constantly washing her hands.

There was still no word about their family, or what was happening to them, or why they were imprisoned, and Ms. Florence didn't welcome questions. Jude hoped something might be developing when a strange man showed up one day, but he turned out to be some kind of repair technician who spent all his time in the little office off Ms. Florence's bedroom and then left.

Cliff was still around, but he was busier outside these days, mowing the lawn and tinkering in the garage. He did grocery runs, which meant their meager fare was a little heavier on snack foods than it had been. He also brought bags that went straight up to his room in the attic – Jude suspected what was in them. He still didn't like Cliff, who continued to watch Martha with those sideways looks whenever he could, which wasn't often. Whenever Cliff showed up, Martha would bolt into the next room or upstairs. Something about the whole situation really smelled.

For some reason, bedtimes were especially difficult for Martha. She'd taken to staying downstairs until the last possible minute, surrounding herself with her siblings until Ms. Florence made them go upstairs. Martha went reluctantly to her room, which seemed strange to Jude. He didn't like being locked into his bedroom every night either, but it wasn't like it was the worst thing that had happened to them.

Martha was dozing fitfully, too jumpy to really sleep but too exhausted to stay awake. She hated the dark, stuffy bedroom. Being in it, on this bed, filled her imagination with horrible memories. Every night she prayed and wept herself into this turbulent, oft-broken slumber.

A creak of the floorboards in the hallway brought her bolt awake. Sitting up and pulling the covers to her chin, she stared in horror at the door.

"No, no, please no," she muttered as she heard the sound of someone fumbling at the lock. "God, please no, please no."

But the door opened. "Hey, baby," came the voice that haunted her nightmares.

Afterwards, Cliff didn't leave straightaway as he had before. While Martha curled against the wall, her back to him, he pulled his jeans back on and sat down at the desk chair, silent in the darkness. The only sound was Martha's plaintive sobbing into her pillow.

"Can I get you...a glass of water, or a towel, or...something?" he asked clumsily. She didn't respond at all, and after a bit more silent waiting he stood to go. "All right then – g'night." He let himself out the door, muttering under his breath, "Bitches."

The next morning, Jude knew immediately that whatever horrible thing happened before had happened again. Martha again bolted for the bathroom, and could clearly be heard crying, almost wailing, through the door. Tabitha and Elizabeth looked at Jude in hurt bewilderment – why was their sister so upset? Was it just the ongoing stress of their separation and imprisonment, or was there more?

When Martha came downstairs, she showed no interest in breakfast, but went straight to the living room where she stayed at the far end, sitting and standing and walking about in agitation. She was totally self-absorbed, paying only the slightest attention to any attempt to interact with her. She stood at windows, gazing out and stroking the glass. She'd sit on the couch, staring into space and biting her thumb, which was an old nervous habit of hers. At one point, Jude was alarmed to see traces of blood on her lip. She didn't settle anywhere, moving restlessly from chair to window to couch to window, never leaving the room, interested in nothing, not even her siblings.

Jude, Tabitha, and Elizabeth kept unsettled vigil with their sister all morning. The girls would try to reach her – Tabitha brought her a glass of orange drink and Elizabeth folded her an origami frog with a scrap of paper she found. Nothing seemed to work. Jude was increasingly frustrated at his impotence. Men were supposed to protect. Men were supposed to take action. He was the only man around, but he was helpless.

After a few restless hours, Martha finally dozed off at the end of the couch, with Tabitha cuddled close and Elizabeth keeping watch from the nearby chair. Jude hoped Martha would get some relief from her turmoil, but the interlude was soon shattered when Cliff came clumping downstairs and she jolted awake like a frightened deer. She jumped to her feet and resumed her pacing, only more frantically, reminding Jude of nothing so much as a sparrow he'd once seen trapped in the barn, fluttering about desperately and beating its wings against walls and windows.

Jude moved to where he could see Cliff skulking about the kitchen fetching some breakfast. He looked like his usual slovenly self, but his eyes seemed more furtive.

"What do you want, kid?" Cliff snarled when he saw Jude watching him. Jude didn't respond, but continued to glower at Cliff. Whatever was wrong with Martha, this punk had something to do with it, Jude was sure. He just didn't know what to do about it.

Just then Ms. Florence made one of her rare appearances, bustling out of the family room and looking about. Spotting Jude in the living room, she frowned.

"What are you doing in here?" she asked, as if they'd been forbidden to be in the living room. "What are you all doing in here?"

"What are you doing to help my sister?" Jude shot back fiercely, even though Ms. Florence was a grownup. "Something's really wrong with her! She needs help, and all you do is watch TV!"

"Watch your mouth, kid," Ms. Florence warned, but she looked at Martha curled on the couch, then, tellingly, to where Cliff was clumping around the kitchen, then back at Martha, then back at Cliff. "Well, then – enough of this," she blustered, as if they'd been doing something wrong. "The kitchen and bathrooms need cleaning, so you girls get busy on that. Tomorrow's trash day, so you collect the garbage, kid."

Jude was just about to protest sending any of the girls into the kitchen where Cliff was, when he heard the back-door slam, indicating that Cliff had gone off somewhere. Disgusted and frustrated, Jude fetched a couple of garbage bags from underneath the kitchen sink and went to gather the trash from the upstairs rooms.

He was back down shortly and started collecting from the downstairs cans. Ms. Florence was outside, engaged in one of her long-winded phone conversations and smoking. Cliff was nowhere around, and the girls were busy about the kitchen. His rounds took him into Ms. Florence's bedroom and the little office. All the time he was wracking his brain for something, anything he could do.

Jude sat on the chair in the office and pulled the trash can out from under the desk. It seemed unusually full, and he saw that it was jammed with a box and some packing material. The box was for a network controller. Ah, that's what the guy had been doing here the other day – installing a new network controller.

Wait a minute.

A new network controller.

Jude sat staring at the workstation screen. Mr. Sam had once explained to him about network controllers when he'd showed interest. The conversation came back with startling clarity, right down to Mr. Sam's slurred speech and funny sideways glances. For one thing, network controllers were devices that routed, managing all the data traffic between the house and the internet. They also handled all the wireless communications on the site, as well as managing the smart devices in the household, like thermostats and appliances.

And locks.

Glancing over his shoulder, Jude saw no sign of Ms. Florence. Hopefully her phone conversation would be a long one. His breath coming fast, he stared at the workstation screen. There was some command that would tell you the network address of the controller, Mr. Sam had told him. Then it came back to him, as clearly as if Mr. Sam had whispered it into his ear. He tapped open a window and typed in the command. Bad command? Oh, he'd mistyped. Trying again, he saw the quick spurt of numbers on the screen. Scanning them, he tried to remember what he was looking for. Oh, there it was: gateway. That number was the address of the controller. He tapped open another window and entered that address. Suddenly he was looking at the control screen for the device.

Jude's elation was short-lived. There was a login screen asking for a user ID and password. What would those be? Then came darting into his memory Mr. Sam's instructions on configuring these things – how they always came from the factory with a default administrative user ID and password, and how the first thing that you wanted to do after you installed it was change the password. Default ID and password – but where? Wait a minute – Jude pawed in the trash can, shuffling through the papers until he found it: the little flyer that always came with electronic devices, the Quick Start Guide that told you how to get the thing up and running. This one was a little folded pamphlet, and Jude flipped through it until he found what he sought: the default administrative ID and master password. Tentatively he pecked the values into the fields and tapped OK.

It worked. He was in.

Jude grinned gleefully. The numbskulls hadn't even changed the default password – but then, they'd not had Mr. Sam to instruct them. His heart was hammering. He had full administrative access to all the devices managed by the controller. He could do anything he wished.

But what to do? And how to do it? Jude took a deep breath and calmed himself. What had Mr. Sam always said? "See what you're looking at." Jude examined the screen. There were tabs along the edge. One said 'Entertainment'. He tapped it, and saw an image of a television with letters and numbers beside it. Ah, so that would be where you controlled the signals to the television. Better not mess with any of this – he didn't want to leave any indication he'd been here.

Another tab said 'Environment', but he guessed that had to do with the heating and air conditioning. Ah, this looked promising: 'Security'. He tapped the tab and was rewarded with a screen that had a column of icons, each with some numbers and colored dots just to the right. Most of the icons had little glowing red dots beside them, but three had glowing green dots.

This had to be it. Jude guessed that the icons with the green dots represented their bedroom door locks, open during the day. The other locks were engaged all the time – that's what he guessed the red dots meant. Beside each icon was two buttons, labeled 'Set Code' and 'Set Schedule'. At the top of the screen were two other buttons, 'Set All Codes' and 'Set All Schedules'.

What to do? He had to be careful not to alert them that the system had been tampered with, at least until it was too late for them to do anything about it. Reset their bedroom codes? No good, unless he reset the external lock code at the same time, and they'd swiftly detect that. Mess with the schedules somehow?

Jude's head hurt as he tried to evaluate all the options. He was keenly aware that Ms. Florence might walk in at any moment. What would Mr. Sam do? Whatever it was, it would be elegant, which was one of Mr. Sam's favorite words. Simple, effective, unobtrusive – that was elegant. But what was an elegant solution here? "Help me, Mr. Sam!" Jude whispered.

Then, somehow, Jude felt like he wasn't alone in the little office. Someone was with him – a warm, friendly, familiar presence that strengthened and reassured him. He looked at the screen with calmer eyes, and it was like someone was whispering in his ear, pointing to what he needed to look at.

Of course! Reset all the lock combinations to a known code, but have it take effect in the middle of the night! He tapped the 'Set All Codes' button, and a new screen opened. There was a field at the top for entering the new code, and several options below. The first option was 'Immediately' – he didn't want that. The next option was 'Delay', where he could tell it how long to wait before making the change. That would serve, but the next option was even better: 'At Time'. One o'clock in the morning should be good. He set the new lock combination to his ZIP code, backwards, entered 1:00 a.m. in the 'At Time' field, and tapped the 'Save' button. A message flicked up, "Changes saved".

Jude went to log off the controller, but something nudged him. "Don't be an idiot," which was another of one of Mr. Sam's favorite sayings. Don't be an idiot? How was he being an idiot? Then he smiled – the same way they'd been idiots, by not resetting the network controller's master password. He scanned the main screen for – there it was, 'Administration'. He tapped through, and right at the top of the screen were the fields for resetting the master password. He did that, then he logged off and closed all the windows, removing all traces of his presence. On another hunch, he poked through the desks drawers and found at the back of one an old, cheap phone with a little sticky note on it.

A phone! Jude was ecstatic. He checked the battery, which was just below half. He was tempted to call home right then. But wait – calling would do no good unless they were clear and safe. If he called now, his family would want to come get them, but that would just make Ms. Florence call the police. No, best to wait and see if his plan worked. He suspected this phone wasn't used often, or was reserved for some special purpose. Hopefully nobody would notice its absence for the next few hours. He tucked it into his pocket, finished emptying the trash can, and slipped out of the office. Passing through the kitchen, he glanced out the back door window. Ms. Florence was still smoking and chattering on her phone. "Thank you," Jude breathed.

The rest of the day passed slowly. Martha was still distressed, but work seemed to distract her a little. Jude was bursting with excitement, but didn't dare say anything to the girls. For one thing, he wasn't a hundred percent sure that what he'd done would work, and he didn't want to get their hopes up. For another, he didn't want them behaving differently, or saying even the slightest thing that might tip off Ms. Florence. It was hard, especially because he wanted to encourage Martha. The best he could do was at bedtime, when Martha showed more reluctance than ever to go upstairs. He patted her hand and whispered, "It'll be okay – just wait." She gave him a puzzled stare in return, but they had time for no more.

Jude settled into his room, staring at the clock. Three hours. He was sure that in his present state he'd have no trouble staying awake that long, but he set the alarm regardless – it wouldn't do to doze off and sleep though their opportunity. He sat on his bed, or paced quietly, watching the numbers on the cheap clock tick away. He thought about what he'd do if they managed to get away. His first instinct was to call home, but he needed to get them located quickly, and Uncle Gil had the equipment for that. He also had to lose the phone once they'd made contact, because as long as they had it, they could be traced. Beyond that, he could make no plans – he didn't even know where they were.

When the clock finally turned past 12:45 a.m., Jude turned the alarm off. He watched it turn 1:00 a.m. and still he waited. At 1:03 a.m. he went to the door and keyed the code.

The lock clicked open.

Silently Jude passed into the hallway and to the girl's door. Again, the code worked, and he stirred his sleeping sisters awake.

"Come on, we're getting out," he whispered. "Quiet as mice, now."

"But how –" Tabitha began, but Elizabeth shushed her. They all crept down to Martha's door – being quiet as mice was something they were good at. Jude keyed the code and eased Martha's door open.

"No, no, God, please not again!" came Martha's muffled cry. She was sitting up in bed, the covers pulled around her, staring in terror at the door.

"Shh, shh, Martha," Jude whispered, running to her. "It's just me! It's Jude."

"Jude?" Martha whispered in disbelief, touching his face.

"Yeah. Come on, we need to be quiet and quick. We're getting out."

"Getting out? But how…"

"No time. C'mon." Jude pulled her out of bed and they all crept down the steps.

"Front door," Jude barely whispered at the bottom of the steps. No good going through the kitchen, past Ms. Florence's bedroom door. They crossed the living room and Jude keyed the code into the front door lock. This was the moment of truth.

The handle turned.

Swiftly and silently, they passed out of the house, turning left at the sidewalk. They were free, but not clear yet. To make better speed, Martha picked up Tabitha, and they passed under the shadow of some trees.

"Where are we going?" Martha asked.

"Somewhere we can call from," Jude replied.

"Call? Where did you get a phone?"

"I stole it. Come on, let's go this way. Do you know where we are?" Jude asked.

"I'm pretty sure it's Port Huron, one of the older sections. Look, you can see more light over that way," Martha pointed.

They passed like ghosts through the shadowed, empty streets. There was a time when these conditions would have frightened them, but now the dark was welcome cover. They made toward the glow, and found it was an all-night gas station. They approached it cautiously.

"There – behind that dumpster," Jude pointed. They angled over and hid in the shadow of the smelly metal box. Jude pulled out the phone – still plenty of charge for one call. He dialed Uncle Gil.

"Hello?" came the response after a couple of rings.

"Uncle Gil, it's Jude."

"Jude!"

"Listen, I need you to locate this phone – the one I'm calling from. We're at some gas station, behind a dumpster. We don't know which city, though we think it's Port Huron," Jude explained.

"Gas station, behind a dumpster," Uncle Gil muttered. Jude reflected that he'd called the right guy. Dad would be going hysterical right now, but Uncle Gil was focused.

"Okay, Jude, I've got my tracker," Uncle Gil came back. "Can I call you back from it? That'd be easiest."

"Sure," Jude hung up, and the phone rang again in a minute.

"Okay, I'm tracking you now," Uncle Gil explained. "You're in Port Huron, all right. South side, west area. You're going to stay there, right?"

"Yes, behind the dumpster."

"Will you have the phone?"

"I thought it'd be safer to ditch it," Jude said.

"Probably, but don't forget to erase the call history," Uncle Gil replied. "Anything else?"

"No – we'll stay here," Jude said, then hung up. It took him a bit to locate where on the phone to erase the numbers, but he found it. He'd been thinking of just pitching the phone in the dumpster, but now he realized that would identify where they last were. Two guys pulling up in a car with music blasting gave him a better idea.

"Stay here," he whispered to the others, then stepped out from behind the dumpster and began walking toward the store so as to pass near the car. He thumbed the phone off as he walked, but as he drew close he saw that all the windows on this side were closed. Rats – he could only hope the doors were unlocked. Changing his course at the last minute, he grabbed the door latch and pulled. The door opened.

Jude had just opened the door enough for his purpose when a voice called out, "Hey, kid, get away from that car!" Looking up, he saw the two guys coming out of the store. Quickly he flung the phone on the floor in the back, slammed the door, and dashed away. Behind him the guys were cursing and yelling, but showed no sign of pursuing him. Jude scooted up the alley and circled back around to where the girls were.

"Why did you risk that?" Martha asked.

"I wanted to get rid of the tracer. Those guys don't even know they have it. They'll drive it all over, confusing the heck out of people. Uncle Gil knows we're here, he's sending someone, we just have to stay put."

"Jude, Jude," Martha cried, hugging him tightly. "How did you ever pull off this miracle?"

"Well, we're not clear yet, but..." Jude explained how he'd found and manipulated the network controller. They were all giddy with excitement but had to keep quiet lest they call attention to themselves.

After about fifteen minutes a car turned into the parking lot and pulled over to the dumpster. An unknown man leaned over, threw open the passenger side door, and looked right at the children.

"Gil sent me to take you to Rivendell. Martha's horse is named Daisy and Jude's hero is Reepicheep."

Martha and Jude looked at each other and nodded, then everyone walked to the car.

"Hi, I'm Jim Walkling," the man introduced himself. "Everyone should lie down on a seat or the floor and cover up with the blankets there. I've got room for one up front. We're going to be taking the expressway for a bit and you need to be clean out of sight. All good? Okay, we're off."

Jude was huddled on the floor in the front while the girls lay hidden in the back. They were soon on I-69 speeding west, and Jim pulled out his phone.

"Gil, I've got 'em. Oh – don't exactly know. Let me ask," he held the phone aside and asked, "Who have we got here?"

"Martha, Tabitha, Elizabeth, and me – Jude," Jude replied.

"Martha, Tabitha, Elizabeth, and Jude," Jim reported, then waited. "Oh. No, just four. I'll ask." Again, he held the phone aside. "Where's Matthew?"

Rescue

Within ten minutes of Jude's call, the Peterson and Schaeffer households, including Derek, were completely awake and moving in high gear. One thing they'd done during the long dismal waiting time was to lay plans against the possibility of the children being miraculously restored to the family. Now, apparently, just such a miracle had happened, and they needed to move quickly in response. A safe house had been prepared for them at a site just north of Gagetown, about an hour away, where the whole family could go into hiding. The house was mostly ready, and the van to transport them was on its way. Kent and Linda were stunned almost to disbelief over this incredible development.

But then came the word that little Matthew wasn't with the escapees and never had been. This introduced an agonizing twist of concern into the euphoria, with everyone torn between joy at the return of the captives and anguish over the whereabouts of the youngest child. Derek felt this keenly, for the bubbly little boy was almost like a son, or younger brother, to him.

At first Linda protested that she wouldn't leave until Matthew was found and returned as well. But Kent put his foot down, forcing her to acknowledge that once they were reunited with the escaped children, they'd be fugitives who'd need to go completely underground. She acquiesced to that, though with bitter tears of grief.

Derek was going to accompany them to the safe house to monitor Linda. Moving her in her current condition was very dicey, and had circumstances been otherwise travel would have been impossible. Cletus Winters would drive the van, a big fifteen-passenger, which was so distinctive that they wouldn't have taken it except that it was the middle of the night. He pulled the van into the Peterson's driveway to await Jim Walkling's arrival with his precious cargo. Kent was jumpy and Linda kept dabbing her eyes and watching the road.

Then a strange car pulled up and the four children piled out, flinging themselves at their parents and brother. There were tears and hugs, but they were quickly cut short. Gil and Janine and Grandpa hustled them into the van and Cletus turned northward.

Derek sat with Cletus in the front while the family clung to one another in the back of the van, catching up on lost time. They said prayers of thanks for the safe return of the children and more for the swift return of Matthew. Kent insisted on hearing Jude's account of hacking the network controller at least three times, beaming with pride at his son's ingenuity.

Joyful as Derek was at this reunion, his immediate concern was Linda and the baby. He watched them carefully in the rearview mirror, apprehensive that the mix of excitement and worry would stress her even more, possibly triggering labor. Of course, they were nearing the window for a full-term delivery even now, but Derek wanted to give this baby every minute of gestation he could.

Derek noticed something else in the mirror: Martha didn't seem her normal effervescent self. Of course, she'd been through a lot, and was certainly exhausted, and had just learned that Matthew had not yet been recovered, but to Derek there seemed something more, a grief that lingered about her eyes.

It was still late at night when they pulled up to the safe house. It was an older-style red brick farmhouse that was showing its years but would serve their purpose. It had been vacant for a while yet never abandoned, so it was habitable, if a bit dirty. The grounds had plenty of big leafy trees which provided abundant cover. Supplies such as linens, towels, and cleaning gear had been placed in the house, along with nonperishable groceries and kitchen utensils. Cletus promised to organize a work crew to come up later in the day to help get the house in order, but for now everyone just wanted to get some rest. Busy hands dusted rooms and made beds, with Linda's being the first. Derek attended to her, monitoring her condition and insisting she let her husband and children do the work while she rested. Despite the turbulent events of the past few days, she seemed to be stable.

The baby had been a bit more active today, but Derek didn't know if that portended anything. He just needed to stay inside mama a few more days.

The eastern sky was lightening when the house was pronounced suitable to bunk in. Kent handed Cletus a list of items to be brought from their house, and Derek confirmed that Fran would stop by later to check on Linda. His heart was torn by the bittersweet expression Linda wore: joy at being once again surrounded by her children tinged with grief that Matthew was still missing.

"I promise you, Linda," Derek said fervently, gripping her hand. "I will find him. If I have to move heaven and earth, I will find him."

"Thanks, Derek," Linda replied with a wan smile. He took his leave and headed out to join Cletus in the van. From her reaction, Derek guessed that Linda had taken his statement for no more than a reassuring sentiment. But in his heart, a fiery conviction was burning. Somehow, he knew that something decisive *had* to be done to locate Matthew, and he was the one who had to do it.

During the weeks when the children had been captured, Derek had been as passionate as anyone about doing whatever he could to get them back. Unfortunately, his particular status severely restricted his options – he couldn't even drive anywhere. Still, he'd pondered several plans, each more desperate than the last. Now, as Derek half-dozed in the passenger seat while turning these plans over in his mind, one particular scheme kept resurfacing and taking firmer shape. It was risky, but dammit, this was Matthew's freedom and possibly his life at stake, and the clock was ticking. That was worth some risk.

"Cletus?" Derek asked. "Would you be able to give me a ride into town tomorrow?"

"Sure," Cletus said. "If I can't, I'll find someone who will. When?"

"Midafternoon."

*   *   *

The clear, sunny morning had given way to a cloudy afternoon, and by quitting time the dark clouds overhead were threatening one of the swift-moving storms for which the area was infamous. Shaundra Nichols never liked dashing for her car under these conditions. Glancing around, she was additionally disturbed to see a hooded punk loitering near the edges of the parking lot. Downtown was peppered with these kids, and they always made her nervous. They usually wanted a handout, and at times could get pushy. Feeling a few spatters of rain, she tucked her chin and ran for her car. Drops started falling more heavily, and when she glanced up to get a bearing on her parking spot, she saw that the punk was moving on a course to intercept her.

Great. Shaundra always tried to be charitable, but she didn't want to be accosted by a street kid with unknown motives in the parking lot during a downpour. She scurried a little faster, and another glance told her she'd make her car well before he reached her. He could see that as well, but it didn't deter him – he kept coming, his features shrouded by his hood. Shaundra reached her car, threw herself in, and locked the doors. The kid kept coming, so Shaundra started the car to make clear what she was prepared to do. But the kid was undaunted, stepping right in front of the car and lifting his head to look straight at her through the now steady rain.

Shaundra's eyes widened and she screamed.

Derek had expected Shaundra to be startled, but he hadn't expected quite that reaction. Hoping that she wouldn't faint or put the car into gear, he tapped his chest then pointed at the passenger door. Her eyes still wide and her hand at her mouth, she nonetheless fumbled with the switch to unlock the doors. Good thing, too – the rain was coming down in earnest now. He ducked inside the car.

"Derek?" Shaundra whispered.

"Yeah, it's me," he admitted with a grin. "As you can see, I'm not quite dead."

"Derek!" Shaundra cried, lunging to embrace him in a crushing hug. It wasn't comfortable across the shift console, but Derek managed it for his friend and former co-worker. It was good to see her, too, but the urgency of his mission tempered his jubilation.

"Shaundra, I haven't much time," Derek said. "Can we get going, by the way?" Derek was grateful for the now-drenching rain, which would make it harder to identify him through the windshield.

Shaundra pulled the car out while Derek gave her a condensed and edited version of where he'd been and what he'd been up to. Shaundra seemed to grasp how delicate the situation was, and how important it was that she maintain Derek's cover. Then he briefed her on the situation with the Schaeffer children. She shook her head sadly.

"I know some people who work for CPS. Caseworkers, the worker bees. They don't like some of the things going on there these days."

"What kind of things?" Derek asked.

"Misuse of resources. Petty politics. Real kids with real needs getting pushed aside so supervisors can assign workers to cases of dubious merit. Nitpicking in some cases while glossing over gross abuses in others. One friend of mine got assigned to a case that she was sure was a vendetta on the part of a supervisor."

"We suspect they're also getting pressure from bigger agencies – being turned into behavior police," Derek suggested.

"That, too," Shaundra agreed. "So, as great as it is to catch up, I'm guessing you didn't return from the dead just to update me on all this."

"No, I didn't," Derek acknowledged. "The urgent issue is this little guy." He handed her a photograph of Matthew. "He's the youngest, and he wasn't at the same foster care home as the others, so he didn't escape. Here's what I need: can you somehow get to the records to see where he's being held?"

"What a cutie," Shaundra smiled, then shook her head sadly. "I'm sorry, Derek, but CPS is one area I've never helped, so I don't have any kind of access to their systems. Besides, even internally they keep their data locked down tight for privacy reasons. Workers can access only their cases, and that's it."

"We don't need much – just a location," Derek urged. "You said you knew people there – any chance you could use some of your renowned charm to get them to slip you some data?"

"Derek, they're tight-lipped about their stuff. If they're caught telling anyone anything, it's not just their job – it's criminal prosecution."

"I know, Shaundra, but this could be life or death. I'm guessing that since the other children have gone missing, which they certainly know by now, they'll soon want to move Matthew to somewhere more secure and watch him more closely. He could be lost forever."

Shaundra sighed. "I'll do what I can. No guarantees, but I'll try."

"I understand. He may be recorded under a pseudonym. On the back of that picture is his birthdate, and the date he was kidnapped. Any other information you might need, contact me and I'll get it."

"Will do," Shaundra said, tucking the photo into her purse.

"And Shaundra?" Derek added. "Prayers are also appreciated."

"Oh, I always be prayin'." Shaundra grinned.

Shaundra was still praying the next morning when she called her friend Terrie and asked to meet for coffee. Since Shaundra never did that, Terrie knew something was up. Shaundra hoped she sounded convincingly furtive and sheepish when she broached the topic.

"I got a friend who's trashed her life," Shaundra explained. "Drugs, guys, the works. Got her son taken from her." She slid the photo of Matthew across the table. "She's starting to get her feet back under her. She knows it'll be a long time before she can even begin proceedings to get him back. Doing that is a big motivator for her, and I'm proud of her progress so far."

"Sure is a cute little guy," Terrie admitted.

"Thing is, it's breaking her heart, not knowing how he's doing. I'm afraid she won't have the stuff to go the distance without some reassurance. So I thought, maybe I could get a status check? No specifics, just general stuff. She's not asking, I am," Shaundra said.

"So, she's had her rights suspended?" Terrie asked.

"Yes. Her lawyer says she'll have to show proof of progress before she can even get visitations."

"Hmm," Terrie mused. "Well, he's not one of mine, so I couldn't get details. But there is a screen in our app that gives an overview of cases with basic data. We use it to determine who's handling who, so we can direct inquiries." She pulled her tablet out of her purse and tapped up something. "Of course, I don't need to tell you how many restrictions there are around our data, and how I can't possibly reveal anything to anyone, especially someone outside the department."

Shaundra tried to appear disappointed, but figured Terrie hadn't gotten her tablet out for no reason.

"However," Terrie continued, placing her thumb on the tablet's biometric pad and opening an application. "If I happened to be working on my tablet while talking to a friend, and were to forgetfully leave it on the table when I went to the ladies' room, I don't suppose I'd know what had happened while I was gone." With that, Terrie got up and walked away.

When Terrie returned five minutes later, her tablet was powered down in the middle of the table and Shaundra was finishing her coffee.

"You're a champ, Terrie," Shaundra smiled.

It was just before eleven in the morning when Derek's phone rang.

"It's Shaundra," came the voice. "The prayers worked, I hope. There's a Tom Doe in the system, matching birthdate, matching intake date. He's resident at a home run by an outfit called Wondercare. They're big in the area. I've messaged you the address. No indication of a change of status."

"My God," Derek whispered, incredulous. He'd hoped for results, but not this much this soon.

"Indeed," Shaundra confirmed. "But another thing – there are four other Does in the system, varied birthdays but the same intake date. They're showing at another Wondercare facility in the area. They don't show any change in status, though. According to the CPS system, they're all still there."

"It's been over a day – they have to know they're gone by now," Derek said.

"Maybe Wondercare does, but they haven't told CPS yet."

"And Matthew's in another one of their facilities. They could shift him at any time."

"Better get moving," Shaundra warned.

*   *   *

Matthew was starting to forget the sound of Mama's voice, and what Daddy's face looked like, and that made him sad.

He hated this place. He didn't know why he was here or why they wouldn't let him go home. When they'd first brought him here he'd missed home so much that he'd cried and cried. Now he didn't cry so much, except at bedtime when he missed home most, and in the morning when he woke up and realized he was still in this awful place.

It was an awful place. There were no books at all, and just a few toys, and none of the other kids wanted to play – they just wanted to watch the noisy screen all the time. Besides, they were mean, biting and pushing each other, and him if he got close enough. And yelling. Everybody yelled here. The kids yelled and Ms. Coates yelled. It scared him.

Every day was the same cereal for breakfast, watery soup and cheese sandwiches for lunch, and hot dogs for dinner. No milk, no snacks of apple slices or carrot sticks, no bananas. Oh, and the terrible juice they gave everyone with breakfast and dinner. It had a funny taste and scratched his throat and made him feel all hot and sleepy. Most of the kids took naps after drinking the juice, but Matthew tried not to, because he'd wake up with a dry mouth and hurting head. Once he'd tried to not drink the juice, but Ms. Coates had yelled at him until he did.

It was a really, really awful place.

Now Matthew was in the living room, playing with toothpicks. The other kids were watching the noisy screen and Ms. Coates was talking on the phone. They'd had lunch, and he'd drunk all his water but was still thirsty. He'd been keeping the toothpicks from dinners, and now had a big enough stash that he could build little houses and barns by sticking them into the living room carpet. He hummed a song Mama used to sing, a song about Mary and Baby Jesus, and tried to remember the sound of her voice.

It was getting harder.

*　　　　　　*　　　　　　*

Kelley Coates only half-noticed the van working its way down the street. Guys in hard hats with clipboards, and a white panel van with a logo on the door and ladders on the roof. They were going door to door, coming this way. Probably the utilities – they were always doing something.

Kelley was on the phone with Charlene, who'd worked in child foster care and understood. It was Charlene who'd coined the phrase "herding brats," which so perfectly expressed how Kelley felt about her job – herding brats. Hell, she'd already been over capacity when they'd dumped another rug rat on her, still without the part-time help she was supposed to have. They'd better hope CPS didn't pull a surprise inspection, or they'd be closed on the spot. Charlene commiserated, telling horror stories of when she'd run her child foster care home.

Then came a knock at the side door, and Kelley saw that it was one of the guys in a hard hat.

"Gotta go, Char," she said, ringing off. Glancing to see that none of the brats were running nearby, she went down and opened the main door, leaving the screen door locked.

"Afternoon, ma'am," the guy said. He was young, clean-cut, and kind of cute. The other guy was behind him, and the van had pulled into the driveway. "We're with the radon detection program, and –"

"Sorry, we're not interested," Kelley cut him off and began to close the door.

"We're not selling anything, ma'am," the guy answered sharply. "This is a voluntary, city-wide program to help with the detection of radon, a dangerous radioactive gas."

The words "dangerous" and "radioactive" caught Kelley's attention, so she didn't quite close the door. Seeing her hesitation, the man pressed on. "We're placing radon detectors in basements and crawl spaces at no cost to the homeowner. These are remotely monitored –"

"Oh, well, this isn't a private residence," Kelley interrupted. "This is a foster care home."

The guy's face grew grave and he examined his clipboard. "There's no indication of that here."

"We don't post signs out front for security reasons," Kelley explained. "But we're properly licensed."

"And you didn't receive the notice?"

"What notice?"

The guy whistled. "Somebody dropped the ball. You're out of compliance, and have been for six months. I'm afraid I'll have to cite you."

Kelley's eyes grew wide. "Cite us? But we didn't even – look, I have to call our compliance office about this."

"Oh, you have a compliance office? That's good," the guy said, clipping a form to his board and starting to jot things on it. "Tell you what – we know this is a new ordinance, and we want to work with you. You've got what, fourteen hundred square feet here? And a full basement?"

"Sixteen fifty, and yes, a full basement," Kelley answered.

"Then you'd need two. Tell you what – let me place them and I can issue you a certificate of compliance on the spot. You can get the certificate to your compliance office, and they can submit it when they answer the citation. I'll note that you were cooperative and aggressively worked toward compliance. That should settle the whole matter."

"I don't know," Kelley wavered. She wasn't supposed to let outsiders through the door without someone from the compliance office present. "I really should call the compliance office about this."

"Yes, you should," the guy agreed. "But if you have the certificate of compliance in hand when you do, it'll go a lot easier. The monitors we place are battery powered and self-adhesive. They take maybe five minutes to place, and you'd be with me the whole time – in fact, you have to be, to show me where you want them. I only need access to the basement."

Kelley wavered even more. She should ask the guys to come back when a compliance officer was here, but would they consider that 'uncooperative'? Seeing her hesitance, the guy started tucking his pen away. "Look, it's all the same to me," he said. "I was just trying to save us both trouble. When this citation goes through, and you don't have a compliance certificate, we'll have to schedule a return visit, and the office might want a full compliance inspection, and there could be violations spotted –"

"All right," Kelley unlocked the screen door. "The basement is right down these steps."

"Great." The guy smiled, waving the box with the monitor unit. "Jim, could you grab another one of these out of the van and bring it down?"

Sixtus Winters had guessed that Todd Beck was a competent operator, but until he saw him in action, he'd had no idea just how good he was. Sixtus listened in awe as Todd smooth-talked the woman behind the screen door, appealing to her self-interest and playing on her fears. The guy should get an Oscar.

Of course, a lot more than a shiny trinket was at stake here.

Todd's casual comment as he headed down to the basement was the cue for Sixtus. He nodded to Jake Kyle in the van and, once the woman was out of sight down the basement steps, he slipped through the screen door and up the half-flight of steps to the first floor.

This was the touchiest part of the plan. They had no idea what to expect inside the house. They didn't know the floor plan, or whether there'd be other staff, or anything. They just had a target to find, and they had to find him quickly and quietly.

Sixtus passed through the kitchen – nobody there. He followed some noise to a room with a big TV and a bunch of kids watching it. A couple of the kids were sleeping, one turned to look at him and then ignored him, the rest were riveted to the screen. None of them were Matthew. His heart began to sink – he knew there was a possibility they would have already moved him.

Sixtus passed quietly toward the front of the house into what looked like a living room. Fortunately, no sign yet of any other staff. The room looked empty, and he was heading for the stairs on the far side when he caught a glimpse of blonde hair. There, behind a chair, asleep on the floor beside a little pile of toothpicks, lay Matthew Schaeffer.

Stooping quickly to pick up the sleeping lad, Sixtus swept from the room. Success, but only partial – they still had to get clear. Passing through the kitchen, he saw a cell phone on the counter just beside the microwave.

The microwave.

Sixtus eased Matthew onto one shoulder while he popped the microwave open and placed the phone within. Fifteen seconds should do it, but it seemed like an eternity while he stood there, listening to the snapping and arcing. He could just hear Todd in the basement, jawboning the lady. Matthew was starting to stir and moan.

"Come on, little guy, just a little longer," Sixtus whispered to him. The microwave finished and Sixtus lay the phone back on the counter where he'd found it. Hopefully that was the only phone around. Wrapping his oversized jacket around the sluggish boy, he slipped down the steps and out the screen door.

Jake had both van doors open, screening the view, and was waiting to take Matthew. Sixtus handed him off, grabbed one of the cheap smoke detectors they were using as props, and headed down to the basement. That had taken, maybe, three minutes. Could be a new record for a snatch.

"Found it," Sixtus announced at the bottom of the steps, waving the device. "It was safely in the van."

"Thanks, Jim," Todd replied. "Just stick it on the wall there at the base of the steps. Here," he said to the woman, taking a piece of paper off the clipboard and handing it to her, "is your certificate of compliance. Thank you for being so cooperative."

Thirty seconds later they were out in the van. Todd took the wheel while Jake called in their progress. Sixtus slipped in back to where a whiny Matthew was waking up.

"Hey, buddy," Sixtus coaxed. "It's me, Sixtus." Matthew only whimpered in response. "We're going to get you home to Mom and Dad."

"Mama?" Matthew moaned.

"Soon, buddy, soon," Sixtus replied. "Does he feel hot to you, Jake?"

"Yes, though it might be because he's just waking up," Jake said.

"Do we have any water?" Sixtus asked, looking around the van.

"No, but I'll ask if Gary does," Jake replied, keying the number of their hand-off contact.

"Banana," Matthew asked.

"And bananas," Sixtus called to Jake.

Derek's phone rang. It was Gil.

"They've got him," Gil reported tersely. "They're headed for the transfer point. They report he might be feverish."

"I'm ready," Derek said, grabbing his bag and heading for the Peterson's. Their swiftly-assembled plan had allowed for the possibility that Matthew might need medical attention. He didn't mind taking another drive up to the Schaeffer's hideout, and since Fran was due to be there later in the afternoon, he could consult with her about Linda's condition.

He waited at the Peterson's with everyone in a mild state of nerves. Though overjoyed that Matthew had been rescued, as long as the team was in the open, matters were still at risk. The plan was that the rescue van would shoot out the expressway, in full view of surveillance cameras, to a small town west of Port Huron. They'd exit there and duck into a little commuter lot just south of the expressway, where Gary Peterson waited in a different car. Sixtus, carrying Matthew, would switch cars, and the van would return to the expressway to drive all the way to Flint. Gary would return to Rivendell by back roads, drop Sixtus off and pick up Derek, and proceed up to Gagetown. For safety, communication was kept to a minimum during this evolution.

At one point, Gil's phone buzzed. He checked the message. "The transfer was successful. They're about twenty minutes out. Sixtus reports that Matthew still feels hot and smells funny."

"'Smells funny'?" Derek asked.

"His words." Gil waved the phone. "They ask we be ready with water and bananas."

"And books," Jan added. "If you're going with him, Derek, he's going to want books."

There was much joy but equal haste when Gary showed up. Matthew was fully awake and excited to see everyone, but mostly wondered where Mama and Papa were. The presence of Uncle Gil and Aunt Jan made a big difference, not to mention Mr. Derek. Derek checked the little boy over while Aunt Jan changed his clothes and gave him as much milk and fruit as he could hold.

"I see what Sixtus meant," Derek muttered to Jan as he packed his gear away. "Catch that sweet, medicinal smell? That's probably the residue from a sedative. They may have been drugging him, and possibly all the kids, to keep them compliant. Unscrupulous, but he should be all right."

Within twenty minutes, they were headed north. Derek was in the back seat with Matthew, reading him as many books as he wanted and encouraging him to keep drinking water. Only when they were safely on the road did they dare call Kent with the joyous news that their youngest child had been rescued and was on his way home. Nearly the whole family was waiting for them when they pulled up beside the farmhouse, and Derek's eyes misted over at the sight of his family once again reunited. Kent carried Matthew in to where Linda was confined to her bed, and a whole new round of sobbing commenced. Derek felt a little embarrassed to be intruding on such an intimate family moment, but they wouldn't hear of him leaving. Right there by Linda's bedside, they knelt on the floor and said a prayer of thanks.

Then the midwife arrived and everyone had to vacate the room. Derek stayed, holding the sheets discreetly while Fran checked Linda and announced that she was starting to dilate.

"Aren't we still a little early?" Derek asked.

"A little, but not much," Fran replied with a motherly smile. "But this could go on for a week. Unless she goes into full-blown labor tomorrow, we should be all right. Frankly, given the amount of stress you've been under, dear, I'm surprised that baby's still in there."

"But today, it's good stress, thanks to friends like this," Linda said, her cheeks wet with tears as she held Derek's hand.

"Stress is still stress," Fran warned. "Try to stay off your feet and keep calm. Things are looking good." Fran bustled out to talk to Kent, but as Derek turned to go, Linda clung to his hand.

"Derek," she said with a distraught look in her eyes. "Thank you for all you've done, but could you do me one more favor?"

"Anything, Linda."

"Could you talk to Martha? Kent and I both think she seems distant. You know her – she's always so bubbly and joyous, and you'd think she'd be more so now, being free again. But she isn't, and she seems to withdraw from us. If Jan were here, I'm sure she'd help, but she's not. Martha loves and trusts you. Can you try to find out what's wrong?"

"Sure, Linda," Derek assured her, a shadow of concern falling across his heart. He took his leave and went out into the kitchen, where the family was preparing dinner. Martha was by the stove, tending pots. Derek went over to her.

"Hi, Martha," he said gently. She looked at him with a quick smile that did not reach her eyes. "Do you have a minute?"

A desperate, hunted look flickered across her face, but she nodded and turned the burner down. Following Derek out the back door, she sat down on the steps. From her posture, Derek could see what Linda meant. Normally, Martha would be looking up and around, smiling and gesturing expressively. Now she sat hunched over, her torso curled almost to her knees, her arms locked in front of her, staring at the ground.

"Martha, are you all right?" he asked flat-out. "Since you escaped, you've seemed withdrawn and...not as happy. Is it just the trauma over what happened?"

Martha sat still for a long time before reluctantly shaking her head. She was still looking at the ground and Derek saw several tears fall into the dust.

"What is it, then?" Derek pressed gently. "Is there anything I can do?"

Again Martha was quiet for a long time, and Derek could almost feel her inner turmoil.

"There was," she finally choked out in a barely audible voice, "a...guy."

"A guy?" Derek asked, not certain he'd heard aright. He knelt on the ground before her and tried to look her in the face. "At the house, there was a guy?" Martha nodded with a choked sob. The chill in Derek's insides grew colder, but he had to continue. "Did this guy assault you?" Martha nodded again, the tears coming freely now. Although Derek hated to push her further, he had to make sure he'd understood. "Sexually?" Once again, she nodded, and stammered, "T...twice."

Derek broke down. His beloved Martha, like his own little sister, the very soul of bright virginal innocence and youthful joy, befouled by some – bastard. He doubled over, and they clung to each other, Martha quietly wailing on his shoulder while he sobbed into her golden curls. He, too, felt soiled, angry and ashamed both as her adopted brother and as a man. That anyone could be so callous to such beauty, such innocence, mystified and infuriated him. That anyone would prey on a captive like that, to rape a defenseless girl...

Rape. His medical training began to grab his attention.

"Martha," he whispered, kissing her head. "Dear Martha, I'm so, so sorry. Oh, precious sister, how can I express how sorry I am?"

She hugged him close, her lips next to his ear. "I've been afraid to tell Mom and Dad, because of Mom's condition, and I wasn't sure how Daddy would react. And I am free, after all..."

"Martha, don't you dare diminish what happened to you," Derek admonished through his tears. "It was a sin and a crime, and you did nothing to deserve it. The fact that you were a prisoner makes it worse. In days past, somebody would hang for this – and some of us think that should still be the case."

Derek let her sob freely on his shoulder while he thought about what he should do, and how he could do it. Martha was probably right about telling Kent and Linda – the last thing they needed just now was another hammer blow like this. They had to learn eventually, but perhaps it would be best after the baby came – and after he'd done what he needed to do.

"Thank you for letting me tell you, Mr. Derek," Martha gasped, recovering from her sobbing. "I've wanted to tell someone, but there's only been Phillip, and I didn't want to burden him with it, and then ask him to keep it from Mom and Dad."

"That was prudent," Derek said. "Martha, dear Martha, my heart breaks for you." He kissed her hands and her damp cheek. "Listen, though, in situations like this, there are some...tests...that should be run. Medical checks. I hate to sound clinical, but –"

"I know, I know," Martha interrupted. "I've been wondering how to ask you."

"Give me a second," Derek pondered. The blood and urine samples were easy, but he should really get a pelvic swab as well. But – on Martha? She was like his kid sister, for Pete's sake.

Derek pulled out his phone and messaged Fran. Was she still here? She was. Could she meet him upstairs?

"Listen, Martha," Derek said. "Can you discreetly slip upstairs to your bedroom? Mrs. Rasmussen is still here. I'll need some samples of a feminine nature, and I can show her how to get them. I'll also need blood and urine samples, but I can do one of those and you can do the other."

"Thanks, Mr. Derek," she said, smiling through her tears.

Derek's heart broke once more. She was so beautiful, so innocent. "Please, just call me Derek," he said. "You're sufficiently adult now." Then he broke down again, unable to bear the pain, and perversely she was comforting him, stroking his shoulder and whispering that she'd be okay.

They dried their eyes and went their separate ways, Martha to her bedroom and Derek to the car for his bag. He didn't have precisely the right equipment, but he would make do, as he always did. The rest of the family was preparing dinner and fussing over Matthew, oblivious to the side drama. He slipped upstairs to Martha's room and took a blood sample, then explained to Fran how to take the pelvic swab while Martha ducked into the bathroom for the urine sample. He left Fran with Martha, composing his thoughts and writing up the tests he wanted run. Fran had a network of supportive providers she used for her lab requirements. When she opened the bedroom door, Derek bagged the swabs and gave her all the samples and instructions. She nodded and departed, leaving Derek a little worried. He appreciated Fran's expertise and decades of experience, but midwives were stereotyped as notorious gossips partly because of people like Fran. She had enough medical knowledge to know what those tests were for, and was familiar enough with the circumstances to guess why he was requesting them. Furthermore, the test results would have to pass through her hands. This was going to be hard enough on Kent and Linda without half the Thumb knowing about it before they did. But Derek had no choice – he needed those results as soon as possible.

Derek sat next to Martha on the bed. "Your mom has been worried about you. You've seemed distant."

"I have been," Martha confirmed. "I think it'll be easier, now that I've talked to someone about it."

"Let's wait until the test results come back, and I'll sit down with you to talk to your parents," Derek proposed. "It should only be a few days. How does that sound?"

"That sounds good," Martha said, leaning against his shoulder. He put his arm around her and hugged her tight. "Thanks for being such a good big brother, Mr. – ah – Derek."

"That what brothers are for," Derek replied, then sniffed a little. "I just can't understand why God would allow such a terrible thing to happen."

"As Grandpa would say, 'Don't go blaming God for the wicked deeds of men'," Martha replied.

"That sounds like Grandpa," Derek confirmed.

Rage

"Melanie, this is Andrea," came the voice at the other end of the line. Melanie's brow furrowed – her friend sounded weary, even exasperated.

"Hi, Andrea. What's up?"

"Well, I have a bit of a...situation going on," Andrea admitted. "It's embarrassing for us, but I figured it was best to come clean with you as soon as possible. We're having a few personnel problems. One of our home managers has not been meeting our standards. There haven't been any incidents, but there might have been if we hadn't caught this.

"We've relieved her of her position and brought in another qualified replacement, but that required reshuffling people at other sites, and...well, you know how it is."

"I sure do," Melanie assured her.

"Again, there's been no disruption of care. Quality care remains our top priority. What there may be, temporarily, is a slight impact on responsiveness. As all our people settle into their new responsibilities, they may drop a stitch from time to time when it comes to responding to requests."

"Oh, I understand completely," Melanie said, internally breathing a sigh of relief that it wasn't something truly serious.

"I appreciate your understanding," Andrea continued. "I know that responsiveness is important, too, and I'll be working with the homes to get back up to speed on that, but I know you'd agree that care comes first."

"Always," Melanie assured her. "Thanks for calling, Andrea. I'll notify my people to have patience with requests for a while."

"Thanks," Andrea said, ringing off. Melanie looked at the phone for a while. Personnel troubles. This was a first for Wondercare. Of course, everybody had them, though usually they were kept quiet. She supposed it was a mark of trust between them that Andrea had felt free to call and apprise her of the situation.

But still.

Melanie looked at the storage chip where it lay in a paper clip tray on her desk. Maybe she shouldn't be so quick to copy those prepared reports into her files. At least, not all of them.

*   *   *

Pa Hubbart glared at the two women seated across the desk from him. One was simply staring at the ground, but the other looked back at him with the same half-defiant, half-terrified look which he remembered from her childhood.

Which, in a way, made him angrier.

"Well, ladies, what do you recommend we do about this predicament? Four – no, five – brats missing before their cases were close to settled. High value cases at that, if we'd been able to hang onto them. But they vanish right under your noses, managing to lock you–" he jabbed a finger at the downcast woman "–in your own room in the bargain!"

"I don't know...equipment malfunction...," muttered Judy Florence without lifting her eyes from the ground.

"That was no malfunction!" Pa roared, picking up a piece of paper from his desk and waving it. "Or the brats would have been locked in, too! The network tech says the controller had been tampered with, so thoroughly that he had to completely reset it! You were outsmarted, under your very nose, in broad daylight, by some kids!"

The woman cowered beneath the burst of rage, almost shrinking in her chair.

"Pa, I've got Andrea running interference on this," the other woman offered, tilting her chin.

"Useless!" Pa rounded on her. "With these cases unsettled, at any time some CPS official could pick up a phone and demand to see those kids before him. What if that happens? What will you do then?" The women remained silent while Pa fumed.

"You!" he barked, causing Judy to look up sharply. "Get out!"

"Yes, Mr. Hubbart," she mumbled, rising quickly and bolting for the door, leaving the other woman alone with the angry old man.

"This problem isn't going away, Suzanne," Pa said.

"Yes, Pa," Suzanne acknowledged.

"It has the potential to do serious damage," Pa continued. "Not just to Wondercare, but to the whole operation."

Suzanne just nodded.

"I want you to come up with a solution. Not just for damage control, but for locating and retrieving those kids."

"Yes, Pa," Suzanne said.

"I want her unit closed," he continued, pointing at the door through which Judy Florence had fled. "Do what you want with her – fire her, assign her elsewhere, whatever – but I don't want her in charge of anything ever again, understand?"

"Yes, Pa."

"Get out, and don't come back without that plan, and a timeline."

Suzanne stood and made for the door.

"One more thing," Pa called as she laid her hand on the doorknob. "Send in my worthless nephew."

Cliff was sweating and his hands were shaking. He knew he was in big trouble. He'd been summoned up here with Ms. Florence, but when she'd been called in, he'd been taken into the conference room just outside Pa's offices by Caleb and that sadistic Joe Pemberton. They stayed with him, talking to each other, while the minutes ticked away.

After a long time, another guy whom Cliff didn't recognize stuck his head in the door and nodded. Caleb and Joe came over and made to take Cliff's arms, but he shook them off and walked out under his own power. It was a short walk to the door behind which lay the most terrifying man he knew.

His great uncle.

Pa was standing behind his desk when Cliff walked in, trying to keep his hands still and his head up.

"Well, well, if it isn't my nephew Cliff!" boomed Pa jovially. Cliff wasn't fooled. He was all too aware of the three brutal thugs behind him. Pa walked around the desk with his hand extended, but halfway around he nodded to the goons, who shoved Cliff forward roughly. He fell on all fours, and they stepped on his lower legs and pulled his arms up so he was kneeling painfully, facing Pa's desk.

Then Pa was there, grabbing him by the hair and yanking his head back. Pa leaned over so his face was inches from Cliff's. "Give me one good reason why I should keep feeding your useless gullet," he snarled. Cliff's neck and scalp were burning with pain, but he didn't even cry out, much less answer. That would have been the worst thing to do. Instead, he just stared anywhere but into Pa's eyes.

"Y'know what my problem is?" Pa asked rhetorically as he shoved Cliff's head down painfully and walked back around his desk. "I'm too soft hearted. My sister comes whining to me, 'Give my grandson a chance! All he needs is a break!' Sucker that I am, I cave in. I give you a chance at the Bay City homes, and you can't even mow the lawns. I send you to the factory, and you screw up left and right. I give you one last shot down in Port Huron, and you can't keep your hands off the damn merchandise! As a result, you've probably caused the most serious crisis we've ever faced – all because I got sweet-talked into giving my bastard nephew too many chances!"

Cliff said nothing, but kept staring at the floor. Two guys, probably Caleb and Joe, were still standing on his legs and twisting his arms up behind him at painful angles. He was in big trouble.

Sitting down at his desk, Pa gave a jerk of his head, and suddenly the thugs were yanking Cliff to his feet and dragging him over to the corner of the office. Cliff cried and writhed, but his captors were too strong. Two of them pinned him down on the table while the third began hammering his head and torso. Cliff's cries ceased as his breath was knocked out of him, but his agony did not as his torturers traded off roles to insure the one doing the beating was always fresh and strong. He tried to curl up or turn away from the blows, but strong hands always pulled him flat so the brutality could continue unhindered. His kicking and thrashing only seemed to goad them to further cruelty, and he knew that pleading would do no good. He hadn't thought that anything could hurt so badly, but the torture continued.

"All right, that's enough," Pa finally barked. They shoved him off the table and he curled into a ball on the floor. "Bring him over here." They grabbed him under his arms and dragged him over before the desk, dropping him in a moaning heap.

"Next time, it's the hogs," Pa said, pointing at Cliff, then to the thugs. "Get him out of here. Have the doc look him over while I decide what to do with his worthless ass." He waved his hand dismissively, and two of them grabbed Cliff and dragged him from the room. They threw him into the conference room and shut the door. Cliff lay curled on the floor sobbing – it hurt too much to think about sitting up. He ached all over his body and had a piercing pain in his side that he was sure was a cracked rib. He didn't know how long he lay there before the doc came in and he had to endure the pain of being stripped and examined.

"Nothing serious," the doc finally pronounced. "You'll be all right in time. I'll send Debbie in with some salve for the cuts and contusions."

Some while later Debbie came in to bandage what she could. She also brought a bottle of water and a sandwich.

"Pa's sending you to Jack's shop in Bad Axe," Debbie explained when she was finished. "He says it's your last chance."

*   *   *

The supervisors were upset. Tyrone could tell. They were edgy and irritable, and talked in whispers among themselves. Somebody somewhere had screwed up, and that meant someone was going to catch it.

"Someone" would probably be a worker like Tyrone, because that's how things were.

He was technically "Tyrone One", because there was another Tyrone in the factory who worked farther down on the other side. That was "Tyrone Two". Their paths didn't cross much – he worked with a different team on a different line – but since they were both Tyrones, they had to get numbers to avoid confusion.

Tyrone and his team were just coming on shift, so his line supervisor Mr. Nathan should be along shortly to give them instructions for the day's work. These days it was brighter in the factory at shift start, with the windows at the top of the walls glowing with morning sunshine. It wasn't always like that – in the cold months it was dark well into the shift, but now it was getting so they started and even ended in the light. Aiden said it was because it was almost summer. Tyrone wasn't sure what that meant, except that it was warmer and brighter, but it seemed to mean something to the older team members like Aiden and Courtney.

Tyrone couldn't remember much of life before he came to the factory. His earliest memories were of rooms he didn't recognize and faces with no names, and a colorful toy that he thought was called a 'clown'. Then there'd been the series of homes, some better than others but all pretty much the same. But all of that was in the distant, fading past. His life now was the factory. He couldn't even remember how he got here, and it didn't really matter. What mattered was working his shift and not making his team members or the supers mad.

They all lived in the broad, open barracks with the big iron beams arching up to the ceiling and the metal walls that were scorching in the summer when the sun fell on them, but frost-coated in the winter. The only windows were high in the walls, up near the ceiling. Those were fine for light but useless for air, at least in the hottest months. Sometimes in those months they'd open the big doors on both ends of the barracks, securing the bars across them, and let the breeze blow through. That brought in fresh air – and bugs – but some of the kids liked it. They'd crowd against the bars just for a glimpse outside. Tyrone didn't bother. The only thing you could see from either end of the barracks was thick woods of tall, leafy trees – as if that was anything special. No, nothing remarkable about the outdoors. The only time they ever went outside was when they were taken to the bleachers, and that was always horrible. It had only happened twice in all the time Tyrone had been here, but he still had nightmares about it.

As far as Tyrone was concerned, the others could go on about the outdoors, he didn't care. His life was the factory, anyway. Every day they got breakfast – sometimes cornbread, sometimes hard-boiled eggs, sometimes porridge, but always with thin milk. Every seventh day they got juice, which he always looked forward to. Lunch was wraps with some sort of goop – Courtney said it was usually tuna – at their stations, and dinner would be soup and crackers, sometimes with peanut butter. Some of the other kids complained about the food. Tyrone didn't know why. It was food, and if they didn't want it, he'd be happy to eat it.

Each day after breakfast they were marched to the factory along the enclosed passage, with metal walls and a roof overhead and no windows. *That* got hot in summer and bitter cold in winter. Once inside the factory, they went to their places on the line and settled in as teams to do that day's work. That's what it was about: hitting your quota and not screwing up and keeping your head down. Because the last thing you wanted was to be called in.

Nobody wanted to get called into the office. Usually you got called in because you screwed up, like the time Tyrone got called in because he dropped a tray and broke a lot of parts. He'd gotten caned for that. If you were really sick you might get called in to see the doc, and that was always chancy. Some who saw the doc got given shots or pills, but others were never seen again. Sometimes Courtney, the oldest girl on his team, got called in. She'd be in the office for a while, sometimes almost an hour, and when she came out she'd be quiet and sad, but she never told him why she got called in.

It wasn't always bad to be called in. A while back, Tyrone had been called in, but they'd just wanted to weigh and measure him and poke his arm. That had been interesting, because when he'd been sitting by the window waiting, he'd glanced out and seen a truck. He'd never seen a truck before – in fact, Tony had had to tell him what it was. A lot more interesting than a bunch of trees. He hoped he'd get a chance to see another truck someday.

Here came Mr. Nathan now, with the day's assignment. The team was all seated and ready, except that Addison still had that cough. Tyrone hoped that would go away soon. He liked Addison – she could always make him laugh – and he didn't want her called in to see the doc.

*   *   *

It was four days after Matthew's return that Fran apologetically called Derek about the test results. It had taken her some time to contact the provider, and then him some time to get the samples, and so on. She was planning to drop in on Linda that evening anyway, and offered to meet Derek at the Schaeffer's, so Derek cajoled Sixtus into driving him and a truckload full of the Schaeffer's household stuff up to Gagetown. He was a little nervous about the test results and even more apprehensive about the discussion with Kent and Linda that had to follow, but he couldn't let Martha go through that alone.

There was something in the glance which Fran gave Derek when she slipped him the test results that suggested she knew full well what they contained. He found a quiet corner and riffled through the sheets. Good, good, the hoped-for array of codes and numbers indicating no infection. But on the last page – there it was, the result he'd feared. Oh God, he winced, why this on top of everything else?

Derek sought out Martha and broke the news. She sobbed into his shoulder, but something about the way she bounced back indicated that she'd been steeling herself against this possibility. They decided to sit down with Kent and Linda once Fran was finished with her checkup. Derek agreed to do most of the talking.

About twenty minutes later, Derek and Martha slipped into the bedroom where Linda lay, enormous with child. Kent stood by the foot of the bed, watching them warily. Martha sat by Linda, who took her hand and gave her a troubled look.

Derek looked at the people who were the only real family he'd ever known and set his jaw. Hard as it was, he had to do this – he couldn't ask it of Martha. "Linda, Kent, I need to tell you something…difficult. While held captive, Martha was assaulted by one of the home staff…twice. And…well, she's pregnant. No infections, but definitely pregnant."

Linda gave a choked sob and held Martha's hand to her cheek. To Derek it seemed like she'd been braced for something like this. But Kent turned white and seemed to quiver. He grasped the bedstead to steady himself.

"Oh, my baby, my baby," Linda sobbed, now hugging Martha.

"No," Kent muttered. "No, no, no – ahhh!" With a cry he burst from the room. Linda looked after him with concern in her eyes, and attempted to get out of bed to follow him.

"No!" Derek said sharply. "I'll go after him. You stay put. Martha, keep her there." He dashed out through the kitchen, where a couple of bewildered Schaeffer children stood. Bursting out of the back door, Derek saw Kent beneath a nearby tree, hammering at the ground with his fists and crying. Derek knew Kent tended to get physically expressive when he was angry or distressed, and was concerned that he'd start slugging the tree if he wasn't stopped.

"Kent," Derek cried, running up and catching his arm. "Kent, Linda's going to need you shortly! You can't injure yourself!"

"Why, Derek?" Kent whirled and grabbed Derek by the shoulders, looking at him with frenzied eyes. "Why would He let this happen?"

"I don't know, Kent, I don't know," Derek answered, his heart aching anew.

"My innocent daughter," Kent muttered, sinking to the ground. "My pure, precious flower, violated by some bastard. Oh, if I ever get my hands on him!"

"I feel the same way, Kent," Derek said, dropping to his knees. The two men leaned on each other, drowning in grief.

"Daddy! Derek!" came Martha's voice from the back door. They looked up to see her coming toward them, concern etched on her face. "Derek, I think Mom needs you." Derek got up and headed inside, while Martha knelt on the ground beside her father. They wept together for a long while, then Martha caressed his hair and kissed his brow. "Daddy," she pleaded. "Please don't stop loving. All the time we were gone, I held tight to the memory of your love. If you stop loving, I'll have nothing. More than anything right now, I need you to love."

"I'll try, sweetheart," Kent sobbed. "I'll try." Father and daughter clung to each other in the deepening twilight.

Inside the house, Derek stuck his head outside the bedroom door. "Has Fran left yet?" he asked Phillip, who was in the kitchen.

It was a long and worrisome night around the Schaeffer home. Phillip and Martha took charge of the little ones while Derek assisted Fran. Under these circumstances he was very much the student of the experienced midwife. Fortunately, Linda had been through five prior home births, because Kent, who'd been her stalwart support through all her labors, was effectively useless this time. He held her hand, but he was emotionally shattered, unable to give anything beyond the most basic support.

It didn't matter. The delivery was uncomplicated, and about 2:00 a.m. Fran was placing a healthy, squirming baby girl in Linda's arms. Kent sobbed anew while Linda beamed. "Derek?" she asked. "Could you go find Martha?" Shortly thereafter the big sister was holding her youngest sibling on her lap, crying with a mixture of pain and joy.

"Kent, I know we've discussed names," Linda said. "But I think I know a perfect one for her: Miriam, the Jewish form of Mary."

"Miriam," Kent repeated as he nodded his head gravely. "Very fitting. The sister of Moses, born into slavery and exile."

"But who lived to see salvation and freedom," Martha whispered hopefully as she rubbed her damp cheek against her sister's downy head.

A couple of days later Derek had occasion to catch a ride back up to the Schaeffer's with Gary and Harmony Peterson. As they arrived, they saw an older couple just departing. The couple looked vaguely familiar to Derek, but he couldn't quite place them.

"Who are those people?" Derek asked.

"Lawrence and Annette Stover," Gary explained. "They have a big family, lots of relatives up this way – kind of like a northern Thumb version of Grandma and Grandpa."

That was it – now Derek remembered where he'd seen the couple. "Were they at the barn dance a year ago last autumn? Where you and I first met?"

"I can't remember, but probably," Gary said. "Whenever the families get together, they like to be around. In fact, here's one of their grandsons now." A dusty pickup pulled into the other side of the circle driveway. "That's Evan Stover, son of Dominick and Julianne, who farm just west of Harbor Beach."

"Well, now, I wonder what he's doing here?" Harmony asked innocently with a mischievous twinkle in her eye.

"C'mon, I'll introduce you," Gary said, so Derek met the venerable Lawrence and Annette, who were indeed the couple he remembered from the barn dance, as well as the smiling, eager Evan. Then Derek went inside to check on Linda and Miriam, Harmony went to hunt down Martha, and Gary found Phillip to help unload the supplies which they'd brought.

Evan went to find Kent, and shortly thereafter they were both sitting down at a table in the shade of a tree. Sorrow and weariness shadowed the older man's eyes, and the usually confident and exuberant Evan seemed subdued and nervous.

"First off, sir," Evan began respectfully. "Allow me to offer my congratulations on the birth of your newest daughter, as well as on the return of your abducted children. At the same time, let me offer condolences from myself and my family for the trials and struggles your family has endured over the past weeks."

"Thank you, Evan," Kent replied. "Please extend my thanks to your parents."

"I will, sir," Evan said. He fidgeted with his hat before continuing. "I'm also aware that your trials are not over, and indeed weigh more heavily than ever on your family."

Kent sighed internally. One of the bitter facts that Lawrence and Annette had just broken to them during their courtesy visit was that Martha's situation was an open secret among the families.

"I...ah...this wasn't a conversation I was planning to have for a few years yet," Evan admitted awkwardly. "But I've never been ashamed of the fact that I find Martha attractive, and I'd like your permission to court her."

"Court her?" Kent hadn't been expecting this.

"Yes, sir," Evan answered firmly, looking Kent square in the eye. "And I hope you don't take this amiss because I've always intended to act honorably toward your family and Martha, but the first time I laid eyes on her, my heart skipped a beat, and I thought, 'That girl is going to be my wife.'"

"Really? How long ago was that?" Kent asked.

"A year and a half, sir, at the autumn dance. Of course, she was far too young at that point, but since then I've been working and saving and studying with the intention of coming calling when she reached a suitable age."

"How old are you, Evan?" Kent asked.

"I'll turn eighteen in September, sir," Evan replied, pulling some papers from his shirt pocket and handing them to Kent. "I work for my father, and he pays me justly. If I do well, he hopes to bring me into partnership one day. There is my most recent bank account statement and my last year's tax return. No, please, look them over. I'm serious about this. Also, I'm halfway to a degree from Michigan State via remote study, and my parents have a small house they're willing to sell me on good terms, provided I renovate it."

"You have put some thought into this, haven't you?" Kent asked, looking over the papers.

"Like I said, sir, I'm serious," Evan answered. "And I hope you'll understand that if you and your wife grant permission, I intend to make this a swift courtship. With no intent to rub salt in your wounds, I'm aware of Martha's condition, and how she got that way. My parents taught me that no woman should have to carry a child without a husband by her side, and no child should be born without a father to raise him. With your kind permission and Martha's assent, I hope to be that husband and father."

"That's...that's very noble of you, Evan," Kent said, his eyes misting over.

"Sir, understand this well," Evan continued earnestly. "Regardless of what some brute did to her while she was captive and helpless, her heart and her soul remain virginal and innocent. The child she carries is innocent as well. I know I'm unworthy of her, but by God's grace I will spend my life becoming worthy."

Kent dropped his head and rubbed his eyes. It was all happening so fast. He wished he could hold it off, to tell this fine young man to return next year, but he knew he couldn't stop time. "Let...let me talk to Linda."

Derek was holding Miriam and chatting with Linda when Kent stepped in, looking sober. Derek ducked out with the sleeping baby to give them some privacy. Not ten minutes had gone by when Kent opened the door, still talking to Linda.

"He's out back. I'll go tell him."

"All right," Linda said, then to Derek, "Do you know where Harmony is?"

"I think she's on the front porch cleaning vegetables with Martha," Derek answered.

"Why don't you see if she'd like to come hold the baby?"

"Both of them?"

"No," Linda replied with an enigmatic smile. "Just Harmony."

Harmony, Derek, and Gary graced that evening's family dinner table, but not Martha, whom Evan had taken to dinner in Port Austin and then out for a drive. Afterwards, Derek and Gary headed back to Rivendell, leaving Harmony, who intended to stay a couple of nights with Martha. Evan brought Martha home by 10:00 p.m., and she slipped in to tell her parents that Evan had proposed, on one knee, on the pier at Harbor Beach. She'd deferred her answer, wanting to talk to them first, and to take time to think and pray. They gave her a tearful blessing, then Martha went to her room to talk with Harmony late into the night.

The next morning, the girls took an ATV down to Gagetown, where they walked around the cemetery at St. Anthony's and spent some time inside the sanctuary. Harmony's heart was heavy, not just for what her cousin had endured and the choices she faced, but for herself as well. She'd looked forward to years of lighthearted girl fun with Martha – dances and sleepovers and horseback rides – before the full weight of adulthood's responsibilities descended on them both. Now none of that would happen, and Harmony was saddened. She tried to keep in mind that Martha was the one with the serious problems, but she couldn't help feeling sorry for herself as well.

The afternoon was getting on and Harmony, who'd left Martha in the church for some solitude and prayer, was just starting to wonder if she should go nudge her. But just then Martha came out, looking lighter and more joyous than Harmony had seen her since her rescue.

"Ready to go?" Harmony asked. "It's getting late."

"Yes," Martha replied as she sat down beside her cousin. "I've made up my mind: I'm going to accept Evan's offer."

"What a surprise," Harmony said dryly. "You and he have favored each other since you first met."

"True, but the situation is different now," Martha explained. "That's what I was praying about. I didn't want to accept out of fear, grabbing at the first offer that came by. I think I'm supposed to marry Evan, and welcome this baby together, so we can give him something his father certainly never had."

"What's that?"

"A loving home."

Savagery

Chip Keller pulled up in front of the house and sat for a while, staring at it and thinking. Then he got out of his car, ducked beneath the yellow police tape, and went up the drive. The side door was open, so he walked into the kitchen. The place had the musty odor of a closed-up house. Chip walked from room to room, noticing only the slightest traces – a hole in the wall here, a brown smear on a baseboard there. The house was filled with a thick, oppressive silence.

A deadly silence.

Chip was standing in the living room, looking around and thinking, when the side door opened again. Startled, Chip wheeled and saw someone in a sheriff's uniform walk in. It was Andy Klein.

"Hey, Chip," Andy said genially.

"Hey, Andy," Chip replied.

"I thought I recognized your car out there," Andy continued.

"Yeah," Chip said. Silence again fell on the room.

"So," Andy said eventually. "Bad business. Never took Gary for the type to do something like this."

"He wasn't the type," Chip said tersely, drawing a suspicious glance from Andy.

"Aw, c'mon," Andy said. "Everyone knew about his marriage troubles, and the problems he had with the bottle. Stuff like that goes on long enough, eventually a man cracks."

"Not Gary," Chip shook his head. "Not Gary. I knew him. Sure, he and Betty had their moments – who doesn't? But he'd put the worst of his drinking behind him years ago. He loved his family. Whatever he might do to himself, he'd never harm them."

"Now you're guessing, Chip," Andy warned. "And being friends with a man can sometimes blind you to his faults."

"I'm telling you, Gary Jennette would never gun down his family and then turn the muzzle on himself!" Chip flared up.

Andy stepped back, momentarily intimidated, but then an ugly look flashed across his face.

"Says you. But you weren't here, and you didn't see the evidence. It was plain as day."

"So that's how it's being filed?" Chip asked. "A murder/suicide, case closed? I tell you, you're making a mistake here, Andy."

Andy glared at him for a minute, then hitched up his trousers. "So you say. But you ain't the sheriff any more – I am. You're just a private citizen, and one who's violating a crime scene, at that. I could cite you, but I won't, provided you leave right now."

Chip bit his tongue, knowing he was cornered. Shaking his head, he turned and headed for the front door. "You're making a mistake, Andy."

"You got any evidence, you bring it on over to the prosecutor," Andy goaded, closing the door behind Chip.

*   *   *

"Sheriff Keller, please, come in, come in," the old man welcomed Chip into his living room.

"Please, Mr. Stover, call me Chip. And I'm not sheriff any longer."

"Well, you were for many years, and have earned the title," Lawrence Stover replied. "And if you're Chip, then I'm Lawrence. Can I interest you in any coffee? Or anything cold?"

"No, thank you, I'm fine," Chip assured him.

"Then how may I help you, Chip?" Lawrence asked as he eased into a large wooden rocking chair.

"Well, that's the tough question, because I'm not exactly sure, though I hope we can figure out something together. I came to you because you're known and respected across the area as a man of integrity and honor," Chip explained. Lawrence nodded and let him continue. "When you've been a cop as long as I have, you develop a gut feel for things. Hard to explain, but it's like an instinct that tells you when matters are right, and when they're wrong. My instincts are telling me things are wrong.

"The most recent example is the Jennette situation. That even made headlines down in Detroit. It's being published as a murder/suicide, and the reports are portraying Gary Jennette as an unstable, trigger-happy nutcase who finally went off and blew away his wife and daughters.

"I knew Gary. No denying, he was a piece of work, and he and Betty had their moments, particularly when he'd had a few. But he loved her, and doted on his girls. They were his pride and joy. And no matter how strained the marriage was, he always came back, and he'd face down a charging rhino to protect his family.

"I haven't dealt much with Gary over the past year, and I know men can change, but they don't change that much. So I chatted with the bartender over at Bill's Bowling in Kinde – a spot Gary frequented. The bartender said he was the same old Gary, so no changes there. But he did say that Gary mentioned that over the winter he was getting pestered to sell his home."

"Sell his home?" Lawrence asked.

"Yes. Unsolicited offers. The house wasn't even on the market, and Gary had no plans to put it there. He and Betty were like that, given to hanging onto things rather than going for the new and flashy. Hell, he still drove that '15 Malibu. The house was the first and only one they ever owned. From the bartender's account, Gary considered the offers an insult, far below anything he'd ever consider for the property even if he was selling."

"Hmm," Lawrence puzzled, looking disturbed. "So, considering all this together, what are you supposing? That the Jennette family deaths were a straight-up murder?"

"I don't have enough evidence to speculate that far," Chip replied. "But I've learned that when your instincts go off like that, you start looking around for more unusual things to see if there might be connections. So we've got unsolicited, unwelcome purchase offers, and then unusual and tragic deaths. I asked Erin to check with the registrar of deeds, and got all the property transfers in the county within the past two years." Chip opened his folio and pulled out a map with dots marked on it. "As you'd expect, the transfers are scattered all over, but almost half of them are clustered in this area."

"Not far from Kinde, north of Bad Axe," Lawrence mused.

"Right. Gary's house is the X here, on the west side of the cluster."

"Do you think there's something suspicious about these purchases?"

"All I can say is that it's unusual to see such a concentration, unless there's some kind of consolidation or economic development effort. Those sorts of things are always announced, and there's been nothing," Chip explained.

"So, this makes what?" Lawrence asked. "Three, possibly four murders, persistent and unsolicited property purchase offers, and an unusual concentration of property transfers in a region of the county? All irregular things, with a tenuous link between them?"

"'Tenuous' is putting it generously," Chip sighed. "'Hare brained speculation' would be closer, from the perspective of hard evidence. But this is one of these instinct things, which brings me to my next point.

"I've had a lot of time to think since I lost the election, and I've concluded that there was something strange about the whole matter. Even during the campaign my instincts were going off, but I kept suppressing them, thinking it was just candidate animosity, or the shock of being challenged at all, and then losing. But once the election was over and I had time to consider everything, the more obvious it was: the whole thing was weird."

"Weird?" Lawrence asked.

"Strange. County sheriff isn't a very political position, but there is some politics involved – working with the local party, getting to know other candidates, and the like. There are few surprises in the political world. People make it known when they've got their eye on a position, they garner support, plan campaigns, line up resources. Everyone generally knows who's planning what.

"Leading up to this last election, there was no indication that anybody was going to challenge me, least of all Andy Klein. Then suddenly, out of nowhere, he pops up with an aggressive and well-funded – and successful – campaign.

"In this area, there are only two reasons to run against an incumbent sheriff: either you really want into the job, or you want the incumbent out. Since Andy doesn't seem very excited about the position – even now, according to some of the deputies – that means that he, or somebody, wanted me out. Since Andy doesn't know me from Adam's off ox, I suspect 'somebody', possibly the same 'somebody' who financed his campaign. Since I've got almost zero chance of figuring out who that is, I have to guess as to why.

"Sheriffs make a lot of enemies during their tenure, especially in rural areas where everyone knows everyone and people have long memories. But only rarely do these enmities turn into vendettas, and even then, it usually goes no further than smashed windows or slashed tires. A well-funded political campaign is out of that class, so I'm guessing it wasn't so much revenge for something I'd done as concern about something I was doing, or threatened to do. I thought long and hard about that, because for years I've had the department doing pretty much the same things: chasing speeders along Van Dyke, tracking punks running opioids up from Flint, breaking up bar fights in Port Austin, usual small-town stuff. The more I thought about it, the more I wondered if it had something to do with the trucks."

"The trucks?" Lawrence asked.

"Yeah. A couple years ago, I began to notice container trucks on the roads around the county. You've seen them – special trailers designed to haul those shipping containers that they load on international cargo vessels. The trailers are pulled by standard semi tractors, and they're getting more common everywhere. I didn't think anything of them for the longest time, but one day I got to wondering: where were those trucks coming from and going to? We don't have a lot of industry here in the county, but what we do have ships their supplies and product using either standard fifty-three-foot trailers or specialty trailers, like tankers. I asked around a bit, and nobody knew who might be using shipping containers – yet there they were, driving through the county."

"Couldn't you just pull one over and ask?" Lawrence said.

"Not without cause, and we never had any," Chip explained. "No speeding, no suspicion of weight violation, nothing. Even if we had, we couldn't have asked details about his load. No, the best we'd be able to do would be to follow one, and we never seemed to have the resources to do that. Besides, there was zero evidence of anything illegal – just unexplained trucks.

"It was just over a year ago now – the early part of last year – when I brought the topic up with my deputies. They didn't know anything about the trucks, either, but we all agreed that it was fishy; that something was going on in the county that we knew nothing about. So I asked them to keep an eye out, and ask around, to see if we could discover where the trucks were going.

"We never turned up anything, but within a month Andy Klein came out of nowhere and filed as a candidate. Even then I didn't see a connection, and I can't say as I have one now, but it's the only thing I can think of that I did out of the ordinary last year," Chip said.

"So, we have mysterious trucks, unexpected candidates, mysterious property acquisitions – and what may be calculated murder," Lawrence summarized.

"And what may be an overactive imagination," Chip admitted. "Only that last factor makes everything a lot more serious."

"Overactive, perhaps, but I wouldn't casually discount the instincts of an experienced law officer," Lawrence cautioned. "But if I may ask, why are you coming to me? How can I assist with any of this?"

Chip sighed. "Being a private citizen, I'm very short on resources. You also are a private citizen, but are well known throughout the area, and have a large extended family and an even larger circle of acquaintances, extending across the Thumb and beyond, by some accounts." Lawrence said nothing, but nodded for Chip to continue. "If you could pass the word among your acquaintances about some of these matters, something might turn up. The trucks might be irrelevant, but information on the property purchases might be more useful, particularly if there's any connection with the murders."

"That very factor may make inquiries a little dangerous," Lawrence warned.

"The word on the street," Chip replied, looking at Lawrence with a level eye, "is that your network of acquaintances isn't put off by a little danger."

*   *   *

"Come in, Kevin," Pa Hubbart waved his nephew into his office. Kevin Bryant took a seat in front of the old man's desk, looking around at the surprisingly Spartan surroundings. The cluttered desk looked like it had been picked up at a garage sale and the worn chair squeaked horribly when Pa sat down on it.

Hard to believe it was the office of one of the most powerful men in the region.

"I want to thank you for your discreet work on the Jennette property," Pa said with a smile. "Apparently the next of kin is an older sister who lives in Warren who isn't interested in owning a home in Huron County."

"Good thing there's already a buyer waiting," Kevin quipped. "Was that the last one?"

"It was," Pa assured him. "There are now no residences within reasonable line of sight of the complex, so that's one less risk, thanks to you."

"Happy to be of service," Kevin replied.

"I called you here to offer you another opportunity – one that sounds suited to your family's particular talents." Pa picked up a paper from the desk and handed it to Kevin. "A friend of George

Klein's works at the Harbor Beach marina, and may have spotted some sort of smuggling operation being run out of there. There's a charter fishing boat that runs a few nights a week. Heads out in the evening, right around sunset, and returns in the small hours of the morning. They appear to load up for a long trip, stocking the boat with a dozen or so coolers before departing. But they must be crappy fishermen, because they never come back with any fish. They never go near the cleaning station there by the parking lot – they just unload their coolers onto a truck and drive away."

"Are you thinking illegal drugs?" Kevin asked.

"Possible, but I don't think it's likely," Pa replied. "No purpose in going to the expense and trouble of marine smuggling your cocaine and heroin when you can just pack it into a truck and drive it up I-75 like everyone else does. Besides, illegals don't need coolers – but prescription drugs sometimes do. That's why I'm thinking it might be medicines."

"Prescription drugs?" Kevin asked, puzzled. "Why not just drive down to the pharmacy?"

"Why not, indeed?" Pa replied. "The answer may be tied to some other interesting rumors I've heard over the years. But that's not important at the moment. What is important is that pharmaceuticals are valuable, and black-market pharmaceuticals even more so, because nobody's tracking them. Not to mention that we could make use of them ourselves, if they're the right kind."

"Ah," Kevin nodded. "So, what would you like done?"

"I'd like to get our hands on one of those shipments. As to how, I leave that in your capable hands. I have enough irons in the fire right now. Keep me apprised, don't take too many risks, and don't leave evidence behind. But then, you know how to do that."

"And…ah…," Kevin asked hesitantly. "What's our stake in this?"

"Fifty percent of gross."

"Fifty percent?" the astonished Kevin replied. "That's…that's quite…thank you very much."

"You're drawing up the plan and doing the work. The risks are yours, so the reward should be commensurate."

"All right, then," Kevin said, standing and shaking Pa's hand. "Let me contact Ethan."

*   *   *

The supervisors weren't happy, and that meant nobody was happy. Nobody knew why they were so upset, but there was a lot more shouting and beating than usual. Tyrone and his team tried to keep their heads down and stay busy working. That was the best way to avoid attention, especially when the supers were walking around swinging their batons and looking mean.

They were assembling little Christmas elf dolls this week. Boxes of plastic arms and legs, torsos and heads, and bags of little green tunics and hats, lay all about them. Tyrone's fingers were sore from pushing parts together, but that didn't matter. What mattered was making quota, and maybe a little over, but not too much over because then they raised your quota.

A couple of stations down the line, one of the supervisors was loudly berating the team, and brought his baton down with such force that it elicited a sharp cry from one of the workers. That caused Tyrone to glance up, so he was looking when it happened. The worker who'd been struck rose up in fury and took a great swing, striking the super on the side of the head and knocking him down.

Tyrone gasped. The worker who'd lost his temper was Connor, who stood stunned, as if unable to believe what he'd just done. Oh, no. This was trouble. This was big trouble. You never, never, never hit supervisors.

The super who'd been knocked down was scrambling to his feet. Connor frantically looked for somewhere, anywhere, to run, but it was too late. Two other supervisors were running toward him, batons in hand. He tried to dash down the line, toward where Tyrone's team was seated, but they caught him and flung him to the floor.

It was horrible. They beat him and beat him, their batons cracking against his body. He screamed and writhed, trying to escape, but they were all around him. Finally, he lay somewhat still, face down, his arms over his head. Then Mr. Nick himself came up with another supervisor who was carrying handcuffs. Mr. Nick looked down at the prone body, then nodded to the supervisor who knelt down and handcuffed Connor. Then they dragged him away.

Tyrone's insides felt light and jangly. He didn't like Connor, who was noisy and pushy, but even Connor didn't deserve this.

"Well," grumbled Aiden. "No dinner for us tonight."

"No dinner?" Tyrone asked. He'd been through this before, but tended to block out the details.

"No, idiot, and no breakfast, either," Aiden snapped. "When the pigs don't eat, we don't eat."

Now Tyrone remembered.

It was a long, difficult night, between hunger gnawing at empty bellies and horror gnawing at young imaginations. Those who'd been here the last time they were taken out remembered; the new arrivals were told what to expect. When morning came there was no breakfast. They were marched out to the bleachers, supers everywhere with their batons, eyeing them all to insure they watched. They'd have to watch, they'd have to watch it all. Anyone who closed his eyes, anyone who turned away, would be next.

The morning was cool and the gray clouds hung low overhead. The bleachers ran along one side of the fenced-in pen. There was no grass inside the pen, only dirt. A big trough of filthy water was at one end and the sty at the other, its doors open, the reek incredible even at this distance.

Across the pen from the bleachers, just outside the fence, was a backhoe. Its bucket was half-raised, and hanging from the hook on the underside of the bucket was Connor. His hands were shackled over his head and he half-stood, half-hung just outside the fence. He wasn't moving, and Tyrone couldn't see from this distance whether his eyes were open or not.

Just inside the fence, jostling and shoving against it hard enough to make it sway, was a herd of large hogs. Being deprived of both dinner and breakfast made them hungry and mean; knowing what a human hanging just outside the fence all night signified made them restless. They squealed and snapped at one another.

Without ceremony or announcement, a man walked out and started the backhoe. The roar of the engine alerted Connor, and he began screaming and thrashing. Two other men approached, and Connor made to kick at them, but it was no use. They grabbed him and stripped his clothes off, leaving him pale and scrawny in the cold morning air.

The men stepped away and the backhoe rolled forward, raising the bucket so that Connor was lifted high in the air. He screamed and writhed at the end of the chain that held him. The operator swung the bucket forward, suspending Connor over the surging, snapping herd of hogs. Then slowly, mercilessly, the bucket began to lower. Connor pulled his legs up and screamed louder, but it was futile. The bucket was dropping steadily, and the hogs were lunging higher.

Then the screams changed in tone. Tyrone looked at the sky above the far trees, unable to watch directly, but he couldn't block his ears. Behind him he heard sobbing and retching, and hoped whoever it was had the sense to keep watching – he didn't want to have to go through this twice in one day.

Swiftly, the cries faded, drowned out by the disgusting snorting and snapping and squealing of feeding pigs. The backhoe rumbled again, and Tyrone saw the bucket lifting with only the bloodied chains hanging down. Below it the pigs jostled, frantically rooting about on the ground. After a while they began wandering away toward the trough to wet bloody jowls in the grimy water. On the dirt in the middle of the pen there was nothing more than a red smear.

The supervisors began to bark orders for everyone to get to the factory for the day. As Tyrone was turning to go, he noticed a man standing at the far side of the pen. He was by the corner where the sty was, and had been watching the gruesome proceedings. His face was brown and wrinkled and his black hair was long and stringy. He wore a shirt and trousers that were too large for him. It was hard to tell from this distance, but Tyrone thought the man wore a satisfied, almost gleeful expression. Whoever he was, Tyrone didn't like the look of him.

Not at all.

Desperation

"So, here's the deal," Kevin Bryant said, sitting down across the table from his son Ethan and dropping an oversized duffel on the ground beside them. "Our contact at the marina has been watching this boat and they seem to follow a predictable pattern. They load up and head out after sunset, which is about 9:00 p.m. these days. They usually return between 1:00 and 2:00 a.m.

"If you figure they're turning between twelve and fifteen knots, that's just the right amount of time to cruise out near the border, meet up with a vessel coming from somewhere like Goderich over on the Canadian side, transfer the cargo, and return. Doing this two or three times a week would mean a lot of cargo."

"How big a crew?" Ethan asked.

"Always three guys. Our contact can't say whether they're the same three. You'll want your crew to be at least four. Here's your go bag," Kevin kicked the duffel. "It's got guns, a portable searchlight, a bull horn, and a tracking monitor. Our contact slipped a location transponder onto the boat, so you'll be able to find them.

"We've got a skiff on a trailer standing by in Harbor Beach. It's a twenty-footer, light and fast, but a little short on range, so be sure to bring extra fuel. Next time the contact sees the cruiser preparing to go, he'll call this number," Kevin slipped a phone across the table. "After that, you call the number stored on there under 'skiff', and they'll run the boat down to the harbor and launch it. You show up with your crew and follow the cruiser."

"What do you want done when we catch up?" Ethan asked.

"Well, make sure they've picked up their cargo first, because that's all we're interested in. Take that, ditch the crew, and sink the cruiser."

"Sink it?" Ethan asked. "Cruisers are valuable."

"We don't have the resources to start dealing in hot boats," Kevin scoffed. "Besides, depending on what they're smuggling, the load might be worth more than the boat."

"Who should I take?" Ethan asked.

"Up to you, but I'd recommend at least two experienced guys. If you can get three, great, but as long as there's you and two others, the fourth guy doesn't matter much. All he does is steer the boat."

"Speaking of the value of the load – what's our cut from this?"

"Thirty percent."

"Thirty!" Ethan whistled. "That's unusually generous, especially for Pa."

"He figures we're doing the work and taking the risks."

"Well, that'll make it easier to round up volunteers," Ethan said.

*   *   *

"Cast off!" Ben Stover called, and the deckhands fore and aft pulled the mooring hawsers off the cleats and leapt aboard. He had experienced helpers tonight, Bob McLean and Todd Beck, and they knew how to get underway smoothly. Ben eased the throttle back, gentling the boat away from the pier and turning the bow toward the north exit from the harbor. He looked around at the nearly empty marina. Poor Harbor Beach. Like so many port towns along the Huron coast, it had been hit by the drop-off in recreational boating over the past several decades. The little harbor had wonderful facilities for pleasure craft – dozens of slips, fueling facilities, and ample dockside amenities – but only a fraction of the space was occupied. Even at peak season, no more than a quarter of the slips were rented.

There weren't as many fishing charters around Harbor Beach as there had once been, but there were still a few, which gave the operation a cover. They were known in the harbor area as Lucky Charters, and even had a handful of business cards printed up to post on bulletin boards in local businesses. They kept a bit of fishing tackle aboard as camouflage, but what they really caught were volume quantities of medicines for the ranches. Ben far preferred these transfers to risky river pickups. They could handle much more cargo, and meeting out in the middle of the lake kept them far from prying eyes. The rendezvous point was off the shipping lanes, and the Border Patrol didn't usually run drones this far up the lake. Even if they chanced to, infrared from drone height wouldn't reveal much. When it was a matter of efficiency, this method was the way to go.

The boat cleared the pier and the lake waves started rocking the hull. Ben eased the throttle forward and came around to the course that would take them to the rendezvous point. Once they were reasonably clear of the harbor they'd turn off their running lights – utterly illegal in these waters but it enabled them to take advantage of the fact that a dark boat at night was practically invisible. They'd have to watch their radar carefully to stay clear of other vessels, but in time they'd have to turn that off as well, so they weren't broadcasting their position. Their locator, tuned to the transponder on the other boat, would guide them to their contact.

All that was routine. Ben set the autopilot and settled into his chair, while on the deck below Todd and Bob arranged the coolers. The sky was clear and the weather was calm. A beautiful night for fishing.

*   *   *

Cliff lived at the back of the shop in a dirty storeroom that had been cleared out for his use. It had a cot with a thin blanket, a cheap card table, and a folding chair. There was an old space heater and an older television, which was his only entertainment. He had to use the shop's bathroom, which meant he never got to shower.

He worked for Jack, who was a cousin of some sort, though Jack just called him "kid". Jack gave him chores around the shop

119

like cleaning or hauling, and at times would let him change oil or flush a radiator. At the end of the week, Jack would give Cliff fifty or sixty bucks in cash, which he would have to husband well. There was an IGA just up the street, where Cliff walked every evening after the shop closed to buy a sandwich and a bottle of juice. He ate half the sandwich and drank half the juice for dinner, and had the rest in the morning for breakfast. He usually didn't have lunch, unless Jack didn't finish his.

That evening, Cliff was sitting in his room watching television when the door flew open. It was Jack, holding a phone in one hand and some keys in the other.

"Here, kid," Jack barked, thrusting the keys at him. "Take the truck. Round up every gas can you can find. Fill them and take them over to Harbor Beach."

"How do I pay for the gas?" Cliff asked.

"Use this card," Jack gave him a credit card. "And there better be only gas on it when I get the statement!"

"Okay. Where in Harbor Beach do I go?"

"To the harbor, idiot. There'll be a boat in the water. Take the gas to them. Hurry!"

Cliff rummaged through the shop for gas cans. There weren't many, but he located three, including an old dented metal one that was rusted all about the bottom. Cliff wondered about that one, but Jack had been emphatic about every gas can as quickly as possible, so into the back of the truck it went. Cliff headed east, stopping at a station on the edge of town to fill the cans and the truck as well, which was nearly empty. In his haste he slopped some gas down the sides of the cans, so he was glad they were back in the bed of the truck rather than up in the cab.

At the harbor, the night was deepening as Cliff drove the truck down to where a boat was tied to a launching dock. It had to be the one, since there were no other boats with people around them. Three guys were near this boat – two inside checking it out and one pacing the dock talking on a phone. Cliff grabbed two of the gas cans and hustled down to the boat.

"What took you so damn long?" snarled one, whom Cliff recognized as Ethan Bryant, his cousin. The other was George Klein, Jack's younger brother. Cliff wasn't sure, but he thought the one on the phone was Owen Hubbart – he seemed to remember seeing him about the factory.

"Is this all you brought?" George asked, looking at the two cans.

"No – one more in the truck," Cliff explained.

"Then go get it!"

Cliff ran as best he could with the old metal can. As he arrived Owen hung up the phone with a frustrated curse.

"Well, ain't that shit? Ted's still south of Sandusky, and won't be here for another forty-five minutes."

"We got to get moving, if we want to get them in the middle of the lake," Ethan cautioned.

"I know that, jackass," Owen looked around in desperation and his eyes fell on Cliff. "Kid, can you drive a boat?"

"A little," Cliff admitted. It was true – one afternoon in his teens he'd been invited out for some water skiing, and he'd had his turn at the wheel in a boat similar to this one.

"You'll have to do. Get in," Owen jerked his head, so Cliff lifted the gas can down to George and clamored down. He almost fell over a big, lumpy duffel that lay on the deck.

"Be careful, you clumsy bastard!" George snapped as Owen got aboard. "Damn, why does this can stink so bad?"

"I…slopped a little gas on it," Cliff explained weakly.

"Figures. Do we have any rags?"

"No," Ethan said as he cast off the lines.

"I ought to make you use your shirt," George said to Cliff. "Just move it farthest back. You sit there on the floor until we call for you."

Cliff found the night breeze a bit chilly as they roared out of the harbor, but he was excited, too. He didn't know what this was all about, but he never minded fast boat rides! The other three stood toward the front of the boat, clustered around where Ethan was steering. They kept watching what looked like a tablet and directing Ethan. Cliff guessed that the tablet-like thing was a navigational device that was guiding them to wherever they were going.

The small boat roared across the lake. Cliff was amazed at how dark it was on the water at night, and how bright the stars were overhead. There were so many, and they looked close enough to touch! After a while, George directed him to dump one of the cans of fuel into the boat's gas tank. Cliff chose the metal one – it was still damp around the rusty bottom, so he wanted to empty it first. Then, since George and Owen had sat down, he sidled forward to where Ethan was driving, the tablet-like thing propped on the instrument panel.

"Is – that where we're going?" Cliff asked, pointing at a red dot on the screen.

"Yup," Ethan replied with a rather mean grin.

"Is it – Canada?"

"No, idiot, it's another boat," Ethan said. Just then the tablet gave a chime and some little figures appeared on the screen next to the red dot. Ethan leaned over and scrutinized the figures, then called out, "Hey, looks like they've stopped."

"Did they?" Owen asked. "How far away are we?"

"At this speed," Ethan examined some figures next to the little blue dot on the screen, "about forty, fifty minutes."

"Okay, slow down," Owen instructed. "We want to give them time to meet their contact, transfer the goods, and start heading back before we move in."

"Okay," Ethan said, easing the throttle so they slowed a little.

"How do you know where they are?" Cliff asked, pointing at the red dot.

"Our guy at the marina slipped a location tracer onto their boat," Ethan explained. Then he realized who he was speaking to and looked at Cliff with disgust. "Stop asking questions! Sit down and shut up!"

Cliff sat down and curled up against the chill. The residual gas fumes were giving him a headache, but the fresh air helped. The other three talked among themselves, ignoring him. Of course they would – they were full-blooded sons of the family, while he was just a bastard, and a disgraced bastard at that. Well, maybe if he was useful on this expedition, whatever it was, he might gain a little more favor.

*   *   *

Out in the center of the lake, the cooler swap between the contact boat and the cruiser was complete. Fortunately, the waves had been calm, so the transfer had executed with less than the usual struggle and risk. The contact boat had headed back to Goderich, and Ben gave him ten minutes or so to get well clear before throttling up and turning back toward Harbor Beach. In another ten minutes he'd be able to fire up the radar, and a few miles after that he'd switch the running lights back on. On this leg of the mission, he wanted to look as normal as possible.

*   *   *

"Hey," Ethan barked. "He's moving again."

The skiff had cut speed two more times, until they were just idling through the water, waiting for the other boat to finish whatever they were doing. The choppy motion of the waves combined with the smell of gas fumes was making Cliff feel uneasy.

"What direction?" Owen asked.

"Just a minute," Ethan said, fiddling with something on the tablet. "Back toward us. At this speed, we intercept in twenty, twenty-five minutes."

"So maybe ten minutes at twice the speed," Owen nodded. "This is it – full throttle. We'll set up while you brief him." He jerked his thumb back at Cliff.

"Listen," Ethan explained as Cliff stepped forward. "In a few minutes I'm going to have to help them, so you're going to steer. It's just like a car, except that this throttle handle is the gas pedal. This notch here is ahead slow, this is ahead one quarter, this is

123

ahead one half. We'll be close in by this other boat, so we'll probably be moving slowly. I'll direct you where to steer it. Got it?"

Cliff nodded. He glanced back to where Owen and George were struggling to mount some kind of portable light along the edge of the boat. They finally got it fastened well enough, then pulled out a bullhorn which they laid on the seat. Then they pulled out the guns.

Guns?

Cliff's mouth went dry and his hands started to tremble as he looked at the men unpacking the weapons, black and evil-looking in the dim light. Guns? What the hell were those for? Nobody had said anything about guns! Suddenly Cliff very much regretted having been brought on this trip. He turned away and focused on the dark water ahead, trying to ignore the ominous sounds behind him of clips being slapped in and bolts being cocked. These weren't hunting pieces, either – these were short-barreled models with large magazines.

What had he gotten himself into?

*   *   *

After cruising in the dark for a while, Ben flicked the radar from standby to active. Like everything else on this cruiser, the radar was aging but still functional, and soon the screen was glowing with dots indicating nearby vessels. There was an upbound lake freighter, a smattering of smaller craft nearer the shore, and the bright line of the land over twenty miles away.

Then Ben scowled a little. One of the dots seemed very close. He clicked the scope to a smaller radius display. Sure enough, there it was, not three miles away – and moving fast. Ben clicked a couple more buttons and scowled more deeply. The contact was on an intercept course.

Ben altered his course forty-five degrees to the west. His hand reached for the switch that would turn on the running lights – with other vessels in close proximity, it was only safe. But at the last minute he hesitated. Their course change should allow the other boat to pass well astern. Best to remain stealthy for a bit longer. He settled into the new course and rechecked the radar after a couple minutes.

The contact had changed course. They were still cruising to intercept, and were now within two miles.

Suddenly this open-water encounter didn't look so innocent.

His heart pounding, Ben clicked the radar scope to a five-mile radius, where he could see the contact moving and turning. Ben swung the wheel over to head directly away from the unidentified boat and rammed the throttle to full, but their pursuer simply followed at a much faster pace, overhauling them easily.

How had the strange boat found them?

"What's going on, Ben?" Bob called up from the deck, feeling the engines change pitch.

"We got company, guys," Ben replied. "Don't know what, but I'm worried. You both get down below the gunwale and don't show yourselves unless I say. Get lifejackets on if you can do it quietly."

"But –" Bob started.

"Do it!" Ben barked. Just then a light came from dead astern, illuminating the cruiser's superstructure. Todd and Bob scrambled about on deck, hidden in the inky shadows, but Ben was in full view up on the bridge, sheltered only by the back of his conning chair.

Ben's innards were churning. At first he'd been worried that they'd finally gotten caught by the Border Patrol or Coast Guard. But now he doubted that. Not only would an official takedown probably use at least two units, there was something about this pursuer that screamed "amateur". For some reason, that scared him even more.

"Hey!" Ben hissed down to the deck. "Under the hatch along the starboard side is an emergency kit. Fetch it out and have it ready."

"All right," Todd replied.

The pursuing boat was starting to overtake them on the starboard side. Ben could hear the whine of their engine start to pierce the rumble of his own. The search light was turning to stay on him, and suddenly the harsh tones of a bullhorn blared across the water.

"Hey! You in the boat! Stop where you are!"

Ben tried to pretend he didn't hear the hail, and turned his course away from the other boat. It was futile, of course – they rapidly altered course to stay with him. Then his heart froze as he heard the sharp popping of gunfire and saw the blue muzzle flashes out of the corner of his eye.

"Oh God," he whispered. "How did they find us?" The other boat was now directly off their starboard beam, maybe a quarter mile away, but already altering course to close with them. Ben cut the throttles and the big cruiser settled in the water, shedding speed.

"Ben, what's going on?" Bob called up from the deck in a hollow whisper. The two others were still below the gunwale, hidden from view.

"Listen," Ben whispered back hoarsely. "In that emergency kit is a signal flare gun. Get it ready. When I call out, pop up and fire it right into their cockpit as best you can."

"What good will that do?" Bob asked.

"It may distract them long enough for us to get a lead," Ben answered. "We have more fuel – we may be able to outlast them."

Bob shrugged and started loading the flare gun. Ben watched the boat closing in. He could now see more of it behind the glaring eye of the searchlight. It was a smaller boat, with a coxswain steering up by the light and three men standing toward the stern, holding automatic weapons.

Ben didn't have the heart to tell his friends the truth. These were pirates. They were probably dead already, destined for a cold, watery grave at the bottom of Lake Huron. The gambit with the flare was a certainly futile gesture of desperation. He prayed as the boat approached, trying to gauge the right moment.

126

Cliff had been nervous enough after taking the wheel of the boat. Then Owen had let off that burst of gunfire, causing him to nearly jump out of his skin. Now he was expected to steer the boat toward the idling cruiser, keep the searchlight directed on it, and watch for anything "fishy".

Cliff didn't like this at all. His cousins were brandishing guns and talking tough. He didn't know what they wanted with the other boat and the guys aboard it, but he was certain it was bad. Very, very bad. He'd been around trouble before, but never anything like this. He struggled to steer with his shaking hands, steady his trembling knees, and watch the other boat. He desperately wished he'd never come.

Then suddenly someone stood up in the other boat, just by the side, and held his arms out as if he was aiming. "Hey –" Cliff started to say, but there was a loud pop and a bright flash and what looked like a small red meteor arced across the water. It fell into their boat fizzling and hissing and blindingly bright, skittering back toward the engine. The others cried out in surprise and confusion, but Cliff turned away, his eyes hurt by the object's brightness.

Then Cliff's world erupted in a deafening roar that felt like giant hands slapping both sides of his head at once. The air was sucked from his lungs and he found himself flying head over heels through the air. He felt his arm strike something with tremendous force and was literally deafened. He could see nothing. His vision was a field of flashing sparks, and he couldn't tell the sky from the lake.

That distinction became clear as he fell clumsily into dark water so cold that it would have knocked the breath out of him if he'd had any. As the icy water closed over his head, Cliff panicked. He couldn't swim! He couldn't swim! Thrashing and flailing, he struggled toward what he hoped was the surface. His head broke the surface of the water and he gulped great breaths, struggling and sputtering as waves splashed onto his face.

Grasping about in panic, he felt things bobbing near him. He grabbed something that felt like foam – maybe part of a seat cushion – but when he tried to pull it closer, searing pain lanced up his right arm. Crying in agony, he let the arm drift. Was it broken?

Clutching the foam as best he could with his left arm, he struggled to keep his head above the waves. But then he noticed that there was something wrong with the air. It was heavy and dark, so thick with a choking, chemical smell that he almost couldn't inhale. Kicking to turn and look about, he saw, to his horror, a flaming slick spreading swiftly toward him, filling the air with thick black smoke. The gasoline! The explosion had ruptured the tanks and ignited the fuel!

Cliff cried and kicked, hindered by his useless arm as he struggled to escape the flames. Suddenly they were all around him, his eyes stinging with the smoke and his throat constricting on the searing gases. A wave sloshed some flaming gasoline onto his head. His face was on fire while his body was freezing, and he clutched at the burning skin, screaming in agony. He slipped beneath the waves, barely holding onto his scrap of foam.

*   *   *

"Go!" Ben yelled. Bob stood up, aimed and fired the flare gun, and dropped back down below the gunwale. Ben rammed the throttle ahead full and the cruiser surged forward. It was a desperate, last-ditch move, but they had to try something. Ben prayed, anticipating that the next thing he'd feel would be hot slugs ripping into his back.

None of them expected the brilliant flash that split the night and the shock wave that knocked them staggering and threw Ben forward onto the control console.

"Holy shit," Ben whispered.

"What was that?" Bob cried. "Did the flare do that?"

"Couldn't have," Ben replied. "Had to have been fuel. If they weren't careful, they may have gotten fume buildup in the bilge –

but still, holy smoke!" Dumbfounded, they stared back at the flaming slick, billowing thick black smoke into the night sky.

"Do you think anyone survived?" Bob asked, but before Ben could answer, Todd, who'd rushed to the stern rail to look at the carnage, pointed back and cried out.

"There's someone in the water!"

"Dammit," Ben murmured, holding the wheel steady on course.

"Ben, I heard cries back there! Someone's alive!"

"Dammit, kid, that explosion will be visible for miles! It'll draw rescuers from all around, by which time we need to be far away!" Ben replied.

"But someone's in the water, right near all that flaming oil!" Todd pointed. "We've got to help! Listen, you can hear him!"

"Those were pirates!" Ben shouted. "They were about to gun us down and dump our bodies in the lake! They deserve what they get!"

"We can't just leave him!" Todd shouted back, pointing astern at the receding wreckage.

"Dammit!" growled Ben, spinning the wheel around in response to the oldest law of the sea. "You get ready with those preservers! We have to come from upwind, or the slick will float down on us!" Ben swung the cruiser in a great arc around the flaming wreckage and played their searchlight across it, trying to penetrate the thick smoke.

"There!" Todd cried, pointing. "Hear that? Over that way!" Ben pointed the light and they saw splashing amidst the waves.

"There he is!" Bob pointed, but Ben was already nosing toward the thrashing figure.

"Steady, now," Ben cautioned, throttling back as they bore down on the man. "Okay, throw!" The two life preservers arced through the air. Todd's went wide, but Bob's overshot the man, who clutched at the line. Both men hauled on the line swiftly, dragging the figure to the side. The flames were dying but there was enough smoke to make the air nearly unbreathable.

"My God," Todd whispered as they pulled the man over the gunwale and dumped him on the deck. He'd cried out when they grabbed his arm, so Todd guessed that he'd sustained some damage there. He stunk of smoke and gasoline, and was gasping and coughing as he rolled on the deck. But most striking was the damage to his head and neck – he'd suffered burns which covered the left side of his head and a good part of his face.

"How did you locate us?" Ben was kneeling beside the man, leaning right into his face.

"Ben, let the guy breathe," Bob urged, tugging at Ben's shoulder. But Ben pushed him rudely aside and nearly shouted at the pirate.

"How did you locate us? Tell me, or I throw you back over the side with my own hands!"

"Tracer," the man gasped weakly. "Guy – at marina – put tracer on."

"Dammit!" Ben swore, then turned to the others. "The boat is locked up at dock, so it has to be somewhere on the weather decks. Check around and under and in things." The two started looking and feeling under the railing while Ben leapt to the bridge and began looking about the coxswain's station.

"What are we looking for?" Bob called through the smoke.

"Anything that feels out of place, something stuck or lodged where it doesn't seem to belong. A box or disc – it has to have a battery, so –"

"Like this?" Todd called out, holding up a small dark object. "It was stuck under the edge of this shelf thing." Ben rushed over and examined it.

"That doesn't belong on my boat," he exclaimed, hurling it over the side. Dashing to the wheel, he pushed the throttle to full and swung the boat around.

"Where to now?" Bob asked. "Back to Harbor Beach?"

"No – last place we want to go," Ben replied tersely. "If they've got a spy in the harbor, we don't want to show up there, especially when they don't return. Right now, we'll steer due west until we get close enough to blend in with the coastal traffic,

130

then turn south to Port Sanilac. That should put us within cell range so we can get in touch with our people. Lord, what a mess. That explosion could already be drawing attention from as far away as Selfridge. They could send drones or helos, and we don't want to be anywhere near when they arrive."

"What do we do about our guest?" Bob asked, pointing to where Todd was trying to help the man lying on the deck.

"That's the question, isn't it? In the short term, there's a spinal board along the port side below. Lash him to that as we get closer to port. I think there might be an inflatable splint in the first aid kit for that arm. Don't be obvious about it, but I want him immobilized when we hit the pier.

"Okay," Bob agreed. "And in the long term?"

"That," Ben said grimly, "is not our decision."

Exposure

It was pushing midnight, and Derek was feeling a bit guilty about keeping Jude out so late, but at least they were heading home now. Besides, it wasn't like Jude was going to get scolded. After his clever subterfuge that had liberated him and his siblings from captivity, Jude was in such good favor with his parents that they let him do just about anything. And what Jude wanted to do most these days was to learn about medicine, so he'd been accompanying Derek on rounds for the past week or so. Derek hardly minded – Jude was cheerful, helpful, intelligent, and eager to learn. But he was still only eleven years old and needed his sleep. That was why he was dozing in the back while Cletus drove north up M-19.

They called it "the ambulance", but it was really an old panel van that had been made over to make it useful for moving guests between the ranches. At first it had only had some ties in the floor for anchoring wheelchairs, but gradually racks and slings had been added to hold or hang medical equipment. Just recently a narrow but serviceable bed had been added along the side, on which Jude was now lying. When he could find a driver, Derek was using the ambulance more and more because he could bring more equipment and medicine on his rounds. They'd just been visiting some ranches in the southern Thumb, which had taken longer (of course) than they'd expected. Had he not had Jude with him, Derek might have opted to stay down there and sleep in his own bed for a change. But he wanted to get Jude home to his parents who were understandably nervous about having their children out of sight for too long. Derek would bunk down somewhere, and tomorrow Cletus would take him on a sweep through the ranches in the northern Thumb and get them home by suppertime. Hopefully.

They had just cleared Yale and were approaching the turn west on M-90 when Cletus' phone rang. He answered and listened in silence for a minute before saying, "All right," and hanging up.

"Change of plan," Cletus announced, looking serious. "We're headed for Port Sanilac. Glad they caught us when they did."

"Cletus, it's getting kind of late, and Jude –" Derek began, but Cletus interrupted him.

"It's an emergency. Something to do with one of the mid-lake pharmaceutical pickups. They didn't want to speak openly, but the code phrases indicated major problems, including severe injuries. They're coming into Port Sanilac rather than their home port of Harbor Beach."

Derek gasped. The smuggling was critical to his medical work, and was usually handled by the experienced team of Ben Stover, Bob McLean, Paul Stover, and recently Todd Beck. "Injuries? Who got hurt?" he asked.

"That's the mysterious part," Cletus answered. "The codes indicate 'team safe', but also 'severe injuries incoming'. Good thing we're not that far away."

As they approached Port Sanilac, they got another call. Cletus listened carefully, acknowledged, and hung up with a puzzled look.

"That's odd," he said. "Though Port Sanilac has plenty of slips in the marina, they want us to go around to the north end of the harbor, to the boat launch ramps. We're supposed to go as far down the ramp as possible and wait for them to come in. That doesn't make any sense. For a mid-lake transfer, they'd be using one of the cruisers. There's barely enough depth for a cruiser at the launch ramps, while there's plenty at the slips. Something fishy is going on."

This made Derek even more nervous, but there was nothing to do but see it out. When they arrived at the sleepy town, all was calm. The evening anglers were long gone and the early morning ones had yet to appear, so they had the ramps to themselves. Derek busied himself making preparations – he had no idea what constituted "severe injuries", but wanted to be ready for anything.

He gently woke Jude and explained what he could, instructing him to stay well away when the boat arrived.

About fifteen minutes after they arrived, another truck showed up. It was Keith Kyle and John Hagerstrom, the team that had been ready to meet the returning cruiser in Harbor Beach to handle the incoming cargo. They didn't have any idea what had happened, either – they'd just gotten a call sending them down here.

Shortly thereafter, the cruiser idled into the harbor, hugging the north break wall. The starboard bow and superstructure were stained and streaked with black. Cletus gave a low whistle. "Why is it so dirty? What is that, soot? Did they have a fire?" Derek's foreboding deepened. He had no idea what he was about to face, but it was probably going to outstrip both his skills and his facilities. He wished he had a real ambulance and a fully equipped EMT team, but he was all there was.

The cruiser approached the docks in silence. Cletus backed the ambulance down the ramp as far as it could go, its rear tires in the water, both doors open toward the pier. The boat nosed toward the dock until it was almost touching, causing Cletus to raise his eyebrows nervously, and then it did an almost in-place swivel that turned the bow away while laying the stern smoothly alongside the end of the dock.

Cletus relaxed again, giving a mild snort of frustration. "That's gotta be Ben Stover – what a showoff. C'mon."

They hastened down the dock to find the shaken-looking pair of Todd and Bob hoisting from the deck someone who looked to be strapped to a backboard. The man's head was half covered with a damp white towel and his right arm was immobilized in an inflatable splint.

"Who's this?" Derek asked.

"Just take him," Todd hissed. "Get him out of sight, get him care, but don't leave until Ben talks to you. We have to get this cargo off."

Bewildered, Derek and Cletus ran the man back up the pier to the waiting van. They wedged him in, unstrapped him from the board, and clumsily lifted him onto the bed. For the sake of both safety and caution, Derek secured him with the bed's straps. The man was half-conscious, moaning and moving slightly. He was filthy and dripping, and reeked of smoke and petroleum.

Derek could hear the busy pounding of feet as the guys bustled the cargo to the waiting pickup. He signaled Cletus to pull the ambulance up off the ramp and to the far edge of the parking lot, under a tree that spread there. Only then did he dare lift the damp towel from the man's face. He grimaced, but what caught his attention was the soft cry from the front seat. Jude, who was sitting in the passenger's seat, had turned around to see what was going on.

"My goodness, Mr. Derek, what happened?" the boy asked. Derek winced – he would have spared the boy this if he could, but there was no taking back what he'd already seen.

"Burns, Jude," Derek explained. "Here, come around to the side, if you have the stomach for it." Of course, the boy did, so shortly Derek was showing him what second- and third-degree burns looked like, and explaining what the primary treatment was. The man was still moaning and stirring a little. Derek wasn't sure if he was conscious or not, but now was neither the time nor the place to wake him.

"Derek," Cletus called from outside the van. "Ben's here, and needs to speak with you."

"Umm – okay," Derek was hesitant to leave a patient in this condition, but it should only be a minute, and he had an assistant. "Jude, stay here by him. If he cries out or starts moving, call me. I'll be just outside here."

Jude nodded, staring with horrified fascination at the raw, scorched flesh on the side of the man's head. Then the man moaned and turned his neck, making more of the unscarred side of his face visible.

Jude gasped.

Out in the parking lot, Ben was giving Derek and Cletus the quick run-down of the attack and the aftermath.

"So that guy's…" Cletus asked, gesturing toward the ambulance.

"A pirate," Ben confirmed. "We don't know who he is or who sent him, though I'm guessing they were after the cargo."

"How would they know about that?" Derek asked.

"Anyone's guess," Ben said with a shrug. "Though it's hard to keep such a widespread operation completely secret no matter how careful people are. Word might have made it into the wrong ears. There was some organization behind the attack, because we were being watched by a contact in the harbor, who slipped a tracer onto the boat. They also had sophisticated weapons, but other than that it was a slipshod operation. They didn't even have life vests aboard."

"So – amateur pirates?" Cletus asked.

"Rookies, is my guess," Ben offered. "Probably some dry-land operation that decided to try their hand at maritime crime. But that brings up the problem: what to do with this guy? We can't turn him loose – he'd go right back to his operation, knowing that his buddies died while we survived. We can't turn him over to the law for about a dozen reasons."

"And he needs urgent medical care, which he can't get through the usual channels," Derek pointed out. "Which reminds me, I need to get back to him. But I have an idea – Cletus, c'mon, I'll explain in the van."

Derek and Cletus headed back to the ambulance where Jude was standing outside the doors looking agitated.

"Mr. Derek, I need to talk to you," he said as the men approached.

"Hop in, Jude, we need to get going," Derek said briskly, opening his door. "Tell me along the way."

"Mr. Derek, I need to talk to you *now*," Jude said.

"Jude, we don't have time. This guy –"

"Mr. Derek, it's *important*," Jude demanded. Derek stopped and looked at the boy. This stubborn insistence was so uncharacteristic of Jude that it grabbed his attention.

"All right, Jude," Derek said, taking the boy aside. "What's so important?"

"Mr. Derek, it's *him*," Jude whispered frantically, pointing to the van. "From the place."

"From what place, Jude? Which 'him'?"

"From the foster care place where we were," Jude explained. "It's the guy who was there."

"What guy?"

"The guy who hurt Martha. His name is Cliff."

St. Anne's House outside Deckerville had once been an adult foster care home, so it was well set up for its new life as a medical facility for the neediest guests from across the ranches. Nonetheless, the small order of medical sisters who ran it were accustomed to having to make unusual changes to accommodate the special needs of certain patients.

But none were so unusual as those received by the sister on night duty in the small hours of that morning.

Yes, they had a secure room that could be locked. It used to be the groundskeeper's room, and was in the basement. No, it only had a small window, and it was primarily used for storage now, but it could be cleaned out. In half an hour? Perhaps, if she woke some of the other sisters to help. Yes, of course, we understand. We'll do what we can.

So the sisters, including their resident helper Janice Boyd, mostly known by her baptismal name of Teresa, busied themselves shifting supplies out of the room and clearing off the frame bed that had been being used as a shelf. They were trying to find a lock to fit the hasp on the door when the ambulance showed up. Janice wasn't surprised to see her friend Derek, but she was surprised to see how brusque and agitated he seemed. She was even more surprised to see them remove a patient on a stretcher and navigate him down the steps to the basement room, with young Jude Schaeffer hovering about.

Janice followed the men down, mystified. Derek and Cletus were lifting the man from the stretcher to the bed, then Derek started using the straps that had secured the man to the stretcher to bind him to the bed frame.

"Can I help?" Janice asked.

"Sure," Derek said, handing her the straps. "I need him tied – ankles, hips, ribs, shoulders, left wrist. I have to get some supplies and the x-ray. Be right back."

Janice tied the straps, knowing what Derek was planning. This man needed the standard ER trauma procedure, which meant getting his clothes cut off and every inch of him inspected for hidden injury. The sealing membrane on the side of his head indicated burns or severe abrasions, and the splint indicated bone damage. Nobody enjoyed this inspection, which had to be done without painkillers lest some injury be masked, so the straps were necessary.

Then Derek was back, trailing Jude, both burdened with bags of gear and the portable x-ray. Jude looked wide-eyed at the man then vanished up the steps. Derek started unpacking supplies, looking tense and unsettled and – angry?

"I can help," Janice offered.

"I got this," Derek replied with unusual terseness.

"Derek, what's going on?" Janice asked. Derek looked up from his preparations, glanced at the patient, then jerked his head toward the door.

"What is this, an accident?" Janice asked once they were outside.

"In a way," Derek replied. "It's a complicated situation with some danger involved."

"Danger?" Janice said.

"Yeah. We would rather not have involved you all, but we had no choice. This guy survived an explosion."

"An explosion!"

"Yes," Derek confirmed. "One that killed three of his buddies. It involved some of our efforts to acquire pharmaceuticals that I can't talk much about."

"Is that why we need a lock for the door?" Janice asked.

"That, and another reason," Derek said grimly. "Turns out that this is the guy who raped Martha Schaeffer while they were held captive in that foster care home."

Janice gasped. "What is he doing here?"

"No idea," Derek admitted. "But I intend to find out. Maybe not today, but sometime soon."

Cliff had been fading in and out, not sure where he was or who was around him. He was terribly thirsty. If he held very still the symphony of pain ebbed to a dull roar. His ears still felt like they were stuffed with cotton. Why couldn't he move much?

A door opened and he turned his head. A dark-haired man came in. Cliff didn't like the look on his face.

"Hello, Cliff," the man said, taking a pair of scissors from a bag and starting to cut at the leg of Cliff's jeans.

"Who are you? Where am I?" Cliff gasped.

"You can call me Luke," the man said, continuing his cutting. "You're in a secure place."

"Is there any water?" Cliff asked. The man paused long enough to squirt some water from a bottle into Cliff's mouth. It was the best drink Cliff had ever tasted.

The man resumed his cutting until the jeans were strips. He yanked them off, none too gently, and then started on the shirt.

"What are you doing?" Cliff said.

"Giving you an inspection, Cliff," Luke answered grimly. "You were in an accident, remember? We know about the burns and the damage to your arm, but you may have sustained other injuries." He lay down the shears and started cutting away Cliff's sleeves with a scalpel.

Then something struck Cliff. "How do you know my name?"

"Oh, I know who you are. In fact, I know more than I want to about your recent history. You see, I'm a friend of the Schaeffer family – a very close friend, almost an adopted family member. That means Martha is very dear to me. To jog your memory, Martha is the girl you recently raped. Twice. And furthermore, she's now pregnant."

Cliff's eyes grew wide and he tugged at the restraints that bound him fast. The man's face turned ugly and he leaned over Cliff, holding up the scalpel.

"Yes, you miserable excuse for a man, that was my sister you violated. You stripped her of her innocence when she was imprisoned and helpless. You have no idea how much I want to start stripping you of every inch of skin and flesh you have."

Cliff gaped, his breath coming in ragged gasps. But the man backed away, though his expression was still hard.

"I am bound by the ethics of my profession to provide you medical care. I am forbidden by the ethics of my faith to do to you with this," he held up the scalpel, "what I'd truly like to do. However," he lay down the scalpel and picked up a couple of other objects. "Our pharmaceuticals are in short supply, particularly anesthetics. After I finish this inspection, I need to debride that burn, and then set your arm. This is a piece of leather for you to bite on. It's the best I can do for you."

*   *   *

"Dammit!" Pa Hubbart swore, slamming his fists on the desk. He'd just gotten off the phone with the search team from Harbor Beach. They'd taken a boat out into the lake, to the last site from which the tracer had transmitted, and had found nothing. Just blue water in all directions. No idea what had happened, no word, no anything all day long.

Fear battled fury within Pa. Had he really lost two grandsons and a grandnephew, reliable men all? Oh, and that worthless piece of crap Cliff, but that was no great loss. What would Nick say? And Judith? How would Kevin respond if Ethan, his eldest, never returned? All this on top of the Wondercare mess.

Was his luck turning?

He needed to talk to Charlie, that's what he needed. He grabbed the phone and keyed Nick's number.

*   *   *

The rabbits rustled in their cages in the bed of the UTV as Nick drove through the woods. Rabbits. He always wanted live ones, too. Sometimes chickens, but always alive, along with the carrots and cabbages and potatoes. Never anything butchered, always live animals.

Nick hated this run, even in broad daylight. Back along the narrow trails to the close, musty little clearing that always seemed to be in shadow no matter how bright the sun. Back to where the tattered, rusty house trailer stood, with the open space before it, centered around the fire trench. Nick had only been inside the trailer once or twice, and it reeked. No electricity, no running water, just Black Charlie living as his ancestors had. Visiting Charlie was like stepping into a different world – a gritty, pungent, sour, shadowed world. Today it was even worse, with the questions and silence about Owen's whereabouts hanging over Nick like a cloud.

Nick pulled into the clearing. There was Charlie, squatting on the ground by the front steps. Always in the same overlarge trousers and stained brown shirt, his stringy black hair hanging down nearly to his shoulders, his wrinkled brown face smudged and dirty. Charlie looked up and nodded, as if he'd been expecting the visit.

"Hi, Charlie –" Nick began, stepping out of the tractor.

"Put it there," Charlie said, pointing to the far side of the steps. "Put it all there." Nick gave the old man a hard gaze, then stomped to the tractor bed and unloaded the boxes of vegetables, buckets of water, and crates of rabbits, stacking them where Charlie had pointed.

"Pa wants to know –" Nick started again, but Charlie cut him off with an upraised hand.

"Tomorrow. Come back tomorrow at this time, and I will tell you the time he can come," Charlie said dismissively. Nick started to respond sharply, but clammed up, got back into the tractor, and roared away from the clearing.

Charlie smiled.

*   *   *

The next afternoon Pa's phone rang. "Nick?" Pa answered.

"Yeah, Pa. Charlie says midnight on Friday."

"All right," Pa replied. "And, Nick?"

"Yeah?"

"I'm sorry about Owen."

"Yeah."

The line went dead. It had been a terrible day. They'd sent out another boat and had even hired a private plane to fly over the area. Nothing. In desperation, they'd called the Coast Guard, pretending that the boat had been on a nighttime fishing expedition. After the duty officer had made clear the folly of waiting two days to report a boat missing, they'd arranged for a helicopter to fly up and search the area. Still nothing. When the duty officer called back to report this, she had also explained that on the night the boat went missing they'd had a call reporting what appeared to be flames on the water in that vicinity of the lake. But it had been some distance from the reporting vessel, and since there had been no distress calls or immediate reports of loss, the Coast Guard hadn't investigated further. The duty officer also informed them that the odds of anyone surviving that long in open water were almost nothing.

Pa was furious. Someone was going to catch hell for this. He wasn't sure who, but someone was.

He hoped Charlie could help with that.

Nick didn't talk much as he drove Pa through the dark woods on Friday night, and Pa didn't know what to say. When they pulled into the clearing, Charlie was sitting by the trench with a rabbit carcass suspended over the fire on a stick. The rabbit's skin was stretched out over a nearby rock. The flickering firelight filled the clearing with dark, morphing shadows. It was not where Nick wanted to be, especially under the circumstances.

Pa went and sat beside Charlie while Nick hung back by the tractor. They looked so incongruous – the tall, neat, silver-haired white man next to the squat, filthy, dark native. But it had always been so. And, Nick noticed for the first time, there was a common streak of ruthlessness that they shared, a detached cruelty that haunted both their faces as they talked in the firelight.

Their discussion didn't take long. Pa waved Nick over as he rose to his feet. "Give him whatever he needs," Pa said as he walked back to the tractor.

"What do you need?" Nick asked Black Charlie.

Charlie looked up with obsidian-black eyes. "One."

Repentance

Tyrone was nervous. The atmosphere around the factory was still tense. His team was meeting their quotas, but the supers were still anxious and touchy. Something was still wrong, or more things had gone wrong, or something. Tyrone didn't like it at all. Making things worse were the nightmares some of the kids were still having after that morning out on the bleachers. Tyrone didn't have them himself, but everyone had been awakened several times by piercing screams echoing through the barracks in the middle of the night as some kid awoke from a nightmare. Nobody ever slept well after that happened. What was more, muttered word was going around among the workers.

Jayden was missing.

*   *   *

Pa drove himself this time, steering the ATV through the dark woods. Old Charlie had said to come alone. Charlie was sitting in his clearing as if he'd never moved. There was no roasting rabbit this time, but a pot of stew simmering over the fire. Pa walked over and sat by him. Charlie didn't say a word of welcome or even acknowledge Pa's arrival – he just stirred his pot and gazed into the flames.

"Did Nick get you what you needed?" Pa finally asked. Charlie just nodded silently. Pa waited a while – he knew Charlie's ways – but his patience was wearing thin. Damned if he'd pay that kind of price for nothing. "Well?" he asked.

Charlie smacked his jaws a couple of times then spoke in his low, gravelly voice.

"You are a strong man, and you are growing great. Great men draw powerful enemies. You have crossed some such, and have drawn notice. Now their gaze is turning on you."

"Who?"

"Old enemies and new," Charlie said in his maddeningly vague manner, waving his hands. "You ventured out lately to your loss. It was foolish. You should have consulted me first. You have not only failed, but have drawn notice, and your foes begin to close in around you."

"Around what?" Pa asked. He had so many operations, so much potential exposure. Charlie didn't reply directly, but pointed away through the woods. "The factory, then? They're focusing on the factory?" Charlie nodded. "What should I do?"

Charlie stared at the fire and worked his jaws a bit more. "Not yet clear. When the threat draws closer, then we can prepare defense."

"But – you'll know, right?" Pa asked. "You'll know when the threat comes closer?"

Charlie nodded slowly. "I will know. I will tell you. But…"

"But what?" Pa asked.

"Defense will cost more."

Pa licked his lips. "All right."

*   *   *

Cliff heard the lock turn and went over to sit on the bed. The day after his arrival, as he was still recovering from the agonizing ordeal of his initial treatment, some men had come to set stronger locks in the door and mount a peephole lens – one that looked inward. Now when the women came he had to sit on the bed while they cleared away his dirty dishes or replaced the bucket in the commode chair or inspected his bandage. Usually there were two, one to do the work and the other to stand by the door, ready to slam it shut if he did anything threatening. There was only one who dared to come alone, and she only came occasionally.

It was her this time. The one with the short red hair and the grave expression, but who could smile so beautifully. She brought in his lunch tray, replaced his pitcher of ice water, and came over to inspect his bandage. She touched some kind of instrument to his forehead and grimaced when she looked at it.

146

"You are taking your pills, right?" she asked.

"Yes," he replied.

She shook her head, pocketed the instrument, and started tidying up the dishes.

"Thank you," Cliff said quietly.

"You're welcome," she replied without looking at him.

"Breakfast was good," he continued. She glanced at him briefly as she stacked things onto the tray.

"I'll convey your compliments to the cook," she said, starting toward the door.

Bleakness closed in around Cliff once more, and in desperation he cried out. "Please don't go!" To his surprise, the woman stopped and turned back, looking at him with a steady, inquisitive gaze. He felt like he had to explain himself, so he continued. "It's like...it's like when I was little, and they'd shut me in my room."

"Who would?" she asked.

"My mom. And grandma," Cliff replied, dropping his head as the bitter memories came flooding back, amplified by his isolation. "They'd get drunk and start shouting at each other, then they'd find something wrong that I did and lock me in my room. It would get so lonely. And they'd forget I was in there, and I couldn't get out for food or the bathroom. I'd be in there for hours and hours, all alone. I'd hammer on the door and howl. But either they wouldn't come because they were sleeping it off, or they'd come and beat me for making noise. But even that was better than being left alone in the cold for hours and hours and hours." A tear seeped down Cliff's nose. He hadn't realized how fresh those memories still were.

To his surprise, the woman sat down in the chair. "I'm sorry you were so badly treated," she said with apparent sincerity. "I can understand why being left alone in a room would terrify you."

Cliff sniffed and wiped his nose. "What's your name?" he asked, just to keep the conversation going.

The woman paused briefly. "You can call me Teresa," she replied.

"Sister Teresa?" Cliff asked.

"Just Teresa," she said. "I'm not even a postulant."

"Okay," Cliff said, not understanding that. "Why – why do you come alone, and all the others come in pairs?"

"Because I'm not afraid of you."

"Afraid of me?" Cliff asked. "Why would they be afraid of me?"

"That shouldn't take much to figure out," she replied. "Most of these sisters know Martha Schaeffer, and a couple are good friends with her family. They know what you did to her, and under what conditions. Rape is a very visceral fear in women."

Cliff winced at the term and dropped his head. He was silent for a long time before speaking in a thick voice. "It was worse than that. It wasn't just her. There were...others."

"Others?"

"Other girls. At other houses I was assigned to, over near Bay City. That's where I – started," Cliff explained. "One of them hanged herself. I still wonder if what I did made it worse for her, until she did that."

"Probably." The room was still for a minute before she spoke again. "Why did you do it?"

"It was like...like here," Cliff waved his arms around to indicate the room. "I was alone in my room, and I got lonelier and lonelier. I'd think about the girls, young girls, alone in their rooms. It was like I was alone in the dark and cold, and they were like bright, warm lights, glowing in their rooms, drawing me. I wanted – I wanted to go to the light, to...to get the glow, to drive away the loneliness."

"So, you raped them because you were lonely? Surely you knew that rape is no way to get a woman to favor you with her company."

Cliff hung his head. "I knew it was wrong, but all I could think of was the light. It was like a hollow part of me that needed filling, a dark hollow part. If I could get to the warm light, it would fill the hollowness. The more beers I drank, the more I thought about those lights in the rooms, and how I knew the combinations to get to them. Besides, in the videos, the women never mind in the end."

"Videos? Porn videos?"

"Yeah. The women always fight at first, but then they start to enjoy it, and end up moaning," Cliff said.

"The videos lie about rape. The videos lie about a lot of things," she said, and Cliff nodded.

"I found that out. It wasn't at all like that, none of it. I hated myself afterwards, and was really sorry. But once I'd done it, it got easier to do. When I'd sit alone drinking beer, feeling all cold and lonely, the thought of those warm lights just grew and grew in my mind. It was like a pressure that kept building until I…gave in. I tried to stop, really, I did. After each time I swore I'd never do it again, but…" he trailed off.

"Sin is like that," Janice said. "Always promising what it can never deliver, and hooking you in the process."

"Yeah, I guess so," Cliff acknowledged. The room fell silent for a minute before she spoke again.

"So, what are you going to do about it?"

"Do about it?" Cliff asked.

"Yes. Several rapes, probably contributing to a suicide – and that's just what you've told me about. That's a lot of sin to carry around. What do you intend to do about it?"

"What can I do? I can't go back home because Pa said he'd kill me –"

"Wait – 'Pa'?" Janice asked.

"Well, he's really my great uncle, but everyone calls him Pa because he pretty much runs the family. Last time I screwed up he punished me bad, and promised he'd kill me if I did it again. He wasn't kidding, either. He's done it before," Cliff explained.

"And this boating expedition you were on: that was Pa's idea?"

"Probably. I got dragged in at the last minute, so I can't really say. He had to know about it, though."

Janice pondered this for a minute. "Hmm. I have some friends who may want to talk to you about this later. But for now, back to the question: what do you plan to do about all the sin you've done?"

"I wish there was something I could do, but I don't know what," Cliff shrugged. "It's not like I can go back and un-rape those girls, or make Martha un-pregnant."

"You're right; you can't," Janice admitted. "But if you're really serious, I can tell you what you can do."

"How would you know?" Cliff asked.

"Because I'm a terrible sinner who's done things at least as bad as you have," Janice said.

"You?" Cliff replied in amazement. "What could you have done?"

"I'll tell you someday," Janice assured him. "But first, about dealing with those sins. You begin by dying."

"Dying?" Cliff asked in alarm. "Well, I've certainly come close to that."

"Yes, you have, as did I," Janice acknowledged. "Which, in a way, makes it easier..."

*   *   *

A few days later, Derek was sitting with Sister Joseph Marie, who supervised St. Anne's House, reviewing the cases at the facility. This was his routine at the end of his periodic drop-ins, and usually there wasn't much to discuss. The patients who ended up at St. Anne's were typically older, in the final stages of life, and beset with ailments for which there was no cure. Treatment options usually amounted to palliative care, which the sisters knew how to do.

But the guest in the basement didn't fit that profile, and Cliff's condition presented a serious challenge for Derek.

"How's Cliff doing as a patient?" Derek asked.

"Better over the past few days," Sister Joseph replied. "Teresa has taken over all his care. That's been a relief to the other sisters, who were always a little skittish about going down there."

"That's understandable," Derek acknowledged.

"It's not just his history, though that's a factor," Sister Joseph explained. "In fact, he's been subdued and compliant. It's also his appearance. One sister admitted it to me, though she knew it wasn't proper for her to react that way."

"Well," Derek admitted ruefully. "That scarring is going to have that effect. The damage to his skin and underlying tissue was severe, and we've no access to anything like reconstructive surgery. He's going to be frightening children for the rest of his life, if he makes it that long."

"Why do you say that?"

"I'm very concerned about secondary infection. I've had him on first line antibiotics, which are all we can get, and those are just barely keeping infection at bay. He's running a constant mid-grade fever which occasionally spikes. That big, open burn is an invitation to infection, and if he picks up a resistant strain – which he has about a fifty-fifty chance of doing – he could go within a few days."

Sister Joseph looked pensive. "So, swift onset sickness and death is a real possibility?"

"Very much so," Derek admitted.

"Well, that changes things."

"In what way?" Derek asked, puzzled.

"Like I mentioned, Teresa has been doing all the interacting with him lately. According to her, he's genuinely contrite about his actions and wants to turn his life around. She's moved a video player into his room and had us scrambling for video chips."

"What kind of video chips?"

"Basic catechesis."

"So," Derek asked skeptically, "she wants to convert him?"

"She wants to bring him to repentance and conversion," Sister Joseph said a bit dryly. "As do I, as should we all."

"Well, sure," Derek admitted. "But a rapist like that –"

"Given her history, Teresa has great compassion for grave sinners, and never gives up hope for any of them," Sister Joseph replied.

"That's admirable, but I'd want to see some real change first," Derek said.

"As does she," Sister Joseph confirmed. "Under ordinary circumstances, we would expect a formation period of a year or so, with accompanying spiritual direction and verifiable change of life. But if he might sicken and die at any time, we should not wait on baptism."

"That's certainly true," Derek acknowledged.

"I need to call Father Gabriel," Sister Joseph said.

"And while you attend to his spiritual health," Derek said, getting up. "I've got some investigating to do regarding his physical treatment. There may be some – unorthodox – avenues to explore."

And so it was that Derek found himself back at St. Anne's a few days later, down in the basement room with Janice, Cliff, Sister Joseph, and Father Gabriel. There was a bowl of water on a stand, and beside the bowl a candle and a baptismal stole. Derek decided he'd keep quiet about the contents of his medical bag until later. Father Gabriel was conducting some sort of interview with Cliff before beginning. Janice was standing at Cliff's shoulder.

"Do you understand the gravity of your sins, and acknowledge that you have caused severe harm to others by them?" Father Gabriel asked.

"I do, sir," Cliff replied.

"Baptism washes away all sins and makes you a new man in Christ, but it comes with the expectation that you will walk in that new life and work to bring healing and charity to a world where your sins have brought harm and hatred. Do you accept this?"

"I do, sir."

"Teresa, as Cliff's sponsor, do you attest that he has received basic instruction in the Faith, and exhibits true contrition and purpose of amendment to the best of his abilities?"

"I so attest," Janice answered.

"I understand," Father Gabriel said to Cliff. "That you and your sponsor have agreed upon a penitential task for you, not as a condition of baptism, which is unconditional, but as a witness to your sincerity and change of heart. Do you accept that task as a solemn commitment?"

"I do, sir."

"Very well, then. We will be using a shorter form of the rite, but it will be a valid baptism. I understand that you will be taking a new name?"

"Yes, sir. Ignatius."

"Good choice," Father Gabriel smiled. "Now, if you're ready, we'll begin in the name of the Father, and of the Son, and of the Holy Spirit. Do you, Cliff, reject Satan…"

Derek watched the ancient ritual proceed in the ancient manner. Cliff was baptized on the right side of his head, away from the bandages, and received the lit candle and white stole. Derek still wasn't fond of the guy, in light of what he'd done, but hoped that he really was planning to change.

After the baptism, Cliff shook hands all around, even with Derek, and Janice presented him with an icon of St. Ignatius, which he hung on the wall. Father Gabriel gave him Holy Communion and the Anointing of the Sick, then packed up and left with Sister Joseph Marie, leaving just Derek and Janice.

"Okay, Cliff," Derek began, then corrected himself. "Or Ignatius, as I guess I should call you now: we're in a fix regarding your care. That big burn poses a severe infection risk, we don't have a sterile environment to put you in, and we don't have access to better antibiotics. That fever you've been fighting indicates that the antibiotics we're giving you are just barely holding off serious infection, and if you catch a resistant strain, even those would be useless. You could die in a matter of days. Understand how serious this is?"

"Yes," Cliff said, looking a little frightened. Good.

"As a result, I'm resorting to unconventional treatment options. The dead tissue around your wound serves as a constant source of reinfection. The problem is that it isn't a big hunk of dead tissue all in one place – it's hundreds of little bits of dead tissue all over the wound. I took off a lot with the initial debridement, but I can't keep doing that, because it scrubs away the new skin growth. You see?"

"I think so," Cliff replied, shuddering at the memory of having the burn scrubbed.

"So, I want to try a very old, rather unusual folk treatment. The problem is, some people find it repugnant," Derek said, reaching down into his bag.

"Repugnant?" Cliff asked.

"Yes," Derek confirmed, pulling out a canister and some bandages. "It's maggots."

"Maggots?"

"Yes − those revolting little white worms. They normally disgust us because of where we usually see them. And it's true, you wouldn't want to even handle maggots you took off a dung heap or carcass, much less put them on an open wound.

"But maggots are useful in this sense: mostly they eat only dead tissue. They'll smell it out and, very delicately, eat just that, leaving the surrounding live tissue alone. Thus, if you can obtain maggots that have been hatched in a clean environment, and figure out a way to apply them to wounds that need cleaning, they can help remove the necrotic tissue while not harming the live tissue. Fortunately, I have a contact who raises maggots for veterinary use, and he's given me some. What I'd like to do is apply them to your burn wound."

"You're serious? Maggots?" Cliff asked.

"I know it's distasteful, but we're running out of options," Derek explained. "It would work like this: we put the maggots in this special bandage and apply it to the wound. We leave it in place for about two hours, giving the maggots time to eat their dinner. In a couple of days, I return and we do it again. Hopefully they'll remove enough of the dead tissue to give your system a fighting chance to grow enough new skin to seal off the wound. Want to try it?"

"Doesn't sound like I have much choice," Cliff said.

"Not really," Derek admitted. "I'm going to show Teresa how to do this, so she can remove the bandage when the treatment's over. Ready?"

So Derek plunged in, trying to remember the tips his veterinarian friend had given him. Cliff tolerated it, and Derek left him in Janice's capable hands. He got a chance to chat with Sister Joseph as he packed to go.

"So," he asked as casually as he could. "Do you have any idea what this task is that Janice and Cliff have agreed on?"

"No," Sister Joseph shook her head. "Such things are unusual, but not unheard of. They were more common centuries ago, when someone might agree to undertake a pilgrimage, or do some deed, when they accepted baptism or confirmation. Whatever it is, it's between those two and God – and possibly Father Gabriel."

"Ah," said Derek. "By the way, is that unusual, to take a new name at baptism?"

"It used to be more common when it was mostly adults getting baptized. It's symbolic of a new identity. In Cliff's case, though, it also has a practical purpose. He can't be seen or known in his old circles again. According to him, his family would literally kill him if they found him alive. Teresa thinks this threat very real, and that only the fact that they think him dead is preventing them from hunting him down."

"Wow – really?" Derek asked.

"Yes. He's thought to be dead, and he has to stay 'dead' if he's going to stay alive."

Derek grinned as he picked up his medical bag. "At this rate, those of you who are truly alive will be spending half your time covering for those of us who are supposed to be dead, but aren't."

A couple of days later, Derek dropped back in to give Ignatius another maggot treatment. A couple days after that, Janice reported that his fever had dropped below 100°. About a week after that, Derek inspected the burn with satisfaction. The tissue had grown sufficiently to form a new, if fragile, skin over the wound surface which would stop most pathogens. The major danger of infection was past.

"Looks like the maggots did the job," Derek said.

"Or the sacrament," Janice countered.

"Or maybe both!" Derek replied with a grin. "I'm sure God's not choosy about what He uses. Anyway, Cliff – or Ignatius – you're doing much better. We should leave the bandages off now to let your new skin air out. Watch your head – no tight hats, and stay out of the sun. You may want to get a loose, light cap to wear, something that breathes."

"So I can go outside?" Ignatius asked.

"Yes, but no football," Derek warned. Despite his ambivalence about Cliff as a man, he couldn't help but rejoice with a patient who'd made significant progress against difficult odds. He stepped back from examining the scalp to look Ignatius full in the face – and inwardly grimaced. Derek had been so absorbed in the clinical concerns of Ignatius' condition that he'd forgotten about the cosmetic aspect.

There was no sugar-coating it: Ignatius was gruesome. The right side of his face was untouched, and even still looked somewhat handsome in a youthful way. But the left side of his forehead, and half of his left cheek, were puckered and an angry red. The whole left side of his head and neck were badly scarred, and his left ear was unrecognizable. Fortunately, the flames hadn't damaged his eye, and had missed his mouth by an inch, but he'd never look normal again.

But how Ignatius would get through the rest of his life looking like an ogre wasn't Derek's responsibility. Derek's job was insuring that he had the rest of his life to get through, and it seemed he'd succeeded at that – with the help of a few maggots.

After Derek departed, Ignatius turned to Janice. "So – I can go out. Should we plan to do it?"

"Certainly," Janice replied.

"When?"

"How about tonight, if that works?"

Ignatius closed his eyes, then nodded. "The sooner, the better, right?"

"That's what I'm thinking," Janice agreed.

"I'm scared," Ignatius admitted.

"I'd be surprised if you weren't," Janice said. "All the more reason to put it behind you."

That evening after supper at the Schaeffer household, Kent and Phillip were sitting at the dining room table going over some schedules. Across the table sat Evan and Martha, quietly planning their imminent wedding. There was a knock at the front door, and one of the kids ran to answer. There was some talking, and then two people came into the dining room.

Kent recognized one of them as Janice, whom he hadn't seen in about a year. The other person was a young man whom he'd never seen before, and he knew he'd remember if he had, because the left side of his head was horribly scarred. Trying to hide his look of disgust, Kent rose, as did Phillip. Behind him he heard Martha gasp, which he assumed was in shock over the man's appearance.

Before Kent could speak, Janice began. "Mr. Schaeffer, this is Ignatius. He has a new life now, but in his old life his name was Cliff, and he did your daughter and your family a terrible wrong. He now has something to say to you."

Realization began to dawn on Kent and the blood began pounding in his ears. He heard Evan step around the table to stand beside him, holding Martha protectively behind them all.

Ignatius' mouth was dry and his heart was hammering. He'd had a little speech memorized, but he couldn't recall a word of it now. The man who stood by the table, and the young men who stood on either side of him were glaring at him with a burning intensity that turned his insides to water. He thought he'd seen angry men before. Now he knew he was wrong. He'd seen mean and spiteful and vindictive adolescents, even if they were seventy

157

years old. Here, he was beholding true anger. These were real men who were righteously furious, and he was the proper object of that fury. They had a right to exact justice from him for what he'd done.

Ignatius' legs buckled and he collapsed to his knees. Still the men held him in their gaze, stone silent, jaws set and breath coming deep and heavy. Behind them he glimpsed the slender form of Martha, but he dared not lift his eyes to her. What could he say to them? What could he possibly say? He fell forward, face down on the wooden floor.

"I'm sorry," he moaned. "I'm sorry, I'm sorry, I'm sorry."

Even from the floor, Ignatius could feel the restraint thick in the air. It seemed that only the presence of the two women was protecting him. Without them, these men would tear him limb from limb, and how could he blame them? His puny words seemed so futile beside the magnitude of his sins. "I'm sorry, I'm sorry," he continued, not because he thought it would do any good, but because it was true. He was sorry; terribly, deeply sorry.

"Cliff, now Ignatius, has repented of his sins before God and accepted baptism," Janice explained. "But he also felt the call to come here and repent to your face."

Ignatius lay silent on the floor, not knowing what to do or say. Then he heard the sound of light footsteps walking toward him, and someone gasping "Martha!" Someone knelt beside him, a gentle hand was laid on his back, and a quiet, beautiful voice said, "I forgive you."

A choked cry escaped him, and tears began to flow, tears like he'd never known. The hand still rested on his back.

"Martha, get away from him!" A gruff voice cried.

"Daddy, he won't hurt me," Martha answered.

"It's not that, it's…it's…" the man stammered.

"He's not unclean, Daddy, not any more. He's asked Jesus for forgiveness and he's asked us. Jesus has forgiven him and I've forgiven him. What cause do you have not to?"

"If you think that just because this worm comes 'round with some mealy-mouthed –"

"Daddy!" Martha cut across her father. "You *must* forgive him. You know that. You taught me that. You *have to* forgive him, especially now that he's asked."

Ignatius felt hands under his arms, and the women raised him from the floor. He let himself be lifted to his knees, but no further. Gasping through his tears, he tried to speak.

"I want to…in recognition…oh, hell," he looked at Janice imploringly, and waved to her to speak.

"Ignatius recognizes that though the spiritual guilt of his sin has been washed away, the temporal consequences remain. Ideally, he would submit himself to civil authorities for trial, for this and other crimes. For a variety of reasons this isn't possible. Therefore, he submits himself to your judgment, Mr. Schaeffer, for whatever sentence you deem suitable for his offence."

"Me?" Kent gasped. "Submits himself to me? I don't want a thing to do with him."

Janice lay a hand on Ignatius' shoulder. "Kent, if you can forgive and accept me, despite what I have done, you must forgive and accept Ignatius, despite what he has done. For, as you know, what I did was worse."

"But…you…that was different," Kent sputtered.

"Not so much as you might think," Janice said. "We leave this in your hands. Ignatius has expressed contrition and your daughter has forgiven him. He isn't asking you to be friends or even to like him. What he's asking for is your judgment. And as your daughter has reminded you, you must ultimately forgive him."

Kent thumped down in a chair. "I can't handle this right now."

"Nobody's asking you to," Janice said. "Take all the time you need." Now Ignatius let himself be lifted to his feet. A soft hand lifted his chin and he looked into the face of the innocent girl he'd violated. Her eyes were calm, her smile was warm, and her hand lay gently on his shoulder. She leaned over and tenderly kissed his cheek.

That was too much for Ignatius. He broke down utterly, torn by sobs, barely able to breathe. Janice led him out to where Sister Elizabeth waited in the car.

"Well," Kent gasped. "I certainly wasn't expecting that."

"I wonder what happened to his face?" Phillip said. "Did he look like that?"

"No," Martha said. "Whatever happened to him happened recently. But now anyone who sees him will know the condition of his heart."

"Yeah – hideous," Kent muttered.

"No," Martha answered. "Scarred."

Revelation

The group sat around the living room of the home just north of Ubly, sipping coffee and waiting for the last one expected to arrive. Derek knew Grandpa Peterson, of course, and Cliff, who he had to get used to calling Ignatius, and Janice, and Gil Peterson. Also present were Lawrence Stover, also called Grandpa by some, and his wife Annette, in whose house the meeting was taking place. Beside Lawrence was a dark-haired man whom Derek had not met, but introductions were being held off until everyone arrived.

Ignatius looked at Derek and grimaced. Ignatius was the reason they were gathered. After speaking to him at length, Janice had called Derek to tell him that Ignatius had much valuable information that should get into someone's hands as soon as possible. Not knowing what to do with that, Derek had spoken to Grandpa, who had contacted Lawrence Stover and arranged this meeting.

There was a knock at the door and a stocky, muscular man with close-cut brown hair and a mustache came in. He was dressed in civilian clothes, but an official air clung to him, as if he was accustomed to being in charge. He accepted a cup of coffee, sat down, and opened a notebook on his lap.

"Thank you all for coming," Lawrence opened. "I'll begin the introductions. Most of you know me, Lawrence Stover, and my wife Annette. This is my son-in-law Steve McLean, and Chip Keller, longtime county sheriff."

"Though not anymore," said the late arriver with an attempt at a laugh. Lawrence gestured to Grandpa.

"I'm Mike Peterson, and this is my son Gil, and my adopted son Luke, colloquially known as 'Doc'. Also with us is Teresa and our new friend Ignatius." Everyone nodded, though Derek could tell they were trying just a bit too hard to ignore Ignatius's disfigurement.

"You are all here at my invitation, but the impetus comes through my old friend Mike, so I'll let him take it from here," Lawrence finished.

"About a week ago," Grandpa said. "Luke here called me in a quandary. Ignatius had come into his care some weeks ago in the aftermath of a terrible accident, and had recovered enough to impart some vital information about activities in this area. Luke didn't know who to pass this along to, so he consulted me. I appealed to Lawrence, who recommended we gather to hear what Ignatius has to say.

"Before we begin, let me explain Ignatius's peculiar status. It should be obvious that Ignatius isn't his given name. He's going to describe illegal and dangerous activities, and he's going to name names. Some of these activities he observed and yes, was even involved in. But he is now believed to be dead, killed in the accident, and it's important that this impression be preserved. If some parties were to learn that he is alive, his life would be in danger even if he were in official custody. That's why he may not answer all your questions.

"That being said, I'll turn it over to Ignatius."

Shifting uncomfortably in his chair, Ignatius cleared his throat. "I – I don't know where to begin. I'm a member of a family up here in the north Thumb area. I'm kind of a fringe member, but I was given jobs.

"Anyway, this family has a lot of things going on. One of them is running a network of foster care homes across the area, down to Port Huron and over to Bay City – I guess to Midland now."

"That's a big network," Chip interrupted. "Does this operation have a name?"

"It's called the Wondercare network," Ignatius replied.

"Wondercare – I've heard of them," Chip nodded, jotting something in his notebook.

"Anyway, this network isn't what it seems," Ignatius went on. "They take the hard cases, the foster children that are an ongoing drain on the system, the ones who can't be sent home

162

and will never be adopted. CPS likes Wondercare because the worst problem cases are taken off their hands. What they don't know is that the homes are just nets to funnel kids into the broader operations."

"What kind of 'broader operations'?" Steve asked.

"It depends. Most of the older girls, and some of the boys, are just – sold."

"Sold?" Chip asked. "You mean – trafficked?"

"I guess so. I heard guys talking about sending them 'down to Toledo'," Ignatius replied. The others looked at him in stunned horror. "It was at one of those homes that I...ran into... Mr. Peterson's – what, grandchildren?"

"Grandnieces and nephews," Grandpa explained. "Sort of."

"Anyway, they were there, and the plan was to ship them out as soon as they could. In fact, they escaped just in time – the doctor was scheduled to show up the next day."

"The doctor?" Chip asked. "For what?"

"To fix them. You know – so they couldn't get pregnant," Ignatius explained. This time there were gasps around the room.

"And this happens to all the children in these homes?" Lawrence asked.

"Not all of them. Some of them the courts are too interested in, so they can't send them away. But Wondercare usually leaves those cases to other homes. They're interested in kids everyone would just as soon forget. The system's overloaded anyway." The room was silent for a minute before Steve spoke.

"You mentioned that only some of the kids end up trafficked. What about the others? What happens to them?"

"They end up at the factory. I don't know exactly where it is because I was always taken there in a closed van. It's surrounded by woods. It's kind of a complex – there's the factory, where they make stuff, and the barracks where the workers live, and the quarters where the staff live, and a few other buildings for storage and stuff. And in the middle, there's the...hog pen."

"Wait – kids," Steve asked. "You mean child labor?"

"I guess so," Ignatius admitted.

"How much are these kids paid?"

"Paid? They're not paid anything. They get fed and they work."

"You mean…they're slaves?" Chip asked.

"I guess so."

"And the staff knows about this?"

"The staff is all family," Ignatius explained. "Nick is the factory manager, and his son Caleb helps run the place. Folks like Eli and Colin are cousins, but everyone's related. That's how I got in for my brief time there."

"And this factory is here in Huron County?" Lawrence asked.

"Somewhere, I'm pretty sure. I think it's north of Bad Axe, but I could be wrong. It's pretty well hidden, back in the woods. There's only one drive to get in and out, and there are cameras all over, watching the fences and the woods. There's a fence all around the place to keep the kids from escaping."

"These cameras – are they always monitored? Is someone always watching?" Steve asked.

"I don't know – I only got into the security shed a couple of times, and I wasn't close to the arrangements," Ignatius replied. "I just did my measly jobs. I know they have a generator shed next to the storage barn, and they can make their own elec– "

"Wait a minute!" Chip interrupted with a roar. "This factory – it has to ship things in and out. Do they use container trucks?"

"Do they use what?"

"Container trucks. Not like regular semitrailers, but like long metal boxes with doors, about forty feet long, eight feet wide, and eight feet tall?"

"I'm not sure about the trucks," Ignatius said. "Everyone had to stay inside whenever a truck came, which happened about every week or so. But I know that materials arrived on the dock, and shipments went out, in boxes that looked like you describe. So I guess that the trucks brought those and took them away."

"I knew it, dammit, I knew it," Chip crowed. "I knew there was something fishy about those trucks!"

"Ignatius," Lawrence asked quietly. "You speak of a family all intertwined in these operations. Is there someone running this family, or is it run by a group of members?"

"Oh, it's one person, all right," Ignatius confirmed. "Pa Hubbart runs it with an iron fist."

That brought another silence as some of the people looked mystified while others gaped in shocked disbelief. Lawrence looked sad.

"Not – not Raymond Hubbart from over Elkton way?" Chip asked in a near whisper.

"I think Raymond is his name," Ignatius said. "We just called him Pa."

Steve gave a low whistle. "But he's...a widely respected businessman. Chamber of Commerce, Rotary, the whole shot."

"It would seem his business interests are wider than we imagined," Lawrence said heavily.

"Wait a minute," Chip said with another look of dawning realization. "Andy Klein, the new sheriff – his brother Johnny is married to Judith Hubbart, Ray Hubbart's daughter!"

"That would explain a few things," Steve confirmed. "So, we've got a foster care network siphoning unwanted kids into either trafficking or good old slavery at the family manufacturing operation. Anything else going on? Drug running? Illegal gambling?"

"Maybe, but I wouldn't know anything about that," Ignatius admitted. "Only places I ever got sent were the homes and the factory."

"Well, that's plenty enough," Lawrence said. "Question is, what can we do about it?"

"Tell you one thing, with Andy Klein sitting in the sheriff's chair, that cuts off a lot of options," Chip explained. "State police, county prosecutor, state attorney general – they're all going to want to work with the sheriff in any local investigations."

"And the factory sounds like a fortress," Steve said. "Seems like the most vulnerable side of this operation is those foster care homes. They have to interface with CPS, the probate courts,

County Health, Community Mental Health – lots of different agencies. Plus, they're across several counties, so it won't matter as much if we can't get cooperation from one county office. If we want to pry this oyster open, that looks like the weak seam."

"We need more expertise," Lawrence admitted. "People who know more about these agencies than we do."

"I know plenty of people in Huron County," Chip said. "But we need to be careful about who we bring in. If Ray Hubbart owns the sheriff's office, there's no telling where else he may have people."

"I know someone," Derek volunteered. "She's trustworthy, and she's from down in St. Clair County. She's very knowledgeable about how agencies work together within a county. She could probably make an evening meeting."

"That's good. Does anyone know any lawyers?" Lawrence asked.

"I know one," Gil offered. "He should be able to make it."

"Shall we reconvene here tomorrow evening?" Lawrence asked.

The little group gathered again the next evening, with the addition of Fitz and Shaundra from St. Clair County. They listened soberly as Lawrence relayed what Ignatius had told them the night before.

"So our question is this," Lawrence concluded. "Given what we know about the foster care operation, and the entities it might work with, how might something like this even be possible? And is there any way to alert proper authorities to what is going on?"

Shaundra answered first. "Ever since Der– since my friend here contacted me some weeks ago, I've been quietly talking to my friends who work in CPS. I've never worked close to that area, and they can't talk specifics, but they can discuss general procedures and operations.

"There are a lot of kids in foster care, way more than the system was ever intended to handle. Everyone from the probate judges to the caseworkers on the line are overtaxed and looking for any relief.

"They tend to think of the cases – the children themselves – as 'messy' or 'clean'. A 'messy' case is one where there's a lot of contention, numerous court appearances, problems with the child while in foster care, and what-all. Even two or three 'messy' cases can make a caseworker's life hell.

"'Clean' cases are where there's no contention and little call for anyone to appear in court. Documents are filed, progress reports are completed, all the boxes are checked. 'Clean' cases are easy. Starting about ten, fifteen years ago, probate judges started preferring those cases where they can just flick through a series of pages, sign a proposed ruling, and get it off their desk.

"These days a judge considers it a good day if he can rule on ten or twelve cases without ever seeing a face or leaving his chambers. That attitude has trickled down to the CPS supervisors and compliance officers. They're evaluated on how much paper they can push, so they focus on that. In today's environment, it wouldn't be hard to have cases that are never actually seen. The data in the system is the reality. The kids themselves are incidental.

"After Der– ah, after I got briefed, I did some quiet asking about Wondercare. They've got a reputation for being really efficient. I know they handle some 'messy' cases because they shuttle them around to hearings and other appointments. To a caseworker, anyone who handles those things looks like a miracle worker, because it's arranging little details like transportation that drives caseworkers nuts. But we've no way of knowing how many Wondercare cases are getting that kind of treatment."

"So you're saying," Steve asked, "that they may keep a 'stable' of kids around to burnish their reputation, but that many, or most, of the children become reduced to pages and files, never seen by any official?"

"Very possible in today's environment," Shaundra confirmed. "In fact, if an outfit like Wondercare gained a reputation for being able to handle problem cases, that would make them a path of least resistance. Caseworkers would send them the cases they didn't want to deal with."

"So having a foster care network that operated as a dragnet to gather kids for unsavory purposes is feasible, especially if they were careful to maintain a clean façade?" Lawrence asked.

"It's a nightmare scenario, but it could happen," Shaundra acknowledged.

"It seemingly is happening," Grandpa said. "Fitz, did you look into any legal avenues there may be for assaulting this mess? Ombudsmen? Complaint lines?"

"I thought over a few," Fitz said, glancing at his tablet. "The most effective route would be for some stakeholding party, like a parent, to file a motion to see a child. If Wondercare couldn't produce the child, that would spark questions. But we don't know which kids are in Wondercare homes, and whether they'll have been moved to other destinations. But even if we knew that, we'd still face the problem of finding a stakeholder and persuading them to file the motion. The reason these kids are in foster care in the first place is that nobody cares about them, and Wondercare probably has ways of figuring out which are the truly lost cases.

"That leaves things like tip lines and abuse reporting sites. Shaundra is probably better positioned than I am to discuss the effectiveness of those."

"You might get some action that way, but it's doubtful," Shaundra cautioned. "First off, you'd need specifics, like a case name or triggering incident, which you don't have. A vague complaint or rumor of misconduct would probably get answered by a compliance officer pointing to a string of clean reports and inspections for Wondercare sites. There's also a built-in reluctance to expose problems, especially with big operations like Wondercare. If problems are uncovered, it has a backlash effect on staffers, reflecting poorly on their oversight. Also, any complaints would certainly be noticed by Wondercare, alerting them that something was up."

Everyone was quiet for a minute before Chip, who looked ready to burst, sat forward and held out his tablet.

"Look, I've done some research. Based on property transfers, which I've spoken to Lawrence about, and Ignatius's information, I think I know where this factory complex is." He pointed to a satellite overview map of some farmland and tapped a thickly wooded area in the middle of it. "Here, along Nathan Road, a few miles east of Van Dyke. It's a half-section, thick with cover, but you can see hints of rooftops among the trees. There's an outline of a curving drive here. This has to be the place!"

"That could very well be, Chip, but what can we do about it?" Lawrence pointed out. "We can't get in there without a search warrant, and you were the one who pointed out that as long as Andy Klein holds the sheriff's office, both local and state law enforcement channels are effectively closed to us."

"Maybe the Feds?" Chip offered.

"The Feds would probably defer to the locals in a case like this," Fitz explained. "We'd need a lot of evidence to get their attention, and our star witness can't take the stand." He gestured toward Ignatius. "Besides, we have numerous reasons to want to keep federal eyes off the area – not the least being that we suspect federal involvement in the recent governmental kidnapping that sparked all this."

"But...think about it," Chip pleaded. "You yourself said the most effective thing would be to have a party demand in court to see a kid that Wondercare couldn't produce, only we've no way of knowing which ones have been removed from the homes. Look at it the other way! What if we were to produce some kids who were supposed to be safely in Wondercare's hands, but had to be rescued from slave labor in a sweatshop? That'd blow the lid off the whole thing!"

"True, Chip, but it boils down to the question of legal authority," Fitz explained patiently. "If you set one foot on their land without proper permission, *you're* the lawbreaker. You know that as well as I."

"Yeah, but..." Chip grumbled, sitting back and tucking his tablet away.

"Chip has a point, though," Steve acknowledged. "If we could get even one of the lost children, the ones that are supposed to be in foster care but are enslaved, that would be all we'd need. Ignatius, about those kids – once they're taken to the factory, when are they let out?"

"Never."

"Never?" Scott pressed. "Of course, not for schooling, but what about other things like medical care? Are they taken to clinics or hospitals? Or back to their foster care homes?"

"Nope," Ignatius shook his head. "Once they're at the factory, they don't leave. If anyone gets sick, they call in the doctor. If he can cure them, he gives them some medicine. If he can't, or if it would be too much trouble, he just gives them the shot."

Everyone, particularly Derek, looked at Ignatius, aghast.

"You mean...he kills them?" Grandpa asked.

"Yup."

"And are they buried right there on the grounds?"

"No," Ignatius said with deep reluctance. "That's...that's what the pigs are for."

There was a general gasp as realization dawned. Annette blanched white and put her hand to her mouth. Lawrence bowed his head and hid his face behind his hand. Only Derek and Shaundra looked puzzled.

"Am I missing something?" Derek asked. "Because –"

"Swine are omnivorous," Lawrence explained in a hollow voice. "They can be trained to eat anything. In rural areas an old dodge for disposing of an inconvenient body was to...there'd be nothing left. Even bones would be chewed to fragments."

Now Derek was stunned, and Shaundra looked like she was going to be sick.

"That's it," Chip announced. "We can't let this continue one more day. With that kind of stuff going on –"

"Chip," Lawrence interrupted. "We all want to stop this as soon as we can. The question is, what is the effective path? Just doing something for the sake of doing something could be totally ineffective and could put the children at even greater risk."

Chip sat back with a mutinous expression, but said nothing more while Lawrence continued.

"We need to consider this further, all of us, from the perspective of our varied experience. I know there are some calls I want to make. Maybe I can talk to Ray."

"Talk to him?" Chip asked. "But wouldn't you…doesn't that risk –"

"I think I could be discreet," Lawrence assured him a little dryly. "I know him passingly, and some members of his family a little more closely. Why don't we ponder and pray on this? I'll get back in touch with everyone during the week, and we'll see what turns up."

Everyone stood and shook hands all around. Chip was one of the first out the door, his mind racing. As much respect as he had for Lawrence Stover, Chip wasn't a member of his family and wasn't under his authority. Furthermore, Chip was a man of action, not given to endless pondering and consultation. To think of these kinds of goings-on, right here in his county! And it was inescapable: this foul operation had been run right under his nose while he was still sheriff. That as much as anything needled his conscience – what kind of law enforcement officer had he been to let this happen on his watch?   This was serious crime – racketeering, interstate human trafficking, enslavement, certainly murder. They didn't have time to dither with this going on!

Chip knew some people, people who were given to action, not just chatter. People with field experience and resources.

Dammit, they had to do something!

Threats

In auto industry parlance, a contract worker was a "jobbie", hired just for a particular job before moving on to other work. During boom cycles, jobbies could make a fair amount of money, enabling them to buy expensive toys like boats. On beautiful summer Fridays, when the sunlight sparkled on the local waters, these workers might be tempted to "pull a nooner" – cut out of work at lunch time and not return until the following Monday morning. Some would head down to their boats on Lake St. Clair and go frolicking among the beaches and islands.

Decades earlier, on the last Friday in June, some of these mischievous types had taken one of their number to a small sandy island in the north of the lake to celebrate a birthday, and the Jobbie Nooner was born. It was a multi-day, informal, unsponsored, ad-hoc assembly of boaters who gathered for drinking, splashing, drinking, ogling, drinking, and sleeping it off. The promoters tried to bill it as "the Mardi Gras of the Midwest," but it was nothing so grandiose or sophisticated. Though economic and demographic factors had reduced its size over the years, the Jobbie Nooner was still a sprawling, chaotic event.

Also, it was just a few miles from an international border, which made it very convenient for anyone wishing to cross that border discreetly.

Grace Kyle and Felicity Peterson had finished their school year at St. Anselm's and were now headed home the same way they'd come over: with just the clothes on their backs. And, given that they were trying to pass unobtrusively through a summer maritime bacchanalia, that meant somewhat less clothing than they'd worn for their last crossing.

The girls were struggling to find swimsuits at the only shop in Wallaceburg, Ontario that still carried them this "late" in the season. Between proper fit and even a semblance of modesty, the selections from remaining stock were slim indeed. They finally settled on a couple of suits, consoled by the fact that they only needed to get them across the border.

"Suitable, suitable," Grace commented as Felicity modeled the suit she'd chosen. "Not exactly your color, but a decent fit. You do fill it out rather well, if I may say so, Miss Peterson."

"Only you may say so, Miss Kyle," Felicity responded with a cautionary look. "Anyone else would get a slap. It's far more high-cut in the leg than makes me comfortable, but it's all that's available. And if I may say so, you present a fine silhouette in the suit you've chosen."

"Thanks," Grace replied wryly, tugging at the suit. "It's apparently a 'monokini', and it's as close as I'm going to be able to get to a proper swimsuit. The one-pieces cut me terribly."

"Well, you are long-torsoed for such a short girl," Felicity said. "Come on, let's go meet our boat."

The slow trip down the river and the leisurely daylight crossing of the lake contrasted sharply with their clandestine arrival the prior August. The girls chatted about the year that had just ended, what they'd learned and what friends they'd made, but their thoughts were ahead, on their homes and families.

"Wow – crowded," commented Grace as they approached Gull Island. Though smaller than in its heyday, the Jobbie Nooner still drew hundreds of pleasure craft to the sandy shallows around the island. The boats were anchored side by side, three or four rows deep, and the partygoers splashed in the water and walked along the beach.

"This is as close as I'm going to be able to get you," advised Tim, their pilot. "You'll have to wade from here. It's three-and-a-half or four feet deep, so be ready."

The girls hopped over the side, plunging nearly to their armpits and wading clumsily ashore. They garnered plenty of whistles and vulgar hails, but kept straight on, assiduously ignoring the scantily clad revelers on all sides.

"Our pickup is on the north end of the island?" Grace asked.

"Yes – it'll be flying a small Vatican flag on the bow," Felicity confirmed.

"Safe bet that it'll be the only one with one of those," Grace grinned. "But that doesn't solve the problem of finding it among all these boats."

"That's for sure," Felicity said, looking around at the crowd of white hulls and partygoers.

*   *   *

Mark Stevens and Joe Pemberton had their tent set up before sunrise, and kept the grill going and the beer coolers visible. This wasn't uncommon – some people camped the whole weekend on the island – but what Mark found unusual was what drew their prey in. It wasn't the beer, which was common at the vast wet party, but the food, which was in shorter supply. As long as he kept brats and burgers on the grill, wafting their scent toward the beach, people would wander over. Oh, he and Joe still had to linger by the water to chat up likely prospects, but usually once they caught the aroma, hunger did the rest of the work.

Four young women lay unconscious behind the tent flaps. Considering what they'd been injected with, they wouldn't awaken until well after dark, by which time they'd be safely in a van headed toward Toledo. Getting them to the boat wouldn't be an issue. Passed out revelers were a common sight, and Ellie made good camouflage. Nobody thought anything of a girl asking help from a couple of guys to get her inebriated friends back on the boat. But the afternoon was lengthening, and the question was becoming whether they should go with what they had, or try to nab one more to make their intended goal of five.

"Well, well, looky there," Mark said, gazing at the two figures walking up the beach.

"What, the brunettes?" Joe asked. "Hot enough, for sure – but two of 'em?" Normally they targeted women moving alone.

"Yeah. And they're virgins, both of 'em," Mark said.

"Pah," snorted Joe. "How can you tell?"

"I don't know, but I always can – something about the eyes," Mark replied. "One of 'em would be worth twice what we've already got, and there are two. C'mon." They started down toward the beach to intercept the girls.

"Got a hypo on you?" Mark asked as they approached the water.

"No – do you?" Joe answered

"Yes, but we'll need another. Signal Ellie."

Ellie was mostly staying near the tent to listen for sounds of movement within, but Joe caught her eye. She nodded at his signal and began fishing in the backpack.

*   *   *

Grace and Felicity were so busy scanning the boats that they didn't notice anything unusual until the two strange men stepped right into their path. The startled girls stopped sharply and stepped back.

"Afternoon, ladies," one said. "You're just in time for dinner – we've got some burgers ready over here."

The girls glanced at each other. Neither of them liked the looks of the two men. The taller one had black hair and wore a knowing smirk, while the shorter, blonde one had an oily manner to him. They were both standing far too close. The girls took another step back, feeling keenly how scant and tight their garb was.

"We're...we're not hungry," Felicity said. "Now, if you'll excuse us." She made to sidestep the pair, but the blonde stranger blocked her.

"We've got cold beer, too – microbrews, good stuff, not the horse piss those other guys are handing around," the blonde assured her, stepping closer and forcing them to retreat another step. Grace noticed that the man was holding his right hand cupped, as if concealing something in his palm.

Panic welled up in the girls. This was bad. Screaming wouldn't help – the beach was echoing with drunken screams. They could try fleeing, but they'd be run down in a minute. To their left a girl in a bikini was coming down from a tent toward them.

"We...we've got somewhere we have to be," Grace said in a shaky voice, grabbing Felicity's elbow and preparing to run.

"Oh, we won't keep you long," the blonde said. The men stepped closer, and the dark-haired one towered over Grace. The girl in the bikini had almost arrived. The blonde man began moving his hand toward Felicity.

"Hey!" called a clear voice to their left. "Grace! Felicity! Glad we found you!"

They all turned to see two men coming over a grassy ridge and down onto the beach. One was tall with long, wavy brown hair and the other was muscular and black, dark as ebony, and wore a broad smile. They waved cheerfully, but the girls looked at each other in mystification. They'd never seen these men before.

The two strange men who had been accosting Grace and Felicity took a step back but scowled at the newcomers. The blonde man in particular looked pugnacious and put off. "Hey," he snarled as the men drew near. "What are you doing here? We were just going to have some beers with these girls."

Grace and Felicity were even more bewildered. This was an unusual reaction to strangers on a public beach, but something about the new arrivals seemed to aggravate the two men.

"Were you, now?" the black man asked with a grin. "I'm afraid they can't stay. They have somewhere they need to be." The newcomers stepped in front of the girls, between them and the threatening strangers. "Besides, you were just leaving."

Now the two strange men stepped back, but with murder in their eyes. "Oh, were we?" the blonde snarled. The black-haired guy clenched his fists and narrowed his eyes, looking ready to fly at the brown-haired newcomer facing him.

"Yes, you were," the brown-haired man replied in a low, calm voice that seemed to shake the earth. Then Felicity gasped quietly. Safely behind their backs, the women could not see the faces of the newcomers, but the two hostile strangers were looking right into them. All combativeness and insolence suddenly drained from the strangers' faces, to be replaced by stark terror. Choking and scrambling, they turned and dashed for the water's edge, where they clumsily splashed out to an anchored boat. Grace and Felicity watched them start the boat, throw the anchor line off without bothering to raise the anchor, and make off as quickly as they could through the crowded water.

Grace and Felicity glanced at each other nervously. They'd been frightened before, but now they knew a different kind of fear as the two newcomers turned to them. But there was nothing alarming in their faces, just warm smiles and kind eyes.

"Thank you," Grace said. "We don't know what those men wanted, but –"

"They wanted no good, but it doesn't matter now," the black man said. "Come, let us look to the others." The men started up the beach toward the tent.

"They...they left me," squeaked the girl in the bikini, looking about in panic. "They went away and left me!"

"Bring her," the brown-haired guy called, so Felicity took her elbow and began leading her.

"I'm Felicity. What's your name?"

"Ellie," the girl stammered, still glancing around frantically. "They left me!"

"It'll be okay, Ellie," Felicity reassured her. The two men stepped to opposite sides of the tent, lifted it clear of the ground, and hurled it aside. The girls gasped to see four young women lying in the sand, flushed and unconscious.

"Here, wake them," the black man pulled a small box from his pocket and handed cloth-covered capsules to each of the girls. They were unsure what to do with them until they saw him kneel, crush one in his fingers, and wave it under nose of one of the unconscious women. She jerked awake with a start and a cry, as did the other woman to whom the brown-haired man was attending. Grace and Felicity did the same for the other two, and presently four dazed and frightened women were blinking in the afternoon sunlight.

"Next time, don't accept the hospitality of strangers so easily," the brown-haired man warned. "Now, go back to your friends."

As the women made off, Ellie was still looking about in confused distress. "They went off and left me!"

The brown-haired man snapped one of the capsules under Ellie's nose. She cried out and shook her head, then gave a violent sneeze. When her head came up she still looked distraught, but the vagueness in her eyes had cleared.

"Ellie," the man said. "You've been rescued. Stay with us. We'll see that you're taken care of. Come along, ladies." The men started walking briskly along the water, bracketing the women between them.

"Thank you again," Felicity said. "You seem to know our names, but we don't know yours."

"Do you not?" the brown-haired man asked with a curious smile. "Well, I'm Mike, and that's Rafe."

"Thank you, Mike and Rafe," Grace said. "Are you taking us to our contact?"

"Yes," Mike confirmed. "We know right where they are."

Gull Island wasn't large, so shortly thereafter they were wading out to a boat with a white and yellow banner hanging limply from its jackstaff. The girls were almost trembling with shock as the magnitude of what they'd been saved from began to dawn upon them fully. They felt safe with their mysterious escorts, even if they were frightening in their own way, but it had been a near thing.

"Felicity! Grace!" called a familiar voice from the boat. They saw Angie Hagerstrom looking at them in perplexity.

"We found them on the beach, and thought we'd escort them here to you," Rafe smiled up at Angie. "Here, let us boost you up." Seemingly without effort, the men lifted Grace and Felicity up into the boat, followed by Ellie.

"Who's this?" Angie asked in confusion.

"A new friend – they'll explain," Mike said.

Grace and Felicity leaned over the side and looked down at the two men. "Thank you again for coming to our aid," Grace said. "I dread to think of what would have happened to us, and those other girls, had you not –"

"Something dark," Mike answered, looking at her gravely. "But this was just a brush with the darkness. Soon, very soon, the time will come when you will have to face it squarely. Remember this: when the darkness rises to cloud all vision, the virgins must walk through it to bear the light and lead the captives to freedom."

Grace and Felicity stared at Mike. His final words had a deep, ringing quality that fell heavily upon their ears. His eyes, which were blue and sparkled with joy, seemed to deepen, and the girls felt like they were gazing across vast spaces thick with intricate patterns dancing about deep, calm regions. Awe and wonder rose within them, and they felt weak and very, very small.

Then the men were gone. They seemed to move quickly toward the front of the boat to duck beneath the bow, but they never emerged from the far side.

"Who were those men? Where did they go?" Angie asked.

"Friends," Felicity explained, still trembling. "I don't know where they went – probably back where they came from. Is there any water?"

They settled in while Angie explained that Todd was off connecting with another contact. It only made sense to take advantage of the proximity and circumstances to pick up a small shipment of medicine. Then Felicity and Grace explained what had happened. They didn't question Ellie, who still seemed confused, but they did wonder what they were going to do with her. Angie wanted to catch up, to chat about all that had happened during their absence and find out how their school year had gone. Normally the girls would have been happy to oblige, but just now Mike's final, mysterious word weighed upon them, and they wanted time to think.

*   *   *

"Dammit!" roared Pa, causing the two men to flinch but Suzanne to lift her chin in her usual defiant posture. "You had four in the bag, and then you just ran off and left them?"

"We wanted...two more...," Mark stammered. "Then there were these guys..."

"So, there were two guys – so what? If they were interested in your targets, why didn't you just let them all walk away? Why did *you* run off, not only abandoning your take but one of your assets as well?"

Mark fumbled and said nothing, staring at the floor. Much as he dreaded getting one of Pa's infamous verbal reamings, the memory of the two mysterious and ominous men was still fresh enough to outweigh it. Pa's ranting might make his knees knock, but the men had turned his insides to water. He couldn't even put a finger on what it was. Once he and Joe had regained enough composure, they'd discussed what about the men had been so intimidating. They hadn't even been frowning, there had just been an air about them that made the two want to put as much distance as possible between themselves and the men. They hadn't thought about the ramifications of their hasty departure at the time, and even on the way home they barely considered them in light of their experience. Scream though Pa might, the men were still quaking from that even greater fear.

"Get out of my sight, you losers," Pa snarled. "I trust you with a simple job and you screw that up."

They fled before Pa could change his mind. Joe, who'd witnessed but never received one of Pa's tongue lashings, pushed down the hall and out the door, probably in search of a beer. Mark stayed beside his mother, stinging from the humiliation.

"Why do we let that petty tyrant run our lives, Ma?" Mark asked quietly.

"Hush, Mark," Suzanne said as she bustled along, glancing around nervously as if his words were unlucky.

Back at his desk, Pa's frustration and anger warred with his rising panic. He'd been counting on the funds from the Jobbie

Nooner take to make up for shortfalls in other areas. Now he not only didn't have that, he'd lost a completely conditioned asset. He should have thought of some suitable punishment for those two incompetents, something to teach them a sharp lesson, but nothing had come to mind. His thinking had been clouded by the rising sensation of being encircled, as if the walls were closing in.

Pa was feeling that way more often these days. He mostly attributed it to the unbelievable number of problems and screwups that had been happening lately, but a deep part of him feared that he was losing his grip, that events were spinning out of his control.

He needed to talk with Old Charlie again. He'd get Nick to take him. He'd had periods like this in the past, and he'd gotten through them with Old Charlie's help. Charlie would advise him, and could do something about those enemies. Maybe it would cost, but it would be worth it.

That night Pa sat by the fire trench beside Charlie, while Nick hung back by the UTV, smoking to mask the foul, acrid odor of the clearing. Nick was still being sullen and uncommunicative. A raccoon carcass was suspended on a stick above the fire, its pelt stretched across a nearby rock, looking eerie in the flickering firelight.

"You are a strong man," Charlie said, drawing an X in the shadowed dust with a stick. "Your circle of influence is wide, affecting many lives." He drew a large circle around the X. "But strong men make enemies, and very strong men make many enemies." He started making little lines pointing at the X like little arrows, some inside the circle and some outside. "You have enemies without and wavering within." Charlie almost glanced at Nick but didn't quite. "Enemies your influence has touched, who are banding together against you. Also, you have affronted parties stronger than men."

"How do I fight them?" Pa asked.

"You need stronger power, ancient power," Charlie said cryptically.

"Like what?" Pa asked. "Like – magic?" He felt foolish, a modern man of business, asking a question like that. But here in this dark clearing in the dead of night, talking to an old shaman by the light of a smoking fire, nothing seemed too uncanny.

"Pah," Charlie spat into the fire. "Strong though you may be, you are a fool in these matters. You use hollow words that have no meaning. I speak of an ancient power, one that was old long before any European crossed the Atlantic. It is chained, chained by water, but I know how to summon it."

"Last time you said you'd be able to see their plans more clearly," Pa said. "Can you?"

"Yes," Charlie confirmed. "It is the workers they want. That is what draws them."

"That's what we'll need to defend, then," Pa said. "What should we do? Move them away? Get rid of them?"

"Make any preparations you wish," Charlie said. "Do what you can. But your enemies are growing and joining forces. They are looking for you, peering into your business, searching you out. Over time they will see more and more of your works, until they can see all. I can provide defense, when you are ready to pay the price."

"What is the price?"

"Three."

"Three?" Pa asked, licking his lips.

"Three," Charlie confirmed. "And the dearer, the better."

Pa looked at the ground and nodded. "Whatever you need, I'll provide. Just – just let me talk to Nick first."

"Strong men have many advisors," Charlie said, scratching in the dirt with his stick. "When you need me, I will be here."

Pa got up and walked back to where Nick leaned against the UTV.

"Seems there's a plot to discover the factory," Pa said grimly as they got in.

"So says Charlie," Nick muttered.

"He says they're gunning for the workers," Pa confirmed. "He says he can prepare defenses. But it'll cost."

"*He* can prepare defenses?" Nick scoffed. "He can't even get his own trailer wired. What kind of cost?"

"Three," Pa said tersely, blanching a little.

"*Three!*" Nick barked, glancing at his father with astonishment. "Pa, don't you think this all has gone far enough?"

"I know, I know," Pa said, chewing his lip and looking conflicted. "It's a lot to ask…"

"Let me try, Pa," Nick pleaded. "Give me a chance to come up with something."

"Nick, if they find those workers, it's all up," Pa cautioned.

"I'll make provision for that, Pa, I promise," Nick assured him. "Just give me a chance to come up with some plans before you…go to Charlie again."

"All right, all right," Pa conceded.

Back at the clearing, Charlie turned his roasting raccoon over the fire and got up. Chuckling to himself, he started walking back around behind the trailer, to where the pen was. At last, at long last, the opportunity had arrived. That greedy fool would place into Charlie's hands the tools to accomplish what his ancestors had been denied so many centuries before.

Ironic that it should happen here – but then, perhaps it was the poetic wheel of history. When his ancestors had been defeated, the victors had commemorated their triumph by carving the tale in rock beside a river. The rock lay not twenty miles from here. For generations after the battle, the victorious tribes had gathered at the rock to recount the tale and caution their children against the perennial danger.

But then the conquerors had come from Europe, bringing their diseases and their wars. The tribes had been wasted and driven from the land, and the memorial stone had been forgotten and overgrown by the smothering woods. Eventually the Europeans had rediscovered the stone, and had built a pavilion over it and a fence around it, and now tourists came to gawk at the carvings and guess at their meaning. Even descendants of other tribes came to perform their ceremonies and speculate about the glyphs, but none could read the tale, so the warning went unrecognized.

Because of this ignorance, he would be able to succeed where his ancestors had failed. Not only was there nobody around to oppose him, there was nobody who understood the threat – and one of the conquerors would actually hand him the tools.

Charlie rounded the end of the trailer and looked over the darkened sty. The stench was thick, but he was accustomed to it. He heard the grunting of the sleeping sow.

"*Wilaktwa-ikwe*, you'll soon have more to eat, and all the darkness you could wish for," Charlie said into the night. There was another grunt and an eye opened, showing a red pupil that glared at him.

*   *   *

Though Lawrence Stover didn't reconvene the informal council, no one was idle. Chip ran the address of the plot he suspected and got it to Fitz, who checked out the registered deed holders. It was owned by a holding company which had offices in a strip mall outside Lansing. The office doors were unmarked, the doors were locked, and the interior was perpetually dark. Fitz wanted to try checking out the tax files, but Chip warned him off. That would involve requesting tax records and payment sources from the county, and since Chip didn't know who in those offices might be connected to the Hubbart family, he didn't want to risk it. Lawrence kept in touch with all parties and alluded to other contacts he was making, but gave no indication of when they might next meet or what they might decide to do.

Todd Beck was a bit surprised when he got a call from Paul Stover requesting he pick up Ignatius in Deckerville and bring him to an address in downtown Bad Axe. The address turned out to be an empty storefront, of which downtown Bad Axe had far too many. Todd parked in back as he'd been instructed. He and Ignatius came in the rear door and found themselves in a large, nearly empty room with debris scattered about the edges. In the center stood a makeshift table made of sawhorses and a sheet of plywood. There were a number of men sitting and standing around, some of whom Todd recognized, like Paul Stover and Gerry McLean (Steve's eldest son and Bob's older brother.) Todd was introduced to Chip Keller, the onetime county sheriff, and to Paul's cousin Tom Stover, who was a county deputy though he wasn't in uniform.

"Thank you for coming," Chip began. "I've asked you here because we need to do something. I have all the respect in the world for Lawrence Stover, and will gladly work with him, but – frankly, he's an old man, and old men get cautious. I'm cautious myself. But when we've got lawbreaking and human suffering on the scale we're dealing with here, you have to balance caution with other considerations." He then proceeded to brief the newcomers on what had been discovered and decided at the two meetings that had been held at the Stover's house near Ubly. He particularly mentioned Lawrence's hesitant response to the crisis.

"Therefore, I want to start discussions and planning for taking more direct action," Chip concluded. "By this I do not mean setting out to harm anyone or damage any property. By this I mean one thing: rescuing at least one of the workers enslaved on that site, and hopefully many more. I think we can all agree that the parties enslaving those kids are abusing the good laws protecting property rights in order to mask a much worse violation of law and human rights. We may have to break some property laws in order to be able to bring these violations to light.

"We all agree that getting at least some kids out will break the whole thing open – the factory, the foster care network, the trafficking, everything. If we trot out three kids who are supposed to be safely in the hands of Wondercare and have them tell the stories of their abuse, all hell is going to break loose.

"Personally, I think that's an attainable goal that's worth a little risk. But I understand if anyone thinks differently, and if you do, you're welcome to leave now. All I ask is that you keep quiet about what you've heard so far."

Nobody moved. Chip nodded. "Tonight, we're only gathering intelligence, with Ignatius here as our primary resource. You others bring a variety of experience and expertise to the table. Gerry and I will take what we learn here tonight to some other friends we know who have experience running operations of this type. If – and only if – those friends judge that we can stage a rescue like this, we'll proceed to the next stage. Understood?"

Everyone nodded. Todd's heart raced a little. He was excited and honored to be included in such an effort.

"All right, then," Chip said gravely, waving at the table. "We have here some enlargements of the section which we're pretty sure is the site of the factory operation which Ignatius informed us of. If he'd be kind enough to tell us what he can about the layout of the factory campus and surrounding grounds, that'll be a starting point."

The men gathered around the plywood table, on which was taped a blown-up overhead photo of a large wooded area bounded by dirt roads and plowed fields. The tree cover was very dense, though there were hints of roofs and clear spaces peeking through.

"Well, if this is the drive in from the gate," Ignatius began, tracing along a curved shadow through the trees. "Then this building here would be the factory, with the loading docks on this end." He tapped where a corner of a roof peeked out from under the greenery. "That means the walkway to the barracks would run about here…"

Preparation

"All right, what's next?" Agent Brian Sanderson asked wearily as his partner Stan Harris flicked through documents on his tablet.

"How about this: couple arrested on several counts of child abuse and neglect, taken to district court and charged, later released."

"Hmm," Sanderson mused. "Any more detail?"

One of the less gratifying tasks which Federal Agents Sanderson and Harris had been pulling over the past couple of years was running down leads that might shed light on the mysterious Imlay City blast. This involved diving down countless "rabbit holes" as Sanderson called them, talking to people about random events and unusual behaviors with no real idea what they were searching for. The governing idea seemed to be that any sort of marginal conduct, from unusual purchasing patterns to odd posting on sites, might provide a thread that would lead to further information. Fortunately, the agents had other duties that helped preserve their sanity, but somehow these pointless, futile leads kept getting thrown their way.

The Imlay City blast had been officially declared an industrial accident at an empty factory that had tragically claimed the lives of two local medical workers, but Agents Sanderson and Harris knew better. Far more than just two people had died in that remote factory from an explosion that had been anything but accidental. Just who the victims were and why they'd been there remained a darkly shrouded secret, but Sanderson and Harris guessed that at least some of them had been serious bigwigs, because Someone Somewhere still wanted to dig up anything that would shed light on the incident.

Unfortunately, it was Agents Sanderson and Harris who got to do most of the shoveling. Since the case was officially closed, the usual operations like the ATF or FBI weren't involved. Nor were there any clues, witnesses, suspects, or hard evidence to go on. But since Someone wanted some kind of ongoing investigation, anything which seemed tangentially related to domestic terror got run down. The two agents had interviewed homeschoolers and survivalists and people who kept online sites about civilian militias, and had never turned up anything remotely connected with the blast. Leafing through area arrest and court records for anything that might look "suspicious" was an ongoing part of this wild goose chase.

The incident Agent Harris had spotted appeared to be another such case. The fact that it was a mother and father who were arrested was unusual enough – usually abuse and neglect filings involved either a single parent or a stepparent – but the fact that there were multiple counts indicated multiple kids. Not much, but just enough movement of the "suspicious" needle to warrant a closer look.

"Okay, this doesn't make any sense," Agent Harris pronounced after half an hour of paging through what police and district court records they could access. "There's a warrant issued for the arrest based on evidence presented by CPS, arraignment on multiple charges, release on bail, and then, two days later, all charges abruptly dropped?"

"I know," Sanderson replied. "With reason cited as 'lack of evidence'. You'd think the judge issuing the warrant would have noticed that little detail. Want to take a drive?"

"Not really, but we might as well," grumped Harris.

The address was in a rural area toward the west-central part of the county. The agents pulled into a circular driveway in front of a well-kept house with a wide front porch. They knocked at the door and a thin blonde woman wearing a floury apron answered.

"Good afternoon, Mrs. Schaeffer," Sanderson began, showing his badge. "My name is Agent Sanderson, and I'd like to ask you a few questions."

"I'd be happy to answer what I could," the woman responded. "But my name is Jillian Hagerstrom. There's no Mrs. Schaeffer here."

The agents looked at each other, puzzled. Harris scrutinized the printout and then the house number prominently displayed by the door.

"I – I'm sorry," Agent Sanderson stumbled a bit. "Mr. and Mrs. Kent Schaeffer don't live here?"

"No."

"Did they ever live here?"

"We rent this place," Jillian explained. "I don't know who may have lived here before. We did just move in, though."

"But – it's the address of record," Agent Harris sputtered, waving the printout of the court document.

"I'm sorry," Jillian said. "You're welcome to come in and look around, if you wish."

"That won't be necessary," Agent Sanderson replied. "Thank you for your time, ma'am."

Back in the car, the two agents sat puzzling. The "suspicious" needle of this investigation had just moved up a couple notches.

"We need to get a look at those sealed records," Agent Harris said, and Sanderson nodded agreement.

Given that the original charges had been child abuse and neglect, that meant minors, and that meant probate court and Child Protective Services – where the charges had originated – and sealed records to protect the children's privacy. The agents had expected that, and hadn't seen reason to try to get into those records. But this unexpected wrinkle of the parents going missing changed the game. It wasn't like they'd jumped bail, because all charges had been dropped. It wasn't even like they'd fled, leaving an empty house. They'd moved out so completely that someone else had moved in.

Who did that, especially when there was court action involving their children in process?

Accessing sealed records was never easy, not even for federal agents. But the magic key labeled "domestic terror investigation" was always effective sooner or later. It would involve petitioning the court, so the agents were soon back at the office, surveying what records they could in order to prepare their case.

"Hmm – stranger and stranger," Harris muttered. "Sure enough, from the time of the Schaeffer's arrest, and steadily across the following weeks, there was a stream of petitions filed with the probate court regarding custody of the Schaeffer children. The court's responses are sealed, but they must not have been satisfactory, because the filings kept coming."

"And they abruptly stop here," Sanderson pointed at the list. "I wonder what happened?"

"We can petition the court about all that," Harris said.

"We have another avenue, unfruitful though it will probably be," Sanderson added. "We could interview the attorney." He started punching up filing details.

"C'mon, you know what jerks attorneys can be," Harris scoffed.

"Yeah," Sanderson said slowly, looking up with a grave expression and turning the tablet toward his partner. "Especially this one."

Harris's eyes widened.

The two agents had dealt with Counselor Gerald Fitzgerald only twice before. Their last meeting was engraved in their memories because it had happened on the very day of the Imlay City blast which still haunted their lives. They hadn't liked Counselor Fitzgerald, whom they suspected of secretly snickering up his sleeve at them, but they met a lot of people they didn't like in the course of their work. But having his name turn up in connection with an already unusual case lent an eerie air to the whole matter.

"Shall we," Agent Sanderson asked, snapping his tablet case closed, "pay a visit to the good counselor?"

"Well, Agents Sanderson and Harris, it has been far too long," beamed Fitz. "How may I be of assistance?" He shook both the agents' hands as he escorted them into his conference room. Both agents noticed that beneath the bonhomie, Fitz looked just a little ragged, and not quite his confident, almost cocky self.

"Thank you for seeing us, Counselor," Agent Sanderson went through the formalities. "We have some questions regarding one of your clients – a Kent and Linda Schaeffer of St. Clair County."

Fitz seemed to freeze, and his eyes narrowed just a little. "What is the nature of your investigation?" he asked.

"A very tangential connection to a domestic terror investigation we're working on," Sanderson explained. "The Imlay City blast. We have no reason to suspect them of involvement, but routine work turned up their case, and we're running it down as a formality."

Fitz eyed the agents cautiously. If they'd had the slightest inkling that Kent Schaeffer knew more than almost anyone else about what had actually happened that night north of Imlay City, they wouldn't be discussing this so casually. But he was wary of even an accidental connection between the family and the incident, and didn't want to encourage further investigation. He had to appear neither eager nor reticent.

"Of course, I cannot guarantee I can answer anything, but I will help as I may," Fitz replied. "What are your questions?"

The agents glanced at each other before Agent Harris blurted out, "What's going on here? We can't make any sense of it. Parents arrested on abuse and neglect charges, all of which are promptly dropped. Probate court records sealed, but you're filing petition after petition on their behalf, until you suddenly stop. And the Schaeffers no longer live at their address of record."

Agent Sanderson expected a caustic reply from Fitz to Harris' outburst. Instead the lawyer looked steadily at the agents for a long while before appearing to come to a decision. He tapped his tablet.

"Kelly, can you bring in the Schaeffer file?" he asked, then turned to the agents. "You're right, there is something fishy about the Schaeffer case. I'll tell you what I can without violating privilege, and then leave it in your capable hands."

Stunned by such cooperation, the agents listened in amazement as Fitz laid out the documents and explained the history of the case.

"So – you have no idea where the Schaeffer parents are?" Agent Sanderson asked when Fitz had finished.

"No idea. The address on the court records is the same one I have," Fitz admitted. This was true – the Schaeffer's new address was a closely held secret that didn't go far beyond immediate family.

"And you have no idea why they might have moved so abruptly?"

"I really couldn't say," Fitz admitted.

"This is beyond strange," Agent Sanderson said to Harris. "Who up and moves without notice when the custodial status of their kids is at question?"

"Who, indeed?" Fitz echoed. "But don't forget that, according to the court, there were no such children."

"That didn't stop you from repeatedly filing for their release," Agent Harris pointed out. "Which reminds me – why did you stop so abruptly?"

"I filed petitions with the court as long as I was requested to," Fitz replied. "When the requests stopped, I stopped filing."

"Would that be when they moved?" Harris asked.

"I couldn't say," Fitz shrugged.

The agents sat and pondered for a bit. "I wonder if any of the kids know anything about all this?" Agent Sanderson mused.

"The kids whom the court contends do not exist?" Fitz asked. "Martha is fifteen, and Jude is a mature eleven. I'm sure you could talk to them – they might be able to tell you more than I."

"But – petition to talk to minors?" Harris wondered. "We might meet resistance."

"From whom?" Fitz asked, spreading his hands. "I can't file anything unless directed by the parents, and they've gone missing. Besides, the court's contention is that the parents have no authority because the children do not exist. If you were to file for permission to talk to the children, I'm sure your federal authority would cut through this pretense. Certainly, no family members would contest the petition."

Again, the agents looked at each other, then stood. "Thank you for your assistance, Counselor," Sanderson said.

"My pleasure," Fitz muttered, looking distracted. He escorted them to the door and stood by the reception desk to see them off. As the agents were heading out, Fitz called in an unusually hesitant voice. "Agent Sanderson!"

"Yes?" The agent turned to see Fitz scribbling something on a slip of paper.

"If you...if your efforts fail," Fitz said, handing him the slip. "You might want to visit this address."

"For what?" Sanderson said.

"For...illumination," Fitz offered lamely.

Looking at Fitz askance, Sanderson nodded and tucked the paper in his pocket. Part of him wondered if the lawyer was pulling his leg.

Back in the car, the two men just sat for a minute, trying to absorb all the developments.

"This case is getting stranger by the minute," Agent Harris finally said. "You'd think...you'd think from the way he was talking that he was encouraging us to file that petition."

"Encouraging, hell, he was nearly goading us," Sanderson confirmed. "Makes me wonder what he knows that we don't."

"Makes me nervous," Harris admitted.

"How so?"

"Think about it. If we file this petition, we'll be doing what he wants. We may actually be assisting Counselor Fitzgerald."

"Yeah," chuckled Sanderson. "Kind of makes you question the whole thing, doesn't it? C'mon, let's get our stuff together and contact legal." As Harris started the car, he pulled the slip of paper from his pocket and glanced at the address. It wasn't even in the county. Hmm – illumination. He tucked the slip into a pocket of his tablet case.

*   *   *

Almost a week after the first meeting, Todd was again summoned to the empty building in Bad Axe. He and Ignatius entered to find more people than there had been last time. Todd recognized Jacob Kyle and Phillip Schaeffer, but there were a few more guys he didn't know, two of whom looked like twins. An image of the wooded section was projected on one of the walls, and by it stood a tall guy who looked so trim and stood so straight that Todd guessed him to be a veteran. Nor was he wrong.

"Gentlemen, thank you for coming," Chip said once they were all seated. "Let me introduce Dan Knight, son of Frank and Deb Knight who live over by Caseville. Dan just ended an eight-year tour with the Marines where he served with their Special Forces. Dan has some experience planning these types of operations, so I brought him in to advise us. He's been reviewing what we learned last time and has agreed to speak to us. Dan?"

The clean-cut man stepped forward and nodded. "Good evening," he said in a surprisingly soft voice. "Chip approached me about this situation, which I find as deplorable as you do. Nonetheless, he asked me to evaluate the goal stringently, in light of the available resources, to answer the foremost question: can this be done?

"Based on the intelligence we have and the goal of the mission, I offer a qualified 'yes'. The site appears to be guarded, but only against casual observation and light law enforcement inquiry. It might be able to deal with something like a SWAT assault, but it doesn't appear to be equipped to handle a targeted incursion. Thus, with proper planning and execution, such a mission could succeed.

"The reason my 'yes' was qualified was twofold. First, I need a clear agreement on the purpose and scope of the mission. The sole purpose would be to liberate as many captives as we could. No other activities would be undertaken. Some minor damage to property would be accepted to achieve mission goals, but not large-scale destruction, and certainly no force against persons, either lethal or nonlethal. No firearms would be taken onto the property and confrontation would be avoided at all costs. If I

194

help plan this mission, it will be with the goal of complete stealth. A perfect mission would be to achieve the goal without being seen.

"Before I get to the second point, I want to be clear about the conditions of the operation. This would be an illegal incursion onto fenced and posted private property. Not only will this make any mission operatives subject to arrest and felony prosecution, but legally the property owners would be justified in using any reasonable means to respond to the incursion, including lethal force. As I mentioned, we will not be using force of any kind against personnel, not even defensively. On this mission, by all appearances, we will be the offenders, the intruders. We have to believe in the goal strongly enough to accept those risks. If you can't, now's the time to step aside."

Dan scanned the room for a good thirty seconds. Nobody moved.

"All right, then, this brings me to my second point. Do we have any veterans here?" Only Chip and Tom Stover raised their hands. Dan nodded. "That's all right – I've been assured that all of you are hard workers who know how to run organized and discreet operations. But for this, we'll have to work as a tight team. That means you come under my discipline, and be prepared to train hard until I say you're ready. The success of this mission doesn't hinge on your willingness and determination. It depends on how ready you are to focus that determination on sound planning and exhaustive training. Being willing to endure that is the only willingness that matters. Are you willing?"

"Yes," came a chorus of voices.

"Good enough," nodded Dan. Turning to the image projected on the wall, he began his briefing. "Based on inside intelligence and drive-by images, there seem to be inward-directed surveillance cameras mounted on every other fencepost. There is exterior surveillance, but it seems to be aimed along the outside of the fences, from cameras at these corners and at this point in the middle of the eastern fence. This pattern is consistent with a primary intent of keeping people inside the compound..."

*   *   *

Melanie Gibs was at her desk when her workstation chimed to signal an incoming message. It was the information she'd been awaiting, so she called Andrea Stevens. The phone rang for quite some time, which Melanie thought odd, since Andrea normally picked up promptly. But just when Melanie expected it to cut to voice mail, Andrea answered.

"Melanie?"

"Hi, Andrea. I just received word that the court has granted our request for a two-week delay on the government's petition to interview. However, our lawyer indicated that the judge was perplexed by the request and seemed unlikely to grant any more extensions."

"That's fine, Melanie. Thanks so much for going to bat for us," Andrea answered cheerily, though to Melanie her tone sounded forced and artificial. "This is so embarrassing for us, but we'll have it straightened out as soon as we can."

"Sure, Andrea. I'll keep you posted," Melanie rang off and stared at her phone in bewilderment. She knew that all organizations hit occasional rough patches, but this response of Wondercare's was baffling. Local management issues notwithstanding, what was so hard about putting two kids on a shuttle to make an appointment?

Back in her office, Andrea took a minute to walk around the office and fight the panic. Then she took a prescription bottle from her purse, tipped some pills into her hand, and gulped them hastily. She finally dialed her mother Suzanne. "Hello, Mom? Yeah, I just got a call from CPS. They got the delay on those agents interviewing the Schaeffer kids, but it's only for two weeks. No, I've no idea why federal agents want to interview them. My contact says the judge is getting impatient. Could we have our doctor write some kind of letter indicating – no, that wouldn't work. Then they'd just want their doctors to look at them. There's been no progress on finding them? Damn, Mom, we gotta do something!"

An hour later, Suzanne Stevens was still sitting at her desk, staring at the phone, fighting the urge to grab her keys, jump in her car, and drive off somewhere, anywhere. Find a road that led far away, take it and never come back. She hated calling Pa with bad news. She hated even more having him find out through other channels something that she should have told him directly. Finally, with trembling hands, she picked up the phone and keyed Pa's number.

"Hello, Pa?" she said timidly.

*   *   *

When the workers returned to the barracks at the end of shift, they were surprised to see project litter on the floor and strange objects around some of the beams. A few of the objects were round and tall, as tall as Tyrone, painted brown and made of metal. Some of the guys recognized them as gas cylinders. There were four of them, tightly strapped with metal bands to the heavy iron beams that arched from floor to ceiling. Just above the cylinders, large blocks of what looked like shiny metal were strapped to the beams. Electrical cables ran to the shiny blocks, and to some apparatus on the top of the cylinders. The cables stretched up the beams to the rafters overhead.

The workers were puzzled by the new equipment, and started talking and speculating loudly until they realized there were still men in the barracks. They were near the end, down by where Tyrone bunked. He was leery of going down near them, especially when he saw his line supervisor, Mr. Nathan, talking to Mr. Nick while the men packed away their tools. But he was supposed to go to his bunk, so he cautiously edged closer, watching the men for a cue as to what he should do.

Mr. Nathan spotted Tyrone, who froze in fear. But then Mr. Nathan smiled and beckoned him over. Tyrone gulped and proceeded slowly, grateful that Mr. Nick and the men were heading toward the far door. He didn't like being near Mr. Nick no matter who was smiling.

Mr. Nathan motioned Tyrone over to where a new switch box of some type had been attached to the wall. Dust and scraps of wire littered the floor.

"Hello, Tyrone," Mr. Nathan said, bending down so his eyes were level with Tyrone's and putting his hand on Tyrone's shoulder. For some reason this made Tyrone even more nervous.

"Tyrone," Mr. Nathan was continuing. "You're a good worker who follows instructions well, and I can trust you, can't I?"

"Yes, sir," Tyrone answered stiffly, not knowing what to make of this.

"Therefore, I'm going to appoint you to a special job, one that I wouldn't trust to just anyone. I'm going to make you barracks safety officer."

Safety officer? That didn't sound too bad. Tyrone was gratified to be trusted, but was still wary.

"It's an important job with lots of responsibility," Mr. Nathan went on. "But I want to explain the first one. Ready?"

"Yes, sir," Tyrone nodded. Mr. Nathan pointed to the new switch box, which had a smooth faceplate.

"This is the main switch for our new safety system," Mr. Nathan explained. "You can feel how the faceplate is a little bigger than the box, so it leaves a little lip all around – see? On the left side, hidden by the lip, is this small catch – feel it? When you lift that little catch, the faceplate pops up like this." The faceplate sprung up, revealing a little button switch inside. He swung the faceplate back down until it latched again. "Here, you try it."

So Tyrone did, feeling around the edge for the catch and springing the faceplate up. It was a little stiff, but he could manage it.

"Good boy," Mr. Nathan said. He pointed to the button inside the box and continued. "That's the safety button. I need you to

198

press that when – and only when – you see the yellow lights on the beams start flashing." He pointed to a spot on the beams just above where the shiny metal blocks were. There Tyrone saw some yellowish globe lights that were currently dark.

"This is a new thing we're doing called a safety drill," Mr. Nathan went on. "If we call a safety drill, we'll want everyone back to the barracks. Once everyone's safely inside, I need you as safety officer to watch for the lights. If they start flashing, you come here, open the faceplate, and push the button. But only after everyone's inside, and you see the yellow lights start flashing. Understand?"

"Yes, sir," Tyrone said solemnly.

"It's a big responsibility I'm giving you, Tyrone," Mr. Nathan went on. "I wouldn't trust just anyone, but I know I can count on you to follow through, can't I?"

"Yes, sir," Tyrone assured him, feeling warm inside about being giving all this responsibility. "You can count on me, sir."

"I know I can, Tyrone," Mr. Nathan said. "One last thing, though: this is a secret position, so you shouldn't tell anyone else. If it became known that I appointed you safety officer, some of the older workers might get jealous. Above all, don't show anyone else how to open the switch box, and if you see anyone messing around near it, run them off. Tell them...tell them it's dangerous, and that I said nobody should go near it. Got that?"

"Yes, sir," Tyrone replied, feeling even more proud that his position of responsibility was not common knowledge.

"Good lad," Mr. Nathan said. "Now, could you get a broom and sweep all this up?"

"Yes, sir," Tyrone said, bustling off to the broom locker. Nathan headed out the door. The workers had departed, leaving Nick standing alone in the evening twilight.

"So, Nate," Nick asked. "Since this is your brainchild, you want to tell me how it works?"

"Simple, really," Nate replied. "We've got four cylinders of industrial oxygen rigged with quick venting valves that are tied into the building's power. When the switch is engaged, the valves open, emptying the cylinders. Within three minutes, the atmosphere inside the barracks will be effectively pure oxygen."

"Okay – what does that buy me?" Nick asked.

"The same circuits that open the valves also power some high-temperature ignition coils mounted under the magnesium blocks that are strapped just above the cylinders. The blocks should start burning within two minutes."

"A Class D fire," Nick mused.

"Right," Nick confirmed. "Impossible to extinguish with ordinary means."

"But that doesn't look like much magnesium," Nick pointed out.

"It doesn't need to be. It's just the starter. The blocks are tight up against the beams. Iron doesn't burn in atmosphere, but in pure oxygen, the ignition temperature is lower than that of burning magnesium."

"So, the purpose of igniting magnesium in the oxygen atmosphere is to get the iron beams inside the barracks burning?" Nick asked.

"That's right. A Class D fire burns so hot that everything will be reduced to powder. No teeth, no bones, nothing but ash," Nate replied.

"Sounds like a hell of a way to go," Nick said, glancing toward the barracks door. Nate looked uncomfortably at the ground.

"Yeah, well – if my calculations are correct, the superheated gases will overwhelm the place quickly. They'll – they'll probably never know what hit them, and will be gone long before any flames get near." The two men were silent for a minute before Nick spoke again.

"So, then, what's the procedure?"

"As you requested, this is a last-ditch option, an extreme scenario. First, we'd make sure all the workers were in the barracks and the doors barred. I've had to throw this together so quickly that I haven't had time to rig up a remote triggering mechanism, though that would have risks of its own. So I picked up some battery-powered intruder warning devices – simple yellow strobes, which I can trigger with this," Nate held up his phone. "I've instructed my most reliable lineman to push the trigger button when the strobes go off."

"I presume your worker has no idea what he'd be doing?" Nick asked.

"I told him it was a safety drill," Nate assured him. "Don't worry, he's reliable. Once we send the signal, he'll come through."

"Yeah, well," Nick said, tapping out a cigarette and offering one to Nate. "Here's hoping we never have to send that signal."

"That's for sure," Nate echoed. "Because once that fire starts, there's no stopping it."

*   *   *

The three friends were chatting and laughing merrily down by the pond in front of St. Anne's House. Janice had been given the evening off to spend time with Felicity and Grace, and they'd spent hours nibbling snacks and sipping lemonade and catching up with each other. Janice wanted to hear all about their studies and life at St. Anselm's, and they wanted to hear how Janice's life at St. Anne's had been going. Grace and Felicity were delighted to see how much Janice had improved since they'd last seen her. Though they still caught little flashes of the somber, distressed Janice, there was far more smiling and buoyancy than they'd ever seen her exhibit. It wasn't that Janice was flippant or giddy, but she laughed and smiled more, and her once-shadowed eyes were calmer and clearer. But there was also a new gravity about her that the two sensed. They felt like she was now more like an older sister, grown in wisdom and maturity and insight.

"How's Ellie doing?" Grace asked casually. The rescued girl had been entrusted to the St. Anne sisters without much explanation. Her situation was so delicate and difficult that it needed to be carefully discussed with her and others before anything could be done for her. Very few knew the story of how she'd come into their midst.

"She's doing all right," Janice said wryly. "Not much in the way of life skills, though she's a quick learner in the kitchen. Sister Joseph is working with her, but we need more skilled medical hands, not more responsibilities."

"I see," Grace said, nibbling a sweet cherry. "The boys are up to something. Jake has been going places with Todd in the afternoons after work, but never says where. They get back late, filthy, and exhausted."

"Is it Jake you're interested in, or Todd?" Felicity teased, eliciting a blush.

"Yes," Janice said in a curious voice, turning slightly to gaze northward with a faraway look in her eyes. "They are preparing."

"Preparing?" Grace asked, a little disconcerted. "Preparing for what?"

"For what is coming," Janice answered without breaking her gaze. "In the north the devouring darkness is rising, and they are preparing to battle it."

Stunned, Grace whipped her head around to meet Felicity's wide-eyed look of astonishment.

Rising darkness?

"Uh, Janice," Felicity said in a wavering voice. "There's – there's part of our year that we haven't yet told you about. It happened at the end, as we were coming home. It's a little frightening for us to think about, even now, but I think you need to hear it."

*   *   *

"We've allocated a shotgun and sidearm for everyone," Nick explained as the UTV bounced along the narrow trail. "We've scattered battery-run, motion activated cameras throughout the woods, in addition to the fence-mounted cameras. We've stepped up staffing in the security shed to 24/7, so the cameras are monitored constantly. We've put round-the-clock armed guards with night vision scopes at the bend of the drive. We've implemented extra precautions in the barracks to insure the workers aren't accessed. All these extra steps and duties are starting to take a toll on the guys, and that's starting to impact production. I tell you, Pa, I'm not sure how much more we can do!"

"I understand, Nick," Pa replied without taking his eyes from the trail. "You've done well, but I still want to talk to Old Charlie."

Nick snorted and attended to his driving, biting back what he truly wished to say. They jolted along in silence until they came to the shadowed clearing. Charlie was sitting in front of his cold fire trench and looked up as if he'd been expecting them. Nick nearly gagged in revulsion – the same filth, the same vile stench, the same random junk cluttering the area. Nick could hear snuffling and rooting behind the trailer. That had to be the enormous sow which Charlie kept back there, which the guys called Molly. Nobody could get near her but Charlie, but then, nobody wanted to.

"So," Charlie said as Pa sat down on the ground beside him. "How are your preparations going?"

"Well enough, according to Nick," Pa answered. "They've implemented lots of new precautions."

"Yet still your enemies tighten the noose around you," Charlie pronounced, prodding the ashes with a stick. "You know this. You have been receiving bad news from all sides. They are searching you out, looking to lay bare your secrets. Your enemies are too strong for you. If they find you, they will tear right through your sturdiest defenses and bring you down."

Pa pinched his lip and stared at the ashes, pondering the array of setbacks he'd already suffered and the numerous threats that still loomed. Charlie was right – of late he'd been receiving bad news left and right. "But – what can you *do*? I know how you've helped before, but what good could that sort of thing do here?"

"You are correct: they are too strong for me to drive off. But I can hide you," Charlie replied. "If you give me enough to work with, I can draw around you a shroud that will shield you from the sight of all your enemies until their interest passes by."

"I...I understand," Pa said hesitantly. "But...well, I was wondering about the cost. You've never asked for three, and–"

"You have never faced a threat this great before," Charlie interrupted. "Yes, it is much, but you need much. If you think the cost too great, then by all means, place your trust in the safeguards which others provide." He waved his stick in Nick's direction. "But I warn you: if you delay much longer, it may become too late for me to do anything to protect you."

Pa pondered that for a minute before getting up and walking over to Nick. "Give him whatever he wants," he said, getting into the UTV.

"But...Pa..." Nick protested, turning pale.

"Do it!" Pa barked.

Abomination

Mark Stevens and Joe Pemberton sat in the truck waiting for the ferry to make it back across the river from the Algonac side. They were hot, sweaty, filthy, and since they'd forgotten to bring water, terribly thirsty. They wanted nothing more than to get back over to the States and drink about a gallon of water each – not even beer sounded as good right now. But nothing could speed the ferry, or the line of vehicles waiting to board, so there they sat roasting in the late afternoon sun.

Mark figured this assignment was another of Pa's calculated humiliations, a pointed reminder of their failure the last time they'd been this far down the river. Algonac wasn't far from Gull Island – in fact, they'd planned to bring the Jobbie Nooner haul back here – so sending them back down was like rubbing their noses in their failure.

Especially for such a menial task.

Nick hadn't told them why a pickup truck load of common dirt was needed, but he was emphatic that it had to be from Walpole Island. The fact that Nick had stressed that so firmly had nipped Mark's first temptation in the bud, which had been to drive to a big box store, buy a pallet or so of black dirt, and empty it into the truck bed. Nick would certainly be tracking the pickup's progress by its locator circuitry to ensure it made the entire trip.

It wasn't that it was hard to get there. For purposes of crossing the border, Walpole Island was part of Canada so it was just a matter of taking the ferry and making it through customs. But within Canada, the tiny island at the mouth of the St. Clair River had a special status. It was a First Nation reserve, and thus it was a nation within a nation, with its own government and sovereign status.

Not that any of this mattered to Mark and Joe. All they needed was dirt, and it needed to be from the Island. They drove around in vain, seeking a store that would sell it in bags, and

finally resorted to driving to the end of a dirt road and shoveling
it by hand from the ditch. It was hot, brutal work, and the sun
was westering before they finally turned home.

"What do you think they need all this dirt for?" Joe grumbled
as they watched the ferry dock.

"Damned if I know," Mark admitted. "Nick said something
vague about it being from 'unceded land', whatever that means."

"There's plenty of dirt where we come from," Joe said. "I'd
sure like to know what's so special about this stuff."

"So would I," Mark replied. "Something else I'd like to
know, too."

"What's that?"

"How we're going to explain this to Customs."

*   *   *

While Mark and Joe were pondering that problem, Chip
Keller and Dan Knight were assembling their team at the
abandoned hut on the property where they'd been training.
Overall, Dan was satisfied with their progress. Chip had been
right: these men were bright, hardworking, levelheaded, and took
orders well. They'd trained hard in the kind of terrain they
expected to have to tackle, learning quickly and showing
initiative. They were as ready as they were going to get.

"All right, gentlemen," Dan called them to order. "We have
some developments to report. Chip?"

"We've been waiting for the best circumstances, and two
nights from now is shaping up as ideal," Chip explained. "It'll be
nearly moonless, and thick cloud cover is expected. It may rain
lightly, which would work to our advantage. Dan tells me you're
ready. If you all agree, we can plan for then."

There was a murmur of assent, and Dan stepped back up and
turned on his tablet. The now-familiar projection of the section
map appeared on the wall.

"We've been able to fine-tune our plan, so this is the final
version we'll be training on. We're going to execute a feint to

206

draw their attention, hopefully allowing the rescue team a clear field. Here's the outline:

"Our first move will be to deny them external power, so yes, we'll have to do just a little bit of property damage. All their power comes in by these lines here near the northeast corner of the plot, so we'll take those down with sniper fire. That'll start the mission clock.

"Losing external power will force them to go to site power – their emergency generator – as well as alert them that something is going on. That's fine, because we want their attention, but first we want to put out their eyes.

"The first set of eyes we'll take out will be the perimeter cameras that watch along the outside of the fence. We know they're monitoring the north, east, and south fences. Conveniently for us, they're doing that from just three locations: here at the northeast corner, halfway down the eastern fence, and on the southeast corner." Dan tapped the points on the projection. "We'll have snipers to take these out, granting us access to the fence. There's also a camera covering the gate, but since we don't intend to go near there, we leave that alone.

"Once we get inside, we'll have to deal with the cameras on the fence posts." Dan tapped his tablet and a different projection appeared, showing a device sitting on a squat box on top of a pole, with a small solar panel sticking up from it. "These are sited on every other pole along the entire length of the perimeter fence. They're hard mounted pointing inward – they don't move in any direction. What they're sitting on there is a battery pack, which the solar panel helps recharge.

"I showed this image to a friend who specializes in security devices. He tells me this is a typical wide-angle security camera designed for small area coverage. Usually you have three or four of these cameras placed around a restricted area like a lumber yard or used car lot. They capture video and send it by short range wireless signal to a centrally located relay device. The relay sends the signals along to a monitoring station."

"The short range is how they can get away with using batteries?" asked Phillip.

"Precisely," Dan confirmed. "The cameras themselves don't use much power, generating a weak signal that only has to reach the relay. The relay is wired for power and amplifies the signals to send over the cable. It's a very handy and flexible configuration for casual surveillance, but not for serious security, because it has an Achilles' heel, which we'll exploit using these." He held up a length of cord with two pouch-like things on either end.

"This looks like a bolo because that's how it's used," Dan explained, extracting a small device about the size of a golf ball from one of the pouches and holding it up. "The magic is in these little spheres, which are multi-channel jammers. They detect wireless transmissions, identify the channel, and start transmitting interference, thus disrupting the signal from the camera to the relay. Now, most of these camera/relay setups are smart enough to detect too much noise on one channel, and will automatically switch to another, so our jammer has to be smarter. It can jam one channel while monitoring others, so when the camera switches to its secondary channel, the device will start jamming that as well. My security friend tells me that these monitoring setups typically use no more than two channels – a primary and a secondary. Our devices can jam up to four, so we should be good.

"We use these by throwing them just like bolos up into the trees in the zone between the cameras and where the relays are likely to be. We'll practice that tonight, because it's important that they catch and hang, not fall to the ground. Once they're hanging, we give them a couple minutes to start their jamming magic, and then proceed.

"We're going to presume they've also placed cameras randomly throughout the woods. We don't have any intelligence of such devices, but we presume it until we know differently. These are likely to be motion-detecting infrared cameras. They lie dormant until something moves within their range, at which point their infrared light panels activate and they start transmitting.

Hunters and forest rangers use these to track the movement of nocturnal animals.

"Since the infrared light is invisible to the naked eye, you won't know it when you've just triggered one of these devices." Dan picked up a device that looked like a small, clumsy telescope. "That's where these come in. This is a standard third-generation night vision monocular. This allows you to see when infrared light is shining. They come with their own infrared lamp, which you'll use for getting through the woods. But occasionally – especially after a move – you'll want to use them in passive mode, with the infrared lamp off, to see if you've moved into the range of a motion-detecting camera. You'll know because your surroundings will be illuminated by a greenish light. If you see that, locate the light source and take it out. Any questions?"

There were none, so Dan returned the section projection to the wall and proceeded.

"After taking down the external power, disabling the perimeter cameras, breaching the fence, and jamming the fence cameras, we proceed as two teams. The larger team, designated Green, will come in from the east. We will be the feint, intended to draw attention. This will be very difficult, for we still hope for complete stealth in the sense of effectively being invisible operatives, but we want the consequences of our actions to be noticed. We'll drive for the emergency generator, with the goal of disabling that. The point group, Green Major, will consist of Cletus and Sixtus, who have sufficient experience with diesel generation to be able to shut down and disable any generator within two minutes. The backup group, Green Minor, will be Phillip and myself. We'll be support and reserve.

"But handy as a blackout will be, the real mission will lie in the hands of the Gold team – Jake and Todd. You'll come in from the west. The drawback is that you'll have to cross the ditch to do it. A narrow access path runs right along the fence, but it has treacherous footing. You wouldn't be able to bring the kids back out that way, so across the ditch it is. The advantage is that they don't have perimeter cameras scanning down the western fence –

I suppose they think the ditch is a sufficient deterrent. Once inside the fence, you'll face the same obstacles as the Green team, but you'll be traveling a shorter distance. Your goal will be the barracks, which is between four and five hundred yards from the fence. This is the team that will need complete stealth. Todd and Jake, are you up to it?"

"We are," Jake answered for them both.

"All right," Dan said. "We'll cover each team's tactics in more detail later. Right now, let's go practice pitching bolos."

*   *   *

Tyrone was busy at his station when he saw Mr. Nick walking down the line with Ms. Charity. He put his head down and attended to his work. Getting noticed by Mr. Nick was bad enough; nobody wanted to be noticed by Ms. Charity. She was awful. She had a fat face and little squinty eyes and always wore a sour expression. She was just plain mean. When she was around, nobody was safe. If she spotted something she didn't like, she'd jump right in and start berating the poor worker right then. She'd even grab one of the super's batons and start beating the worker – Tyrone had seen it happen. Not even Mr. Nick liked being near her – you could see it in his expression – but she was important for some reason.

Tyrone glanced sideways and saw that they were both still coming down the line toward his team, with Ms. Charity pointing from time to time. *Please let them turn*, Tyrone pleaded, but they kept coming. They stopped just far enough away that Tyrone couldn't hear them. To Tyrone's horror, Ms. Charity seemed to be looking at him, and even pointing in his direction. But then Mr. Nathan walked up and began talking to her and Mr. Nick. They talked for a while, and Mr. Nathan kept shaking his head. Finally, he called Tony over, and Tony followed Mr. Nick and Ms. Charity as they walked away. Tyrone watched as two other workers were called away from stations farther up the line to go with them. He couldn't shake the feeling that he'd just dodged something terrible.

But he also couldn't help feeling sorry for Tony.

Nick drove the three workers up to Black Charlie's. They were seated in the bed of the UTV, their feet hobbled, their hands tied, and burlap sacks over their heads. Nick grumbled and muttered rebelliously all the way, but what could he do against Pa? He drove as smoothly as he could, so the workers weren't jostled against each other more than they already were. Wouldn't want one of them to topple out and get bruised.

Nick laughed grimly.

As he pulled into the clearing, Charlie rose from where he'd been sitting on his trailer steps and came over, chuckling and grinning. But when he saw the worker's coveralls, he frowned a little.

"I said the dearer the better. Was this the dearest he had?" Charlie asked Nick. Nick said nothing, and Charlie shook his head as he fingered one of the worker's sleeves. "His life's work at risk, and he sends me his property. Had he sent me his blood, I could have protected his line for five generations. As it is," he shrugged. "I will shield him as I can."

Nick walked around and dropped the gate on the UTV's bed. "Where – where are we?" asked a tremulous voice. A girl. Nick wouldn't have chosen her, but Charity had insisted.

"Just hop down and sit over here. You'll be all right," Nick lied for about the hundredth time that day as he eased the girl out of the bed.

"Put it over there," Charlie said, pointing to a spot by the trailer. Nick saw the three large garden trailers filled with the requested Walpole Island soil parked near the edge of the clearing.

"Good, good," Charlie said as Nick helped the last worker out of the bed and over to where the others sat blindfolded and helpless. "You come back at sunrise tomorrow with a vehicle that can tow these." He pointed to the trailers.

"Yeah, yeah," Nick growled as he started the UTV and turned it toward the trail.

"Hey!" called one of the workers through his burlap face cover. "Where are you going?" The panic in the kid's voice was thick. "Come back! Don't leave us!"

Nick just gritted his teeth and stomped on the accelerator.

It wasn't Nick who returned the next morning, but Eli. He pulled into the clearing as the sun was about to rise. The three trailers stood ready to be towed, and Charlie was roasting a slab of some kind of meat over the fire trench. From behind the trailer came a gross snuffling and gobbling sound. The acrid stench of decay mingled with a heavy, sickly sweet odor that hung about the clearing.

"You ready?" Eli asked.

"Soon, soon," Charlie smiled. "Just having breakfast. Want some?"

"No."

"So, your boss didn't come this morning?" Charlie asked, pulling the nearly blackened meat off the fire and starting to gnaw at the edge. "Why not?"

"Because he sent me," Eli snapped back. He'd only taken this assignment under protest; damned if he was going to converse with Black Charlie.

Smiling like he could read Eli's mind, Charlie kept chewing at the slab of meat with an inordinate amount of smacking and chomping. Finally, he threw what remained of the slab into the fire and pushed himself to his feet.

"Hitch up one of these," he pointed to one of the trailers. Eli complied, reconciling himself to the revolting reality that he was going to have to ride beside Black Charlie. The disgusting little man hadn't even wiped his mouth. The grease from his barbaric meal smeared into the dirt in the seams of his face.

"We come back for the others," Charlie announced as he got into the passenger seat, waving at the other two trailers. "Now – to the gate." Eli noticed that in one hand Charlie was carrying what looked like a gourd cut in half lengthwise, so it looked like a big scoop, and in the other a curved thing with pointed sections on the end that looked for all the world like a broken-off section of deer antler.

The horrible task that followed took nearly the entire day. Starting at the gate, they made a tedious round of the perimeter of the property, staying about fifty yards inside the fence. Charlie walked behind the trailer, scooping out the soil and scattering it in a loose line as they went, moaning and muttering all the way. It was like he was laying down a great loop of the dirt encircling the complex. Charlie was meticulous about his work, sometimes doubling back to insure he'd left an unbroken trail. Every so often he would stop to perform a crude ceremony, which consisted of kneeling on the ground and jabbing at his left forearm with the antler-like thing, and then using it to stab and dig at the dirt he was laying down. It looked like he was working the dark, polluted dirt into the ground. He made no attempt to explain this strange behavior.

Navigating the UTV through the woods was hard enough for Eli, not to mention the times he had to run back to the clearing to fetch the next trailer full of dirt. Slowly, tediously, they worked up the west side of the property, across the shorter north side, back down the east side, and ultimately back over to the main gate. There, with much muttering and chanting and bowing, Charlie sprinkled the last of the dirt on the first scoopfuls he'd laid down that morning.

Eli detested every minute of this. He didn't want to be anywhere near the filthy, smelly old man. He'd heard the rumors and had seen how distraught Nick had been. He guessed why the dirt was so dark and wet, and fell from Charlie's gourd in great sticky clumps. He guessed why it stank and swarmed with flies. He was never so glad to finish a workday as when he turned the

UTV from that grim clearing and headed back to quarters for a shower. A long, hot shower.

Eli hoped it would get him clean.

History

Derek was just settling into the guest room at his host family's house when his phone rang. He was tempted not to answer – he'd had a full day of rounds and had no intention of heading out again to attend to a problem that a couple of painkillers would hold until morning. But when he saw it was Grandpa, he answered quickly.

"Hello, Luke?"

"Hi, Grandpa," Derek answered. "What can I do for you?"

"Is your evening free?"

"For you it is. Do you need me to come down there?"

"No, no," Grandpa replied. "Where are you?"

"Just north of Sandusky," Derek said. "I've been working east from the Caro area today."

"That's good. I hate to ask this after your full day, but can you meet me at St. Anne's?"

"Sure, Grandpa," Derek replied, puzzled. "It's not that far from where I am. Are you at home?"

"No, actually, I'm already en route. I'm north of Yale, approaching Peck," Grandpa explained.

"Oh – well, then, I'd better get going," Derek said. "If I start now, I should arrive there about the same time you do."

"Bring your medical equipment," Grandpa added.

"I always do," Derek replied. He rung off, more puzzled than ever. Grabbing his jacket and helmet, he ducked out to explain to his host family and reload his travel bags. Good thing he'd remembered to refuel the ATV.

Derek arrived at St. Anne's House a little before Grandpa to find an equally puzzled Janice waiting on the front porch. She confirmed that Grandpa had called her, too, requesting her presence but offering no explanation as to why. They waited in the sultry evening air. The westering sun was hidden behind a sullen gray bank of clouds that was creeping steadily eastward, promising at least rain and possibly storms by morning.

After about ten minutes a car pulled in, out of which came not only Grandpa but Grandma. They all greeted each other warmly, but with an air of urgency Grandpa gestured Derek and Janice into the car while Grandma went into the house.

"Thank you both for being available on such short notice," Grandpa said as he pulled out of the drive.

"Grandma's not coming?" Janice asked.

"No – she'll be doing her support from here," Grandpa replied.

"Grandpa, do you mind telling us what this is about?" Derek asked. "And where are we going?"

"We're going first to Lawrence Stover's," Grandpa explained. "Where we go from there – some or all of us – depends on what we decide then."

"Is this connected with the – ah – situation we've been discussing?" Derek said.

"Probably," Grandpa confirmed. "Earlier today, Fr. Gabriel called me with some interesting news. It seems a good number of young men from our circles – including some of my grandsons – made a point of attending daily Mass this morning, and then requested appointments for Confession immediately thereafter. This despite the fact that regularly scheduled Confessions are only a few days from now.

"That by itself is only atypical, but combined with other things I've been hearing…"

"I've been hearing things, too," Janice admitted.

"It doesn't surprise me. Secrets can be kept from officials, but tend to slip out in close families," Grandpa replied.

"What are you speculating?" Derek asked. He'd heard nothing.

"It was clear at the meetings we held that some of our participants were impatient with the pace of our response to the situation we uncovered," Grandpa explained. "The magnitude of the offense seems to call for swifter action, even if that action skates close to, or over, the line of legality and prudence. For all I know, they may be right. But it appears that they have decided to move independently, planning and training for some kind of operation against the suspected site – and may be executing that plan soon, possibly tonight."

Derek looked at him in amazement. "So, what are we going to do?"

"Well, after the call from Fr. Gabriel I called Lawrence to convey my suspicions. He confirmed that he'd been hearing similar rumors, but he also said that he'd at last gotten in touch with a person he'd been trying to reach. At Lawrence's request, that person is coming up to speak with us about the situation – in fact, he's already in Ubly. Lawrence tried to contact some of the others, but they were unavailable this evening, which made him even more suspicious."

"Did he say who this person was?" Derek asked.

"He was reluctant to discuss it over the phone, but said it was urgent that we meet and talk to him, especially if some of us are planning precipitate action," Grandpa answered.

"But…what do we do? Try to stop them? Threaten to expose them? Wait and see?"

"I posed that same question to Lawrence, and he seemed to think it was important to talk to this party before making any decisions. So, I agreed to come up promptly, bringing as many of you as I could."

"Including Grandma?" Derek asked.

"She insisted on coming as far as St. Anne's," Grandpa explained. "Whatever happens, she wants to be backup support, so she'll be in the chapel."

Janice had been listening to all this while looking northward out the windshield with one of her faraway gazes. Suddenly, she turned to Grandpa.

"Do you mind if I make a phone call?"

"Of course not," Grandpa replied. Janice pulled out her phone and keyed a number.

"Hello, Felicity? Can you pick up Grace and meet us in Ubly? Yes, it's urgent. I'd guess an hour and a half, maybe two hours. I'm not exactly sure, but I'd rather have you nearby in case of any developments. Thanks. Call me when you get close." She tucked her phone back in her purse and turned to Grandpa. "Backup support," she offered by way of explanation.

They pulled into the Stover's driveway to find themselves nearly the only ones there. A strange car with Indiana license plates was the only other vehicle. Lawrence greeted them and escorted them into the living room where stood a tall, heavyset man with a long face, gentle smile, and warm brown eyes.

"Permit me to introduce my old friend Mike Peterson," Lawrence said to the man. "His godson Luke and his goddaughter Teresa. Friends, this is an old friend of mine, Tyler Barton. He's driven up from Indianapolis to help us as best he can."

"So – Indianapolis?" Grandpa asked as they were all seated. "Rather a drive all the way up here."

"Yes, but I'm accustomed to it," Tyler explained. "I grew up here, though I don't come back often, and need to be discreet when I do."

"Really? You grew up in this area?" Grandpa asked with some surprise.

"Yes," Tyler confirmed. "You see, I'm Ray Hubbart's stepson." Smiling a bit at the shocked expressions, he continued. "I am, as it were, the white sheep of the family. I'm the eldest son of Ray's second wife Cheryl. Ray tolerated me for her sake, but made it clear that his blood children, especially Nick, were his favorites, and that I wouldn't be cutting them out of anything. I would be allowed a place if I wanted to do things the "Ray Way," but if I didn't, I'd be marginalized.

"That was a lot for a middle-school kid to handle, especially when I saw how overbearing Ray was, and how harshly he dealt with everyone, especially my mother. But a kind pastor and his very wise wife helped me come to terms with my situation. In time I came to better understand, and even at times to pity, Raymond Hubbart and his family.

"Ray comes from a long line of Hubbarts who settled in Huron County in the mid-19th century. He is extremely intelligent and very motivated, with interests that range from economics to politics to history. However, he's no academic dilettante. His education is very practical; everything has a goal. He got a bachelor's degree at Michigan State and an MBA at the University of Michigan. With those in hand, he moved to Chicago to try his luck. Within two years he was back here, and some were snickering up their sleeves that the farm lad couldn't make it in the big city. They couldn't have been more wrong.

"Ray played the big city game and decided that it was a losing gambit, destined for ultimate failure. He concluded that associations like corporations, cities, and even nations were all artificial constructs that had no long-term staying power. And you must admit, given the social turmoil of the last generation, it's a compelling argument. Ray returned to Huron County convinced that he'd seen the future, which was essentially the past: mankind's only hope lay in families. That, he concluded, was the only social construct that would ultimately endure. He'd become convinced that Western civilization began its decline when it forsook a family-centered culture for government based on abstract political and social theories. He studied ancient societies obsessively, especially the Roman, the Carolingian, and the Egyptian cultures.

"His actions matched his words. Soon after returning to the area he married and began having children. He encouraged his siblings to have children, too. When his first wife only bore him four children, he divorced her and married my mother, who gave him four more. He took child raising seriously, too, only sending his children to public school through the eighth grade, and ultimately not even that. He hammered into their heads the centrality and importance of family.

"Of course, his biggest struggle was economic. Not much money flows into Huron County. His family was rich in acreage but not much more. But here his economic studies came into play. He foresaw the disorder that would overtake Asia, and America's currency collapse in the international markets. He knew millions of Americans loved the cheap goods produced by foreign labor markets, and understood that that demand would remain even after the eroding value of the dollar made that labor prohibitively expensive. He looked for ways to tap that demand. In his cunning he also saw opportunity in the collapse of families, and a society that would be flooded with inconvenient children which it would rather not bother with. He seems to have combined those two concepts into his current...venture."

"So, you knew about this factory staffed by slaves?" Derek asked.

"I knew something was going on," Tyler sighed. "I didn't realize it was this bad. You see, I've always been on good terms with Nick, and even after I made my escape, we've stayed in touch. I think I act as a relief valve for him – he says things to me he wouldn't dare say to anyone else because he knows it would get back to his family. He never told me anything flat-out – security around family operations is much too tight – but from our conversations I gathered that something dubious was taking place. I guessed it was a sweatshop, exploiting the poor under harsh circumstances. But from what Lawrence has told me, it's clearly something much worse.

"But that fits with Ray's vision and his ruthlessness. He sees governmental structures tottering and crumbling all around, and he's sure he's got the vision to replace them. He wants to build a broad enough family base to control the entire region."

But...I don't understand," Derek interjected. "He knows not much money flows to this area. Even if he controlled it all, it wouldn't be much."

"It's not about money, Luke," Lawrence explained. "It's about controlling the lives of others, making them live on your terms. That's what tyrants are always after – money is just a means to that end."

"Exactly," Tyler confirmed. "That's Ray's conscious and deliberate end: to raise a dynasty that will rule."

"Sounds kind of old-fashioned," Derek said.

"Ray would agree with you," Tyler replied. "But he'd contend that things like legislatures and plebiscites and corporations are the newfangled ideas that are destined to crumble and collapse. As long as society is built on families, it thrives and grows. Once it departs from that foundation, the decay begins."

"At least he's consistent," Grandpa admitted. "He's feeding, scavenger-like, on the debris of decaying families, sweeping abandoned children into his operation. He's also exploiting the detached, impersonal world of corporate production. His clients didn't care about the conditions under which their goods were produced when they were made in China or Malaysia. They're not going to start caring now, as long as the goods come in on schedule and at price."

"That's his vision: to milk what he considers a collapsing social order to help build his new one. It's the oldest ethic in history: those who are in the family exploit those who are not. But there's another element you need to be aware of: Black Charlie."

"Black Charlie?" Derek asked.

"Yes. He was a fact of life by the time I came onto the scene, but later I started asking questions and doing some investigating. What I learned was at least disturbing, and even diabolical, if you look at the world that way.

"Charlie is of Native American stock, though nobody knows exactly which tribe. Ray met him on Walpole Island about thirty years ago, when Ray was over there doing research on Anishinaabek tribal structures. Ray brought him back as an "advisor" or "spiritual counselor", and Charlie has haunted the fringe of Ray's life ever since. Ray always makes sure he has a home. Charlie doesn't require much materially – he says he likes to 'live native', which in his case appears to mean 'live filthy'. He eschews modern conveniences like running water and electricity, lives in squalor, and has eating and hygiene habits that would shock a Viking.

"But Charlie seems to have an almost hypnotic hold on Ray, to a point that has some of his family concerned. Ray knows his family loathes Charlie, but won't hear a word spoken against him. Ray calls Charlie his 'totem' and his 'good luck charm', and always consults with him before making major decisions. Ray attributes much of his success to Charlie's assistance.

"And, indeed, there are some who would concur, at least in the sense that Charlie brought good luck to Ray by seeming to bring bad luck to any who opposed him. Now again, what I'm about to say will only make sense if you look at the world a certain way, but shortly after Charlie came into Ray's life, word started getting around that it was unlucky to oppose Ray Hubbart. If Ray wanted your field, you'd better come to terms, or your crop would fail, and you'd have to settle for what you could get. If you were bidding against one of Ray's businesses for a contract, your wife might be diagnosed with cancer. If you didn't agree to supply his operations on his terms, one of your kids might get in an accident."

"So, you're saying that Charlie was cursing people for Ray, or something?" Derek asked.

"Perceptions are funny things," Tyler answered. "They may not be reality, but they shape how we look at it. I researched some of these incidents, and found out that in many instances where some party opposed Ray Hubbart, something did happen to or near that party, usually causing them to withdraw their opposition. Were there more dire incidents than would have occurred in the normal course of events? Who can tell? What was certainly true that it came to be thought that opposing Ray was unlucky, and that was ultimately effective enough. But there's something else I've learned in my long years, studying this and other things."

"What's that?" Derek asked.

"That there are things in this world that cannot be explained by rationalistic materialism. Things that are ignored, or scoffed at, or dismissed as having some yet-unfound rational explanation. And I'm sure that in a good number of cases, that's true – the rational cause has simply not yet been found. But I'm equally sure that for some cases, it's not true. There are things which materialism cannot explain; which brings me to the rest of what I learned about Black Charlie.

222

"When I finally flew the Hubbart coop, I researched a lot of things, including Charlie. That was easy – Walpole Island is close, so I went down there to ask around. This was about twenty years ago, so that would have been about ten years after Charlie left the island with Ray. I thought it would be easy to find people who remembered him, but that proved false. I found almost nobody who knew anything about him, which I thought was strange considering that he claimed to hail from there. I had almost concluded that his claim was a hoax when I ran into two older guys in a store. They remembered Charlie. When I started asking questions, they politely but forcefully requested I refrain from mentioning his name and the tribe's name in the same breath. Proceeding more tactfully, I learned that Charlie had appeared on Walpole years earlier, supposedly on a pilgrimage to Tecumseh's grave. Nobody knew where he had come from. He was certainly Native American, but never told which tribe, or even from which side of the international border. One of the guys mentioned that, from some hints Charlie dropped, he may have been from the Munsee tribe, some remnants of which live in southern Ontario. But it didn't matter – he just showed up one day and, to the chagrin of the islanders, hung around for a couple of years.

"Charlie's head was full of grandiose ideas about the First Nations. He made much of the fact that Walpole was unceded territory that had never been conquered by Europeans. Of course, this is a poetic fiction. There may never have been a Battle of Walpole Island, but it is as much under Canadian jurisdiction as Toronto is, and the tribal leaders are fine with that. Charlie put on airs as some kind of shaman, a repository of ancient lore, which disgusted both the historians and the true lore masters. Apparently, Charlie had constructed an entire history out of his own imagination and bits and scraps of Anishinaabek legend. He spoke of pilgrimages to Michipicoten and Manitoulin Islands, and worshipping ancient spirits he met there. He would hold some people spellbound with tales of ancient civilizations and long-lost powers, and claim to have descended from tribes that there is no evidence ever existed. None of this bore any relation to either legend or known history.

"The two men made another thing coarsely clear: they considered Charlie a depraved pervert. The crude joke about him was that when he came around, you locked up your kids and your livestock. The consensus was that he was mad, but they used an interesting idiom to describe him, one that was difficult to translate. They referred to him as having "dined with demons". From what I could gather, this meant that he was mentally and spiritually unhinged, but in a morally culpable way, because he had done what was known to be forbidden and opened himself to things no man ever should. The islanders scoffed at him but also feared him.

"The men freely admitted that Charlie had a forceful personality, and could be very persuasive if heeded. In fact, the islanders most feared him for this influence, attributing it to more than eloquence. The tribe had about decided to run him off – "ship him up to Nunavut where he could molest the seals" was how one put it – when Ray Hubbart had showed up and relieved them of the burden. Though there was general mirth at the stupid white man, I gather there was also a bit of genuine concern for Ray's welfare, that he had no idea what he'd let himself in for.

"When I explained what had followed Charlie's arrival in Ray's life, they nodded grimly and congratulated me on getting out of that situation. They urged me to encourage other family members to get away, and one even hinted that I would be justified in killing Charlie to protect my family. White man though I was, they came close to apologizing to me, hoping I understood that every people had their bad apples and asking me not to let someone like Charlie influence my understanding of what the First Nations stood for. I thanked them for their concern, and passed what I could back to Nick."

"Wait," Derek asked, "if they thought his claim to mystical powers was all sham and pretense, why were they so worried for you?"

"Just because Charlie's head is full of vain imaginings doesn't mean that he isn't in touch with some dark stuff," Tyler replied. "Christians like Lawrence here affirm that there is a reality that's unseen – it's the basis of their salvation. They also understand that there are malevolent as well as benevolent forces. I don't make any claims to know what is going on with Charlie, and what he can and cannot do. But I find it interesting that his own people described him as having "dined with demons.""

"Regardless of these matters about which we can only speculate, since that day I've worried about those two ruthless, self-centered old men, each lusting for greatness in his own way, using each other with no regard for anyone around them. If you're contending with that, you need to know the full context."

Everyone in the room sat in stunned silence as Tyler finished. Outside the big front window, the sky was almost completely dark, with occasional flickers of distant lightning on the western horizon.

"That's certainly some story," Lawrence said at last. "It fills in a lot of things for us. As far as…ah…contending, some of us have been considering ways to address the situation. We hadn't yet decided what to do, but it's possible that some of our party have chosen to take more immediate action. In fact, they may be executing that action tonight."

"If so, they need to understand that Ray has many resources," Tyler warned. "And – how to put this? – they may face opposition of a type they're ill-equipped to counter."

Just then Janice's phone rang. It was Grace, reporting that she and Felicity were in the area. Janice gave them directions to the house while Derek closed the curtains against the deepening darkness.

"So," Lawrence said with some apprehension. "Do we have any plans, particularly in light of all this background information?"

"I think the first thing we need to establish is whether anything is actually going on tonight," Grandpa said. "All we have now is speculation."

"What would these parties be attempting, if they were doing anything?" Tyler asked.

"Good question," Lawrence replied. "I'd guess either an attempt to sabotage the factory operation, or to somehow expose it, or to rescue some or all of the enslaved workers, or some combination of those."

"Knowing some of the parties, I'd guess a rescue," Grandpa added. "That would accomplish the last two of those goals."

"How can we find out?" Tyler asked.

"Simple enough," Lawrence shrugged. "We can go to the site we suspect and see if anyone's there."

Grandpa had been musing for a bit and suddenly spoke up. "Lawrence, if I may suggest, I don't think you and I should go up there, at least not yet."

"Why not?" Lawrence asked.

"We know these lads. If they're attempting something, it's not going to be some undisciplined scramble-and-charge. They've been training, and probably have a plan, and certainly leadership of some type. If you or I show up, that'll precipitate an authority crisis, a situation of divided loyalties. Whatever we do, we don't want that."

"Good thinking," Lawrence observed. "Then what do we do?"

"Send us as an initial contact," Janice volunteered. "We were planning on going anyway."

"We were?" Derek asked in surprise.

"Sure we were," Janice confirmed. "Medical personnel. Whatever's going on, if someone needs attention, you'll get the call anyway. Might as well be nearby."

"Let's hope it doesn't come to that," Derek replied.

"That's a good idea," Grandpa said. "Let's send an advance party to see if there's anything even happening. If there is, they can convey our concern, and we can decide what would be an appropriate response."

Just then there was the sound of a car pulling into the drive, and Janice jumped up. "I think a couple more volunteers have arrived." She went out to greet Felicity and Grace and brief them on the salient points.

"So that's it," Grace said with a slight smirk when Janice had finished. "The boys have decided to play soldier."

"Our brothers may have undertaken a dangerous task with a noble and honorable intent," Janice corrected gently. "We would be going to advise and aid them, should that prove necessary." Grace looked chastened. "Besides," Janice continued, looking northwest toward the pitch-black clouds. "Tonight may be the night we need to walk."

"Um…ah…" Felicity and Grace murmured, looking at each other uncomfortably.

"Sisters," Janice said, turning to them with the wisp of a smile. "I am a great sinner who has done terrible deeds, but I am still a virgin."

Rising Darkness

The gathering clouds blotting out the sunset enabled the team to advance the schedule by twenty minutes or so. The action was planned for after dark, but there still needed to be enough light for the precision shooting that would kick off the party.

Three snipers wearing ghillie suits had crept to their places in the ditch. Between the suits and the tall reeds and the gathering dusk, they were confident that they lay unspotted in the greenery – except by the mosquitos. Dan, the most experienced sniper, watched the fading light carefully and whispered updates into his microphone. Finally, he judged conditions to be ready.

"Green Major, Gold Teams, stand by," he said, sighting in on the first target. "Shooters, stand by, on my mark."

The two other shooters only had one target each: the perimeter cameras pointing along the fences. Dan had a camera to target as well, but first he had to take out the power. Fortunately, they'd made it easy: the site drew everything through a conveniently placed transformer sitting on a pole just outside the north fence. Once he'd dealt with that, he'd take out the cameras on the northeast property corner – or, more accurately, their power cables. All the cameras were shielded by metal plates, doubtless to hide them from sight and protect them from plinkers. But their power cables ran right down the outside of the posts, dark black against weathered wood. Easy targets.

Dan peered through his scope at the red laser dot dancing on the insulator at the top of the transformer. "I am taking out power – now." He squeezed off a shot and saw a satisfactory spray of sparks. Without stopping to admire his work, he shifted his scope to the camera power cables. "Camera takeout – three, two, one, fire." Another echo of three shots that sounded almost simultaneous. Through his scope Dan could see pieces of shattered cabling driven deep into the post. No power was getting through there.

"Second shots?" Dan asked.

"East cable blown through," Phillip Schaeffer reported.

"Southeast cable totaled," Paul Stover whispered.

"Green Major, go, go. Gold, stand by," Dan said, shrugging out of his ghillie suit and tossing it over his rifle. Stepping out of the ditch, he began quick-walking south along the road to meet up with Phillip. Cletus and Sixtus were already at the fence cutting the wiring. It went against Dan's military training to put twins on the same team, but he couldn't deny that they moved like one man and could almost read each other's minds, which was why they'd pulled the difficult assignment on this mission. Dan and Phillip were just along to insure they made it there and back.

"Inside the fence, throwing jammers," came Sixtus's voice in Dan's earpiece.

*   *   *

"What the hell?" growled Riley Bryant as the lights went out and the battery backup under the desk started beeping.

"Storm moving in," Eli said. "Shut that damn thing off and sit tight – it should come back on in a minute." They waited while Riley groped in the dark to find and silence the shrill device. After a minute or so, Riley's phone rang.

"That was Nate over at the factory," Riley said after a brief conversation. "They're down over there, too. Better get the generator going." Grumbling, Eli felt his way through the dark room and out the door. Fortunately, the security shed was right off the storage warehouse, just around the corner from the generator hut. After a couple more minutes Riley heard the rumble of the engine and the lights flickered back to life. He began the tedious task of bringing the monitors back up.

"Well, crap," Riley pronounced as Eli returned.

"What?"

"Looks like we've got some kind of damage on the east side," Riley said. "The perimeter cameras are clean out, and some of the fence cameras are acting flaky."

"Flaky?" Eli asked.

230

"See for yourself – ghosting, snow, signal loss," Riley pointed. "I wonder if we got struck by lightning."

"I didn't hear any thunder," Eli began, but Riley's phone rang again.

"Yeah, Nick?" Riley answered. "I was just showing Eli – we may have taken a hit. The perimeter cameras are gone, and some of the – what? No, nothing, just blank screens." He listened for a minute. "Look, I'm sure it's just related to the outage. We can – all right, all right." Riley hung up with a curse.

"What?" Eli said.

"Nervous Nick there is spooked by the power outage – as if we don't get those all the time. He wants us all to head out into the woods to listen for intruders. Armed."

"Armed? Even that fool Pemberton? He's gonna blow somebody's head off."

"He wants us all out there. He's shutting down the line and getting the workers back in the barracks. And I don't think you have to worry about Pemberton – he's got gate duty."

*   *   *

The Gold Team of Todd Beck and Jake Kyle had waded across the reed-clogged ditch and were at the west fence when they got word that Green Minor, Dan and Phillip, were inside the east fence. That was their cue. Todd switched on the jamming balls while Jake made short work of the fencing with wire cutters. They slipped through the gap and Todd began scanning for low branches while Jake tied one end of the twine securely to the fence. As the rescue team, they had a unique problem: getting the workers out. Todd and Jake were wearing locating transponders and earpieces, and could be guided by the Control Team with their tracking tablets and mapping programs. But a hundred or so kids groping through moderately thick woods wouldn't have such devices, and might go astray. This problem was solved with the time-proven expedient of a long trace of tough twine which the men could unroll behind them as they went. Even confused and frightened kids could follow a line through dark woods to freedom.

"Gold Team in, jammers hung," Todd reported.

"Gold, go," Control replied. The two men began working their way toward the barracks with the help of their night vision devices.

*　　　　　*　　　　　*

Charlie sat in the clearing before his fire pit, which was cold ashes just now. It would not do to have a fire lit, not this night. Since his trailer sat on a slight rise, he could look down the slope into the woods, where he could see the headlights of vehicles moving and hear men shouting. So it always was – men would holler and bluster and threaten. But take away their sight and sap their strength, and they were nothing more than whimpering cowards. Charlie closed his eyes and reached out to the earth beneath him.

*　　　　　*　　　　　*

The Green Team was making creditable progress through the trees. The two groups were "leapfrogging" past each other, with one group watching while the other moved ahead. They found some ATV trails that allowed them swifter progress along some stretches, but couldn't stay on them long. For one thing, there were ATVs out, ridden by men bearing guns of some type. For another, the trails veered away from their target, so Control kept directing them off the trails and back into the woods. Occasionally, one of the ATVs would come close, and they'd lie flat in the brush until it passed.

"Green, we show you about two-fifty, three hundred yards east southeast from target," Control reported.

"Moving," Dan answered. Everything was proceeding smoothly.

Nick and Nathan barged into the security shed to find the room vacant, the monitors illuminating empty seats.

"What the hell?" Nick growled, pulling out his phone and dialing Riley. "Yeah, it's me – where the hell are you? Yes, I did tell you to get into the woods, but I didn't mean leave the monitors unmanned. I don't know – anybody. What good is having security cameras if nobody's watching them? Yes, I know, but some of them are working. No, don't worry, I'll take care of it." He hung up with a muttered curse and started examining the screens. "Help me out here – we've got to get a handle on this situation."

"This bank of monitors here seems to be the perimeter cameras," Nate pointed out. "The gate camera is working, but the others aren't – blank screens."

"Here are the fence cams, it seems," Nick pointed at another array of monitors. "They mostly look all right, except for these few along the east fence."

"And a couple on the west," Nathan pointed to some white and shadowy screens.

"This makes no sense," Nick muttered. "I'd think damage from fluctuating power, but it's sporadic – some of them are working fine. Has anyone reported anything? Do we even have contact with anyone out there?"

Nathan shrugged and pointed to another bank of monitors. "What are these ones? They look like they're kind of propped here. Are they new?"

"Maybe," Nick dialed Riley again and asked a few questions. "Seems they're the monitors for the new cameras we placed in the woods. Doesn't anyone know how to label things around here? Why are they all dead?"

"They're motion-activated, so they don't transmit unless something moves to turn them on. That one's running," Nate pointed to a screen. "But it's not showing anything but underbrush."

"Can we scroll it back?" Nick asked, so Nate swiped the film back to where the camera flicked on. The video clearly showed a figure passing across the camera's field, then another.

"Are those our guys?" Nick asked.

"Can't be sure," Nate replied. "I think all our guys are on ATVs, but they might have dismounted. Who else would be out there?"

"Where is that camera?"

"Dunno. All we've got is these numbers in the corner of the frame," Nate pointed out.

"Damned incompetents!" Nick barked, rummaging through the papers on the desk for anything like a document that identified the camera locations. He finally gave up with a curse. "Look, most of these anomalies are to the east. Get everyone into those woods. And see if we can find some locations for these cameras!"

*   *   *

Back in the control van, Paul Stover and Chip Keller were watching the tablet that showed the map of the half-section, with the building locations overlaid onto it and the team members showing as bright green or gold dots.

"Roger, Gold," Paul acknowledged, then turned to Chip. "Gold Team reports a stall – couple of ATVs in the woods ahead. Guys riding, parking, walking around. Gold is holding position, don't think they've been spotted."

Chip grimaced. "Hope they can get moving again soon." Then into his mic, "Green Minor, you're veering a little south. Bear more to your right as you can."

Todd and Jake were waiting in the underbrush while the minutes ticked by. The two guys with the ATVs weren't doing much besides talking to each other and swinging their shotguns around. They weren't searching anywhere, and their headlights weren't even pointed into the woods. But they were barely thirty yards away, and were parked right across Gold's path.

Todd was just wondering if it would be worth trying to circle around them when one guy's phone rang. He answered, had a brief conversation, and then (thank God!) both men slung their guns on their backs, got on their ATVs, and roared off into the darkness.

"Control, Gold," Jake reported quietly. "Roadblock removed, proceeding."

"Roger, Gold," Control acknowledged. Todd took a quick sweep with the night vision scope and then remembered to flick off the IR lamp and look again. Up ahead to his right he noticed a patch of wood lit by a greenish glow.

"Control, Gold, I think I've spotted one of the woods cameras," Todd said. "Getting infrared illumination that's not ours."

"Did it spot you?" Paul asked.

"Doubt it – it's well off to our right. We'll be swinging left, though, and watching for more," Todd replied. "Advise Green that there are definitely cameras out here."

"Roger," Control acknowledged.

*   *   *

Charlie wasn't even hearing any more. He felt, all through the ancient earth, the black earth, the blood-soaked earth. He'd united with the sacrifices before the ritual, mingling his blood with theirs, so that it was not just their blood out there encircling the compound, it was his – and it was not just his blood pulsing through his veins, but theirs as well. He could feel on the earth the weight of the fallen leaves and needles, centuries of accumulation. He could feel the roots of the trees and the slow seeping of the groundwater, trammeled and subdued. He could feel the lumpy boulders scattered through the soil, mixed in by the glaciers that had buried and crushed the land not long before. He could feel the light and prickly weight of the buildings, like that of an itchy wool blanket on his back. He could feel the bustling feet of men rushing about, harried and hurried, full of their own power and self-importance. Power! Huh. What did they know of power? They made so much of fire, with their roaring, stinking engines and their power cables and their guns. All the while swarming about the surface of the earth, oblivious to its importance. Huh! He would show them power. They'd see how frail their fire was when he called on the power of the earth beneath their feet.

There, now – Charlie could feel the intruders. Quiet, disciplined, focused, very unlike the chaotic men who sought them. Stealthily they proceeded toward their goal, whatever it was. A shame they would never reach it.

Breathing deeply, Charlie began to chant the ancient words, the forbidden words, the words it had cost so much to learn. As he sang, he named the darkness, willing it to rise from the rocks and the soil, to cling to the boles of the trees as it had so long ago in the far north. By dint of the unconquered soil and the sacrificial blood and his own bitter will, he named the darkness, summoning it to him.

The darkness responded, drawn from the earth, seeping up from it, extending his senses above the ground. He reached out, seeking the intruders. He could feel the others, the fools, the supposed guards, but he ignored them. He wanted the intruders, and with his will flowing through the earth and up into the darkness, he found them. Strong men, determined men, but men nonetheless. Men born of the earth, whose bodies were made of earth, who ate only that which came from the earth.

And earth was his element tonight.

They were inside the border now, well within the circle of earth and blood, and thus within his power. He willed downward, toward the earth, drawing their strength from them, back to the ground from which it had come. In the darkness he could feel his will surrounding them, enfolding them, enmeshing them, dragging them down.

Only – his hold was slipping. What was this? The bonds would not cling to them – well, most of them. There was one, but the others seemed only lightly affected. Charlie set his teeth and made to try again when he remembered what the shaman had told him. The invocation would work on all but the Blackrobes and their followers. Bah! The cursed Blackrobes! But they were no longer a force in the land – what made they here? Charlie tried again, but with the same effect. No use wasting any more effort on that – it wasn't going to work, except on the one. Very well, he would concentrate on intensifying the darkness. It would take longer, but would serve just as well in the end.

*   *   *

"Todd, is this fog?" Jake asked from behind. Todd, who had been scanning with the monocular, looked about. The dim woods seemed hazier than they had been, thick with a heavy murk that seemed to cling to the lower tree trunks. But it didn't look light and misty like nighttime mist. What little light there was seemed to die in it.

"Looks like fog, but very dark and dense," Todd acknowledged. "Control, Gold, were we expecting fog?" The air was thick and damp with the oncoming cloud line, and weird things could happen under these circumstances.

"Stand by, Gold," came Control's response.

"Todd, this is getting weird," Jake said in an edgy voice. Todd glanced back to see Jake looking about sharply at what looked like opaque mist that reached up to his waist. With alarm Todd saw the same dark vapor swirling about his own hips. He couldn't see even his knees. Reluctantly he swung his hand through it, looking at his fingers as if expecting them to come out stained. They weren't, and the stuff hadn't felt any different, but it was definitely heavy and opaque – and rising. Todd could no longer see his belt buckle.

"Todd, man," Jake said, close to panic. "What is this?"

"Calm down, Jake," Todd said, though he was alarmed to see that the dark fog had risen to Jake's chest. "Just stay where you are." He lifted the night vision scope and saw Jake clearly, but the fog was just a dark bank – he could see nothing within it.

"Gold, Control," came a faint and raspy voice in Todd's ear. "Can you describe what you're seeing? We're getting descriptions of atmospheric phenomena from Green Team."

"Like fog, but dense, very dense," Todd said. "Not light like mist, but dark like very murky water. The night vision scope can't penetrate it. It's…it's rising fast."

"Todd!" Jake exclaimed sharply. Todd could see the mist nearly to his neck, and he was lifting his chin as if it was rising water.

"Grab that tree, just to your right," Todd directed. "Don't drop the twine!"

"Gold, Control, please say again, you're breaking up," came the faint and rough response.

"You're breaking up, Control," Todd replied, his own heart hammering as he noticed the rising mist approaching his neck.

"Todd, I can't see, man, I can't see!" Jake nearly screamed. Todd looked his way and saw nothing but dense mist.

"Stay calm, Jake, and stay quiet," Todd urged. "We still have enemies out here. Have you still got the tree and the twine?"

"Yeah," came the shaky response. Todd tipped his chin up a bit as the mist swirled higher, but then reassured himself – you could breathe in fog. Jake clearly was, if he could call out. Todd's whole body was immersed in it, and it didn't feel any different from the night air. But Todd still felt a moment of panic when the mist finally rose above his head, totally blinding him.

"Jake, you there, man?" Todd called. The mist was impossibly dark, thick with a blackness that seemed to be pressing in on his eyeballs.

"Right here," came the answer.

"How far can you see? Lean toward the tree."

"About four, maybe six inches," Jake reported.

"That's about what I'm getting, too," Todd said, moving his hand toward his face until he could just discern its outline.

"This is really strange fog," Jake said.

"It is – let me check with Control. Control, Gold, we're closed in with this fog. Please report our positions relative to goal." There was nothing but whispering silence in Todd's ear. "Control, Gold, do you copy?" Todd waited a minute before trying again. "Control, Gold, do you copy?"

"Damn. Todd, they're not answering!" Jake said sharply.

"Jake, listen," Todd said firmly. "Calm down. I don't know what's going on or how long this will last. I'll keep trying to raise Control. If I don't succeed within three minutes, I want you to follow the twine back out to the fence. Understand me?"

"But – what about you?" Jake asked.

"I don't want to start groping around for you in this murk. I'd probably get really lost, and then you'd get lost finding me. Under these circumstances, our first priority is to reestablish contact with Control. If the earpieces don't work, our fallback is you walking back out to them. I'll just stay right here until this lifts or someone comes to get me."

"But what about the mission?" Jake asked.

Todd sighed heavily in the darkness. "We may be able to salvage the mission if this lifts soon enough, but we can't complete it in this. We can just pray, and hope this all blows away soon."

"All right," Jake acceded.

"Control, this is Gold, do you copy?" Todd began to hail in the swirling darkness. "Control, this is Gold."

*　　　　　*　　　　　*

"What the hell was that?" Nick barked. He and Nate were still in the security shed, talking to the guys out in the woods, trying to impose some sort of order on the chaos. Now they were getting reports of some kind of thick fog that was complicating matters, and there had just come a grinding crash from outside.

"Don't know," Nate said, sticking his head out the door. "Damn, it's thick out here, Nick." Through the open door they could still hear banging and crashing intermingled with a noise that sounded like screams.

"Are those pipes clanging?" Nick asked.

"Nick," Nathan said, pulling the door shut and looking at him with an ashen face. "I think the hogs are out."

*   *   *

"Green, Control, do you read?" Chip called again, to no avail. "Dammit, now we've lost the entire Green Team as well! What's going on?"

"I don't know, but it's more than just comms," Paul said gravely, pointing to the tablet screen. A flecked haze was spreading across it, obscuring the glowing dots.

"What the hell?" Chip cried in dismay.

Just then a car that had been coming up the road pulled over in front of them, its headlights shining right into the van's windshield. Then the headlights were doused and four people got out – three women and a man.

"Is that Doc Peterson?" Paul asked.

"I think so," Chip confirmed. "Who are the girls? I think I recognize one, but not the other two."

The man Chip knew as Luke came around to the van window. "Hey, Chip! I thought this van looked familiar. So, is this where it's happening? Where the action is tonight?"

"I don't know what you're talking about," Chip answered shortly. "And if you don't mind, we're dealing with a situation here."

"Of course, you are," said the girl at Luke's shoulder. Chip remembered her now from Lawrence's place, where she'd been introduced as Teresa. "You're trying a rescue, but you've run into – unexpected opposition? Unusual conditions?"

Chip and Paul stared at each other in stunned silence.

"It's okay," Janice reassured them cheerily. "We're here to help. Just guide us to the – what, driveway? Main entrance? – and we'll take it from there."

Chip and Paul looked at each other with more consternation. Derek smiled and patted Chip's arm. "It's all right. We received intelligence that you might be attempting something tonight, but also learned that you could encounter more than the usual opposition. So, we're the reinforcements – or at least they are." He pointed at the women. "I'm here in case I'm needed, which hopefully I won't be."

"But...you...what can...?" Chip stammered.

"Look," Janice continued in the same cheery tone but with just a hint of firmness. "We've got a job, and time is running out. Are you going to take us to the main entrance or not? You aren't responsible beyond that."

"The main gate is locked and monitored by a camera," Chip explained.

"I'm confident you'll be able to deal with those obstacles," Janice replied.

Paul and Chip looked at each other again, then at the hazed-out tablet. "Bolt cutters are in the back," Chip said, and Paul got out to open the door and grab the heavy-handled tool. He also clipped a pistol onto his belt.

"C'mon," Paul said. "It's just up around this corner. We'll walk rather than draw attention by driving." They walked quickly up to the corner and then west along the road, with the fenced and posted property to their right. The western sky was still dark and ominous, but the clouds in the east were catching enough reflected glow to cast a little light on the road.

"There's the gate," Paul pointed. "The camera monitoring it is on the post just above and to the right."

"What are you going to do about it?" Derek asked.

Paul handed Derek the bolt cutters and drew his pistol. "You hold these while I get a little closer."

As they drew near the gate, Paul stepped off the road and through the brush until he was standing almost directly beneath the camera. With a couple quick shots, he shattered the lens and body. "Now," he said, taking the bolt cutters up to the gate, which was chained and padlocked.

"Wait – what's that?" Felicity asked, turning to look down the fence to their left. Soon they all heard what sounded like someone thrashing through the weeds. Paul held his pistol ready, but the panting young man who came stumbling into view was clearly no threat.

"Jake!" cried Grace, running to her brother.

"Grace?" Jake asked, clinging to her. "What are you –"

"We're here to help," Grace interrupted. "What's going on?"

"In the woods...couldn't see..." Jake gasped. "Todd told me...follow twine out. Darkness all around."

"Darkness?" Janice asked sharply.

"Yeah," Jake confirmed. "Like fog, rising from the ground – except black like smoke."

"Get that gate open," Janice ordered, then turned to Grace and Felicity as Paul cut the chain and swung the gate away. "Ladies – sisters – it's our time. May I ask who your patronesses are?"

"Catherine of Siena," Felicity said.

"Rose of Lima," Grace answered.

"And mine is Teresa of Avila," Janice smiled. "May they walk beside us into the darkness, that we may be six."

"Or, who knows?" Felicity said with a grin. "Since it seems to be Virgin's Night Out, we might get a seventh."

Virgins' Walk

The Green Team had drawn close together as the darkness had risen, mainly because Dan had suffered some kind of attack. He'd collapsed to the ground, his heart pounding and his breath labored. Thus, the men were within arm's length of each other when the thick murk filled the woods. They, too, debated what to do once their communications failed. The urgency of their situation was hastened by the sounds they now heard in the darkness around them – roaring motors, human cries and screams, other high-pitched animal noises, and the occasional roar of shotguns or crack of pistols.

Dan wanted the others to try to get out, to retrace their steps by groping through the trees. They refused to do this, insisting that wherever they went, Dan would go with them. But Cletus and Sixtus wanted Phillip to stay with Dan while they went on, completed their mission, and then went for help.

"What?" gasped Dan. "You can't see a foot in this fog, and you've no guidance. How can you find your way to the target, much less back out to the road?"

"We can," Cletus said, and Sixtus nodded. "I can't explain it, but we always know the points of the compass, and we always know where we are in relation to each other. It's always been that way. You can't see, but I'm currently pointing due north. Our last fix had us two hundred and fifty yards southeast of the generator. That means it's northwest, which is that way," he pointed into the murk. "Together we can make it through and back."

"But to what end?" Dan asked. "The mission has failed. Control reported that Gold was experiencing similar conditions. They're stopped, too. There's no mission to complete. The best we can hope for is to get out intact and try another day."

"There's still a mission," Sixtus said emphatically. "We've been stymied temporarily, but there are other resources coming in. We just need to do our part, which is shutting down that generator."

"What resources…?" Dan began, but Cletus cut him off.

"Phillip, stay with him no matter what. We won't be long. C'mon, Six." And they were off, quickly swallowed by the fog.

*   *   *

Caleb Hubbart and Joe Pemberton had been assigned to watch the main drive. They'd seen the dark fog in the woods around them, but it hadn't seemed to rise as high across the cleared space of the drive. It surged and flowed like shadowy syrup, but never even got to their waists. The two thought it no more than curious. The distance kept them from hearing the growing cries and other alarming noises among the thick trees farther north. Their job was to stay at the curve and guard the drive. For this they'd been given the finest rifles on the site, with precision scopes and laser targeting.

"Hey – I think we got something coming," Caleb said. He stood up from where he'd been leaning against the UTV, and Joe pitched his cigarette aside. They peered down the shadowed drive and listened carefully.

"Definitely," Joe affirmed. "You can hear 'em on the gravel."

"Then they can hear how we deal with trespassers," growled Caleb, shouldering his rifle and sighting down the drive. "They're coming around the bend now. Looks like three of them."

"You sure?" Joe asked, sighting in. "Seems like more – five at least, maybe six."

"You're right," Caleb affirmed. "But some of them look – lighter? In fact, I think seven – see the one out in front – ahhh!"

The men collapsed, dropping their rifles and clutching their faces. Their eyes were seared by white images which looked like people, but which glowed with fierce intensity. The brilliance persisted no matter how tightly they closed their eyes, clawing at their nerves, piercing their tissues, filling their eye sockets with agony.

*   *   *

The virgins hadn't even noticed the men, much less the rifles aimed at them, when the screams of pain tore the night.

"O dear," Janice said. "I think I hear our opponents. We must go help them."

"But –" Grace began, pointing to the roiling cloud of dark fog hugging the ground around them.

"That's what we're here to pierce," Janice assured her. "This is only the leading edge – it's much higher and thicker farther along. But we will bear the light through it. And speaking of light, these lads have had a bit too much." They were now beside the writhing men, and Janice knelt. Felicity and Grace saw that where Janice was, the dense fog thinned, or at least permitted more light through.

"Here, here," Janice was instructing Joe, grabbing his wrist to stop his rolling about. "Let me see your eyes." She forced her hand under his, laying it across his eye sockets. His struggles immediately ceased.

"You do it for him, Grace," Janice instructed, pointing to Caleb. "Don't be afraid, Rose will help." Skeptical but willing, Grace slipped her hand over Caleb's eyes, stilling his trembling.

"Who – who are you? And what did you do?" Caleb asked, but the women were already standing to go.

"I can't see a thing," Joe said, groping about.

"We'll deal with that on the way back," Janice said, picking up the rifles and pitching them into the woods. "Stay by your vehicle." Just then a phone on the dash of the UTV started ringing. Janice nodded to Felicity, who threw the phone into the woods as well.

"Come, sisters, we haven't much time," Janice urged, and they resumed their walk. As they proceeded, the trees grew thicker overhead, cutting off even the dim reflected glow from the eastern clouds. The dark mist was pouring out of the woods on either side and was deepening along the drive with every yard they advanced. Grace and Felicity were a little hesitant as they moved into the fog, but emboldened by Janice's confidence, they kept striding. As they passed completely into the mist, they were surprised to find that they could see – in fact, the area around them was illuminated by a faint golden glow. They could see the mist, but they could also see through the mist, at least a short distance. Grace could see the road ahead, and trunks of trees on either side.

"What's happening?" Felicity asked in amazement.

"We're walking in the Power, even as our patron sisters did," Janice explained. "Light is what we need to complete our task, so light is provided. 'This is the night of which it is written: The night shall be as bright as day'!" Janice laughed and twirled as she walked.

"But – how?" Felicity persisted. "Humans don't glow."

"It's not our light, we're just bearing it," Janice replied. "It's coming with us, as our Companions are. Don't be concerned with it just now. Watch the road and attend to our mission."

"Okay," Felicity responded. "Where are we going?"

"Up ahead," Janice pointed. "Not the first building we see, I think, but one of the ones beyond it. We'll know it when we see it."

"All right," Felicity said, shrugging and glancing at Grace. But just then there appeared a flicker in the glow.

"Oh!" said Grace with a startled cry. "What – what was that?" She suddenly felt more exposed and vulnerable.

Without breaking stride, Janice gazed forward into the mist. "One of our Companions has gone on ahead – she's needed. Don't be afraid, we are still many, and the beings of the darkness will not approach the light. But we must hasten."

*   *   *

"Dammit! Now the gate camera is down!" Nick snarled. "What the hell is going on?"

"I dunno, Nick," Nate said nervously, glancing at his phone battery level. He'd been calling the guys out there in the field, trying to get reports. Very few were answering, and those that did told of nothing but a thick fog that obscured vision and hindered movement. There was no sign of any intruders, and phone reception was weak and shaky – there seemed to be some kind of problem with the signal. Nate's battery was almost dead and Nick's was close to twenty percent. Nick scanned what few monitors seemed to still be working for any sign of movement.

"Oh!" Nate suddenly cried as one of the monitors showed something moving into its field. It was one of the fence cameras in the northwest corner of the property. It had been showing nothing but tree trunks fading into the thickening mist. Suddenly, a man on an ATV came charging through the trees, moving far too quickly for being off trail. He kept glancing back over his shoulder, and therefore didn't see the fallen log that lay across his path. Spotting it too late, he tried to veer sharply, but only succeeded in toppling the ATV on its side and throwing himself to the ground. He scrambled back to his feet immediately, pushing through the brush with almost frantic haste, continually looking back toward the woods.

Watching in numb horror, Nick and Nathan saw two great hogs come charging through the trees. They were partly shrouded by the low mist, but their goal was clear, and the man knew it. He tried to run but kept stumbling, and the hogs closed in quickly. He was making for the fence, and so passed under the camera's field, but the monitor showed the pigs closing in on a spot, charging and trampling.

Nick reached over and yanked the monitor's cable out. It was collapsing, crumbling all around. It was over. Only one thing remained.

"Nate," Nick said hollowly. Nathan turned to him with horror-stricken eyes. "The code to activate those lights in the barracks. Send it."

"You...you sure, Nick?"

"I'm sure. They're not getting out. None of us are getting out. Better it should be quick and clean than...that." He pointed at the dark monitor.

With trembling hands, Nathan tapped up the app and punched the code to trigger the lights. Tyrone – trusting, dutiful, doomed Tyrone – would do the rest. Then Nate's phone began flashing the red exclamation point that signaled a nearly dead battery. "Nick, I'm gonna…I'm gonna go, before those things move this way."

"You do that," Nick said, leaning over the table and staring with hollow eyes. "Goodbye, Nate."

Without a further word, Nate bolted for the door and out into the pitch-black night.

                    *   *   *

Cletus and Sixtus were feeling a little less confident about their directional instincts, but they kept moving doggedly onward through the mist-shrouded woods. They'd adopted the leapfrog strategy, where one would remain stationary while the other groped and stumbled beyond him, stopping just at the edge of audible range. Then the stationary one would come along, following the calls until he reached and passed his brother. They'd given up any pretense of stealth, figuring that whatever noise they made would go unnoticed against the backdrop of cries, screams, and occasional gunshots that echoed through the woods. These were eerie and terrifying, but they tried to ignore them and focus on their goal.

"Right here! Keep coming!" Cletus was calling when a familiar hand reached through the fog. "There you are!" he said, grabbing it and pulling his brother close. Sixtus was panting and had a scratch on his cheek. "You okay, man?"

"Fine – just took a tumble," Sixtus said. "How much farther you think we've got?"

"I'm hoping we're within eighty yards," Cletus replied. "That way, right?" He pointed off into the mist.

Sixtus stood for a moment, orienting himself to north. "Yes," he confirmed, pointing in the same direction.

"All right, then, off you go," Cletus said, and his brother plunged into the darkness. "Marco!"

"Polo!" Sixtus's reply came through the fog.

*   *   *

There was something in the air, something not right. Everyone was on edge. They were all in the barracks, but nobody had come to turn out the lights. Some workers were dutifully under the covers, in case a super came walking through the door, but others were standing around near bunks and in corners, talking in low, nervous whispers. Something was going on.

Tyrone was splitting the difference, sitting on his bunk but chatting with Jackson, who was hovering about. They were both speculating about what might be happening when there was a collective gasp, and one of the girls gave a little shriek.

The yellow lights had started to pulse.

The yellow lights.

"What's that?" Jackson asked, but Tyrone ignored him. Rising to his feet, he stared at the flashes hypnotically. So that was it. This was a safety drill. Something was going on with the safety of the barracks. Mr. Nathan had appointed him safety officer.

He had a job to do.

"Hey, where you goin'?" Jackson asked, as Tyrone began walking to the end of the barracks. Tyrone ignored Jackson. As instructed, he hadn't told anyone he'd been appointed safety officer, and nobody had even noticed the new switch box on the wall. He focused on it as he walked.

Suddenly, a girl appeared along the wall, just by the switch box. Where had she come from? She had to have been moving fast for Tyrone not to have noticed her approach. Who was she? Tyrone knew all the workers, and he'd never seen this girl before. For one thing, she wasn't wearing the blue coveralls that workers always wore, but a black skirt, plain white blouse, and rough brown shawl. She had dark black hair that was pulled back and her skin was dark – not as dark as Tyrone's, more like Fredrico's.

She was the most beautiful woman Tyrone had ever seen.

"Who are you?" Tyrone asked. She looked at him with kind but slightly sad eyes, smiled gently, but said nothing. "Are you supposed to be in here?" Still she made no response, but kept looking at Tyrone as if she wanted him to understand something.

"Can't you talk?" Tyrone asked. "Look, there's something I need to do," he said, stepping toward the switch box. The girl still didn't speak, but she stepped in front of the box and waved her hands as if warning him off.

Tyrone was in a quandary. There was something about this strange girl that made him want to trust her, but he had his instructions. "Look," he pleaded. "Mr. Nathan told me to – it's about safety." But the girl stayed in place, blocking his way and shaking her head slowly. "Please move! The lights are flashing, and I'll get in trouble if I don't!" But she wouldn't step aside, and Tyrone didn't know what to do. He didn't want to just push her away, but he needed to perform his task. But she just stood there, blocking his way and looking at him with those dark black eyes and sad expression.

Then all the lights went out.

Several people screamed as the room was plunged into darkness. The yellow lights continued to flash, filling the room with an eerie flickering.

"Oh, great," Tyrone said in self-reproach, rushing to the switch. The girl had vanished, and in the pulsing light he found the switch box. Opening the plate, he punched the button frantically. Nothing seemed to happen. "Oh no, oh no," Tyrone muttered, holding the button down. He'd blown it. He'd really blown it. Mr. Nathan had entrusted him with a safety job, and he'd let himself get delayed. Whatever the button was supposed to do probably needed power, and the power was down again! He'd let himself get delayed, and now it was too late, and who knew what kind of problems were going to happen. Mr. Nathan would probably strip him of the job now, and make somebody else the safety officer.

Behind him, the workers were getting noisier as their panic grew in the darkness, aggravated by the eerie flashing of the yellow strobes. Tyrone sweated and panted, pushing the button again and again and praying for something to happen.

Then there was some noise by the door at the south end. Everyone looked as it swung open. They were expecting a couple of supers to come through, and maybe the lights to come back on. Instead they saw a soft golden glow coming through the doorway. A woman stepped in, a shadow against the glow.

"Hello?" the woman called into the dark barracks.

* * *

"Got it," Sixtus said, coming out the door of the generator hut and dropping to sit beside Cletus.

"What'd you do?" Cletus asked.

"Found a valve in the fuel line leading to the filter. Closed it and smashed the handle. Even if they find the damage, they'll have a hell of a time fixing it, and they'll need to for the engine to start," Sixtus explained.

Cletus grinned and held up his hand for a high five, which Sixtus returned.

"So – what now?" Sixtus asked.

"First, we rest a bit. Then, I think it best to head due east until we hit the fence. From there we can work southward until we find the break, then get out and get help. We've zero chance of finding Dan and Phillip in this fog. Best thing we can do is go for help, and maybe wait until daylight."

"Maybe," Sixtus said ominously. "Always providing they survive that long in…all this." He looked around at the thick fog. The horrible noises had tapered off, but the woods now seemed full of a malicious, brooding silence.

"And always providing we make it out ourselves," Cletus added grimly.

* * *

Black Charlie sat immobile, his hands still, his eyes closed, his consciousness dissipated through the earth and up into the thick fog that now nearly filled the woods. He could feel the fury of the rampaging swine, the crunch of bone and the salty taste of blood. They were no man's plaything! The panic and desperation of the hunted men was like a drug, intoxicating and absorbing him.

Charlie was so deep in his trance that he didn't hear the restless motion from behind his trailer, or the angry grunting and heavy sound of weight being thrown against the pipe fence. Only the great crash of its fall managed to get Charlie's attention, and by the time he'd brought himself back, there was nothing to hear but a vague scuffling. Charlie turned to peer at his trailer.

All he saw was a pair of red eyes glowering back at him through the fog.

*　　　　*　　　　*

On the road outside the gate, everyone was waiting with growing impatience. After the three women had walked through the gate into the fog, no one heard anything from anyone. The tracer equipment was still displaying snow and none of the phones were working. With the gate camera destroyed, Paul and Chip felt safe in bringing the vehicles around to park them across from the gate and await developments. Derek took advantage of the lull to lay out some medical equipment on the floor of the van, making his best guess as to what he might need when the girls reappeared.

They were still pacing the road when another van pulled up. It contained Lawrence, Annette, Grandpa, and Tyler, along with some crates of hastily assembled supplies. Derek was glad to see the boxes of fruits and snack bars, cases of water, and piles of blankets. They were likely to be of more use than his bandages and splints – or at least he hoped so.

"Good thinking on the supplies," Derek complimented Lawrence.

"It was Annette's idea, not mine," Lawrence admitted. "She has great faith in the outcome of tonight's events."

"I'm glad somebody does," Derek muttered.

*   *   *

The girls were escorting the liberated workers back down the access drive as quickly as they could. Fortunately for the circumstances, the youngsters complied with any instructions given by adults, even strangers. The girls organized them into a long group stretching down the road with Janice leading, Grace about halfway back, and Felicity bringing up the rear. The youngsters were warned to stay together, not stray to the sides of the road, and to move quickly. The mysterious glow seemed to accompany the whole parade of them as they moved briskly past the dark buildings and through the shadowed woods.

Grace found herself walking beside a black lad who was almost as tall as she, though very wiry. He was looking about with wonder and curiosity.

"Are you the safety people?" he asked Grace.

"The what?" Grace replied with a smile.

"The safety people," the lad repeated. "Mr. Nathan made me the safety officer, and I was supposed to press the button when the yellow lights flashed, but when I went to, the pretty girl didn't want me to, so I didn't know what to do. Then the lights went out, and the girl went away so I pressed the button then, but nothing happened, and I was worried. But then you opened the door and let us out, so I was wondering if you were the safety people, and if you came because I pressed the button."

Grace understood almost none of this, but the boy's simple enthusiasm made her grin. "Then I guess we are the safety people, because we're here to take you to safety."

"Good," the lad broke into a big smile. "Was the pretty girl a safety person, too? I never saw her before, but she really didn't want me to press that button. You remind me a little of her."

"Why, thank you," Grace replied. "I don't know about anyone in the building, but this seems to be a night of wonders, so it wouldn't surprise me. I'm Grace – what's your name?"

"I'm Tyrone. Tyrone One, because there's another Tyrone. He's up there, so they call him Tyrone Two to tell us apart –"

"Help!" came a frantic cry from the darkness to their left. "Oh, God, please help!" There was a crashing noise and the girls halted the column. Janice came back to stand by Grace.

"Hello?" Janice called, and a man came stumbling out of the woods, gasping and choking.

"Light! Are you real?" the man cried.

"We are real," Janice replied clearly. "If you wish to escape the darkness, you are welcome to come with us, but we must hurry."

"Escape?" the man pleaded as he staggered up to them. "Oh, God, yes – please take me with you!"

"Mr. Nathan?" Tyrone asked in amazement as the glow fell on the man's face.

"Tyrone? You're alive? You escaped – all of you escaped? Thank God – I felt so terrible, asking you –"

"We must move," urged Janice. "Come with me." She took Nathan with her up to the front of the column and soon they were all moving again.

"It was Mr. Nathan who made me safety officer," Tyrone continued his rambling. "He was our line super. He was nice – for a super, that is. He tried to be fair, not like some of them, who were just mean. He sure looked bad. Why was he in the woods? Why are the woods so dark?"

"I don't know," Grace admitted, then changed the subject. "Where are you from, Tyrone?"

"Flint, I think. At least, people would talk about Flint, before I came here to the factory."

"Is that where your family is?"

Tyrone looked troubled. "I don't know about a family. There were just the homes. Mrs. Jacobsens' was nice, but the

Courtney's not so much. That was the last one before they brought me here."

Grace's heart almost broke hearing this matter-of-fact recounting of the lad's bleak existence. With tears in her eyes, she laid a hand on his shoulder. "Tell you what, Tyrone – you're never going to have to go back to the factory again."

Tyrone looked at her in stark amazement. "Really? Never?"

"Never," Grace promised. "And I'll tell you what else – if you want a family, we'll find you a family."

"Really?" gasped Tyrone. "Can – can I live with you? You're really pretty and seem really nice."

Grace smiled. "Thank you. I'm not sure about my family exactly, but I promise you this – we'll be good friends and live as close as we can, and I'll come visit you often. Will that do?"

"That's great!" Tyrone said, seizing her hand in gratitude. "You safety people are terrific!"

Up ahead, the column was slowing as they came upon the curve in the drive and the UTV standing there. The two men clung to it, listening intently to the sound of the approaching crowd.

"Who's there?" Caleb called.

"Keep moving, kids," Janice urged, directing them along the other side of the path. Some of the kids recognized Joe or Caleb, and were hanging back out of fear. "Don't worry about them, just keep moving. Grace, can you come up and lead?" Janice dropped back to deal with the men, and Nathan stayed with her.

"Caleb? Joe? Is that you?" Nathan asked.

The men looked about in all directions. "Is that you, Nate?"

"It is," Nathan answered. "Guys, it's all gone to hell in there. Everything's busted, the power's gone, the hogs are loose. It's over. I'm getting out."

"The hell you say!" barked Caleb. "Who are you to be talking like that, Nate?"

"It's over, I'm telling you! They're letting the workers out – that's them going by now."

"What?" Caleb snarled, grabbing with one hand so that Nathan jumped back. "Damn you! The workers? Where's Riley? Where's my dad?"

"Your dad's back in the security shed in the dark, last I knew," Nathan replied. "The woods are full of darkness and the hogs are out. I'm getting out now, and to hell with it all."

Caleb started a profane response to this, but Janice interrupted him sharply. "We have no time. If you would come, you must come now. Your blindness can be healed, or you may remain in the darkness."

"I'm coming, I'm coming," choked Joe Pemberton, reaching out. "Nate, I know we haven't been friends – in fact, I've been a jackass. But help me now, and I'll thank you forever. I can't see a thing."

"I'll help you, Joe," Nathan said, grasping his hand. "I won't leave you in this darkness. I know what it's like. I wouldn't leave any man in this darkness no matter what. You coming, Caleb?"

"No, damn you, you effing traitor!" howled Caleb. "You come back here! You take me to my dad, or I'll –"

"Come," Janice urged the men along the drive, leaving Caleb screaming curses at their backs. They followed the column of workers around the curve and out through the gate onto the road.

The workers were milling about in joy and mystification. Paul, Annette, and Derek were moving among them, while Lawrence and Grandpa were on phones calling for more help. Janice urgently sought out Grace and Felicity, and took them to Chip.

"Our work is not yet finished," she explained. "Have you heard from the teams?"

"Not yet," Chip admitted. "Still dead air and snow on the screen."

"We must find them. Where are they?"

"One team in two groups entered through a cut in the fence here, about halfway up on the east side," Chip pointed to the display. "Another team of two men, the rescue team, went in from the west, about here. Of those, Jacob came back, leaving only

Todd. There should be twine tied to the fence that will lead you right to where he'll be, if he hasn't moved."

"Grace, why don't you take the west side, while Felicity and I take the east?" Janice asked.

"The guys went in across the ditch, but there's a very narrow track that runs along the base of the west fence. It's all dirt and weeds, but one person could do it," Chip explained to Grace. She nodded and ran off toward the corner.

"Call for help for these," Janice said, waving at the workers. "But no authorities until we return with the teams."

Grace made the best time she could along the narrow trail that Chip had mentioned. Though it was fully dark and the black bank of clouds in the west was drawing closer, she could still see well enough to get by. She supposed the glow was still accompanying her – she must still need it.

Grace found the cut in the fence and, sure enough, there was the twine tied right where Jake said it would be. The dense fog still swirled just inside the trees, and it looked more intimidating to her now that she was alone instead of with a team. But she steeled herself with the thought that Todd was in there by himself.

"Okay, St. Rose, help me now," Grace whispered as she took the twine and plunged into the fog. Her vision was curtailed, but she could still see well enough to trace the twine leading through the trees. After following the twine for about ten minutes she began calling out, figuring she must be getting near. Her voice seemed to fall flat and dead in the heavy air, but eventually she thought she heard a response.

"Hello?" the dim voice called.

"Todd? Is that you? It's me – Grace."

"Grace?"

"Yes – are you by the twine?"

"I am – I haven't moved since Jake left."

Grace hurried along and soon came to the end of the twine. She could see Todd about ten yards beyond, leaning against a tree.

"Todd!" she cried, running toward him. He turned to look at her, and stood in amazement.

"Grace? Why I can see you? I haven't been able to see anything in this fog, though I've heard the most terrible things. My eyes were beginning to play tricks on me."

"A special light – no time to explain, and I don't understand anyway," Grace said, grasping his hand. "Come on, we've got to get out of here."

"Gladly," Todd replied.

On the eastern side of the woods, Felicity and Janice were pushing through the brush, calling out to the men. Eventually they heard a responding call, and angled over to find Phillip and a prostrate Dan.

"He's had some kind of attack," Phillip explained. "I don't know what it is, but he's weak and his breathing is becoming more labored."

"First thing is to get him out of these woods," Janice said. "That should improve things greatly. Where are the others?"

"They went on to shut down the generator. They said they could find their way because they have an uncanny sense of direction. I don't know if they succeeded," Phillip said.

"They did," Janice affirmed, motioning Felicity to take Dan's other arm. "So we can trust that same sense of direction to get them back to the fence."

Phillip wondered how the two women were going to lift the tall, heavy man, but some of his strength seemed to return as they helped him up. He was unsteady on his feet, but he was standing.

"That's better," Dan said. "Who are you two ladies? And how is it that I can see you?"

"Later – we need to get moving," Janice said. "Can you walk?"

"Now I can – I think," Dan replied.

"Let's go, then," Janice urged, and they started back the way they'd come. With the two women on either side of him, Dan seemed to gain strength as they proceeded. Before long they were at the fence, a little south of the break. Working their way north, they heard cries that didn't sound like desperate screams.

"Cletus? Sixtus?" Phillip called.

"Hey!" came a familiar voice in response. "Where'd you get the light?" Soon they arrived at the cut in the fence, and the tired and battered twins emerged from the fog to meet them.

"Hey, Dan! Back on your feet, I see," Sixtus said.

"Still weak, but compared to how I've been feeling, I could take on a lion," Dan replied.

"Gentlemen, we need to move," Janice pointed through the gap in the fence.

"Gladly," Cletus assured her.

By the time the teams returned to the gate, the assembly was beginning to resemble a block party. More support, summoned by Lawrence, had arrived with supplies. Grace had returned with Todd, and Dan had almost completely recovered his strength. Derek had offered to examine any of the children who needed it, but they were all in reasonable health and far more interested in the edibles than in being prodded and questioned. Word had spread among them that they wouldn't be returning to the factory, and the resultant disbelief and giddiness were infectious.

Lawrence, however, came bustling over to the women with concern etched on his face. "Have you got a minute?" he asked Janice, and led her over to a truck where the still-blind Joe Pemberton sat on the tailgate, with Nathan, Tyler, and Chip standing by. Tyler looked agitated.

"Nathan here tells me that Nick is still in there," Tyler pointed to the woods. "I wanted to wait until you were back before doing anything. Can we get him?"

"Do we know where he is?" Janice asked.

"I left him at the security shed," Nathan said. "But he may have moved."

"Does he have a phone? Can we call him?"

"He had a phone when I left him, but it may be dead by now," Nathan replied.

"And phones have been kind of sketchy in there," Lawrence added.

"Does anyone have his number?" Janice asked.

"I do; it's right here," Tyler punched up something and handed the phone to Janice. She hit dial and listened for a minute, then handed the phone back to Tyler. "It's ringing," she said. Tyler listened for a pickup.

"Hello?" came a weak and scratchy response.

"Nick? This is Tyler."

"Tyler? What are you – why are you calling?"

"Listen, I'm right outside here. I'd like to come get you."

"Outside?" Nick asked. "What are you doing up here? How did you get outside?"

"Never mind that. You need to get out of there," Tyler said.

"Get out? Tyler, I can't get out, not now," Nick said with a sigh that sounded like a moan. "Not now, not after what I've done."

"Nick, don't talk rubbish," Tyler said sharply. "Yes, you've done wrong, but you can still get out. We can come get you." He looked at Janice and Grace, who nodded.

"No! Don't come in here! You'll get lost in the dark, and they'll find you!" Nick replied sharply. "There's nothing to come for, Tyler. It's all crumbling, collapsing into darkness. It's over, Tyler, it's all over."

"No, Nick, we can –" Tyler tried to interrupt, but Nick continued, though the signal was weak.

"I deserve this, Tyler. I took them up there, three of them, three innocent kids. I left them with that butcher, knowing what he was going to do to them. I left them in the hands of a monster and drove away, though they called to me for help. I've done a lot of terrible things, but that was the worst. For that, and for all the rest, I deserve to die in the darkness."

"Listen, Nick, it's not about what you deserve," Tyler started, but Nick was continuing.

"I always caved, Tyler, you know that. Pa would demand, and I would cave in. I never stood up to him, even for things I knew were right. I was too afraid of his anger, of his disapproval. Every time it was a choice between what he wanted and what I knew was right, I gave way. Now there's nothing left. There's no 'me' here, there's just a hollow shell with Pa's will inside. Don't come in for that. I deserve this."

"No, no, Nick," Tyler was nearly crying. "You are there, the man I love, my brother! Please let me come get you!"

"Don't come – I deserve this," Nick repeated, though his voice was fading. "Listen, you can hear them outside. They're thumping against the door, trying to get –"

The signal dropped. "Nick! Nick!" Tyler cried into the phone, then tried redialing. The line rang and rang, then cut to the voice mail message. He looked pleadingly at the women, but Janice shook her head.

"We cannot bring him out if he will not come."

Tyler nodded. Tucking his phone away, he hung his head and sniffed, while the others stood in sad silence for a minute. Then Janice turned to Lawrence.

"We're not done yet," she said. "How are the kids doing?"

"Well enough," Lawrence said. "Some say they want to go back to their families, but most say they never want to see the system again. We're trying to make arrangements for them – we've got calls out across the Thumb – but it will take some time. People should start arriving within the hour, and then we can sort things out. Once we've made provision for the kids who want to vanish, we can make the official call. Several children supposedly in the custody of Wondercare found wandering a country road."

"That'll give Andy Klein some heartburn," Chip chuckled.

"More than just him, I'm thinking," Janice said, turning to look at the fence and the darkened woods beyond. "Which leaves only one final matter."

"Yeah, what is that stuff?" Chip asked. "It looks unnatural."

"It is," Janice replied. "It's diabolical."

"I'll bet Black Charlie had a hand in it," Tyler said. "I'd bet my last dollar. But how do we get rid of it?"

"I don't know if we can," Janice said. "The most we may be able to do for now is contain it."

"Okay – how do we do that?" Lawrence asked.

Janice stood in thought for a moment, then smiled. "I have an idea. Since this seems to be our night, I think we can address this – but we may need the kids to help. Grace, can you hunt down Felicity? I'll see if I can get their attention." She walked away calling to the children, leaving the men puzzled.

"The kids?" Chip asked Lawrence.

Janice conversed with Grace and Felicity for a bit, then the three of them walked into a cluster of the liberated workers, where they were greeted with raucous cheers.

"Hey, guys, who wants to come on a parade with us?" Janice called out. "A celebration parade, a victory dance?" When the kids cheered in response, Janice went on. "Okay, you'll have to follow us. It'll be a bit of a walk, but who wants to go to bed anyway? Cheering, running, and dancing are allowed, but you need to stay reasonably together and follow us. Let's start off with a song, shall we?" There were more cheers, and the girls began clapping and singing:

I will sing unto the Lord, for He has triumphed gloriously,
The horse and rider thrown into the sea...

Before long all the children were clapping and singing at the tops of their voices. Janice began leading them toward the dirt service drive that ran along the ditch to the west of the property. The kids followed, singing, with Grace and Felicity walking on either side.

The Lord, my God, my Strength, my Song,
Has now become my victory!
The Lord, my God, my Strength, my Song...

"What is this, some kind of white magic?" Tyler asked as they watched them go.

"You could call it that," Lawrence smiled. "Three thousand year old white magic."

"Where are they going?"

"Not sure," Lawrence admitted. "But I'd guess around the property. That may be what she meant by containing. I don't know if or how that darkness can be cleansed from those woods, but maybe it can be hemmed in. And this night, they're the ones with the power to do it."

Judgment

By the time the parade returned from its circuit around the property, the kids were good and tired, though still exuberant. They didn't usually walk for over an hour, and it was well past their usual bedtime, but they were accustomed to pushing through difficulty. By that time, the flurry of calls and messages initiated by Lawrence and Grandpa had produced a near-flood of cars and vans to convey the children wherever they needed to go.

While the parade had been circling the woods, a hasty series of conference calls that included Lawrence, Annette, Grandpa, Chip, Fitz, Gil, Steve McLean, and Tyler had formulated a plan of action. No child would be required to return to the foster care system. For any who wished a home, one would be found. Those kids who had loved ones with whom they wished to reunite would be the "found" children, the explosives that would rend apart the web of deceit.

Fitz pointed out that any children who were witnesses in a prosecution of the slave operation at the factory would have complications in their lives, with subpoenas and court appearances and depositions lasting years, keeping old wounds open. After some hashing about, Tyler came up with an elegant solution: forget the factory. Make no attempt to expose it right there and then. Take the kids a reasonable distance away to "find" them. They could say they'd been forced to work at a facility somewhere, but they didn't know exactly where it was. The factory was already shut down, more thoroughly than any legal effort could have done. The exposure of the Wondercare fraud would be more than enough for the prosecutors to run with, and any connections that ultimately led to the factory complex would be a development of the foster care investigation, not a separate prosecution in its own right. This would keep the kids' involvement minimal, hastening their return to normal life, and would reduce the involvement of the tainted sheriff's department in the immediate aftermath. Besides – though nobody came out

265

and said it – they were sure that with the exception of the two who'd escaped with the liberated workers, the worst perpetrators of the atrocity of the slave factory had already received their judgment somewhere in those shadowed woods.

Derek was standing beside Lawrence and Annette as the crowd of liberated children rounded the final corner, some of them still clapping and skipping but most just trudging along. Lawrence sniffed a little and wiped an eye.

"It is a touching sight, isn't it?" Derek asked.

"Yes," Lawrence affirmed. "But I was also thinking of the poor victims who went through those gates never to come out, and those who got sent down I-75 into the sex trafficking network. Who will free them? We have failed, Luke. To let an evil this black exist undetected in our midst for so long – we have failed."

The plan decided upon was quickly executed. Most of the children were put into vehicles and driven away to host homes, which might or might not be where they eventually ended up. Grace escorted Tyrone to the car that would take him to his temporary housing and promised to come visit within a couple of days. This left only the eighteen workers who had volunteered to be the "found" ones. They were taken to a site a few miles south of Verona. There, Lawrence and Annette met up with Amy Shank, a friend who worked at the county mental health organization. It would be Amy who would call the sheriff's office with the report of a group of youngsters found wandering a country road, tired and confused. That way the mental health organization would have a record of all the children and be involved in their handling by the sheriff and the courts.

While all this was being sorted out, Derek sought out Janice, who looked exhausted.

"Good job, sister," Derek said, giving her a hug.

"Maybe, but it's not quite finished," she replied. She straightened her back and walked over to where Nathan and Joe Pemberton sat on the tailgate of a pickup. As she went, she beckoned Felicity to join her. Nathan stood at the approach of the women.

"What's your name?" Janice asked Joe.

"Joe. Joe Pemberton, ma'am," he replied.

"Do you wish to come out of the darkness and see again?"

"I...I do, ma'am."

"Then let us take your hands and touch your eyes," Janice instructed.

Felicity, who'd mostly been watching Janice, now looked more closely at the blind man. She gasped and drew back a little – in the ambient light cast by the various headlights, she saw that he was one of the men from the beach at Gull Island. The memory of that terrifying incident came flooding back, and her heart pounded in panic.

"Felicity," came a quiet voice. "Felicity!" She turned to see Janice watching her closely. "He cannot harm you now, and his healing lies in your hands."

Drawing a deep breath and rubbing her face, she looked again at the stricken man. There was no trace of the arrogance and lust his expression had worn the last time they'd met. His eyes stared helplessly into the air, and his countenance was heavy with fear and dejection. Steeling herself, she took his hand in her right hand and laid her left hand over his blind eye. Janice held his other hand and covered his other eye, and spoke in a clear voice. "See again, Joe Pemberton. Look upon evil no more, and no longer turn your hands to wickedness. Come out of the darkness and into the light." When they took their hands away, tears were streaming down his face.

"I think I can see something," he said. "It's all gray and blurry."

"Well, it is nighttime," Nathan pointed out.

"Your sight will return gradually," Janice explained. "By sundown tomorrow it should be mostly restored."

"I want to thank you for rescuing me – us – from that darkness," Nathan said quietly. "I don't know what your light was, but I thought I was lost until I saw it through the trees."

"It wasn't our light – we were just bearing it," Janice corrected. "It was sent to bring out of darkness any who would come, but your journey to the light has only begun. What are your plans?"

Nathan looked at the ground in shame. "We've done terrible things, worse than you know. We've been talking to Chip and Dan about it. We're going to stay quiet for a while at a place they know until they decide what to do. They're worried that it won't be safe for us once all this starts coming apart. We'll do what they tell us, we promise." Joe nodded in agreement.

"Very well," Janice said, then turned to Derek. "Is there any water around here?"

"That pickup over there," Derek pointed. He and Felicity walked together for a little before she stopped and slipped her arms around his neck, just leaning against him.

"Long night, eh?" he asked.

"Unbelievable," she answered. "Derek, I have so many questions, and so much to ponder. How could all this be? What happened here tonight?"

"You're asking me?" Derek chuckled. "I've no idea, and I don't think you're in any condition to discuss it. I'm prescribing a good night's sleep for you, and a full breakfast in the morning."

"Mmm, can I start right now?" she murmured, leaning her head against his chest. "You're a good brother, Derek. It's been a while since I leaned against you like this."

"Nearly two years," Derek confirmed.

"And then we were all worried about Janice," Felicity added. "Look at her now. She was the real heroine tonight – Grace and I just followed her lead."

"She's come a long way," Derek said, looking to where Janice was discussing details with Annette. "Who knows how far she'll go?"

"As far as she can, I'm thinking," Felicity said.

*   *   *

The next morning the local news sites were abuzz with the bizarre tale of a dozen and a half youngsters, supposedly safely in the hands of state-sponsored foster care, wandering rural Huron County roads in the middle of the night. Before long, the major sites in the state had picked up the story, and probate judges from St. Clair to Bay counties were demanding that foster care homes physically produce every child in their custody for visual verification. It quickly became clear that only the Wondercare homes were the problem, and county prosecutors started to gather evidence for indictments. Then the national news sites picked up on the scandal breaking across Michigan's Thumb, and all hell broke loose. Police were visiting Wondercare homes to remove children and home operators were falling all over themselves to offer testimony about the abuses and violations they'd been pressured to keep quiet.

In St. Clair County, this maelstrom was swirling around Child Protective Services Inspector Melanie Gibs, who was frantically trying to deal with demands from her supervisors, state officials, probate and district courts, county prosecutors, and the press. Most damning were the discoveries by officials visiting the Wondercare homes that their conditions were at sharp variance from what had been described in the last several audit reports which Melanie had submitted. Melanie had given up trying to contact her friend Andrea – none of her numerous earlier messages had been returned, and later messages could not be left because Andrea's voicemail box was full. Calls to Wondercare headquarters likewise got only to voicemail. In desperation, Melanie scrambled to assemble what evidence she could to present to the CPS executive, who was demanding to know how several dozen children supposedly under her oversight were simply missing. This same scenario was playing out in agencies and courtrooms across the region.

By early afternoon, warrants had been issued for the arrest of several Wondercare executives, including Suzanne and Andrea Stevens, both of whom were missing without explanation. Just a few hours later, word came from Phoenix Sky Harbor airport that the mother and daughter had been arrested while waiting to board a flight to Mexico City, and were being extradited back to Michigan to face charges.

* * *

At the end of that terrible day, Pa Hubbart sat in his office, staring at the walls. He was alone in the building. When he'd come in that morning some of his workers had asked him for directions, for orders. He'd simply closed the door in their faces and turned off his phone. By noon they'd stopped knocking, and soon afterwards, they'd all fled like rats from a sinking ship.

There'd been no word of any kind from the factory complex. The last report had been of a power outage that had forced them to fire up the generator. After that, not a word in or out. Nick had been there, as had Caleb and Charity and Mark and so many others. Not a word. He'd seen the videos on the sites of Andrea and Suzanne being escorted through Detroit Metro Airport in handcuffs, holding their arms up to shield their faces from the cameras. How long before that trail led back to him?

It was over. It was all over. His hopes, his dreams, his vision for the future, all shipwrecked on the pettiness of lesser men. His family members, shackled and paraded for public humiliation. His life's work shattered and crumbling to dust.

He needed to talk to Nick. Nick was good for ideas. And maybe Charlie, too. His good luck charm, his benevolent totem. He needed to talk to them. He stood and went out to his car.

* * *

Chip's phone rang, and he saw that it was Tom Stover. "Hey, Tom, what's going on?" he answered cheerfully.

"Chip, are you sitting down?" Tom asked in an unusually grave voice.

"Oh, no – what's wrong?"

270

"Grim news all around," Tom replied. "It has a silver lining for you, but I don't think you're going to like the cost."

Chip braced himself as Tom continued.

"First off, I did a drive-by of the factory site yesterday evening to see if everything was quiet. It was, but there was a sedan stopped on the road across from the gate. The keys were in, the engine was running, and the driver's door was wide open, right into the road. The gate to the property was open a little."

"Did you go in?" Chip asked.

"No, but there was a segment of cut chain there, so I looped it around the post to hold the gate shut," Tom said. "The car is registered to Ray Hubbart."

"Oh, no," Chip whispered. He'd had nightmares last night about the screams and cries he'd heard from those woods.

"Ready for the rest?"

"There's more?" Chip asked.

"Yeah. Angela came back from lunch today to find Andy gone and a resignation letter on his desk. Her inner alarms went off – you know how Angela is – and she drove to his house. His door was unlocked and he was slumped over his kitchen table. He'd...he'd blown his heart out with his service pistol."

Chip gasped and pressed his hand to his face. He had no reason to be fond of Andy, but he'd never...

"No sign of his wife, but one of the cars was gone and their room showed signs of 'hasty packing', as Angela put it," Tom went on.

"Oh, God," whispered Chip.

"Obviously we've been occupied dealing with all that, but I talked to Jennifer about the situation." Jennifer Vincent was the county administrator.

"What did she say?"

"She's going to recommend to the County Commission that you be offered the office of sheriff on an interim basis until they can arrange a special election," Tom explained. "So, it looks like you've got your job back."

"You're right," Chip confirmed. "I don't like the cost."

"We'll be glad to have you back," Tom said. "I haven't wanted to talk about it, but the department has been going to hell."

"Yeah, well, stands to reason, doesn't it?" Chip replied. "Keep me posted – I've got some calls to make."

"Keep your phone handy. Jennifer will probably be calling you tomorrow."

*　　*　　*

"Hey," Chip hailed Dan Knight as he walked into the coffee shop just north of Bad Axe. He came over and sat down across from Chip with a little wince.

"You okay?" Chip asked.

"I'm fine," Dan assured him. "I think I wrenched my shoulder when I fell the other night."

"Yeah, that was strange, you having that attack just then," Chip said. "You sure you're okay?"

"I'm fine," Dan assured him. "But you're right, it was strange."

"Strange atmospheric conditions, too," Chip mused.

"And electrical interference," Dan added.

"Must have been that approaching storm line," Chip suggested.

"Maybe," Dan said. "Yeah, that makes sense. The storm line."

"Anyway, there have been some – developments – that are going to affect things. Some will soon be public knowledge, but others are kind of quiet, so I ask for your discretion. First, Ray Hubbart's car was found outside the factory gate, engine running. No sign of him then or since, but the property gate was slightly open.

"Secondly, Andy Klein resigned his office today, then went home and blew a hole in his chest."

Dan gasped. "Any reason given?"

"Not that I've heard, but his brother is married to Ray Hubbart's daughter, so we can assume he was at least somewhat involved."

"Do you think he knew about the factory?"

"No way to know now," Chip replied. "But I'd guess not. Andy was a braggart and a buffoon, but I think the factory was a closely guarded family secret. Anyway, they're thinking about offering me the sheriff job on an interim basis until the next election. If they do, I won't be able to help with our guests anymore."

"That's no problem, Chip," Dan assured him. "I'm happy to deal with them by myself."

"How are they?"

"They're fine – amazingly so," Dan said. "Perfectly compliant, so much so that I think we wouldn't even have to lock the doors. Nate is helpful, and Joe's vision has almost completely returned. Lawrence has dropped by several times, and keeps sending people to talk to them, including a priest."

"Wow," Chip shook his head. "Maybe they really intend to change."

"Yeah, those…atmospheric conditions…seem to have really shaken them," Dan said.

"Have you explained their options? Did they agree to the special hearing?"

"I did, and they did. They don't see as they have much choice – the alternatives are too messy all around."

"They've got that right," Chip said. "And they've agreed to abide by the verdict?"

"Yes."

*　　　　*　　　　*

Agents Sanderson and Harris were frustrated. It came as no surprise that the Schaeffer children were among those reported missing from the hands of Wondercare, but it got them no closer to their original goal of interviewing the parents. The inordinate amount of complexity and delay they'd encountered down this particular "rabbit hole" – not to mention having again encountered Counselor Fitzgerald – had them hoping that they'd find something useful at the bottom. But it was starting to look like it would all come to nothing.

While pondering this, Agent Sanderson remembered the paper that Counselor Fitzgerald had given him, the slip with the address on it which he'd tucked into his tablet case and forgotten. He pulled it out and looked at it, then handed it to Harris.

"Way up north of Bad Axe?" Harris asked. "What good would this do?"

"Dunno," Sanderson replied, tapping the address into his tablet. "But the counselor said to try it if everything else failed, so let's give it a shot. We can go first thing tomorrow and be back by lunch."

So it was that about the middle of the next morning the government sedan was cruising back and forth along Nathan Road, checking house numbers. After passing the gate a couple of times, they finally stopped in front of it.

"No numbers or mailbox, but this has to be it," Agent Harris pointed out as the men walked to the gate. "Looks locked," he added, pointing to the chain.

"It does, but it isn't," Sanderson said, pulling the looped chain off the gates. They looked at each other – who would just loop a chain like that?

"Shall we take a look?" Harris asked.

"Umm – sure," Sanderson replied with a bit of reluctance, as if he wished the gate had been locked. They slipped through the gates and started up the drive, looking around cautiously. The silence was almost ominous, and the shadows under the trees all around looked darker than normal, unbroken by any daylight filtering through the branches.

"What's that?" Harris asked as they rounded a bend in the drive, pointing ahead at where a UTV lay in the trail.

"Looks like one of those carts that hunters and groundskeepers use," Sanderson said.

"What's it doing on its side?"

"Dunno."

The men passed up the drive in silence. "Looks like something up ahead," Harris finally said, pointing at what looked like a loading dock. Sure enough, the woods opened out onto a clearing of some sort. There was a big structure like a pole barn on their left, to which the docks were attached, and a large open area before them with fencing around part of it, and other buildings beyond and to their right.

What shocked them was the air of dereliction. Large stretches of pipe fencing were knocked down and scattered about. Many doors stood open to the elements, and they could see an ATV run up against a tree on the far side of the clearing.

"What the hell is all this?" Harris asked in the ghost of a voice.

"No idea," Sanderson replied, slowly drawing his service pistol. Harris followed suit.

The air was deathly still, and both men felt chilled despite the summer sunshine. There seemed to be a lot of flies in the air, and a faint odor of decay wafted about. The skin on their necks was prickling. The shadowed woods and dark, vacant doors looked heavy with brooding malice.

"What's that?" Agent Harris asked as something that sounded like a low grunt came from the far side of the building.

"Probably just a branch rubbing against the siding," Sanderson offered. "When the wind – oh!"

They'd just rounded the end of the building. There, where the concrete of the docks joined the metal of the building side, was a weedy patch. Half-buried in the weeds lay what was clearly a human spine and half a human skull.

"Oh, my God," Harris whispered. The low grunt sounded again.

"Let's go," Sanderson said. The men started walking briskly back down the drive, away from the hellish buildings. There was another grunt, and some rustling in the underbrush to their right. The men broke into a run, and by the time they reached the UTV were sprinting as fast as they could. Harris reached the gate first and stood holding it open while urging his partner on. Once Sanderson was safely through, Harris slammed the gate shut and wrapped the chain tightly around the center bars.

"Isn't there some way to lock this damn thing?" Harris swore.

"It'll do, it'll do," Sanderson said, leaning against the fencing and panting.

"That little prick," Harris muttered. "I oughta –"

"No, no," Sanderson said, pulling out his phone. "Fitzgerald is mischievous, but I don't think he's malicious. He wouldn't – hello, could I speak to Counselor Fitzgerald? Yes, thanks. Hello, Counselor Fitzgerald? About that address you provided –"

There was an audible gasp at the other end of the line. Agent Sanderson heard what few ever had: the glib Gerry Fitzgerald rendered speechless.

"Oh, my God," Fitz said in a horrified whisper. "You...you didn't go there, did you?"

"Actually, we did –"

"Are you all right? Did you get out okay?" Fitz asked frantically.

"Yes, we did, but –"

"Oh, thank heavens! Gentlemen, I am so terribly sorry. It totally slipped my mind that I had given you that address. Please, please forgive me. Had I remembered, I would have called you immediately – I'm so glad you got away safely. Please tear up that slip and never go back there again."

Taken aback by this outpouring of humility and contrition, Agent Sanderson stammered, "Um – sure, we didn't see anything useful there anyway. But...ah...Counselor...just what is that place?"

"I've no idea," Fitz responded. "I've never been there myself. It was an address of interest in some matters I was handling that I thought might be useful to you. But a few nights back, some things – changed – and it's now a place to avoid at all costs. If I'd had my head screwed on, I would have called you the first thing the next morning. I am so sorry for any distress you might have suffered. Are you sure you're all right?"

"We're fine. Thank you, Counselor," Agent Sanderson signed off and they both got into the car. Neither man wanted to talk about what they'd just been through.

"I recommend," Agent Harris suggested. "That we close this line of inquiry."

"Agreed," Sanderson replied.

*   *   *

The following day, the Huron County Commission voted unanimously to offer Chip Keller the job of interim sheriff until an election could be scheduled. Chip accepted the offer. The day after that, a couple of workers in an unmarked van showed up along Nathan Road. They securely mended the fencing on the east and west sides of the property and arc welded the gates shut with heavy angle iron.

*   *   *

The week afterward, there was a solemn gathering in an old meeting hall just outside Harbor Beach. Derek was there as one of about a dozen observers. Behind a long table sat Lawrence, Grandpa, Kent Schaeffer, and Steve McLean. Nathan and Joe stood before them. The hearing had taken an hour, and was coming to an end.

"These are grave crimes and sins you have admitted to," Lawrence said. "But we all agree that commending you to the civil authorities would cause immense complications, and possibly endanger you and others. Understanding that we are not a civil authority, do you agree to abide by the ruling of this council and submit to our authority?"

"We do," Joe and Nathan said.

"With regard to your sins, that is between you and God. We commend you for the choices you have recently made, and encourage you on the path you have begun. We hope to see you receive baptism in time.

"With respect to your crimes, this is our ruling: many of the liberated children have been taken in by families who do not have adequate accommodations for them. You are to help remodel, modify, and add onto those dwellings so there is sufficient living space for all the children. You will be provided tools, vehicles, food, and shelter, but you will labor until all have adequate housing. Do you understand?"

"Yes," Joe and Nathan answered.

"Do you have any questions?"

"No."

"Do you consider your sentence just or unjust?"

"Just."

"Very well, then," Lawrence said. "Details of your sentence will be worked out. For now, you are dismissed."

The men filed out, along with some of the observers. Shortly thereafter, different people came in. Martha and her betrothed, Evan, slipped in to the observer seats, but Ignatius walked in through a different door and stood before the long table. This time it was Grandpa who spoke.

"Ignatius, you have freely confessed to your sins and crimes. Do you have anything to add or retract?"

"No, sir," Ignatius replied.

"You have repented and received baptism," Grandpa continued. "Thus, you have been forgiven your sins, and we welcome you to the Family of God and encourage you to diligently continue in the path of holiness."

"Thank you, sir."

"But there remain the temporal effects of your actions, and the matter of what you can do to help right the wrong you have done in the world. In this, you have submitted yourself to Kent, and have sworn to abide by his judgment. Are you still intent on that?"

Ignatius swallowed and set his chin. "Yes, sir, I am."

"Hear, then, your sentence," Grandpa said, nodding to Kent, who gestured to Paul Stover. Paul ducked out a side door, returning shortly with a young woman.

"This is Ellie," Kent said. "Through no fault of her own, she has not learned the basic skills of how to care for herself. You are to provide for her. Your work will pay for her housing, her food, her clothing, any medical care, any education – all her basic necessities. I understand you have an interest in mechanics?"

"Yes, sir."

"We will arrange for a job for you. You will have housing, clothing, and food, but her needs will always come first. We will move you to another part of the state where we have resources. You will have families to guide and mentor you both, but the work will be yours. This is your sentence. Do you understand?"

"Yes, sir," Ignatius answered.

"Do you have any questions?"

"Yes," Ignatius said, looking at Ellie with his horribly scarred visage. "Will Ellie accept my help?"

"A fair question," Kent said. "Ellie?"

Ellie said nothing, her eyes flicking from face to face around the room, but she nodded.

"Very well. Ignatius, do you consider this sentence just or unjust?"

"Just, sir," Ignatius said. "And merciful."

"So be it," Kent said. "Paul, if you'd take Ignatius and Ellie, we'll arrange details of their move." The two were escorted out, glancing shyly at each other.

"Well," said Grandpa, leaning back in his chair and gazing at the door through which the two had just exited. "I'd give that a year or so."

"Definitely within two," Lawrence concurred.

*   *   *

Later that day Chip slipped into a booth across from his old friend at a coffee shop.

"Good to see you back in uniform, Sheriff," Lawrence said.

"Good to be back, though I could wish for different circumstances than those which brought it about," Chip replied.

"The hearings were held this morning. Nathan and Joe have been sentenced to hard labor helping families expand their dwellings to accommodate the adopted workers, and Ignatius has been assigned to work to provide for a woman who was rescued out of sex trafficking."

"Man, you guys work fast," Chip said.

"We're working with a simpler set of laws," Lawrence said.

"I've been wanting to say something since that night," Chip said almost reluctantly. "I hope it didn't seem like we were doing an end run around your wishes. I understood that you wanted to be prudent and effective, but some of us wanted to move a little quicker."

"You hardly answer to me, Sheriff," Lawrence raised his hands. "We were all doing the best we could, and I think everything came together just as it should have."

"Well, maybe," Chip said, shaking his head. "For all the good we did."

"C'mon, Sheriff, your efforts were vital," Lawrence admonished. "You took out the surveillance cameras. Your teams drew the staff away from the complex and into the woods. And I'm sure Nate has told you what had been set up in the barracks. Had your teams not cut the power when they did, those workers might have met a horrible death. You made the girls' work possible. You had no way of knowing that you'd encounter that fog and electrical interference."

"Yeah, that was quite something, wasn't it?" Chip said. "Well, I thank you for your concern and your help. If there's anything you ever need help with, you know where to find me."

"Actually, there are a couple of small things," Lawrence answered. "First, there's a family I know. Here's their address, but they'd rather their name not get around. They live just inside the county line, a little north of Gagetown. They're law-abiding citizens, but they've been troubled by some unscrupulous people misusing the law, and have to lie low. If you catch wind of any official interest in or movement on this address, could you let me know? I'll pass the word along to them."

"Sure thing, Lawrence," Chip tucked the slip of paper with the address into his pocket. "What's the other thing?"

"Well, you met Luke, or Doc, as he's commonly called," Lawrence explained.

"Yes – nice guy."

"He makes medical rounds through the counties, including up here into Huron. Usually he travels by ATV, but he gets around however he can. But one thing he's short on is documents."

"Documents?"

"You know – driver's license, library card, credit cards, that sort of thing. Could you quietly pass the word to your deputies that this is normal, and not to give him any trouble if they ever chance to meet him?"

"Oh, sure thing, Lawrence," Chip assured him. "You tell Doc Luke that he's got free run of Huron County so long as I'm sheriff, and thank him for his help."